Best fake Fiancé

USA TODAY BESTSELLING AUTHOR
ROXIE NOIR

Cover: Najla Qamber Designs
Editor: Sennah Tate

CHAPTER ONE

DANIEL

The officer waves me forward, one hand on his belt, and I step through the metal arch again.

It beeps before my foot hits the floor on the other side. I go through my pockets again, nerves already jittery, resolutely ignoring the line of people forming behind me.

"Keys, cell phone, wallet, beepers, watch, jewelry, belt, no weapons in the courthouse," the guard drones. "Do you have any artificial body parts?"

"No," I say for the second time that morning.

I dig to the bottoms of my pockets. Nothing. I pat my back pockets, but there's nothing there either; nothing in the pockets of my suit jacket.

Someone behind me in line sighs loudly. I ignore them.

"Could be your shoes," the guard offers, still speaking in a monotone. "Those steel-toed?"

I look down at the wingtips I spent an hour polishing last night.

"No," I tell him. "They don't even make — wait."

I pat the breast pocket of my suit and realize what the problem is.

"Found it," I tell him, and walk back through the metal detector. It beeps again, and I pull a charm bracelet out of the pocket. Another guard holds out a small plastic bowl, I drop the bracelet in, and he runs it through the machine.

I finally step through without issue and gather my things on the other side: wallet, phone, belt, keys, briefcase. At last the charm bracelet comes through, all alone in its small plastic bowl. It's still warm from my body heat, and I pick it up and tuck it safely back into my chest pocket.

I feel its small, heavy weight as I head for the elevators. I know every charm on its short length by heart: a book, a ballet shoe, a musical note, a tree, a heart, a tiny Eiffel Tower, a radiant sun. Her mother gave her the Eiffel Tower. I gave her the sun.

Rusty nearly missed the school bus this morning because she almost forgot to give it to me to take to court. She was already out the door and halfway down the driveway when she came sprinting in, backpack bouncing up the stairs, out of breath as she shoved it into my breast pocket saying *Dad I almost forgot!* before sprinting back down the driveway just as the bus pulled up.

I take the elevator to the second floor, walk along the polished marble floor to Courtroom 220. I'm twenty minutes early, so I sit on one of the wooden benches outside and wait.

A moment later, my phone buzzes.

Charlie: Break a leg.
Me: I'm going to court, I'm not in a play.
Charlie: Then don't break a leg.
Charlie: Unless you think it would get you sympathy with the judge. Then maybe it's worth a shot?
Me: Or he decides that having a broken leg makes me an unfit parent and takes custody away.

Charlie: I thought it was a visitation hearing, not custody, can he even do that?
Me: If he's in the mood, probably.
Charlie: How about if I just say good luck?
Me: Thanks :)
Charlie: So picky.

I put the phone back in my pocket, smiling to myself. Charlie — short for Charlotte — is terrible with dates, but she's always remembered every court hearing I have. She must write herself a million reminders. The thought always makes me feel a little better.

People are walking by, congregating in small knots throughout the hall. Most are wearing suits. Some are wearing what are clearly the nicest clothes they own — khakis and polo shirts, sometimes a button-down shirt. Then there's the small smattering of people who could barely be bothered, wearing jeans and t-shirts, sweatpants, hoodies.

I pace. There's no way I can sit still. It doesn't matter that I've been here, in this courthouse, for the exact same reason, at least twenty times. I still get anxious. I still need to move back and forth, do *something* other than sit.

It's just visitation, I remind myself. *Crystal's going to bitch about something or other, you'll all agree to some new schedule, and next month she'll be making excuses again about why she can't see her kid.*

Just then, a man wearing cutoff jean shorts and flip flops wanders past, and I stare after him.

His outfit isn't what gets my attention. It's the giant tattoo on his calf.

I swivel my head, blatantly staring after him, double and triple checking that I'm seeing what I think I'm seeing.

Then I grab my phone, because I *have* to tell Charlie about this.

Me: Someone in this courthouse has a huge tattoo of Barney the dinosaur butt-fucking a unicorn.
Charlie: Please tell me it's a lawyer.
Me: He's wearing cutoffs. Unlikely.
Me: Also, he has a tattoo of a beloved children's character having anal sex with a unicorn, so he may not have graduated from law school.
Charlie: You say that like lawyers can't be perverts.
Charlie: Also, how can you tell it's anal? Is it that detailed?
Me: I don't know. He's gone now.
Me: Barney had a REALLY dirty look on his face.
Charlie: I have so many questions about this.
Me: I have no answers.
Charlie: Was it a good tattoo?
Me: Depends on what you're into.

"Thanks for being on time," a voice says behind me, and I turn.

"I know you're always on time," Lucinda, my lawyer, goes on. "But lately I've been trying to encourage good habits in my clients. You look good. Half-Windsor?"

I touch the knot in my tie.

I like Lucinda. I've liked her since the moment I first walked into her office, six years ago, and we've been a team ever since. We're a somewhat odd pairing — a middle-aged black woman and a white man in his late twenties — but Lucinda's a godsend, as far as I'm concerned.

"It is," I say.

"That's a good choice," she says, then finally smiles. "How are you doing, Daniel?"

"I'm well, Lucinda," I say, smoothing one hand over the front of my jacket. "Yourself?"

"Also well," she says, then sighs and gestures to a bench along a wall. "We should sit."

My palms suddenly start to sweat, my heart rate jumping up. Lucinda never tells me to sit for good news, but I do it anyway, the wooden bench cool.

"Holden Hughes is going to be the judge on this case," she says bluntly, her tone of voice making it clear that this is bad news. "I'm sure opposing counsel managed that somehow, and I don't like it, but we can't change it."

I simply nod, spine perfectly straight, hands folded in front of me, and wait for more.

"Judge Hughes has a certain reputation," she says, matter-of-factly. "He's old school, conservative, and frankly he wishes it were still the Eisenhower administration, so he doesn't like me much," Lucinda goes on.

I detect the tiniest of eyebrow quirks, as if somewhere, deep down inside, she takes pride in that fact.

"Most pertinent to our current issue, he has a long history of siding with mothers over fathers," she goes on, and she looks me dead in the eye as she says it.

I nod sharply. Lucinda never sugarcoats things, and I love her for that.

"It's widely known that he believes in a traditional family structure," she says, waving a hand. "The usual, married parents, father goes off to work at the office, mother stays home with the children, she vacuums while he golfs, et cetera. And he's not exactly keen on updating his views, from what I've heard."

The corner of her mouth twitches. There's a sharp look in her eye.

Shit, Lucinda *hates* Judge Holden.

The buzzing anxiety in my chest starts to rattle, like

someone's taken my heart and is shaking it. It feels like it's going to shake a hole straight through me, and I realize that I'm rubbing my hands together over and over again, trying to calm the feeling.

"What do we do?" I ask, amazed at how calm my voice sounds.

"We do exactly what we were going to do," she says, steely-voiced. "We show the visitation logs, how often she's cancelled at the last moment, how willing you are to meet her more than halfway."

I nod, my heart still rattling.

"We show the court your daughter's report cards, her school records, the statements from her teachers, her dance instructor. We prove that she's thriving in her current situation. And Daniel," she says, lightly touching my arm. "We remember that this hearing is only a petition to change the current visitation arrangement."

I nod, swallow. I'm still rubbing my hands together. I can't stop.

"Of course," I say. I still sound perfectly cool, calm, and collected, even though I'm anything but.

Going to court rattles me like nothing else. It always has. Every single time I put on a suit and walk through these doors, I'm instantly and inescapably aware of two things:

One, I don't belong here, wearing a suit and tie, looking like a stockbroker or something. This is the only suit I own. This tie took me at least twenty minutes to get right. I may look the part but really, I'm a fraud. I don't know how to tie a tie very well and I don't know how to parent any better, even though I thought I would by now. But I don't. Every single day I'm making it up as I go along, even though everyone else at the PTA meetings seems to have a plan.

Two, they could take her away.

That's it. That's the very worst thing that could happen to me, and it could happen here, ten minutes from now, and the judge that Lucinda hates could be the one to do it. I can tell myself a million reasons that it's unlikely, but that doesn't change the fact that it's a possibility.

I could walk into that courtroom with full physical and legal custody of Rusty, and I could walk out with nothing.

It's unlikely. I know that. But as long as it's even possible, I'm going to hate coming to this place.

"Don't worry," she says lightly. "This is all perfectly routine."

· · * * ★ ★ ★ * * · ·

AT TEN FIFTY-FIVE, they let us into the courtroom for our eleven o'clock time slot. Before I enter, I text Charlie one last time: *going in*. She texts back a string of emojis, hearts and smiley faces and crossed fingers, and I shut my phone off.

Opposing counsel isn't here yet, so I soothe myself with my pre-hearing ritual, taking all my notes, the statements, the documentation, everything I've collected in my favor, and stacking it neatly in front of me on the wide wooden table. Having the weight of evidence right there, within easy reach, always soothes me.

Last but not least, I take out the drawing.

It's a different drawing every time, because Rusty's always making new ones, but I always bring one. This one's got the two of us as stick figures — her, small, long-haired, wearing a bright green skirt, me twice her height and wearing only shoes for some reason — along with several trees and a small blob with feet that she told me last night was a wombat.

Rusty's really into wombats right now. Last week I told

her that she couldn't have one as a pet, and ever since then, she's been casually mentioning various wombat features that would just happen to make them *perfect* pets. For example, their poop is square, so it's stackable.

She couldn't believe it when that tidbit didn't sway me.

"Did you get a dog?" Lucinda asks, glancing over at the drawing. She's seen plenty of Rusty's artwork over the years, though this is the first time in about eighteen months, since things with Crystal have been relatively quiet lately.

"It's a wombat," I explain.

"Did you get a wombat?" she asks drily.

"Not yet," I say. "Though if Rusty has her way…"

She chuckles. A door opens.

Pete Bresley, the bailiff, steps in. He sees me and nods quickly, then steps to his usual spot and folds his hands in front of himself.

"All rise for the honorable Judge Hughes," he intones.

We rise. The stenographer rises. The officials sitting off to one side rise.

The plaintiff isn't here yet, and I admit to feeling a not-small amount of satisfaction on that account.

Before I can gloat, Judge Hughes sweeps into the room. Not all judges wear robes for a visitation hearing, but this one does.

Judge Hughes is on the short, stocky side, but I'd bet money that he's ex-military. He's silver-haired, white, his face lined but still stern.

"Be seated," he commands as he sits, then finally looks up at everyone in the room. His face betrays nothing as he glances over Lucinda and me, but his gaze settles on the empty desk to our left.

He laces his fingers together.

"The plaintiff isn't here yet?" he asks, pointedly looking at the clock on the back wall.

"No, Your Honor," answers Pete the bailiff.

The judge is still glaring at the clock.

"Well, thank you to everyone who managed to make it on time today," he says, more than a note of irritation in his voice. "If the plaintiff has not shown up by five after, then we'll have to table this matter and reconvene—"

The door swings open, and we all turn.

It's a man I don't recognize. He's got on a dark gray suit with a dark blue tie. His briefcase is black and shiny. His shoes are black and shiny. He's white, tall, probably in his fifties, and he smiles easily at Judge Hughes.

The judge's face softens.

"Apologies, your honor," the man says. "You know how it is with all the construction on the roads these days."

For a moment, I think that Crystal's just sent her lawyer and hasn't come herself. I actually let myself get optimistic.

Then the door swings open again, and she comes through.

Belly-first.

My jaw nearly hits the floor. I barely even notice that she's followed by another man, this one younger but just as well-dressed as the lawyer.

Crystal's pregnant.

Crystal's seriously pregnant, far enough along that it's obvious, though the way she's got both her hands splayed over her swollen belly does call attention to it.

When the hell did that happen? I think. My heart is rattling again, inside my chest, faster and more desperate than before.

I just saw her six weeks ago, when I dropped Rusty off for a few hours. Was she pregnant then and I didn't notice?

She must have been.

The belly's not the only thing.

It's not even the thing that alarms me the most.

Crystal's wearing a suit. It's a full-on pinstripe pantsuit, complete with heels, a nice-looking purse, and a string of pearls.

The woman who once left a six-month-old Rusty home alone in her crib so she could go out and get hammered with her friends now has a brand-new lawyer and looks like a Stepford wife. The last time we came to court, a year and a half ago, her lawyer was considerably shabbier, and she was wearing torn jeans.

My palms start sweating. I have to remind myself to breathe. My heart feels like it's being wrung out. Something is going on, and I don't know what.

"The hearing began at eleven o'clock, Mr. Winchester," Judge Hughes says, but his voice doesn't have the same stern note that it did a moment ago. "Is everyone prepared?"

Crystal, her lawyer, and the other man sit. The judge moves some papers around.

"Yes, your honor," her lawyer finally says.

"All right," the judge says, and picks up a piece of paper, looking at it through reading glasses. "I hereby call to session the matter of Partlow vs. Loveless, Virginia case number..."

He goes on for a moment with the formalities, and Lucinda finally catches my eye, raising both her eyebrows the tiniest fraction, an expression that I'm pretty sure means *Did you know?*

I shake my head ever so slightly. She turns her attention forward again.

"...so if counsel for Ms. Partlow would please begin?"

"Thank you, your honor," the other lawyer says. He stands. He buttons his jacket in a smooth, practiced gesture, then stands behind the podium between the two desks.

"First, as Ms. Partlow is now known as Mrs. Thornhill, I move that we include that in the record."

I sit bolt upright, my head swiveling toward Crystal, across the room. She's looking back at me, a smug, satisfied look on her face.

I look down. There's a huge diamond ring on her finger, the man sitting next to her patting her hand comfortingly.

I feel like the courtroom is tilting. Now I'm sweating everywhere, not just my palms. Crystal getting pregnant is one thing. If she got knocked up again by accident, I — the first person to accidentally knock her up — wouldn't exactly be surprised.

But getting married is different. That takes at least some amount of intention and forethought, two things I wasn't sure Crystal was capable of.

I couldn't care less that Crystal's married. Good for her. But if I don't know, that means she didn't tell Rusty, either.

She didn't tell her own daughter that she has a new stepdad.

She didn't tell her daughter that she's going to have a new sibling.

Cold prickles travel down my spine.

"Furthermore," continues her lawyer. "I'd like to make an amendment to the petition."

"What is the amendment?" asks the judge.

"I'd like to change this from a visitation hearing to a custody hearing," the lawyer says.

I feel like the floor falls from under me. Lucinda's already on her feet.

"Your Honor," she says, but the judge holds up one hand.

"That's highly unusual, on what grounds?" Hughes drones on, like a bomb didn't just go off in his courtroom.

"Mr. Thornhill has accepted a job offer in Denver, and the Thornhills would like to amend custody in light of that," the lawyer goes on.

I'm out of my chair before I know it.

"No!" I say.

Lucinda's grip is on my arm like steel, but I ignore it.

"You can't take her to *Denver*," I say, my voice already rising. "She lives here. Her life is here, her family, her friends, her school, you can't just—"

"Ms. Washington, *please* control your client," the judge booms over me.

"Daniel," Lucinda says, her hand even tighter on my arm.

I close my mouth, mid-word, but I haven't broken eye contact with Crystal's lawyer, my heart pounding wildly out of control.

Denver. It's two time zones away. A thousand miles. Fifteen hundred?

"*Daniel*," Lucinda says again, and I swallow hard. "Come on."

I sit, slowly. I'm amazed that my hands aren't shaking.

"If I may continue?" the lawyer asks in a tone of voice that makes me want to commit violence. "We're requesting full custody, with Mr. Loveless getting the standard ninety overnights of visitation per year."

I can't breathe. I can't. I bring one hand to my mouth because I think I might vomit, the courtroom closing in around me, but I don't say anything. Already I'm afraid that I fucked myself over with my outburst.

"Your Honor," Lucinda is saying, still on her feet. "This is highly unusual. Mr. Loveless has been the sole legal and physical guardian for nearly six years, and a change of this magnitude would be incredibly—"

"Thank you, Ms. Washington," the judge says, and

Lucinda presses her lips together, eyes blazing. He redirects his attention to the slimeball behind the podium.

"I do happen to agree with opposing counsel on this, Mr. Winchester," he says. "This is an extraordinary request made with no warning. I'm sure you're fully aware that the court is in no way prepared to make a ruling at this hearing?"

"Of course, Your Honor," he says, smoothly as ever.

Denver. Ninety overnights. That's three months; that means that they'd have her during the school year, and maybe I'd fly her out for vacations and the summer.

I can't imagine it. I can't imagine a life where I don't wrangle her out of bed and onto the school bus every morning, a life where I don't help her with homework at the kitchen table, a life where she doesn't complain while I try to untangle her hair after she bathes.

"May I briefly go over the change in circumstances?" the lawyer asks.

I sneak another glance over at Crystal. She's rubbing her belly like it's a crystal ball, like she's trying to draw attention to it.

"Proceed," says the judge.

The lawyer clears his throat. My undershirt is damp, clinging to me with sweat.

"There are several major life changes of note," the lawyer begins. "First, my client was married one month ago to Mr. Thornhill, an executive at Prometheus Mining. They're currently residing in Holmes Creek, where they own a home."

I glance at Lucinda. She's taking notes, and circles *Holmes Creek*. My stomach writhes. The houses there start at six hundred grand, and I have no idea how high they go.

"In addition, Mrs. Thornhill is currently several months

pregnant with her second child and plans to be a stay at home mother to both of her children."

At the other table, Crystal nods piously. She's still rubbing her belly.

It feels like a hand grabs my heart and twists with jealousy. Not for me, but for Rusty. I can't imagine Crystal ever rubbed her belly like that when she was pregnant the first time. I can't imagine that Crystal made a single accommodation for her first daughter.

Hell, she *admitted* to drinking and smoking pot through her pregnancy with Rusty. God only knows what she didn't admit to.

"In Denver, Mr. Thornhill will be a Vice President of Prometheus, and they've already selected a home in an exclusive neighborhood. Rustilina is on several waiting lists at top private schools, where she would be taught by some of the state's best—"

The judge holds up a hand.

"You don't need to advertise the schools to me," he says. "Are there any other life changes?"

"Mr. Thornhill has a brother in Denver, so both girls would grow up with their cousins," he finishes. "Again, family is very—"

"Important, yes," says the judge. "Thank you, Mr. Winchester."

The other lawyer gathers his documents and leaves.

"Ms. Washington, would you mind answering a few questions on behalf of your client?"

She steps smartly to the podium. I lace my fingers together on the table in front of myself, hoping that I look cool, calm, and confident, even though I feel like someone's taken a wrecking ball to my insides.

"Let me just run down a few facts here," the judge says,

looking at his papers. "Does Mr. Loveless still reside with his daughter in the house owned by his mother?"

Lucinda clears her throat.

"Yes, Your Honor," she says. "Mrs. Loveless is a strong presence in—"

"Thank you," he cuts her off. "And she's attending Burnley County Public Schools?"

"Yes."

"Is Mr. Loveless still in the liquor business?"

"He co-owns a brewery with his brother, Your Honor. In fact, Mr. Loveless has four—"

"Thank you," he cuts her off again. Lucinda's lips thin, but she stands there patiently, respectfully. "And has Mr. Loveless experienced any life changes not noted in these documents? He isn't also married and expecting, is he?"

He's half-smiling, like this is some joke. Like the possibility of taking my daughter away from me is somehow *funny*.

"No, Your—"

"I'm engaged," I say, standing suddenly.

I say it before I can think, the lie out of my mouth and in the courtroom before I can claw it back.

Total silence follows. It feels like my heart stops beating.

"Congratulations," says the judge, barely looking at me. "It seems that you didn't inform Ms. Washington?"

I button the button on my sportcoat to give my hands something to do while my mind races, going ten thousand miles a second while Lucinda looks at me, one eyebrow raised.

Instantly, I know I fucked up. I fucked up and I can't take it back, because I just lied to a judge who's considering taking my daughter away from me.

I take a deep breath and dig my hole deeper.

"I had understood this to be a visitation hearing," I say. "Your Honor."

"My client didn't realize it would have any bearing on this matter," Lucinda says smoothly.

"May I have the lady's name?" the judge asks, pen poised.

I hesitate, but only for half a second.

There's only one name I can possibly say.

"Charlotte McManus," I say.

From the corner of my eye, I see Crystal's head whip around to look at me.

Don't panic.

Even though you just told a judge that you're engaged to your best friend.

"And what is Ms. McManus's occupation?"

"Carpentry," I answer.

"Are you cohabitating?"

"We're not," I say, the first truthful thing out of my mouth since I stood. "We believe in waiting until after marriage to live together."

That part's just to make myself sound better. I've never thought about it before. I've never been in a position to cohabitate with anyone and definitely not with Charlie.

Charlie, who is going to kill me.

"Do you have a wedding date?" he asks.

"We're thinking next summer."

The judge just nods, writing.

"Is *that* all, Mr. Loveless? Ms. Washington?"

"Yes," I say.

"Yes, Your Honor," Lucinda quickly adds.

"All right, then," Judge Hughes says. "In that case, I'd like for the plaintiff to write up another petition and have it to everyone no later than…"

I look down at the table, at Rusty's drawing of us with a wombat.

I just fucked up.

I panicked. I never panic, except that I did just now, faced with losing Rusty to exclusive neighborhoods and private schools, to a mom who's suddenly claiming to be someone I know she's not, to a stepdad who could probably afford to actually purchase and house a wombat if he felt like it.

I, who live with my mother and own a business based around alcohol, lied to a judge.

I, who send my child to public schools and will only ever be able to afford public schools, lied to a judge.

Fuck. Fucking fuck fuck fuckity fuck.

I'm nauseous. My undershirt is soaked with sweat, because I just told a bald-faced lie to the man who'll decide whether my daughter stays here or moves across the country.

Unbelievably stupid.

I try to listen to what the judge is saying now, what the next steps here are, but I can barely hear him over the pounding of blood in my ears. I grab a pen and write down a word, a phrase, here and there, but I can barely listen.

Maybe it will be fine.

It doesn't have to be a big deal. No one outside of this courtroom knows, and Crystal doesn't even live in town anymore.

Get Charlie a fake ring, talk her into coming to the next hearing with you, and it'll all be fine.

Totally fine.

No big deal.

"Dismissed," the judge says, and everyone else stands. A moment later, I stand, and the judge leaves the room through a back door.

Lucinda turns to me immediately, her lips still a thin line.

"Congratulations," she says.

"Thank you," I say automatically.

At the other table, Crystal, her new husband, and her lawyer all stand. They file out, one by one, Crystal glancing over at me, her hands no longer on her belly now that the judge is gone.

We lock eyes. Hers are cold, blank, unreadable.

"Daniel," Lucinda says, her voice grave.

The knots in my stomach tighten so hard I think they might break. I feel like a kid about to get chastised at school, but I also know that I deserve it.

I clear my throat.

"Yes?"

"You know that lying to a judge during a custodial hearing would reflect far more poorly on you than being a single father, don't you?" she says.

I swallow hard. I shove one hand through my hair, my nerves jangling anew.

Fuck. Fuck!

"I panicked," I admit, closing my eyes. "I didn't mean to. But he was talking about letting her bond with her baby sister and having a real family and sending her to private schools and giving her ice-skating lessons and buying her ponies and—"

"—all of which is simply talk from the plaintiff, they've got nothing to back up those assertions—"

"—and I panicked," I finish. "That's all. I panicked and said something stupid and — oh, fuck me running, I can't believe I said that."

Lucinda sighs.

Then she puts one hand on my arm.

"Is Charlotte at least a real person?"

I just nod, mutely.

"Think she'd be willing to put on a ring and come to a hearing?"

I take a deep breath.

"I think I could talk her into it," I say.

CHAPTER TWO

CHARLIE

I t's been ninety minutes. Still no text.

I snap my goggles back onto my face, make sure that my hair's all properly secured, and turn the lathe on again, the low hum filling the air around me. I lower the chisel until it's biting into the spinning wood, a gap widening.

I let up on the chisel, do it again on another point, slide it down the length of the wood as it spins, cutting the square piece round. This is the ninth baluster that I've turned today, so by now I'm doing it on autopilot.

He can't possibly still be in court. It's been an hour and a half.

I frown at the wood as it takes shape: a lump here, an elongated lump in the middle, tapering off toward the top and bottom. Another bump. A line.

Usually, I revel in this sort of thing. I like turning a lump of wood into art, coaxing a form out of nothing. I like using my hands and creating something I can hold, touch, feel. It's why I like my job.

Except today I can't focus on it to save my life. I'm a bundle of nerves, my mind everywhere but in front of me.

He forgot to turn his phone back on, I tell myself. *He was out of there in twenty minutes, everything is fine, he just forgot.*

I narrow the taper at one end, careful not to press too hard. I've already had to scrap one of these today.

Right. When was the last time Daniel forgot something?

I can't even think of it. I know he's not perfect. He must forget things all the time, but compared to me — someone who routinely goes to warm up a forgotten cup of coffee, only to discover *yesterday's* forgotten coffee already in the microwave — he seems like a machine.

I shake my head to focus on the task at hand, particularly since it involves sharp objects, dangerous machinery, and expensive stuff.

The balusters are for a staircase on a yacht; balusters are the spindle-things that hold up the handrail, a term I didn't learn until the second year of my carpentry program. I learned that some yachts have staircases last Friday, when I discovered that I'd be hand-making the parts for one.

I have no idea whose yacht it is. I have no idea where on earth this yacht even is, since Sprucevale is in the middle of the Blue Ridge Mountains, several hours inland, and I strongly doubt the river is deep enough for a boat that big. There are some lakes around, but they don't seem like yacht lakes.

They seem much more like fishing-from-a-rundown-motorboat-with-a-case-of-beer-in-a-styrofoam-cooler lakes, but I'm not a lake expert.

I examine the baluster carefully, then flip the lathe off. The whine dies down, and I take the wood off of it, put it down next to the first eight that I made.

Then I frown.

"Dammit," I hiss out loud, just to myself. The lathe is in one corner of the Mountain Woodworks building, which is

21

big and open-plan and constantly noisy, because someone's always running a power saw.

These don't match. I fucked up. The big lump tapers the wrong way, because I was worrying about whether Daniel was still in court and wasn't paying attention. You'd think that after making eight of the exact same thing, I could have another thought for one second without screwing up, but apparently not.

I grab the bad baluster, put it on a work bench, and take another square length of red cedar. I pencil the markings on it — cut here, here, here, and here — then load it onto the lathe and throw the switch, irritated with myself.

I haven't gotten any further than the first slice when in the corner of my vision, my phone lights up. I grab it instantly, chisel on the table, shoving my goggles onto my head.

Daniel: I need to talk to you.
Me: What happened?
Daniel: I'm coming by.
Me: It's almost lunch time, can we meet somewhere?

No response. I fidget with my phone, shove my other hand in the pocket of my coveralls, start fiddling with a wood chip there. Nothing. He's not even typing.

Me: What happened?!?
Me: Just tell me, I hate surprises. Come on.

Still nothing.

Me: Please??????

Daniel doesn't respond, no matter how hard I stare at

the phone. I bite my lip, watching my screen, a thousand bad possibilities flickering through my mind.

Behind me, the whine of the lathe stops. I whirl around.

William, my boss, is standing there.

"Best not to leave that running," he says, solemnly. "Could catch something on it by accident and that'd get ugly."

I swallow hard, my face flushing red. I shove my phone back into the pocket of my coveralls.

"Sorry," I say, biting back *my best friend just had a court hearing about his daughter, and I think something went bad and he won't tell me what and my mind wasn't really on carpentry,* but that's way too much information.

Besides, I just left machinery going while I looked at my phone. I don't need to seem even *less* professional, and God knows I'm aware of what can happen when you forget something is on.

"Just be careful," he says mildly. "How are these going?"

William is middle-aged, serious, looks like he's spent a lot of time outdoors, and is a man of very few words. I was convinced that he was always angry with me until I figured that out.

"They're going well," I say, omitting the fact that I've ruined two. "This is my last one, and then I've got to start on the bannister itself…"

We talk shop for a moment. If William's mad that I left the lathe running or upset that I've used two more lengths of red cedar than necessary, nothing about his manner gives it away. We go over some plans. We go over some drawings. We go over a grainy photograph that the client gave him, showing the exact bannister that he wants to imitate.

I'm only half paying attention.

"That's the best photo we could get out of him," William is saying, his drawl low and slow.

As he's talking, the door at the far end of the workshop opens.

A Daniel-shaped being enters, silhouetted by the bright sunlight outside. My heart leaps and then falls, the silhouette putting its hands into its pockets, standing just inside the door.

He wouldn't be here if something bad hadn't happened.

"Seems that his ancestors came over from England as guests of the crown in seventeen-something," William is still saying. "Now he's trying to outfit his yacht with the same details that their ship had."

I glance up at Daniel. He's still standing by the door, clearly waiting. My heart shakes in my chest.

"Minus the scurvy, I imagine," I say without thinking, looking back at the photo, my mind utterly elsewhere.

William says nothing.

I silently scold myself for making dumb jokes to my boss.

"I'll leave you to it," he says, nodding once. I nod back, and William walks off to another portion of our massive workshop.

I count to ten, then put the photo down.

"I'm going to lunch, I'll be back in an hour," I announce to absolutely no one in particular, and then I practically run toward the door where Daniel is standing.

"What happened?" I practically shout when I'm within ten feet of him.

"C'mon," he says, pushing the door to the outside open again and holding it for me. I step through into the sunlight, blinking, and whirl on him.

"I need a big favor," he says, the moment we're outside, his voice low and serious.

My heart's in my throat.

"Sure, anything," I say instantly.

He pauses, his hands back in his pockets, his jacket open, and he studies my face for a long moment, looking more serious than I've seen him look in ages.

Finally, he looks away for a moment, pushes his hand through his slightly-floppy hair, then looks at me again. Daniel's got some of the bluest eyes I've ever seen, deep and clear, and they're dead fixed on me.

He's also wearing a suit. He never wears a suit, which is a shame, because the man looks *good* in a suit, which feels inappropriate to notice right now.

"It's gonna sound weird," he says, his voice still low.

"What *happened?*" I ask for the thousandth time. "Look, whatever it is, I don't care, I'll do it."

"I need you to come to the next hearing and say we're engaged," he says.

It catches me off-guard.

I thought he'd need me to give Rusty a ride to summer camp next month, or put sugar in Crystal's gas tank, or secretly shadow her to prove that she's having weekly meetings with Satan. Something like that.

"To each other?" I ask, after a moment.

"Right."

"At a hearing?" I say, still thrown for a loop.

"I fucked up," he says, folding his arms over himself. "And I may have told the judge I was getting married. To you."

"Okay," I say, my stomach suddenly in knots. "Yeah, sure, just let me know when it is, I'll take off work and come... lie to a judge, I guess?"

He closes his eyes, takes a deep breath, exhales and straightens, like there's a weight off his shoulders.

Then he grabs me and pulls me in for a rough hug.

"Thank you," he says into my hair, which is currently piled in a knot on top of my head. "Jesus, Charlie, you're a lifesaver."

I hug him back, my arms around his tall, rugged form, not that I notice how tall or rugged he is.

Nor do I grab him one percent tighter than I probably should. I sure don't think about the muscles underneath his clothes, or the fact that I've seen him hoist full five-gallon buckets overhead like they weighed nothing.

Most of the time I'm used to the extreme attractiveness of my tall, rugged, very handsome best friend. It's just one of those things: the sky is blue, grass is green, Daniel is hot, et cetera. I'm over it.

The suit, though. *Hello.* It's jarring enough that I've been jolted into noticing the rest of the hotness all over again.

It's a long hug, not that I mind. I'm probably getting sawdust all over him, though.

"Did you just volunteer this?" I ask when he releases me. "Or was there a specific question, or...?"

For the first time since I've seen him today, he smiles.

"Want to get lunch?" he asks.

· · · · ★ ★ ★ ★ ★ · · ·

"HOLY *SHIT*," I say. "Does Rusty know her mom got married?"

Daniel shrugs dramatically, still chewing a bite of his turkey club.

Crystal might be Rusty's mom, but she's not Daniel's ex. She's someone that Daniel got blind drunk and had sex with a few times when he was twenty-one, dumb, and going through a rough time.

He likes to make that distinction very, very clear.

"Does her husband have cloven hooves?" I ask, gesturing with my own sandwich. "Did you see an ultrasound? Does the baby have horns?"

"He's a mining executive," Daniel says, swallowing.

"So I'm not that far off."

Daniel snorts, taking another bite.

"How the hell did she meet him?" I ask. "Did he seem hypnotized? Maybe under some sort of mind-control drug?"

"I don't think Rusty knows," he finally says, answering my first question. "She'd have told me if she did, she can't keep secrets."

"True," I say.

It's not exactly true. She probably couldn't keep a big secret like that, but just last week I hung out with her one afternoon and we got ice cream sundaes *before* dinner. I'm pretty sure she kept the secret, because I never heard about this horrible breach of protocol from Daniel, and I usually do.

Also, last winter I took her sledding at Suicide Hill, the steepest sledding spot in town, and never heard about it from Daniel, even though he did specifically say we shouldn't go there.

He can be a little overprotective. The kid had a blast.

Daniel finishes his sandwich, sighs, and leans back in his chair. He took the tie and jacket off, so now he's just wearing a white button-down shirt, both sleeves rolled up, the top two buttons undone.

It's an even better look, or at least it would be if I were noticing how Daniel looks, which I'm not.

The man does shine up like a new penny, though.

"Anyway, that's why I panicked," he says, shaking his head slightly. "I know I shouldn't have, but they were going on about gated communities and private schools and raising her with her sister, and shit, Charlie, I've got none of that."

I lean in, push my empty plate out of the way.

"Yeah, but none of that shit can make Crystal a good parent," I say, keeping my voice low.

"Tell that to the court."

"You want me to?" I ask, taking a sip of water. "Want me to go in there and tell everyone exactly what I think?"

He rubs his hands over his face, laughing.

"Please don't," he says. "As much as I'd love to see her reaction, I don't need my fake fiancée reprimanded by a judge."

I just shrug, smiling into my water glass.

"You sure that's all you need?" I ask. "Should we mockup save-the-dates or a registry or something?"

For a split second, I wonder what we would put on our registry, what our invitations would look like if we really *were* engaged. It's not the worst thought.

"I think that's overkill," he says. "Besides, how do we explain if someone finds it?"

"True," I concede.

"It's probably smartest to keep a lie simple," he says. "I'll find you a fake ring, you'll show up for a single court date, and—"

He cuts off mid-sentence as someone steps up to our table, and we both turn.

"I am so sorry to interrupt y'all," Shirley Crest says.

She settles one be-ringed hand on each of our shoulders, like she's about to lead us in prayer. Daniel and I trade a quick glance, then look back at her.

"But I just heard your good news from Mavis and then I saw you sitting over here, and I knew it was a sign," she goes on. "I am *so happy* for y'all, and I just know you've got years of love and happiness ahead of you."

Shirley smiles, her frosted hair swaying ever-so-slightly on top of her head. I stare at her with my mouth open, literally speechless.

There's a brief pause. Daniel collects himself first.

"Thank you, Shirley," Daniel says, covering her hand with his.

"You two were always so sweet together," she says. "Not to mention that now Karen Rogers owes me fifty dollars. Blessings!"

Then she waves, turns, and she's off.

My mouth is still open. I close it, jerking one thumb after Shirley's retreating form.

"Daniel," I hiss.

His face has turned to stone, and he's still looking after Shirley, like he can undo the last thirty seconds with the force of his mind.

"Daniel, who was in that courtroom?" I ask, my voice low and deadly serious. "You, Lucinda, Crystal, her people, the judge? *Who else?*"

He presses his lips together and swallows, his Adam's apple bobbing slightly. Then he takes a deep breath, sighs, rubs one temple like he's just remembered something.

"The bailiff," he says.

I just wait.

"Pete Bresley."

I put my face in my hands, my BLT now rolling in my stomach. I'm slightly nauseous. I force myself to take a deep breath, my mind going a thousand miles a minute.

"You told the town gossip's gossipy-ass son that you and I are engaged?" I ask. I'm trying my best to keep my voice low and steady, but it's definitely not working.

"Maybe it won't get out," he says. "Plenty of people get married in Sprucevale, there's no—"

My phone buzzes in my pocket, and I pull it out while he's still talking.

It's my mother. I show Daniel the screen. He stops talking. I put the phone down on the table very gingerly, then softly tap the *decline call* button, like being gentle will help.

"She's calling to ask why I didn't tell her first," I say, and look frantically at Daniel.

He leans forward, blue eyes blazing, forearms on the table.

"Tell her," he says, his voice low, steady. "That we were keeping it a secret, but the judge asked me a direct question, so I couldn't—"

"You want me to tell *my mother* that we're engaged?" I whisper-shout.

He says nothing, just looks at me steadily.

"No," I say, holding up both hands like I can ward him off. "What? *No.*"

"It's not that—"

"It's a huge deal!" I hiss, as my phone rings again. It's Mom. I decline the call. "This is fucking insane, Daniel, I can't—"

I swallow hard, force my voice lower.

"I can't tell everyone I know we're engaged," I say.

He swallows again. His fists clench, then relax.

"Look, I'll lie to a judge," I say. My voice is shaking. "Fine. Sure. But I can't lie to everyone I know, Daniel. I'm not that good of an actress, they're going to figure it out, they're not going to believe us, they're—"

My phone rings for a third time.

"Fucking fuck shit goddamn it—"

I clear my throat and pick it up.

"Hi, Mom," I say. "Right now's not really a good—"

"MAVIS BRESLEY!" my mother exclaims, right in my ear.

30

I jerk the receiver away, my heart already sinking, and glare at Daniel.

"I just had to find out from MAVIS BRESLEY that you're engaged to Daniel Loveless, you couldn't even tell your own mother? I didn't even know the two of you were dating, you didn't say one single word about it and then I hear from MAVIS that you're engaged and getting married and—"

She takes a breath. I already feel like dirt, even though for once, the disaster isn't my fault.

"Mom," I say quickly, squeezing my eyes shut, the back of one fist to my forehead. "Listen, Mom, I know this seems sudden but it's actually not a good—"

"We're so happy for you," she interrupts.

I freeze, a lump suddenly forming in my throat. I clear it away.

"Thanks, but it's kind of a complicated situation," I say, my eyes still closed.

You see, I'm going to kill Daniel, I think.

"There's been a mis—"

The phone is lifted from my hand, and before I can react Daniel's leaning back in his chair, the phone held to his ear.

"Hi, Mrs. McManus," he says, smoothly.

I grab for my phone as subtly as possible, trying not to make a scene in this cafe. I'm pretty sure it's not working.

"Can Charlotte call you back in a minute?" he asks, his eyes boring into mine. "Today didn't quite go as planned and we're still ironing out a few details."

I make another lunge, but Daniel just grabs my wrist and lowers it to the table. God, he's got strong hands, and he covers mine with his and puts them both on the table, next to our empty plates.

"Of course," he says, into the phone. "And, Mrs.

McManus, I'm so sorry about this. It's not at all what we intended."

I kick him under the table, though not too hard. He frowns at me.

"She'll call you back in a few," he finally says. "Thank you."

At last, he hangs up my phone, puts it on the table, and just looks at me. He hasn't let go of my hand. I haven't tried to wrest it back, even though my heart is threatening to burst out of my chest.

"Two months," he says.

"Insane," I tell him.

"The case will be over in two months, maybe less," he says. "Then it'll all be over, and we'll tell people we're breaking up—"

"You. Are. *Crazy*," I whisper. "Everyone will know that this is some bonkers story, no one is going to believe us—"

"Shirley believed us," he says.

I stop short, blood rushing through my ears.

Then I shake my head.

"I can't lie to everyone I know!" I say, quieter this time. "I can't lie to my mom, and my sister, and all my friends. You sure as *shit* can't lie to your brothers."

"Charlie," he whispers. "Please. I'm fucked. If they find out that I lied they're going to take her to Denver, and... I can't."

"Remember when Eli thought that no one knew he was banging Violet?" I ask.

"This is different."

"It's not," I say, but my voice is suddenly unsteady. "I'm a bad liar. You're a bad liar. Everyone will know and it will only make it worse."

He gives me a desperate, pleading look that stabs me straight to my core.

I take a deep breath and stand my ground anyway. I know, deep in my heart, that this is way too crazy to work.

"Doubling down on some crazy lie isn't how you fix things," I say. "Look, just — tell people we broke up, or tell people that there was a misunderstanding, or tell people you got flustered and confused, I don't know."

"Think about it," he says, his hand still on mine. He squeezes a little tighter. My chest constricts to match it, and I ignore it.

Then he gives me a look that nearly stops my heart.

It's raw. Searing. Searching. Pleading. I feel like I can see straight through to the bottom of his soul right now, and I falter.

"Please?" he asks, his voice low, private.

I hesitate for the first time, my hand in his. I hold my breath.

I want to say yes. I do. I know that if he loses Rusty, it'll destroy him, and I'd do anything to keep that from happening.

And I don't hate the idea. We've been best friends since we were eleven. Daniel knows me better than anyone. I'm friends with his brothers. I'm his kid's cool aunt.

Except that *this won't work*. I know it won't work, because it's crazy. Somewhere, deep down, Daniel must know it too, that doubling down on a lie isn't the way to solve his problems. Just because Shirley believed a rumor doesn't mean anyone else will. It doesn't even mean she'll still believe it next week.

"I can't," I say. "It's not gonna work, Daniel. Just go back and tell the truth, it'll be fine."

I pull my hand back. I stand. I feel like everyone else in The Earl of Sandwich is looking at us, and I ignore them as I walk out the door, leaving Daniel behind me, sitting at the table.

CHAPTER THREE

CHARLIE

I stare at the box of Lucky Charms.

The leprechaun stares back.

Lucky Charms or Froot Loops? I think, sliding my gaze over to the brightly colored toucan.

Do I want marshmallows, or do I want loops, or do I want to fuck over my best friend?

There's the guilt again, deep and heavy in my chest. There it is clawing its way up my back, perching on my shoulder, whispering in my ear: *it's your fault if Rusty has to move to Denver.*

I swallow hard. I'm still standing in front of cartoon-covered cereal boxes, but I'm staring at them blindly, one hand resting on my shopping cart.

He'll be fine, I remind myself. *He's had sole custody for six years. He's doing a great job. She's reading at a least a fifth-grade level, she's learning fractions, she knows what all the parts of an insect are called...*

It's the same litany that I've been repeating over and over in my head ever since Daniel left my job this afternoon. There are a thousand reasons that Rusty's mom won't be able to suddenly take her away, and none of them are 'Daniel has a fiancée.'

He doesn't need the lie to keep her. He's doing just fine on his own.

But what if the judge doesn't believe that?

I sigh and grab the Lucky Charms, toss them into my shopping cart. It's otherwise full of guilt groceries: strawberries and spinach and organic radishes and the fancy, sprouted-grain bread. I even bought kale, because when I feel bad about something, I suddenly have the urge to eat the most guilt-free diet possible.

Except the Lucky Charms. I need this, okay?

There is no way that lying to everyone we know makes everything better. Literally no way. When has lying fixed anything, ever?

I push my cart along the aisle, toward the checkout. I'm pretty sure I'm doing the right thing, but *wow*, the right thing feels bad.

Just as I reach the end of the aisle, I hear a voice call my name.

"Charlotte! Is that you?" a woman calls, and I tense. Of all the days to run into someone at the grocery store.

I turn. I smile.

"I thought I recognized that hair!" Priscilla Hayes exclaims, fluttering down the aisle toward me.

Automatically, one hand goes to the unruly mess on my head. I discover that it currently contains not one, not two, but *three* pencils. No wonder I can never find anything to write with.

"Hi, Priscilla," I say. I don't even remember how I know Priscilla, I just know that I have for most of my life.

"I heard your news," she says, coming in closer, putting one hand on my arm. "And I just wanted to say that I am *so* happy for you two."

I suck in a sharp breath. The guilt on my shoulder digs its claws in.

"I never wanted to say anything, but I suspected for a long time," she goes on, keeping her voice low. "I understand why you'd want to keep a relationship quiet, but I can always tell when people are in love."

I open my mouth. I shut it.

Then I open it again and say something I shouldn't.

"Thanks," I tell Priscilla.

It's the wrong thing, and that knowledge shoots adrenaline through my veins. The hairs rise on the back of my neck, but Priscilla doesn't notice. She just smiles, comes in a little closer.

"I'm so glad that Rusty's going to have a stepmother like you," she says quietly. "That precious angel deserves it, after everything she's been through. I was her social worker, you know."

I just nod.

"And you know, normally, making the decision to take a child away from a parent is absolutely gut-wrenching," she goes on. "But getting that poor little girl out of her mother's house was one of the easiest decisions I've ever made, and of course, Daniel's done an absolutely fantastic job. She really seems to be thriving."

"He's great," I echo, relieved that I get to say a sentence that isn't a lie.

"You two will be very happy," she says, squeezing my arm. "Congratulations, sweetheart."

Then she drifts away, back down the grocery store aisle, and I'm left standing there, feeling even worse than I did five minutes ago.

I don't know much about Rusty's early life. Daniel doesn't like talking about it, so I don't press him for details.

I just know that one day, Child Protective Services came

to the gas station where he was working and told him he had a one-year-old daughter. They told him his daughter's name was Rustilina and that she was currently in a foster home, because they'd removed her from her mother's care.

A week later, he moved back in with his mom. A week after that, he brought Rusty home for the first time, and within three months, he had sole physical and legal custody.

And now the mother she was taken away from is angling to get her back, and I'm refusing to help him.

Fuck. Fuck.

Fuck.

· · · ★ ★ ★ ★ ★ · · ·

WHAT PRISCILLA SAID rattles around my brain as I drive home from the market, even though I try to think about it rationally. I tell myself that there's no way a judge is going to send Rusty back to a home that CPS took her from in the first place; I tell myself again that they almost always side with the custodial parent; I remind myself about her report cards and the fifth grade reading level and the fractions and all the proof that Daniel's the best thing for her.

And I remind myself ten thousand times that trying to fix this *with a bald-faced lie* is stupid and wrong and will never, ever work.

But I still feel bad, a little black storm gathering in my gut.

Would it be such a lie? I think.

Would two months of pretending be so hard, or so bad?

My apartment's right in town, above Blushing Bonnie's Bridal Boutique, which is a lot of name. There's a small lot right behind it, and as I park there, I realize someone's sitting on the steps leading up to my place.

Before I get out of the car, I look at my phone. There are so many missed calls and texts that I can't even scroll through them all. I shut my phone off again, guiltily, without answering a single one of them.

That's probably why someone's lurking at my apartment. I glance up at them.

In the fading light, I can just make out a head full of curls.

"There you are," Elizabeth says as I tromp up the wooden steps, carrying a grocery bag in each hand.

"Were you sent?" I ask.

"I'm here of my own free will," she says, neatly putting her phone in her purse. "Though Mom and Dad were *very* relieved when I said I'd come over. You don't have the reusable bags?"

I look down at the plastic grocery bags in each hand and feel guilty. That seems to be today's big mood.

"I forgot them," I admit.

"Keep them in your trunk," Elizabeth says, like it's just that easy.

"Then I use them and have to remember to put them back in my trunk."

"Keep them by the front door."

"Are we going to play this game all night or are you going to move so I can go inside?" I ask.

Elizabeth rolls her eyes but stands and lets me pass, then follows me into my apartment. I put the groceries down in my small kitchen, put the yogurt and milk into the fridge, decide everything else can wait until I feel like dealing with it, and grab a beer.

"You want one?" I ask, holding it up so Elizabeth can see it.

"Sure," she says, leaning against my kitchen table.

I grab another, get the tops off, and hand her one. She looks at the label before taking a swig.

They're both Loveless Brewing Sprucevale Ale. Daniel brought some over last week and these two were still in the fridge.

"Mhm," Elizabeth says to the beer label, like it's confirming all her suspicions.

We both drink.

And then she gives me that older sister look, eyebrows raised, lips slightly pursed, that says *I know everything you've ever done and everything you'll ever consider doing, so don't even bother fucking with me.*

I hate that look.

"I hear congratulations are in order," she says.

I clear my throat, because I still haven't exactly figured out what to do about that yet. Am I telling people we're engaged? Am I lying to everyone? Am I leaving Daniel to fend for himself and maybe leaving Rusty for the wolves?

I could kill him. I really could.

"Thank you," I finally say.

"I didn't actually congratulate you," she points out.

"Then un-thank you."

"Because it did seem strange that you'd go from being completely platonic friends with someone to being engaged to them without so much as a hint to your family and in particular, your sister," she says, pointedly.

I sigh, head into my living room, and drink some more. Elizabeth follows me.

"The same sister," she goes on, following me, "Who has *never* told anyone one of your secrets in her entire life. Your sister who knows that you borrowed Mom's tennis bracelet once and then lost it, and never ever told on you. Your sister who covered for you constantly when you were sixteen and dating Steve Fisher, even though Mom and Dad explicitly forbade you from seeing him. Your sister who bought you booze when you were underage, who taught you which concealer was the best for covering hickeys, who—"

"Okay!" I say, flopping onto my couch. "I get it, Betsy."

"And yet you *get engaged* to someone and never once hint about it *to your own flesh and blood.*"

"Would you also like to invoke the pinkie promise I made to you when I was eight?" I ask, gesturing with my beer bottle. "Or maybe the time I got you high when I was twenty and we made a blood pact by pricking our fingers with safety pins and dabbing it on the back of a gas station receipt? Or perhaps the time you told me that—"

Elizabeth bursts out laughing. She laughs so hard she snorts. Satisfied, I take another long pull from my beer.

"I forgot about that," she says, sighing. "What was our blood pact about?"

"Sisterhood, I think."

"That's it?"

"We were *really* high."

"That remains the first and last time I've done drugs, you know," she says, leaning her head back against my couch, her curls squashing against the fabric. We've got exactly the same hair, but somehow hers is always neat and orderly and mine is…

…not.

"You mean you're not up all night doing eight balls?" I ask.

"I can tell you're kidding but I don't even know what that is," Elizabeth says. "Other than it's some kind of drug thing."

"Cocaine."

"Yikes."

"Yup."

I tried cocaine exactly once, when I was nineteen, dumb, and hanging out with a rough crowd. When I woke up the next morning, I couldn't walk because the bottoms of my feet were bruised and cut to shit. Apparently, I'd insisted on running several miles home, barefoot. I never tried it again.

There's a long pause.

"You were about to tell me what's going on with Daniel," she prompts.

"Was I?" I ask.

"You were," she says.

For a second, I wonder if all big sisters are this bossy, or if it's just mine.

"I know something's up," she finally says, tucking one foot under her. "And if the next words out of your mouth are 'Daniel and I are engaged' you can just get right the fuck out of here because I'm not going to believe you."

"It's *my* apartment," I point out.

"Then don't lie to me," she says.

I hold my breath and stare at her for a long moment. I have no idea what to do. I was all set to make up some other version of the truth, one where the rumor was wrong and something that Daniel said in court got twisted.

But I'm having a hard time getting that version out of my mouth, mostly because I know she won't believe me for a second.

"Charles," she says, her eyes still holding mine.

I let the breath out in a rush.

"Daniel had a hearing today, and it was supposed to be about visitation but then Crystal made it about custody, and also she's married and pregnant and respectable now and the judge they got always sides with mothers, and so apparently Daniel panicked and told them we're engaged so he'd seem more respectable," I say.

"Oh, shit," she murmurs.

"And at first, he thought that if I just put on a ring and came to the next hearing and we, like, held hands or something it would be fine, because he only told the people in the courtroom, right?" I go on, rubbing my knuckles against my forehead. "Which would have been fine, honestly, I don't want him to lose custody either. Except of course nothing in this stupid town stays secret for even two seconds, and the next thing I knew Mom called me, shouting about Mavis Bresley."

Elizabeth considers this seriously, looking into her beer bottle.

"Did that make sense?" I ask.

"So now, if you tell people you're *not* engaged, it'll come out that Daniel lied to a judge in a custody hearing," she says.

"A judge who apparently has a long history of siding with mothers over fathers," I say. "The fuck do I do, Betsy? Besides kill Daniel for putting me in this position, though that would also mean that Crystal gets custody of Rusty so that would render the whole point moot."

She stares at the blank space of my TV for a long moment. Too long, absentmindedly clinking her wedding ring against the glass beer bottle.

"I mean, he's had full custody for years, and Rusty was taken away from Crystal by CPS, and she's doing so well with Daniel that even if it did come out that he lied, it wouldn't matter, right?" I say.

She's still frowning, clinking, staring.

"Earth to Betsy."

"I had this student a couple of years ago," she says. "The sweetest little boy you could imagine. He was kind of quiet, but he was really smart, got along well with all his classmates, very polite. Just a great kid. At the first back-to-school night I find out that he's being raised by his grandparents, this absolutely lovely older couple, and as I get to know him a little better, I learn that his parents were meth heads who'd neglected him until he wound up in the hospital."

I swallow hard.

"Well, his mom got clean," she says. "And, long story short, she sued the grandparents for custody and won. We all left for winter break and I never saw him again."

The story feels like a punch in the gut.

"That was grandparents, not an actual parent, so I'm sure it's different," she says quickly. "But…"

I lean forward, elbows on knees.

"…Daniel probably needs everything he can get," she says quietly.

"Betsy, I can't act engaged," I say. "I can't just tell everyone I know that we're, you know, in love and getting married. I'm a terrible liar. I'm a terrible actress. This farce is going to last exactly one point one seconds, and then we're going to get found out and it's going to be even worse than if I just said no."

"Chuck," she says slowly. "Everyone already thinks it's true."

"Only because they heard the rumor," I say. "Once we have to actually—"

"They think it's true because it's believable," she says. "Admittedly, it's been like six hours, but everyone who's called me has been like *oh my God, finally*, not *I think this is a farce.*"

I look away from the floor and over at her, and I can feel the heat creeping into my face.

"You're the only one who thinks this is some crazy, unbelievable lie," she says. "Well, and me. I didn't think you guys were a thing, for the record. But I think that telling people you are will raise exactly zero eyebrows."

"What about Mom and Dad?"

Elizabeth looks at me steadily.

"I've fielded some inquiries," she says.

"I don't know how to act engaged," I protest. "What do I do? Do I have to kiss him in front of people? Hold hands? Do... engaged stuff?"

I can tell that my face has gone flaming red as the images float through my mind: holding hands. His arms around me.

Kissing.

I pretty much break out in a sweat at that one. A memory tries to surface, and I frantically push it back down.

Elizabeth just shrugs.

"Hold hands once in a while, give him a peck on the cheek, act like you normally do, and you're fine," she says. "It's not like you're a medieval queen and everyone needs to watch you get deflowered."

I just stare at her, and she waves a hand.

"Sorry. It used to be a thing. And yes, I know that your v-card got swiped long ago," she says.

"My vag is not a credit card reader," I mutter, then finish off my beer.

When it's gone, I look down at the label: Loveless Brewing Co., Sprucevale, Virginia. My mind feels fractured, like I'm trying to have a thousand thoughts at once, but none of them can form more than halfway before being shoved aside by the next one.

"What happened to the kid whose mom got him back?" I finally ask, voice quiet.

"I don't know," Elizabeth says. "I never followed up."

She leaves *I couldn't bear to* unspoken.

I stand. I take her empty beer bottle and walk to the kitchen.

"I'm getting some water," I call. "You want anything?"

* * * ★ ★ ★ ★ * * *

TWO HOURS LATER, after we have a mishmash of leftovers for dinner, Elizabeth leaves and I finally gather the courage to look at my phone. I've had it on Do Not Disturb mode this whole time, but even so, the battery is at 5%.

I have more texts than I can read. Texts from people I haven't talked to in years. Texts from numbers I don't recognize. There are two texts from international numbers, because apparently my fake news has even made it overseas.

It would be sweet if it weren't so nerve-wracking.

Congratulations!

The two of you are soooo good together!

Can't wait for the wedding - I knew something was up!

So happy you're engaged! You guys are perfect.

Haha, I always thought you guys were up to something! Congrats.

They're endless. They're unfailingly positive. They're emoji-filled. At least fifty percent of the people who've texted me claim that they just *knew* that Daniel and I were secretly dating.

Reading the texts has the weight of certainty. Elizabeth

was right. She usually is, a fact which has been annoying me my entire life.

I bite my lip. I shut my eyes for a moment, because what I'm about to do seems completely, utterly, and totally insane.

Then I text Daniel.

CHAPTER FOUR

DANIEL

"The door opened," I intone. "Inside the cave were vast piles of gold, silver, and gems, and to one side, an enormous desk. Sitting behind the desk was the biggest — and first — dragon that the Princess Ophelia had ever seen."

Rusty is sitting bolt upright in bed, eyes the size of saucers, watching me.

"'Hello, Ophelia,' said the dragon. 'I believe you're here to apply for a job.'"

It's so quiet I could hear a pin drop as I take the bookmark off Rusty's side table, place it gently in *Apprenticed to Dragons*, and close the book around it.

"One more chapter," Rusty says, breathlessly.

"I already read you two," I tell her, ruffling her curls gently. "It's past your bedtime."

"*One*," she says, and holds up one finger as if she was unclear. "Please?"

"Sorry, kiddo," I say. "You'll have to wait for tomorrow night to see if Ophelia gets hired."

She sighs dramatically, but accepts this and scootches

47

down into her bed, pulling the sheet up to her chin. These sheets are jungle themed, and she's wearing robot pajamas. Seems like the robots might rust in the jungle, but these are the sorts of questions you don't ask a seven-year-old before bed.

"Night, chickpea," I say, leaning over and kissing the top of her head.

"Night, Dad," she says, already sounding half-asleep.

I head out, flipping the light switch by the door. Her light goes off and the stars on the ceiling start glowing as I close the door gently. Thankfully, Rusty's always been a pretty good sleeper — every now and then she'll make an appearance an hour after her bedtime requesting water or something, but overall once she's down, she's down for the night.

I stand at the top of the stairs. Laughter floats up, and I close my eyes, rubbing my temples with both hands.

The laughter is the reason that Rusty got two chapters tonight instead of the usual one: both of my older brothers showed up, unannounced, along with Eli's girlfriend, Violet. I managed to get them not to say anything in front of Rusty, but the second I go downstairs, they're going to have a *lot* of questions and I don't really have any answers.

At least my mom is at the telescope tonight, so I don't also have to deal with her questions.

I can't even be mad at Charlie for refusing to do this. She's right. It's completely insane to pretend we're engaged to everyone we know, it would never work, and when we got found out it would only make everything worse than if I just stopped this farce right now.

There's more laughter. I wonder, briefly, if I could somehow escape out of my bedroom window and just sit outside in the flower bed until they leave, though I'm sure that sooner or later, they'll search for me.

Since I have no other real option, I go downstairs. The three of them are on two couches, Eli sitting with his arm around Violet, Levi across from them, one ankle perched on a knee.

"There's the man of the hour," he says, watching me descend the last few steps.

Eli and Violet both turn.

"Shit, I wasn't ready," Violet says, and pops up, darting into the kitchen.

I take a deep breath and shove my hands into my pockets.

"Congratulations," Eli says smoothly.

"Indeed," adds in Levi.

I glance after Violet, who's got the fridge open.

"What's she doing?" I ask, jerking a thumb in Violet's direction.

"She brought a bottle of champagne," Eli says, levelly. "So that we can celebrate your engagement to Charlie in style. Since you're engaged. To Charlie."

I glance from Eli to Levi and back.

Neither looks remotely convinced.

Time to start the damage control, I guess.

"There was a misunderstanding," I say.

Expectant silence from the brothers. I steel myself and forge ahead with the bad excuse I made up, even though I can feel a light sweat breaking out on my palms.

At least I'm getting my toughest audience over with first, I think.

"Was there?" Levi prompts.

"I said that Charlie was an important female role model in Rusty's life," I go on. "I guess that *someone* in the room misinterpreted that as Charlie and me being—"

"Ta-da!" Violet says, coming back into the room. In one hand she's got a bottle of champagne, and in the other, she's got four wine glasses.

"I couldn't find the champagne glasses," she says.

"I doubt that there are any," Levi says. "We're rarely champagne people."

"Daniel was just explaining that he and Charlie aren't actually engaged, it's all just a big misunderstanding because she's a *role model* for Rusty," Eli says, getting off the couch.

"It was very believable," adds Levi.

Eli takes the wine glasses from Violet, sets them on a side table, and holds out a hand for the champagne.

"No," I say, shoving one hand through my hair, looking at the champagne. "We're not engaged, nothing happened, save the champagne for something real. It's all a big misunderstanding. Charlie and I aren't together, we've never been together, we're not *going* to be together —"

Levi makes a noise that I don't appreciate.

"*What*," I say, starting to get annoyed.

"I didn't say anything," Levi goes on, in that *we both know perfectly well what that noise meant and I'm not going to say it out loud* tone that older siblings always seem to have.

"We are not. Together," I say, punctuating it so that maybe he can understand me a little better. "There was a *misunderstanding*, and—"

There's a loud bang, and I jump. Violet's holding the uncorked champagne, wispy fog streaming from the top of the bottle.

"Fuck it," she says, grinning. "Now I want champagne. Y'all?"

She doesn't wait for us to all grumble *yes* before she starts pouring. Eli and Levi come grab glasses, still both watching me expectantly, like I'm going to break into a musical number any moment now.

"Here's to Daniel and Charlie very definitely not being together," Levi says, holding up his glass.

His eyes light up and his beard twitches like he's smiling. I don't like it.

"We're not," I say.

"Here's to nothing at all weird happening today," Eli says, and he's definitely smirking like an asshole.

"Here's to champagne because we like champagne," Violet says calmly.

"That one," I agree. "I like that one."

We clink glasses. I take a sip, then another sip, and then before I know it, I've guzzled a wine glass full of champagne and it's empty.

Everyone else just looks at me.

"You want to talk about it?" Eli offers, just as my phone dings in my pocket, and I sigh.

"The hearing was shitty besides everyone thinking that I'm engaged now," I say, pulling it out of my pocket. "Crystal's married, and she's *pregnant*, and—"

I've got about a thousand texts, but it's the most recent that stops my sentence in its tracks.

Charlie: I'll do it.

I have half a second of perfect blankness, where I can't remember what we were talking about earlier that she's agreed to.

Then it hits me, and I have a thousand thoughts all at once: *shit I just told my brothers another story thank God for Charlie maybe I'll have a chance now oh my God how do you act engaged and especially engaged to Charlie what face do I make? Do we get to kiss? Will people know?*

Everyone will know.

"Do what?" Eli asks, craning his neck around so he can see my phone.

I shut it off as fast as humanly possible.

"It's take your daughter to work day next week," I lie, my mouth running ahead of my brain, moving my phone back to my pocket. "I'd asked Charlie if she'd take Rusty, since—"

My phone dings again in my hand, and then, suddenly, it's not in my hand.

"Hey!" I snap, whirling around as Levi steps back, holding my phone up in front of himself.

"She also says she wants a ring the size of Texas," he says.

"You can't just take my phone!" I hiss, still trying to keep my voice down because Rusty's asleep.

I lunge at Levi.

"Seems like I can," he says, and smoothly tosses it to Eli, who catches it one-handed.

"Give me that," I order him, whirling around, my hand out.

"Tell us why Charlie wants a ring the size of Texas for take-your-daughter-to-work day," Eli says.

"I don't know. Maybe she'll explain it in another text," I say.

I grab for the phone.

Eli throws it back to Levi, just out of my reach. I ball both my hands into fists of impotent rage and stand there, every muscle in my body tense, seething.

"Fucking stop that," I tell them.

"What are you guys, ten?" Violet asks, sipping her champagne and leaning against the side table.

Levi glances at me, then looks down at my phone again. I force myself to stand still, because I've played this game far too many times before in my life, and I know the only way to win is not to play.

"But she thinks you should go to some wedding cake tastings for real," he tells me.

"I know all the good places," Violet volunteers.

Levi tosses my phone in his hand, flipping it end over end. I watch it, tempted to lunge again, though I know exactly what will happen if I do.

Having two older brothers really sucks sometimes.

"So you're going to go taste wedding cake for take-your-daughter-to-work-day," Eli says cheerfully, because he's a dick. "While Charlie is wearing a ring the size of Texas and all of Sprucevale thinks you're engaged."

"Which no one will think after you shop for wedding cake together," Violet volunteers. "That will definitely make people think this was a misunderstanding."

"You two deserve each other, you know that?" I snap.

Violet and Eli just clink their glasses together. I glare.

"Would you like to tell us the truth or should we continue meandering into this increasingly ludicrous web of lies?" Levi asks, stoically as ever.

I look from Levi to Violet to Eli, and I know one thing for certain.

There's no way I'm getting out of this. I'd prefer to begin our charade with as few people in on the secret as possible, but this will have to do.

They can keep a secret. Right?

I hold my wine glass out toward Violet, who reaches behind her, grabs the bottle, and gives me a refill. I drink about half of it down, then take a deep breath and try to figure out where to begin.

"I lied to a judge at the hearing today," I start.

· · · · · ★ ★ ★ ★ · · · ·

I TAKE another sip of my black coffee and fiddle with my phone. I'm sitting at one of the back tables in the Mountain Grind, the coffee shop in downtown Sprucevale where

Charlie told me to meet her this morning. I've got about twenty minutes to waste — I was ten minutes early, she'll be ten minutes late — and I keep rereading her texts from last night.

Charlie: Fine, I'll do it.
Charlie: I want a ring the size of Texas, though.
Charlie: And we should go wedding cake tasting for real. FREE CAKE.
Charlie: Mountain Grind at 8 tomorrow morning? After Rusty gets on the bus, before work?

Right now, I'm nervous as a long-tailed cat in a room full of rocking chairs, as my mom would say. Already this morning at least five people have congratulated me on my recent engagement, and they've all said variations on the same thing: we're so happy! You're perfect together! We always thought that there was something between you and Charlie!

It should soothe me, but it doesn't, because now I'm thinking about her, us, how we are together, what we've done to make everyone think we're an item. If everyone thinks it's true, what are they expecting?

PDA? A lot of PDA? Handholding? Kissing in public? Intimate, candlelit dinners where we hold hands over the table, stare deep into each other's eyes, and coo sweet nothings while ignoring the food in front of us?

Well, we won't be doing that because there's no way Charlie makes it more than ten seconds of cooing without cracking up. I don't think I'd make it more than ten either.

We're going to have to do the other stuff, though. Holding hands. Kissing.

The thought of that last one makes my stomach feel like it's on a roller coaster without the rest of me. I frown at my phone, tapping it restlessly on the table, ignoring my reflection in the black screen as a flicker of a memory comes to light.

Just as quickly, I shove it away, because it's completely irrelevant to the current situation.

"You're not even watching anything," her voice says.

I look up from my blank phone screen, sitting bolt upright at the table. Charlie's standing next to me, coffee cup to her mouth, both eyebrows raised.

Should I kiss her? Do engaged people kiss when they see each other?

Is it weird if we do? Is it weirder if we don't?

"Just zoning out," I say, and she sits across from me. No kiss. I can't tell if I'm relieved or not.

"Why, something on your mind?" she teases, her cup between her palms.

"What could possibly be on my mind?" I deadpan, taking a long pull from my own coffee cup, and she laughs.

It's a good sound. It makes my stomach feel less like it's on a roller coaster and more like it's on a lazy river.

"So," she says.

"So," I echo, looking across the table at her.

Charlie's pretty. She's distractingly pretty. Confusingly pretty. She's got a mane — that's the only word for it, a mane — of deep brown curly hair that goes gold in the sun. She's got hazel eyes that always look like they're laughing, a spray of freckles across her nose and cheekbones, and full lips that somehow always make her look like she's up to no good.

Even in the wintertime, she looks like she's just come in from the sun. She looks like she could shake her head and sunbeams would sprinkle the floor around her. She's always in motion, fiddling with something, talking with her hands, tapping her feet. She's more fidgety than my seven-year-old.

I don't understand why there isn't a line of men following her at all times, begging for a date. I've never understood that.

"I had some thoughts," she says, and reaches for the canvas bag that seems to be functioning as her purse today.

"At least one of us has a strategy," I say.

"I didn't say it was a strategy," she says, bringing out several loose pieces of paper with fringe on one side, like they were ripped from a notebook. "I said I had thoughts."

She reaches in again and grabs a receipt, covered in writing, and then an envelope. A sturdy-looking napkin. A piece of a cardboard box.

"The notebook I was writing in ran out of paper and I couldn't find another one," she says.

I reach over and grab the piece of cardboard box.

"Backpacking with Caleb?" I ask, squinting as I try to decipher her handwriting.

"Don't look at that yet," she says, grabbing it from my hand, then frowning at the various pieces of writing-covered stuff in front of her. "I thought I numbered these," she says to herself.

Patiently, I take a sip of my coffee.

"Here's page one," she says, finally shuffling her pile together. "For some reason I numbered all the other pages, but not the first one, so I—"

She looks up at me, then laughs.

"Right. Anyway. I need a ring."

"The size of Texas," I supply, and she grins.

"I actually don't care what size it is," she says. "And it can be cubic zirconia or whatever. But everyone's going to ask to see it. I had to explain to three people already this morning that we hadn't planned on announcing yet so I don't have a ring, but you got surprised at the hearing and couldn't bear lying to a judge."

She rests her chin on her hand, eyes laughing.

"That's our backstory now?" I ask. I feel like I should be taking notes. "Good to know."

Charlie looks down at her notes.

"Sorry, I got put on the spot," she says. "Also, you always have to let me win at horseshoes."

"But you're terrible at horseshoes," I point out.

She just shrugs.

"That's the price of my acceptance," she says.

I glance around us, but no one is listening. We're sitting at the only table against a wall in the back, and the rest of the Mountain Grind is bustling, the ambient noise too loud for anyone to overhear.

"Okay, you can win at horseshoes," I say, begrudging. "What else?"

She glances down at her notes.

"Wait, is that your list of demands?" I ask, grabbing for a piece of paper. She pulls it away.

"It's not *all* a list of demands," she says, shuffling. "There's other thoughts in here too."

"How much is demands?" I ask. "What am I getting myself into?"

Charlie ignores my question and continues on.

"Next, I want first crack at your mom's strawberry pie," she says.

"Not blackberry?"

"Nope. Strawberry," she says. "Any time a strawberry pie appears, you will save me a piece."

I swallow some more coffee.

"All right," I say.

"Third, free beer for life from Loveless Brewing."

"For *life?*"

Charlie just nods very seriously. I narrow my eyes, like I'm thinking about negotiating.

In reality, I don't remember the last time she paid for a beer from my brewery. This pretty much just formalizes the arrangement.

"Ten years," I say.

She presses her lips together, thinking, and I don't notice the way it gives her a slight, soft, supple pout, nor do I think again about the fact that we're going to have to kiss.

My stomach does a little flip.

"All right," she says, shrugging, and flips over a page. "Meatballs upon request from your brother Eli."

"I can't guarantee that," I protest. "You know I have zero say in what Eli does."

"Didn't you talk him into infiltrating his own place of work to get a security video last year?" she asks, tilting her head to one side.

"I didn't talk him into that," I say.

"You just suggested it and he did it?"

"I didn't even suggest it!" I say. "I just… gave him advice when Violet was pissed at him."

She's looking at me with those eyes, tapping her fingers on the side of her coffee cup. We lock eyes for a long moment.

"Fine," I finally say. "Meatballs."

"I want Seth to do my taxes."

Seth's my next-youngest brother. We co-own Loveless Brewing; I do the beer parts, he does the business parts.

"How many more of these demands do you have?" I ask.

"Two after this one," she says.

I take a deep breath, drink some more coffee.

"All I can do is ask," I point out. "You do know my brothers are separate entities from me, right? We're not all branches of the same massive organism, like an aspen stand or something."

She gives me a puzzled look.

"Aspen trees are actually all shoots of one massive root system," I explain. "There's one in Colorado named Pando that's the world's heaviest living organism. Levi got real excited about it once."

My eldest brother is the chief arborist of the Cumberland National Forest. The man knows a *lot* about trees.

"Yes, I know you're not an aspen," she says. "But I bet you've got some influence with them, my taxes are going to be hell once my LLC is formed, and I know Seth does the brewery's."

"Fine," I say. "What are the last two?"

"A backpacking trip with Caleb to the best secret spot he knows in the Blue Ridge," she says, and I'm already frowning before she finishes the sentence.

"You want to go backpacking with my little brother?" I ask, already imagining the two of them, alone together on the trail for a few days. Laughing over a campfire. Sharing one of those tiny backpacking tents, sleeping inches away from each other.

Caleb's the youngest, currently getting his Ph.D. in Mathematics, and when he's not in school he's usually hiking some very long trail. He did the Appalachian Trail while he was in college, and he finished the Pacific Crest Trail last summer.

At least it's not Seth, I tell myself. *Caleb knows how to keep his hands to himself. I think.*

I still don't like it. I don't care that this engagement is fake. I don't like it one bit, and I frown into my coffee.

"You can come if you want," she says, shrugging.

"I will," I mutter. "What's the last one?"

Charlie takes a deep breath, holding the envelope in her hands, and my heart does a little hop inside my chest.

She wants to practice kissing, I think, feeling the blood rise to my face. *She thinks that I should start sleeping over sometimes, in the same bed, to make it more believable—*

"Our fake breakup has to be mutual and amicable," she says, still not meeting my eyes. "However we decide to end it, it has to be the nicest, most civil breakup in the history of Sprucevale. You can't tell people I cheated on you or something, I can't claim that you stole my credit card and bought ten thousand bouncy balls, you can't run down Main Street posting flyers of my face that say 'this woman is a jerk,' et cetera."

I pause, mid-sip. I hadn't thought about this part. To be honest, I hadn't gotten much further than *we're going to have to kiss,* but there's a pang, somewhere deep down inside, at the thought of having to break up with Charlie.

Even though it's fake. I'm not saying it makes sense. Just that it's happening.

"It's not that big of a deal," she says. "I just think we should figure out how we're going to end things now, before we actually have to do it. That'll make it more believable, if we can start planting the seeds of our eventual breakup now instead of suddenly going, 'He puts mayonnaise on french fries, we can never marry' in two months."

"You would dump me over mayo on fries?" I ask, trying to sound light, even though my heart is still thumping unpleasantly in my chest.

"You're a red-blooded American," she says, taking a long swig from her cup, her eyes glimmering with a smile. "Use ketchup and don't get ideas above your station."

I just laugh.

"I forgot we'd have to break up," I admit.

"We can't actually get married," she says. "I mean, obviously. This is not— I mean, we're not— you know—"

Suddenly she's flustered, the light gold skin under her freckles pinkening.

"We're just us," she says. "We're not really a thing, no matter what everyone in town seems to think."

I glance down at my nearly-empty coffee, and there's a flicker — just a flicker — of years ago, the two of us sitting on the hood of my car, beers in hand, my arm around her as she laughs, her curls brushing against my cheek, we're so close.

I shake it away and drink. The past is past.

"We'll have the world's most amicable break up," I agree. "It'll be so fucking civil that the United Nations will ask us to lead a seminar."

"In front of everyone," she says. "All the gossips. I only want to do it once, Daniel."

There's something in her voice, her look, and I think for a second about Charlie saying *I don't love you enough to make this work* a few months from now and despite everything, despite the fact that we're sitting here talking about our fake engagement, it hurts.

"Me too," I say.

We're both quiet for a moment, drinking, glancing around the coffee shop, sitting in our mutual, comfortable silence.

"Did you have any more demands?" I ask. "I don't think you've got anything that Levi has to do yet."

"I'll think of something," she says evenly.

"You can't make more demands after we've agreed."

That just gets a catlike smirk that lights up her hazel eyes.

"Can't I?" she teases.

CHAPTER FIVE

CHARLIE

As Daniel's walking me to my car — something he always does, even though it's eight-forty-five on a sunny morning in the middle of downtown Sprucevale, and I don't think even the Vatican could possibly be safer — my phone rings, and I pull it out of my pocket.

It's Daniel's mom, Clarabelle Loveless.

"Hi, Clara," I say.

Daniel just watches me, one eyebrow raised.

"Charlie!" she exclaims. "I only just heard your big news, I was at the telescope all night. You and Daniel! I have to admit, I had absolutely no idea."

We stop on the sidewalk, and I turn, look into Daniel's ocean-blue eyes.

"Well, we kept it pretty secret," I say. "Thanks, Clara. We're really happy."

"*Very* secret," she says. "So secret that no one suspected a thing."

I give Daniel a slightly alarmed look, and he frowns.

What? He mouths.

I just shake my head.

"Well, you know how gossip around town can be," I say, the words starting to tumble over each other, the way they always do when I get nervous. "And we didn't want to tell anyone until we were super sure, because, you know, rumors and Rusty and everything so we just decided to keep it secret for those reasons! Secret reasons."

Daniel closes his eyes and rubs his knuckles against his forehead. I bite down on my lip so I can't talk any more.

"Whatever your reasons, I'm positively delighted," Clara goes on. "You'll have to come over for dinner tonight, of course. I've already talked Eli into cooking, and of course all the boys will be there. Even Caleb is driving down from school for the night."

"Dinner? Tonight?" I ask, and Daniel's eyes shoot open. He shakes his head.

"The usual time, six o'clock," Clara says.

Daniel shakes his head harder, making the *cut it off* gesture across his throat, and I make a face back at him that means *it's your mom, you know I can't say no, are you crazy?*

"Six o'clock it is," I confirm, a little more chirpily than necessary.

Now Daniel's making that motion with both hands at once, shaking his head at the same time.

"See you!" Clara says, and we hang up.

Daniel just sighs.

There's a heavy weight inside me, something that feels like it's dragging my lungs down into my stomach. *Daughter-in-law. Stepmom.* This faking thing is bigger than just Daniel and me, and when it ends, there are going to be a lot of disappointed people.

Now I feel guilty.

"For the record, this?" Daniel says, shaking his head and doing the cut-it-off neck-slicing motion with his hands, "means no, stop, don't, that sort of thing."

"I can't say no to your mom," I tell him, like he's crazy.

"I do it all the time."

"She's *your* mom!" I say. "I can't say no. Besides, everyone's coming, Eli's cooking, it's gonna be a whole thing—"

"Eli always cooks," Daniel points out. "And everyone comes all the time."

"Sorry," I say. "I spazzed."

"It's okay, I just gotta tell Rusty first," he says.

Of course. Rusty. How could I forget?

I wait a beat, putting my phone back into my pocket.

"The truth?" I ask, softly, and he nods.

I bite my lips together.

"I can't lie to her about this," he says, and I nod in agreement.

I don't love the idea of entrusting this enormous secret to a seven-year-old, but I *hate* the idea of telling her that I'm going to be her stepmom only to take it back in a few months.

"I gotta get to work," I say, gesturing at my car.

"Me too," he agrees.

Then he pauses and just looks at me, his eyes searching my face, and I look back. He's dressed casually today — jeans and a Loveless Brewing t-shirt — but he's still astonishingly handsome, tall, built, and intense. I swallow, momentarily lost for words.

I could pretend to be attracted to that, I think.

Pretend?

"Charlie, thank you," he says, his voice low and quiet, pitched so that only I can hear. "I know this isn't ideal, but... thanks. You're a lifesaver."

Daniel makes it easy to smile, and I do.

"You're welcome," I say, and gather my courage.

Then I walk up to my fake fiancé, put one hand on his

arm, stand on my tiptoes, and kiss him on the cheek, my heart beating like a flock of starlings.

His skin is warm under my lips, his short beard surprisingly soft. He smells a little like shampoo and a little like something sharp and earthy.

Then it's over, and it was no big deal except my whole body feels like a live wire.

"See you tonight," I say.

His other hand skims my waist as I step back.

"See you," he echoes.

· · * * ★ ★ ★ ★ * · ·

THE MOMENT I pull into the driveway, Daniel comes out of the house. By the time I've parked he's walking toward me, the gravel under his bare feet not bothering him in the least.

"I'm not that late," I say, getting out of the car. "It's like five after six."

"It's ten after, but you're fine," he says. "I wanted to prepare you."

As if on cue, Eli's girlfriend Violet opens the screen door, waves, then walks back inside.

"She knows," Daniel says, his voice low. "Her, Eli, and Levi... found out."

"You told them?" I ask.

"No, they're a bunch of nosy assholes," he says.

"Language," I tease, and Daniel rolls his eyes.

"Rusty's inside, she can't hear me. I told her today. She was kind of confused, but I sold it to her as a fun pretend thing that we're doing, and I think she's on board for now," he goes on. "My mom, Seth, and Caleb don't know."

"Yet," I say, still looking up at the big house. We start walking.

There's something on the small of my back, and it takes me a moment to realize it's his hand, just barely brushing against me, like he's guiding me up the driveway.

A slow, warm tingle travels up my spine, from his fingers to the nape of my neck. It's nice. This is nice.

I ignore it.

"Yeah," he agrees, his voice low and slow. "I see Seth every day at work, and Mom... you know how she is." he mutters.

"You mean, 'possibly psychic'?" I ask.

"She's not psychic," he says. "She just pays attention."

"So this secret is just between us and four other people, one of whom is in second grade," I say.

"Right."

"What could go wrong?" I ask, rhetorically.

We reach the porch steps. Daniel's hand is still there, on my back, and I'm doing my damnedest to pretend that this is perfectly normal, that I'm used to his light, strong fingers guiding me, that this has been happening for ages now and somehow, no one else has noticed.

Then Daniel stops.

"Charlie," he says, my foot on the bottom stair. "Hold on."

"You need a minute?" I ask, stepping back. I couldn't blame him if he did. The Loveless clan is delightful, but they can be intense.

"Sort of," he says. He takes my hand. "C'mere."

There's a half-smile in his eyes that matches the one on his lips, and he tilts his head slightly to one side. I raise an eyebrow and let him lead me away from the porch steps, around the side of the old farmhouse that's been in his family for generations.

Surrounding the house is a strip of grass, then the forest. He leads me in on a barely-there path, and even though now I know where I'm going, he doesn't let go of my hand.

A hundred feet later we're there: a small grove of cedar and pine trees, the last of the day's sunlight filtering through, the ground covered in pine needles.

"Don't tell me you stole your dad's whiskey again," I say, looking around.

Daniel laughs.

"No, and I didn't pinch a bottle of Boone's Farm from the 7-11, either," he says, and I involuntarily make a face.

"Well, unless you bought pot from Silas, I give up," I say.

Let's just say that Daniel and I spent some time in this little clearing while we were teenagers, and we were never doing homework. Frankly, I'm amazed we didn't burn the whole forest down.

"Nope," he says, and reaches into a pocket. "Got this, though."

Before I can answer, he steps in front of me and pops open a small, gray box.

"Holy shit," I gasp, both my hands going to my mouth.

It's a ring, and it's *gorgeous*.

I'm not a jewelry girl. I think I own one bracelet and two necklaces, and my ears aren't even pierced, but I'm momentarily struck dumb by this ring.

It's stunning. It doesn't look a thing like I was expecting an engagement ring to look like. The central stone is square and red-orange, set into a gray metal, two tiny white stones set into the band on either side.

The metalwork is beautiful, delicate and solid all at once, faintly art deco.

Even in the dim light, it flares like it's burning from the inside.

"Where the hell did you get this?" I breathe.

"I think you're supposed to jump up and down and say yes," Daniel teases.

"I think you're supposed to give me a speech about how much you love me and actually propose," I tease back, still staring at it. "Is that... real?"

I'm kind of afraid to touch it. It looks expensive and delicate, and I have a certain bull-in-a-china-shop tendency.

"It's real," he says, taking it out of the box and snapping the box shut. "It's a garnet. My great-grandfather proposed to my great-grandmother with it."

My heart plummets.

"No," I say, shaking my head. "Nope. No way. I can't take that ring."

"Char—"

"I'll lose it, or I'll maim it, or I'll accidentally feed it to a dog—"

"You don't even have a dog."

"Doesn't matter," I say. "Daniel, you can't give me your *family engagement ring*. Doesn't that technically belong to Levi or something? Or Eli? At least he's dating someone."

"It's first-come, first-serve," Daniel says. "Come on, you're not going to lose it."

"I can't be trusted with that," I insist.

Daniel just sighs. He spins the ring in his fingers, looking down at it, thoughtfully. Then he looks back up at me.

"I trust you," he says simply, and holds out one hand.

I hesitate, my eyes still on the ring. The problem is that I don't trust me. I know how I am. I shouldn't have nice things.

"Come on, Charlie," he says softly, and I take a deep breath.

Despite all my misgivings, I reach out, put my hand in his.

"Other one," he says softly.

I laugh and give him my left hand.

"Will you fake marry me?" he asks, his tone light, teasing.

"Nothing would make me happier," I answer.

"Thanks," he says simply. "It probably needs to be resized, but— oh."

He slides the ring onto my finger, and it fits perfectly. I flex my fingers experimentally, to see if it's a fluke and the ring is actually going to fly off so it can be eaten by a magpie, but it stays on.

It stays on and... I *like* it. It looks good on my hand — not too big, not gaudy, not small. Just right, even with my calloused fingers, lightly scarred knuckles and short nails.

Daniel's still got his hand under mine, and he runs his thumb up my ring finger, over the ring, along the back of my hand, and sparks scurry up my arm.

Then I swallow hard and look up at him.

"We should go back in," I say. "I don't want to make them wait for us."

· · · * ★ ★ ★ * · · ·

DANIEL OPENS the door for me, his hand lightly touching my back.

"Congratulations!" several people shout at once, all out of sync.

Then a kazoo blows.

I start laughing.

There's a banner. Seth and Levi are waving little flags. Eli and Violet are wearing party hats, and Caleb is cranking a noise maker next to Rusty, who's playing the kazoo. Clara's just standing there, beaming in the middle of it all.

Then I look back at Daniel and see the look on *his* face, and it tells me that even though he was just in here, they've somehow managed to surprise him as well.

I laugh harder. I can't help it. This is ridiculous, and also, there's a kazoo. And flags. I don't know why they're waving flags, but it's hilarious.

"Thank you," Daniel manages to say after a moment, sounding somewhat bewildered. "Thank you for this. Were you hiding it somewhere?"

"It doesn't take too long to pin up a banner," Violet volunteers, straightening her hat. "Besides, we thought we ought to do something special for your surprise engagement announcement."

I try to make myself stop laughing, and snort quietly instead.

"It's beautiful," I finally say.

"We won't even make you pick a best man right now," says Eli, a smirk hovering around his mouth. "We'll let you wait until after dinner."

"I should set up some kind of competition," Daniel says, deadpan. "Make you guys fight for the honor."

All four other brothers look at each other, like they're considering who'd win.

"Certainly not," says Clara. "I've had enough of you fighting to last me three lifetimes. Daniel will choose his best man however he likes and there will be a *minimum* of complaining from the rest of you."

"It's just work, you know," Seth chimes in. "You have to plan a bachelor party, help with the wedding, keep track of the rings."

"So you don't want it?" Caleb asks.

"I'd plan a great bachelor party," Seth says, grinning.

"No," says Daniel, glancing quickly at Rusty.

She's frowning slightly, hanging onto every single word that comes out of Seth's mouth.

"We'd go out, get steak, have a good time," Seth goes on, leaning forward, a grin on his face that means he's needling Daniel. "We could even stay up *past midnight*."

"That's crazy," says Daniel.

"You could have *two* drinks," adds in Eli. "Maybe three!"

"Wow," deadpans Daniel.

"You're gonna have fun, whether you like it or not," finishes Seth.

"Mandatory fun, the best kind!" says Caleb, grinning.

They keep harassing Daniel about his bachelor party, and even though he's acting annoyed, I can tell he's secretly enjoying it. Besides, if this were one of them, he'd be right there alongside the others, dishing it out.

We sit. The boys keep talking. Clara tries to keep the peace, but she doesn't try that hard. At one point, Daniel drapes his arm over my shoulders, and no one says a word about it. They act like it's normal, expected, routine. I lean back into his warmth, laughing along with them.

And I think: *It's too bad they're not really going to be my family*.

CHAPTER SIX

DANIEL

E li made spaghetti and meatballs, along with garlic bread, roasted brussels sprouts with goat cheese, and a salad with fennel, asparagus, sesame seeds, edamame, and some citrus fruit. I think it's grapefruit, but I wouldn't be surprised if it were something crazy I've never even heard of before.

Whatever it is, it's delicious.

"Have you given any thought to a fall wedding?" Violet is saying, taking some more salad with the tongs. A piece of asparagus falls onto the table, and she picks it up and pops it into her mouth. "It's a beautiful time of year here and venues tend to be a little less booked, though of course whether or not the trees will be in full color is kind of a crapshoot."

"We're considering it," Charlie says. It's the most neutral answer possible. "We haven't really had a chance to actually plan much yet."

Violet licks some goat cheese off of one thumb.

"Right, sorry," she says. "Force of habit to quiz brides-to-be about all the details."

Until last year, Violet was an event coordinator at a high-end wedding venue outside town, so she knows weddings backwards, forwards, and upside down.

If we were actually getting married, she'd probably be very helpful.

Charlie just laughs lightly, winding spaghetti around her fork.

"Right, of course," she says, and my eyes flick to the ring on her finger. It's easily the fanciest thing I've ever seen Charlie wear.

To put it lightly, Charlie isn't girly. I could count the number of times I've seen her in a dress on one hand — she looked nice, it was memorable — and I don't think I've ever seen her wear jewelry.

She wears a lot of coveralls, mostly for work. She wears a lot of jeans and t-shirts, a lot of sneakers, a lot of cutoff shorts in the summer and men's button-down shirts in the winter. When we were kids, we ran around the woods together, always getting dirty, covered in sticks and twigs and mud. I used to help her pick the leaves out of her wild hair.

But the ring looks good on Charlie, makes her hands look delicate without taking anything away from her.

I already feel bad that we're going to have to give it back.

"Have you picked out a dress?" asks Seth.

Everyone looks at him.

"I can't ask about wedding dresses?" he says, fork halfway to his mouth.

"You can ask about wedding dresses and we can be surprised that the question occurred to you," Levi says.

"Don't be sexist," Seth says, laughing.

"Yesterday you referred to a necktie as a head noose," I point out. "I'm a little surprised you know the word *dress*."

"I had a brain fart and forgot what they were called," he says. "You're all jerks. Charlie, take me dress shopping. I'm an expert."

"No!" I say, more forcefully than I mean to.

Great, now they're all looking at *me*, but I can't handle the thought of Seth being anywhere near Charlie while she's in a state of undress, and isn't that what dress shopping is? Getting naked repeatedly and then putting on dresses?

Charlie raises both eyebrows, making a *so you're going to try and tell me what do to* face. I regret my outburst instantly, even as the thought of Charlie getting naked again and again to try on dresses is... a nice thought.

"You wanted to go with Betsy, right?" I ask, naming her older sister.

"It was a joke," Seth says, eyeing me.

"I hadn't given much thought to my dress shopping support team yet," Charlie says, staying remarkably cool. "But I'll probably take Betsy and my mom. And I assume it'll be... a wedding dress?"

She clearly hasn't thought about this, because why would she?

"That is typically what women get married in, yes," Seth deadpans.

"You're the expert," Levi adds, and Seth just sighs.

"When you're ready, I have spreadsheets and lists of everything," Violet says, ignoring the boys. "I don't want to overwhelm you, so just say the word. I can even walk you through them."

"But there's no rush, right?" Eli says, giving me a *look*. It's a very annoying look, and I give it right back. "Enjoy your engagement. It's such a special time in your life."

Seth and Caleb both look at him like he's suddenly sprouted a second head. Levi continues methodically winding spaghetti around his fork. I think Violet's trying not to roll her eyes. Rusty's picking the soft, butter-soaked part out of the middle of her garlic bread and eating it, totally ignoring the adults.

"Thank you, Eli," I say, as sincerely as I possibly can. "It's a lot to do, but we're excited."

Suddenly there's warm denim beneath my palm.

Half a second later I realize I've got my hand on Charlie's thigh, her muscles tense under my hand. I didn't mean to. I swear my hand just moved of its own volition, but now it's there, I can't go back, and I definitely can't pull it away and apologize in front of my entire family, half of whom think we're really going to get married.

Instead, I just give her a quick squeeze. After a moment, she relaxes.

I keep my hand there.

The subject finally turns away from our not-actually-impending nuptials to some tree problem that Levi is having, and I stop listening for a moment, eating with my right hand while my left is still touching Charlie.

I've never touched her like this before, not in the almost twenty years we've been friends. Not this intentionally. Not for this long, or in this place, or with no other reason for touching her than just to touch her.

I've never touched her like we're lovers.

For all that, it feels oddly right. My hand feels like it fits to her, like it's supposed to be there, her warmth melding into my fingers.

After a moment, while one of my brothers is going on about something, she gives me a quick, questioning glance.

I give her a slight shrug, and she goes back to the conversation. After a while I pull my hand back, already missing her warmth.

· · · · ★ ★ ★ ★ ★ · · · ·

AFTER DINNER, I try to help with the dishes, but Caleb chases me out of the kitchen, and I let him.

When I find Charlie, she's in the front hall, hands in her pockets, looking at the wall, hung with pictures. I step up behind her, and she glances back, acknowledging me. Neither of us says anything.

The pictures are mostly my brothers and me. High school graduation photos, a few kids' sports pictures, a few where we're in boy scout uniforms. Levi, Seth, and Caleb all have their college graduation pictures up there, too, and there's one of all five of us plus Rusty, who looks about four, taken at a waterfall.

Further up on the wall, just above eye level, are the pictures of my father. They're older. Slightly faded, and Charlie's head tilts up slightly as she looks at them.

There's one of him in his police uniform, looking solemn in front of an American flag. One of him and my mom, somewhere sunny, in t-shirts and jeans, laughing. There's their wedding photo, which is pure eighties — her dress has both a train and poofy sleeves, and Dad looks like he's rocking a slight mullet — but they look *so* happy.

I never look at these pictures. I walk by them a couple times a day at least, but I never stop and look. Here's one with all five of us and Dad, piled into the back of a pickup truck, grinning away.

I'm in that gangly, awkward phase in the photo. Caleb's still a kid. Levi looks close to how he does now, so he must be sixteen, seventeen.

That can't have been taken long before the accident, I think.

I put one hand one Charlie's shoulder, and she puts her hand on top of it.

"I forget how much Eli and Seth look like him," she

says, still looking at the wall.

"They really do," I murmur.

"Those two are the spitting image of their father," my mom's voice says behind us.

There's a moment of silence.

"It's a little eerie sometimes," she admits. "Last year when Eli was staying here, I walked into the kitchen one night and nearly had a heart attack, because for a moment I thought your father was standing there, raiding the fridge. Had me believing in ghosts."

I wonder what it means that I think the opposite. That every so often, I walk by these photos and wonder why Eli's wearing a police uniform, only to remember the truth half a second later.

"Seth sounds exactly like him, too," I say. "It really weirds me out sometimes. I'm always afraid he's about to get the belt."

My mom sighs.

"That only happened once," she admonishes me. "He felt so bad about it afterward that he burned the thing and never laid a hand on any of you again."

"What did you do?" Charlie asks.

We're all quiet for another moment.

"Daniel," my mom says pointedly.

"I sneaked into the school and put glue in all the classroom locks," I say. "No one could open their doors. They had to cancel school that day."

"Eight years old," my mom says. "It's a wonder I survived the five of you all the way to adulthood."

"Sounds like more of a wonder that we survived," I say, and my mom laughs.

"I had my moments," she admits. "But now you're all grown and I'm free to drink whiskey, travel the world, and spoil my granddaughter."

She holds out one hand to Charlie.

"Can I see the ring?" she asks.

"Of course," Charlie says, and starts to tug it off.

"No, no, keep it on, it's yours," my mom says, taking Charlie's hand gently. "I wanted to see how it looked on you. Did Daniel tell you that my grandfather had it made for my grandmother?"

Charlie flicks me a glance.

"He did?" she asks.

"He sure did," my mom says. "My granddad Lowell gave it to my grandmother when they got engaged in 1930. I don't know where he got the stone, but he had it made by a jewelry maker in Richmond."

She twists it slightly on Charlie's finger, the garnet still fiery.

"He went all that way on horseback," she goes on. "He owned a car, but it was apparently in the Sheriff's possession at the time. Took him a week to get there, a week to get it made, and a week to get back. She wore it every single day for the rest of her life. After she died his father—" she nods at me, "proposed to me with it, and now it's your turn. I always thought it might look nice on you."

Charlie's eyes go wide, and she glances at me again, past my mom's head, bent slightly over the ring.

"Thank you," she says softly, after a beat. "It's beautiful."

"I'm just glad someone's wearing it," my mom says. "It wasn't doing anybody any good sitting in my jewelry box for all those years. Welcome to the family, Charlie. Officially, anyway."

She pulls Charlie in for a hug, and a moment later, I get one too. Then my mom reaches up and tousles my hair.

"I'm going to go see what's going on in the kitchen,"

she says. "Apparently there's been some to-do about ice cream."

With that, my mom leaves us alone together with the pictures and each other.

· · · ★ ★ ★ ★ · · · ·

THE TO-DO about ice cream is that Levi made some from the wild black raspberries he found growing along a creek, not far from his cabin. Eli tries to tell him that they're just blackberries, not black raspberries, but he picked an argument with the wrong person because Levi shuts it down almost instantly.

My mom apologizes that she didn't have time to make some pies, since this was on such short notice — she throws me a look when she says that and I ignore it — but promises that she'll do celebratory baking soon.

There's a final round of congratulations. I tell Rusty to go brush her teeth and put on pajamas while I walk Charlie to her car. Charlie waves as she steps outside, beaming, the ring on her left hand and her right weighed down with leftovers for lunch tomorrow.

And then, suddenly, it's quiet. The house isn't exactly in the middle of nowhere, but it's surrounded by the thick Virginia forest, and there are no other buildings in sight. There are no other visible lights, so even though we're only fifteen minutes from town, it feels like we could drive for hours and never see civilization.

"I shouldn't have taken the ring," Charlie says, our feet crunching along the gravel. "I already feel awful."

She holds up her left hand. The garnet flares, even in the pale moonlight. Without thinking, I alight my hand on her lower back. Charlie looks up at me.

"I don't think anyone's watching right now," she says,

her voice low and melodic. I swear her eyes reflect the stars above.

"You never know," I say. "They're a bunch of nosy assholes."

The ring catches the light again as she fiddles with it, worrying it with her thumb, spinning it around her finger.

"It's gonna be bad when we break up," she says as we reach her car. She puts her leftovers on top of it and turns to me.

"Don't leave those there, you'll forget them when you drive off," I say.

Charlie rolls her eyes at me, but she opens her door, sticks the leftovers on the passenger seat. Since I've watched her break at least three coffee mugs by driving off with them on the roof of her car, I feel justified.

"I'm serious," she says, shutting her passenger door and moving her hair out of her face.

"I know."

"Your mom just gave me her grandmother's ring and told me she'd always hoped I would wear it," she says, her voice lowering even further. She takes a step closer. "What happens when I give it back? We didn't think this through very well."

Her freckles look like stars, scattered across her cheeks, and I'm struck by the urge to take her face in my hands and run a thumb across them, see if they contain the same fire.

I settle for shoving my hands into my pockets.

"Let's cross that bridge when we get to it," I say. "It's months from now. Maybe something will happen that makes it all easier."

Charlie gives me the world's most skeptical look.

"Such as?"

I roll my lips together and glance toward the house, because I have no fucking clue.

"Maybe it'll turn out that we're actually second cousins," I offer. "Actually, that one's not bad. It could work."

"For that to work we'd have to actually be second cousins," she says. "That particular information is pretty verifiable."

"Maybe I'm adopted," I offer, and Charlie just snorts.

"Go look at those pictures again," she says. "You're not adopted."

"We'll think of something," I say. "I'll take the blame. I'll tell my mom, I'll tell everyone. I'll say I got cold feet and I wasn't ready. I'll say—"

"You don't have to," she cuts in. "You're right, we can figure this out later. I should head home."

She's still looking at me, the stars still scattered across her face and reflected in her eyes as she raises her left hand tentatively, the ring flashing and glimmering.

"They're probably watching right now," I murmur.

My hands are out of my pockets, one on her right hip, her warmth underneath her clothes flooding me.

"Because they're nosy assholes?" she asks, a slight smile lighting up her face.

"Exactly," I say.

My heartbeat is fast, hard, a frantic rhythm I've never felt before.

Correction: a rhythm I've only felt once.

Her eyes dart between mine. I move closer, her hand on my arm, her face tilting up slightly.

"Make it look good," Charlie teases, and I lower my lips to hers.

It's a quick, momentary kiss, over in a flash, but it makes my bones shake. It's a lightning bolt of a kiss, over in a second but when I pull my lips away from hers, I can still feel it jolting through my veins.

I take her face in my hand, thumb gently stroking along the scattered freckles. The movement isn't intentional, isn't calculated for an audience. It just *is*, because the need to touch her again right now is more than I can deny.

Charlie tilts her head into my hand, hazel eyes watching me, guarded and curious and shocked and a thousand things at once.

I want to kiss her again. I want to kiss her properly, harder and longer. I want to push her up against the side of her car and feel her body against mine as she kisses me back.

It takes everything I have not to kiss her again.

Just friends, I remind myself. *Just for show.*

Stepping away from her feels like wading through concrete, but I do it. The ring flashes one more time as we separate, her hands lowering, and then suddenly it's over, the spell broken. Charlie looks away, at the trees, at her car, glances over at the house.

"See you later?" she asks, already fiddling with the ring, turning it around her finger again and again, the movement unconscious.

"Of course," I say.

Charlie looks like she's about to say something else, but then she gives her head a little shake, smiles at me, gets in her car. I watch from the driveway as her taillights disappear toward the road, as she turns left, leaves.

Finally, I exhale, still rattled. Still shaken from half a second of touching my lips to hers, my mind racing.

I'm thinking that this is a worse idea than I knew. I'm thinking that we can never keep this up, that this lie will come out no matter what we do, that our inevitable breakup will tear everything we know into pieces.

But mostly, I'm thinking that I can't wait until I see her again.

CHAPTER SEVEN

CHARLIE

That wasn't our first kiss.

I'm driving fast, too fast, along the dark winding rural roads back to town. Headlights in front of me, darkness behind me, his great-grandmother's garnet ring around my finger.

It flashes, even in the darkness.

I don't think Daniel remembers the first time. It's been six years and he's never brought it up — not a look, not a glance, not an oblique reference, nothing.

Not that I've brought it up either. It was only one kiss.

We were twenty-three and drunk at a bonfire. There'd been cases of shitty beer and a few jugs of moonshine passed around, and the two of us were on the hood of his truck, lying back against the windshield, watching the sparks from the fire swirl up into the sky.

We were laughing about something. We clinked beer cans together. He was three-quarters of the way through his first year at community college, and I'd just gotten accepted into a two-year carpentry program.

I remember it felt like we were floating, celebrating, the

wasteland of the past four years behind us. We'd both pulled through bad times and bad company, and there we were, making something of ourselves, letting go for the first time in ages.

I don't remember what happened next. He turned and looked at me or I turned at looked at him, or maybe both. It must have been both.

But I remember being suddenly breathless with desire. I remember the feeling that my brain had bubbles rising through it, like champagne, and I remember the way that everything but Daniel faded, and I remember that it felt like if we didn't kiss right then I'd die.

So we kissed. It was gentle, slow, tentative. It was surprising. It felt like walking into an air-conditioned building on a hundred-degree day: wonderful and bracing, with that sense of bone-deep satisfaction.

Either he deepened the kiss, or I did. It doesn't matter. I just know that it felt righter than any other kiss in my life.

Then I spilled my beer all over both of us. The kiss ended and we were laughing, flicking beer off. Not long after we both went home, separately, because I didn't want to rush anything. I needed time to consider the fact that I'd just kissed my best friend of thirteen years, process it, decide how best to proceed.

The kiss rattled me, but in a good way. A tambourine, not a rattlesnake.

And then, the next day, Burnley County Child Protective Services showed up at Daniel's door and told him that a woman he knew was claiming he had a one-year-old daughter, and suddenly, nothing else mattered.

I couldn't blame Daniel for getting hit by a tornado, even though I was hurt. I couldn't blame Rusty for being the tornado. I was sad and upset and disappointed, but what could I do? Life moved on. I got over it.

Okay, I *did* make a voodoo doll of Crystal. It was a really bad one — just a vague human shape that I carved from a block of wood that I had lying around — but believe me, I stabbed the shit out of that thing. I think it made me feel better, though eventually I threw it away. Having a voodoo doll of your best friend's baby mama is fucked up.

I'm probably lucky that he forgot, or pretended to, or that we both decided to ignore it forever. Everything would be different now, and we'd have wrecked the friendship that we have. I wouldn't hang out with his family every Sunday at dinner. I wouldn't be Rusty's cool aunt who buys her stuffed animals of deep-sea fish and secretly let her drive her own bumper car once at the state fair.

Daniel doesn't know about that last part, mostly because before I took her, he gave me an extensive rundown of what rides she should and shouldn't go on.

I ignored the list and we went on all of them. We ate cotton candy, too. It was a blast.

When I finally pull into my parking space behind my apartment, I don't really feel better. I still feel a deep, layered guilt over wearing his great-grandmother's ring. I feel the same about lying to his mom and half his brothers, not to mention my own parents.

And I sure feel something about that kiss, something big and spacious and impenetrable, something taking up almost all the room I've got for feelings and leaving no room for anything else.

I head up. I glance into the kitchen, decide that there's nothing in dire need of cleaning before tomorrow. I brush my teeth, wash my face, turn out my apartment lights, and get in bed.

The ring catches on the sheet as I pull it up — just

slightly, no big deal — and my heart skips a beat. I sit upright in bed, turn on the bedside lamp and pull it off.

Then I hunch over the ring in the not-very-good light, heart still thumping, as I assess it for any possible damage — a prong torn off, the gem fractured, I don't know — but it's fine.

I sit there, staring at it, for a long moment. I tell myself that literally millions of people own engagement rings, that plenty of them probably wear them to bed, and that these are made to go on hands. They can probably stand up to cotton sheets.

I close my hand around it and get out of bed, because I can't wear this while I sleep. I'll wake up every forty-five minutes to double check that I haven't somehow swallowed it or something, and that's no way to live.

I need a ring receptacle. What I really want is, I don't know, a wall safe with a thumbprint scanner, because while you can lose keys and forget combinations, you can't lose or forget a thumbprint.

I don't have a wall safe. I don't even have a fireproof lockbox, even though my mom keeps telling me to get one. My 'important documents' are just in a cardboard box under my bed, a fact that made both my mom and my sister briefly close their eyes and breathe deeply when they found out.

In the absence of something that locks, I head into the kitchen and grab a mug. I have about two thousand too many, because whenever I find a particularly weird one, I can't help but buy it. That also means that other people buy me weird mugs, so appropriately, I find one that Daniel gave me last year.

It's got a cartoon illustration of several pinup-type women facing away from the camera, wearing thongs, and in goofy all-caps text it says VIRGINIA BEACH: NO BUTTS ABOUT IT!

First, no butts about what? 'Virginia Beach' isn't really a statement.

Second, there are clearly *some* butts about it because the butts are right there on the mug. I guess the argument could be made that the butts aren't really *about* Virginia Beach, because butts simply exist and aren't really about anything, but then it might seem like I've given this dumb mug way more thought than I should have.

I drop the ring in, and it lands with a satisfying clink. Then I double-check the locks on my door, put the mug on my dresser, and get back into bed.

After congratulating myself on actually finding a proper spot for the ring instead of sticking it wherever and telling myself I'd deal with it in the morning, I fall asleep.

CHAPTER EIGHT

DANIEL

I unlock the side door to the brewery, step inside, and take a deep breath. Instantly, it relaxes me: the smell of grain and malt, the sweet bready aroma that comes from boiling wort, the sharp tangy afternotes of hops.

It smells like work, and thank God for that. Loveless Brewing feels like the one area of my life that's going well right now: we're increasing production and expanding perfectly in line with Seth's business plan. Whatever he's doing, in terms of advertising and distribution and all that, it's working.

I pretty much just make the beer, talk us up to potential vendors, and stay out of his way.

I head to my office, checking the pressure gauges and thermometers on the huge, upside down cone stainless steel tanks as I do.

In my office, I fire up my computer, put on some coffee in the break room, then come back and open the brewery's spreadsheet.

Beer operates on a very specific schedule — even more so if you want to maximize efficiency and profit, like we obviously do. The master spreadsheet is half me (the beer schedules) and half Seth (the profit maximizing). It's also complicated, color-coded, partly automated, and a thing of beauty.

Today I'm dry-hopping a batch of IPA, filtering and bottling a lager, and making a very small batch of an experimental amber ale that I've been wanting to try. Easy. Straightforward. Beer can't protest. It's not my seven-year-old daughter waking up late and then stomping off to the bus, furious at me because she couldn't find the right glittery headband.

I offered her a different, shiny headband, but did she want it? No. No, she did not.

It's not my best friend wearing my great-grandmother's ring and kissing me outside my mom's house and... no.

I'm not thinking about that this morning. I'm not wondering if I really buried the past as well as I thought I did.

I'm thinking about beer and nothing else. I pull my to-do list for the day up on my screen, give it a quick read over, and then head for my office door so I can get started.

Just as I'm almost there, the phone on my desk rings. I frown and check the caller ID, because it's just past nine in the morning and beer people don't tend to call that early.

SETH LOVELESS, reads the small, blocky screen. I roll my eyes.

"WHAT?" I shout, not bothering to pick up the receiver.

"COME OVER HERE!" a voice shouts back. "PLEASE."

The phone stops ringing. I walk the seven feet from my office door to Seth's and lean against his doorway. He's in his office chair, leaning back, hands laced across his midsection like he's a movie villain about to say *I've been expecting you.*

"I called because I was trying to be polite," he says.

"You could've just walked over," I point out. "I just did that and I'm fine."

"Yeah, but I needed you in here," he says, and shifts his computer screen toward me.

It's... a spreadsheet? A flow chart? There's also a graph.

"Tell me you didn't redo the brewery spreadsheet," I say, darting a glance at my younger brother. "You can't just do that without—"

"Chill, I didn't," he says. "Take a closer look."

I lean in until I can read the small text on the screen, and I realize something: the spreadsheet is full of names and times. Up in one corner, the only two things in that column, are DANIEL LOVELESS and CHARLOTTE MCMANUS.

"What is this?" I ask, though I half-suspect the answer.

"This is my analysis of your engagement announcement," he says, swiveling in his seat to face his screen. He looks incredibly smug right now.

I fold my arms and wait, because apparently, he thinks he really is a Bond villain and wants to explain his entire evil scheme to me.

"I thought the timing and manner of your engagement announcement was kind of strange," he says.

"I explained that," I say, patiently, readying the story that Charlie came up with. "We weren't going to tell anyone yet, but then at the hearing—"

"Nah, that's not it," Seth says, waving one hand at me. "Because that happened at what, approximately eleven-thirty in the morning? Yet the first confirmation of the engagement from you is hours and hours later, at Mom's house, at approximately eight p.m."

"Why do you know this?"

"I asked Eli and Levi."

I want him to get to the point, but I don't want to give him the satisfaction of asking questions, so I continue to wait.

"On the other hand, it seems that Mavis Bresley had heard the news and was informing others of it by approximately twelve-thirty that day. I myself heard it from Patricia Yardley—"

"Did you?" I smirk. "Does Trixie know where you're *hearing rumors* from?"

"Trixie and I were never exclusive, and besides, we're no longer seeing each other," he says, like he's impatient to move on.

"Doesn't mean she's not mad," I point out. "When do I get to start tracking *your* rumors?"

My brother Seth is tall, charming, good-looking, and on account of those qualities, he's been to bed with a sizeable chunk of Sprucevale's female population.

As this spreadsheet proves, he's also a huge dork.

"—*anyway*, I heard it from Patricia around two, still long before either you or Charlie had broken the news to anyone."

"Congratulations," I deadpan. "You've got the insider track on town gossip."

"Except I should have known long before that," Seth says, raising his eyebrows.

He temples his fingers together, really getting into this whole Bond villain thing.

"Even if what you're saying about keeping it a secret and informing the court due to extenuating circumstances is true, you should have been on the phone telling your family the moment you stepped out of there," he says. "Not saying anything for hours is highly atypical for you."

"I've never accidentally shared news of a secret engagement before," I protest.

"Even so, not the sort of behavior I'd normally expect," he says. "Anyway, I did some analysis, and it turned out that the primary vector of the news was Pete Bresley, who just so happens to be a bailiff at the Burnley County Courthouse."

"Yes, he was there," I say.

"Furthermore, this regression suggests that Charlie *herself* was unaware of her own news until mid-afternoon, though it's more difficult to pin down an exact time," he goes on.

"She had her phone off."

"And finally, there's the most important data of all," he says, swiveling back to me. "And that's that the two of you *haven't been in a goddamn relationship this whole time* and I don't know who the hell you think you're kidding, Daniel."

There it is. Frankly, I'm surprised that he waited this long to confront me about it. I can fool a lot of people, but fooling my brothers is difficult, to say the least.

Doesn't mean I won't make him earn it.

"Yeah, that's what secret means," I tell him. "That people didn't know."

"I'm not saying people didn't know," he says. "I'm saying that maybe you can tell everyone else you and Charlie have been together for ages, but you can't tell *me* that. So would you like to tell me what's really going on?"

I look at the spreadsheet one more time, and I admit I feel a little bad that he's clearly spent hours on this.

On the other hand, Seth *really* loves spreadsheets and formulas. Maybe he had fun. I don't pretend to understand any of my brothers.

"Fine," I admit, uncrossing my arms, sitting in the chair opposite him.

He leans forward, both elbows on his desk, satisfaction written across his face.

"I lied to a judge," I start.

· · · ★ ★ ★ ★ ★ · · ·

"ALL RIGHT, KID," I say into the rear-view mirror. "You got any questions?"

Rusty kicks her booster seat a few times, like she always does when she's thinking.

"Can I tell people I'm the flower girl?" she asks.

"Sure."

"What if a police officer asks me whether you're really engaged?"

I put my car into park, sigh internally, and turn around to face her. It's the next day, Saturday, and we're picking Charlie up before we go to RiverFest.

Everyone I know will be at RiverFest. Everyone. It's the event of the year in Sprucevale.

I'm somewhat apprehensive about it, but it is what it is and there's no going back now.

"If a police officer asks, tell them the truth," I say, as seriously as I can muster. I wonder if I'm going to regret telling her that, but on the other hand, I don't want to be the dad who asks his kid to lie to the police.

Just everyone else she knows, that's all.

"What about a fire fighter? Or a doctor? Or my principal? Or—"

"Do you think any of them are going to ask you?" I say.

I thought we'd covered this, since I took her out to lunch for burgers and fries today and had a long talk about the fake engagement. She's surprisingly excited about getting to play pretend for an extended period of time, but she made me promise again and again that Charlie would still like her afterwards, and that we wouldn't *really* break up.

As usual, I felt awful. Rusty *adores* Charlie, and even though I reassured her a thousand times that Charlie's not going anywhere, I think she's still a little worried.

"Probably not," she admits.

"Then how about we talk about that if it happens?" I ask, and she nods.

It's Saturday afternoon, and we're parked outside Charlie's apartment, here to pick her up for our first date.

Sort of. It's our first public appearance, so I offered to pick her up and she said yes. I'm not sure if it's a date if my entire family, her family, and my kid are all going to be there with us, but it'll sure be something.

I get out, get Rusty out of her booster seat, and head up Charlie's stairs. She shouts to come on in when I knock, so we do.

Rusty goes instantly to her corner of Charlie's living room that Charlie set up for her and regularly stocks with cool new stuff. I don't think there's anything new over there today, but within seconds Rusty is wearing enormous purple sunglasses, sitting on a fuzzy blue pillow, and reading a chapter book with a mermaid on the front.

"Sorry, give me a few," Charlie calls. "I was about to get into the shower but then my mom called, and she wanted to know what our plans were for tonight, and then she started grilling me again about..."

She keeps explaining herself, but Charlie's running late because that's what Charlie does. It's annoying sometimes, but I learned to deal with it long ago, so I lean to one side and glance at her bedroom door, wondering if it's okay for me to go in.

It's open about six inches. I lean more, and then I see her.

It's *not* okay for me to go in, because Charlie's not dressed yet.

Her back is to me. She's wearing a bra and panties, and I should definitely turn around and look at something else, but I don't.

In fact, I do absolutely nothing besides stand perfectly still. My mouth might fall open.

Charlie looks *good* almost naked. Even with her back to me, her body's feminine and powerful all at once, a combination of curves and muscle that appeals directly to my lizard brain and shuts any higher functioning down completely.

Half a second later she slides something over her head, and then all of a sudden she's decent, wearing a sleeveless mint-green dress that comes down to her knees, but the image of her undressed is already burned into my mind: the way her muscles flex lightly under her skin as she arranged her dress over her head, the gentle curve of her waist, the way she cocked one hip and then the other.

Furthermore?

The bra and panties matched. They were both black, but even in the half-second I saw them, I could tell they both had the same lace around the edges, and that simple fact makes my heart race like nothing else.

"Hey, Daniel?" she calls.

I take a quick step to the side and jam my hands into my pockets, glancing over at Rusty. She's completely absorbed in her mermaid book.

"Yeah?" I ask, pretending I'm Mister Casual as Fuck.

"Can you come tie this for me? I'm completely incapable of tying bows behind myself," she says.

"Sure," I say, and walk into her bedroom. It's controlled

chaos as usual: laundry in big piles, but only in one corner. A precarious stack of books on her bedside table. Her bedside light sitting atop another, smaller, stack of books, also precarious. Her bed unmade, but cozy-looking.

"Thanks," she says as I take one end of her sash in each hand. "Whenever I do it myself, I wind up looking like a Christmas present wrapped by a blind toddler."

I focused every ounce of concentration I can muster on tying the mint green sash, because otherwise I might think more thoughts about unwrapping Charlie, and my daughter's in the other room so I will not be thinking those thoughts today.

Not even some.

Her hair smells tropical, like coconut and pineapple.

None of those thoughts, I remind myself.

I finish the bow, adjust it, and step back. Charlie looks over her shoulder at herself in a full-length mirror.

"Holy shit," she says.

"She's *right* outside," I remind her.

Charlie wrinkles her nose in apology.

"Sorry," she says. "But every time I need a bow tied, I'm coming to you from now on."

"I've had a lot of practice," I say, nodding my head toward the seven-year-old in her living room, and Charlie just laughs.

"Right," she says. "Maybe you can teach me how to French braid, too."

"You might be surprised."

"You guys ready?" she asks, dropping to her hands and knees.

"Yep," I confirm. I don't point out that yes, we're ready, of course we're ready, we showed up to her apartment exactly when we said she would and she was the one still getting dressed. Pointing that sort of thing out to Charlie doesn't make any kind of long-term difference, and mostly just makes her feel worse.

"All right," she says, lowering her head to the floor. "Let me grab my shoes and we can head out."

I look away.

It takes all my willpower, but Charlie's clearly not used to wearing a dress — I didn't even know she owned one — and so instead of memorizing the way she looks with her ass in the air while she searches for her shoes under her bed, I look away.

I deserve a medal.

"I'll let Rusty know," I say, and saunter out of the room. She's still sitting on the pillow, wearing huge purple sunglasses and reading her book. I don't know how she can see to read, but it's not my problem.

"You ready to hit the road again, kiddo?" I ask.

"Can I take the book with me?"

"Sure," calls Charlie from her room.

"Thank you!" Rusty calls back.

A few seconds later, Charlie comes out. She's wearing sandals, her hair down and cascading around her neck and shoulders. I think she's got lip gloss or something on, and my great-grandmother's ring is sparkling away on her finger.

And her bra and panties match.

I wish I didn't know that last part. It's not helping anything.

"You're wearing a dress?" Rusty says. She sits up, cross-legged, and lifts her giant sunglasses up to get a better look at Charlie, who grins at the gesture.

"Yup," says Charlie. "You're wearing shorts."

"Yeah, that's normal," Rusty says. "I didn't know you *had* a dress."

"I didn't know that either," I say, casually.

So, so casually.

I also didn't know that she had matching—

Jesus, stop it.

"Betsy took me shopping yesterday after work," she admits.

Then she twirls once. The skirt flares out briefly, then swishes around her legs when she stops.

I've never seen Charlie look like this. I've seen her in coveralls and jeans and cutoffs and cargo pants and swimsuits and dressed as the planet Saturn, once, but never in a sundress that nips in at the waist and flares at the hips, that accentuates her breasts like this or that shows off her upper back—

"You look pretty," Rusty says.

"Thank you."

"Yeah, you look nice," I offer.

"Thanks," she says, one eyebrow raised, and I regret it immediately. Is there a lamer compliment than *you look nice?*

Fuck no, there is not.

"It's a good dress," I try again. "It's got. You know. It twirls, and it's good on your skin."

Good on your skin. I sound like a serial killer.

What I'm *really* thinking is that she looks beautiful, breathtaking, that she's always been pretty but there's something about this simple summer dress that's knocked me on my ass and all I can think of is the word *nice.*

I want to touch her. The feeling isn't new but it's surprisingly intense right now, the urge to brush my fingers along her arm, slide my hand around her waist, plant my lips on one sun-kissed shoulder.

"We should go," I say, before I can accidentally say something like *your eyeballs look delicious.* "Ladies first."

Rusty gets off the floor, puts the sunglasses back where she got them, and heads for the door in front of Charlie.

"*Do* I look okay?" Charlie asks under her breath when Rusty's out of earshot. "I feel kind of weird—"

"You look incredible," I say, the truth rolling off my tongue before I can think it through.

"Oh," she says.

"I meant it. You look really nice," I say, using that awful word *nice* again.

She looks down at herself, like she's forgotten what she was wearing, and when she looks up, her cheeks are faintly pink.

"Thanks," she says. "But you have to promise me that you'll tell me if I come out of the bathroom with my skirt tucked into my underpants or something."

It takes a heroic effort, but I don't visualize Charlie, her skirt tucked up inappropriately, black panties with lace edge on partial display.

Nope. Not at all, and definitely not while my seven-year-old daughter is impatiently waiting for us on Charlie's steps.

"As long as you tell me if Rusty dumps glitter in my hair again," I say, and Charlie laughs.

"Deal," she says, just as Rusty's face pops back around the door frame.

"Are you *coming?*" she asks, and I hold the door for Charlie as we leave her apartment.

CHAPTER NINE

CHARLIE

According to town legend, Sprucevale was founded in 1775 by Heath McCoy, a highwayman, brigand, rapscallion, and all-around guy of questionable-yet-rakish character. He'd either stolen several chests of gold coins from the British or absconded with the Governor's daughter — maybe both — and after being on the run for a few weeks, he found himself holed up in this holler when the first snow fell.

Apparently, Heath was also a strapping Daniel Boone-slash-Johnny Appleseed type, because he made friends with the local natives, built himself and his possible paramour some shelter, found food, and made it through the winter.

Spring came, everything thawed, and in the meantime the British became fairly preoccupied with that whole 'the colonies are fomenting revolution' *thing*, forgot about Heath, and thus, Sprucevale was born.

There's a statue of him in front of the library, standing heroically in some old-fashioned clothes, looking off at the horizon with a rifle in one hand, its butt resting on the ground.

He's pretty dashing for a statue. If I were a British governor's daughter in 1775, I'd probably let him abscond with me.

Anyway, Riverfest celebrates the date of Sprucevale's supposed founding, on that day in 1776 when McCoy first broke ground on the farmhouse that would grow into his homestead, and later, this town. The whole story of the founding might be apocryphal, but if it is, I don't want to know that he was actually just some surveyor sent out to map the wilderness who decided to stay and blah blah blah.

Riverfest is your standard small-town carnival. There are stands serving food on sticks. There's cotton candy. There are not one but *two* bouncy houses. There are tchotchke booths. There are two stages set up, one at either end of the several-blocks-long festival area, that feature local performances.

It is, fittingly, next to the Chillacouth River that runs through town.

Right now, we're watching a stage full of pre-teens in leotards, pointe shoes, and long, floaty skirts do some sort of ballet. They all look deadly serious, and, bless their hearts, they're not that good.

"She doesn't know the steps," Rusty mutters critically, her eyes trained on one ballerina in particular. "She keeps messing up."

"Maybe she's got stage fright," Daniel says. "It's scary to perform in front of people."

"No it's not," says Rusty. "It's no big deal if you practice."

"Some people find it really hard," Daniel says, ruffling her hair slightly and shooting me an amused look over her head.

You can't say that Rusty's not confident, that's for sure.

She's got all the self-assured, cocky swagger of a Loveless in a pint-sized package.

"I get stage fright sometimes," I tell her.

"You do?" she asks, still watching the dancers.

"Sure," I say. "When I was in high school, my softball team won the regional championships, and they voted on me to accept the award at this banquet in front of all the other teams. I had this whole speech ready, but when I got up there, I totally froze, so I just said 'thank you' and pretty much ran back to my seat."

"Did you practice?" Rusty asks.

She's currently in ballet and piano lessons, and I know Daniel's been emphasizing practice over talent a lot with her. He read it in some parenting book.

"Probably not as much as I should have," I say, and Rusty just nods.

The dance ends. The dancers flit offstage. Someone gets on the microphone to tell us that in fifteen minutes, the elementary school clogging team will be gracing the stage, so we drift off toward the rest of Riverfest.

It's a beautiful spring day. It's sunny and warm, but not *too* warm. There's a pleasant breeze and plenty of shade from the trees growing along Sofia Street, where this is taking place.

And my stomach is in knots. For starters, I'm wearing a dress and I think I regret it. Daniel keeps giving me weird looks, and I think maybe I'm overplaying this whole 'engagement' thing. I should have stuck to shorts and not made a big deal of it, but I let Betsy talk me into dressing up for our first date, and now I'm pretty sure that everyone is town is staring at me behind my back.

Surreptitiously, I smooth the back of one hand over my butt, just double-checking that my skirt's covering it. The dress is a little longer than knee-length, but I'm still paranoid that somehow, I'm showing someone the goods by accident.

I'm not.

I'm also nervous because everyone I've ever met in my life is probably here, and I have to convince *all of them* that Daniel and I are so in love that we're going to get married. No matter how many times Betsy told me to chill, and that engaged people pretty much just act like regular people, I'm anxious.

As if on cue, a shrill whistle cuts through the noise of the crowd. Daniel and I both stiffen and turn our heads at the exact same time, and even though it's a small town I'm ready to flip someone off when I see Silas waving his arms in the air at us.

"Oh," I say, and Daniel laughs.

"That was rude," Rusty points out, but we make our way through the crowd and toward Silas.

Along the way, Daniel takes my hand in his, and instantly I step on the back of my own shoe, stumbling for half a second. He just holds my hand a little tighter and looks over.

"You okay?"

"Fine, just clumsy," I tell him, fighting the redness I can feel creeping into my cheeks.

Bang up job so far, I think.

"I'm not eating all the powdered sugar parts," Silas is saying when we make our way over to him. "It's funnel cake. It's all powdered sugar parts."

"Yes, you *are*, and stop it," the woman next to him says, taking a forkful of fried dough and tugging it off the plate they're sharing. "I swear I'll tell Mom and Dad."

"What, that I offered to share my funnel cake with you, and you complained? Hi," Silas says, that last part to us. "You know June, right?"

June waves her fork in greeting, her mouth full of funnel cake.

"You visiting for Riverfest?" I ask.

Silas is Levi's best friend, three years older than Daniel and me, but his younger sister June was in our class. We were friendly in high school, though she went to college and then moved to Raleigh, so we haven't talked much since then.

She shakes her head, still chewing.

"June moved back to town," Silas says. "She's exploring some promising opportunities in Sprucevale, considering a few other options, and taking some downtime to weigh her next career move."

June raises both her eyebrows at Silas and swallows.

"Can you write my resumé for me?" she asks. "That sounds way better than 'I got fired so I moved back home.'"

"You got *laid off*," Silas protests, tugging more funnel cake off the plate. "It's completely different."

"Still unemployed," she says, then turns her attention to us. "Hey, guys. How are you? Engaged, right? Congrats!"

"Thank you," Daniel says, and squeezes my hand. "We're excited."

"Who won the betting pool?" she asks.

"Betting pool?" I ask.

Silas shoots her a look, and she ignores it.

"I think it was at like five hundred bucks or something," June says. "There was maybe a five-dollar buy-in, and you had to name the month and year that you two would finally go public — what?"

Silas is giving his little sister a *look*.

"You're not supposed to tell *them*," he says.

"Why?"

"You're just not. It's manners."

"Is it also *manners* to have a betting pool in the first

place?" June asks. "Or is it perfectly all right to wager money on people as long as you never tell them what you're doing?"

"It's complicated," Silas mutters, and June rolls her eyes.

"Besides," she goes on. "I knew about it and I was in another state, how did you two not know?"

"No one told us," I say, trying not to laugh at them.

Even in high school, June was straightforward, fearless, and unafraid to speak her mind to whoever was listening. It got her in trouble more than once, but I always liked that about her.

"You can't tell *them*, because then they could win the pool by rigging it," Silas points out.

"So don't let them enter."

"They could easily use a proxy," he says, and then nods at something over my shoulder. "For example, they get Levi to enter them, tell him the day that they're going to go public with their relationship, and then split the winnings with him."

"What did I win?" says Levi's voice. "I hope it's not another lifetime supply of Capri Sun, that was a complete — hello."

He stops next to me, a huge pink puff of cotton candy in front of his face, and suddenly looks lost.

I'm not sure I've ever seen Levi look lost before.

"Silas. Daniel. Charlie. Rusty. Ma'am," he says, forced casualness back in his voice.

Every head in the circle turns toward Levi.

Did he just call June ma'am?

He's blushing. Behind the beard, I swear he's blushing.

"Miss," he corrects himself, standing stiff as a statue.

June cocks her head and narrows her eyes.

"You forgot my name again," she says.

"Of course not," Levi says quickly, lowering the cotton candy a few inches. "June. It's June. I know your name is June. I was being proper."

"Nice save," June says, laughing.

"It wasn't a—"

"He thought my name was Julie for like six months," she explains to Daniel and me.

We're still holding hands. He hasn't let go. I haven't let go.

It's starting to feel... normal?

"When Silas was in Afghanistan and they were writing each other letters all the time, Levi would ask how Julie was doing, or say he'd seen Julie in the market and said hi, stuff like that. Silas didn't bother telling him that my name was actually June until poor Levi actually *called* me Julie and I corrected him," she says. "So the moral of the story is that Silas is a jerk."

"Levi's got bad handwriting," Silas protests.

"It's not that bad," Levi says. He hasn't moved a single muscle since June accused him of not knowing her name.

"It's pretty bad," Daniel says.

"And Julie's not that far off," I point out.

"Oh, it's a really close guess," June says, still laughing. "And, to be clear, I'm making fun of Silas for not correcting him. Because Silas *definitely* knows my name and just felt like being a dick."

"What do men need to know your name for?" Silas says, and June rolls her eyes again.

"Ignore him, he thinks it's the middle ages and sisters should be traded for several goats and a brood mare," she says, stabbing more funnel cake.

"I'd trade you for more than one brood mare," Silas teases. "Shit, June, you're worth a couple hogs, too. Don't go undervaluing yourself."

"So," June says, pointedly ignoring him. "You guys buy your duck for the regatta yet?"

· · · · ★ ★ ★ ★ · · · ·

"He's got a mask and a cape so he can be sneaky and sneak past the other ducks in the water," Rusty explains excitedly, drawing on her rubber duck with a Sharpie. "And then I'm going to give him laser eyes so that he can zap them out of the water and win."

"That sounds like a good plan," I say. "You know, they say the best defense is a good offense."

"And stripes," she says. "Because stripes make things go faster."

"Exactly," I agree. I'm pretty sure Seth's the one who told her that, once, when he was explaining why his mustang had a single racing stripe down the side. The real reason, of course, is that Seth thinks it looks badass, but he and Rusty both get a kick out of his tall tales.

"Lemonade," Daniel announces behind me, and a second later, we've got plastic cups with straws in front of us.

"Thanks," I say, as Daniel moves to sit next to me at the table.

As he does, he puts his hand on my upper back, his fingers alighting on bare skin, cold from bringing us drinks.

I swear the shiver courses through my whole body. My toes clench in my sandals. I sit up a little straighter, sharpie still in hand where I'm decorating my own rubber duck, and before I can stop myself, I turn my head and look at him.

He looks back, eyes blue as the Caribbean Sea.

There's a moment, a single tiny moment when I think *what if?* and then he sits and takes his hand off my back and drinks his own lemonade and the moment's gone, only the cool spots on my spine lingering a few more seconds.

"What's your strategy?" he asks me, leaning both his elbows on the folding table in front of us, the top strewn with markers, other people sitting around decorating their rubber ducks.

"Mostly to just act normal," I tell him, bringing my own lemonade to my lips.

And to keep pretending that it does nothing to me when we touch, I think.

Daniel raises one eyebrow.

"I guess that's a start," he says. "How about your duck regatta strategy? Looks like Rusty's got laser eyes, so you're gonna need shields."

Right. Obviously that's the question he's asking, my mind is just somewhere else.

"Well, you know," I say. "We're gonna go out there and give it our all, really focus up and lay it on the line. Give a hundred and ten percent. Do our best. Stick to the inside lines."

I take a sip of my lemonade, trying to recover some dignity as I also try to remember more of the pep talks my high school field hockey coaches liked to give out.

"Gonna leave it all on the field," I deadpan. "And also, shields for the lasers."

"Smart," he says. "Very sportsmanlike of you."

He tips his lemonade toward me, and we cheers them together.

"Thanks," I say. "I think I've really got a shot at it this year."

"Not against lasers," Rusty says, still coloring furiously, mostly to herself.

"We'll see," I tell her.

"Better hurry up with those," Daniel says. "Five minutes until it starts."

"Plenty of time," Rusty says, her brow furrowing.

The duck regatta is technically a competitive event, in that only one duck will win, but it's definitely not a sport.

At one end of the race, everyone dumps their rubber duck into the river. When it starts, the floating barrier goes up, and all the ducks float downriver.

The first duck to the finish line wins. Pretty much all you can do is stand on the bank and shout at your duck to go faster, so it gets pretty boisterous.

"You didn't get one?" I ask Daniel.

"I figure if you win, I get half anyway," he says, his blue eyes laughing.

"Who says I'm sharing?" I tease, even though my heart thumps one percent harder.

"What's yours is mine, right?"

"Not *yet*."

Not ever.

"Isn't the prize a gift certificate to La Dolce Vita?" he says. "Who else are you gonna take on a fancy date?"

"Someone's being presumptuous," I say. "I've got a sister. I've got friends. I could even take Rusty."

La Dolce Vita is the swanky Italian restaurant downtown. It's candlelit. It's got a long wine list, good tiramisu, and mood music, and I don't hate the thought of going there with Daniel.

Just the two of us. No Rusty. No Betsy, none of his brothers, just us trying to act couple-y across a candlelit table. The spots where he touched my back a moment ago prickle cool again, even under the warm sunlight.

Daniel grins.

"Yeah, but you'd take me," he says. "You're just talk."

He's right, so I stick my tongue out at him. If Rusty weren't here I'd flip him off.

The loudspeaker crackles.

"One minute until the race starts," Hank Rogers's voice booms out. "Please bring your ducks to the starting line."

Rusty takes her duck in both hands and blows on it, a look of total concentration on her face.

"You ready?" Daniel asks her. Rusty nods very seriously and stands, her folding chair scraping across the asphalt below it. He points at the uncapped Sharpie still on the table, and she sighs dramatically, but puts the cap back on.

We head to the starting line. Before we toss our ducks in, we turn them upside down and check the number.

"Fifty-seven," Rusty says.

"I'm fifty-eight," I tell her. "Can you remember that for me?"

"Yes," she says, as serious as can be, and we both toss our ducks into the river behind the floating barricade.

The racecourse is maybe two city blocks long, and the finish line is another floating barricade, right before some rapids begin. Every year a few ducks escape and get away, and every year the day after Riverfest, at Daniel's house for Sunday Dinner, I have to hear about it from Levi.

"Come *on!*" Rusty calls, darting ahead.

"Stay where I can see you!" Daniel calls, taking my hand again. There's a paved bike path along the river here, a wooden fence separating it from the water. Right by the finish line there's a spot with a few benches and a low stone wall, and Rusty's making a beeline for it, Daniel and I following behind.

Any time she disappears for a split second, his grip on my hand gets tighter, then relaxes when she reappears. Even though she's not fifteen feet away. Even though we know pretty much everyone here.

"No one's going to steal her," I tell him, keeping my voice low. "They all know what a pain in the ass she is."

That gets a laugh out of him, another hand squeeze, and I think he relaxes. Then she's up ahead, again, heading into the area with the stone wall by the finish line.

The wall's only about three feet high, and she goes up to it, standing on her tiptoes, leaning over as far as she can to see the ducks. We're ten feet behind her, the ducks coming on quickly.

"Rusty, be careful," Daniel calls out as she leans a little further over.

"Stop it, she's fine," I tell him.

"I don't want her to fall in," he protests.

"She's barely taller than the wall, she's not going to," I point out.

"I just—"

"Besides, Hank is right in front of her, and the water's barely to his knees," I say, pointing at Hank Rogers, who's in the river, wearing waders and a hat with a rubber duck glued on top. His outdoors supply store, Bear Hollow Sporting Goods, sponsors the duck regatta every year.

Daniel just sighs.

"Relax," I tell him, and squeeze his hand. He squeezes back.

We stand there, together, keeping one eye on the oncoming ducks and the other on Rusty, who shows no sign of falling into the river. After a moment, I lean my face against his shoulder, my cheekbone against soft cotton and thick muscle.

He shifts his hand, laces his fingers through mine.

What if? I think again.

"I think the lasers might be broken," Daniel murmurs to me, a smile in his voice.

"They probably got wet," I say.

"We should've warned her to use the waterproof lasers."

"Too late now," I say. "Remember it for next year's duck regatta."

Now the ducks are coming on fast, little yellow dots bobbing furiously up and down on the river. Up against the stone wall, Rusty's bouncing with glee, her ash-blond curls sproinging in the sunlight.

Daniel's gonna have a hell of a time untangling that later, I think.

"How long do you think we'll have to listen to Levi go on about the environmental impact of escaping ducks tomorrow?" Daniel asks, his voice low and slow, even over the rising hubbub.

"He's not wrong, you know," I point out.

"Hank always goes on a duck cleanup mission the next day," Daniel says. "He's very conscientious. Levi just doesn't like him."

"I think it depends on whether Silas brings June," I say, and Daniel snorts.

"Levi *has* seen a woman before, right?" he asks, rhetorically.

"He went to college," I say. "He has a master's degree. There must have been some women somewhere."

"He's been in the woods too long," Daniel says. "Too much communing with birds and bears and squirrels and poof, you're calling your friend's little sister ma'am."

"I should go get drinks with her," I say. "I didn't know she was back in town."

"For some reason, that's been relegated to the second-hottest gossip this week," he says, and he flicks the engagement ring with one finger. "I don't think she minds too much."

The ducks sweep past the observation area, Rusty

hopping up and down, surrounded by other kids who are also hopping up and down.

"Yeah, she probably owes us for that," I say.

There's a furor at the finish line, mostly of kids. Hank holds a duck up, and he's shouting something, but it's too loud to make out what it is, and besides, I'm making sure I keep track of Rusty.

Suddenly, she comes tearing out of the knot of kids, hair wild, face lit up like a lantern, breathless.

"CHARLIE," she practically screams. "YOUR DUCK WON!!!!"

CHAPTER TEN

DANIEL

You'd think that Charlie had won an Olympic medal. Rusty can't stop shouting. Hank Rogers pulls Charlie up to a podium — an honest-to-god winner's podium — and presents her with a golden duck statue. There's a medal. The mayor shakes her hand. Hank shakes her hand. She has to hold up the winning duck for a photo from the newspaper. The owner of La Dolce Vita gives a quick speech relating duck races to Italian food, and then he presents her with a $200 gift certificate to his restaurant.

Naturally, during all this, my brothers appear.

"She should use her platform to call for the end of the duck regatta," Levi says as they walk up.

"Congrats on your fiancée," Seth tells me, ignoring Levi. "She need a date to the restaurant?"

I shoot him a glare. He grins, because he's an asshole sometimes.

"Instead of complaining about the ducks, you could go on the duck hunt tomorrow morning," Caleb says to Levi.

The duck hunt is for stray rubber ducks, not actual ducks, but Levi harrumphs anyway.

"I'm going," cajoles Caleb. "I'll pick you up."

"Come on, Levi," says Eli, who of course is also there, just because. "Put your money where your mouth is."

"Money's filthy," Levi says.

"It's just an expression," says Caleb.

"He knows that, he's just being difficult," says Eli.

"You're one to talk," mutters Levi.

"I heard June is going," I say.

I didn't hear that. I just want to see what Levi does, because I'm enjoying not having all the attention on me.

Levi arranges his face. I swear I can see his features moving one by one, until they're all in the most neutral possible position, like he's studied it.

"Oh?" he says, staring off into the middle distance.

"Who's June?" asks Caleb.

"Silas's little sister," I say. "She was in my class in high school."

"I remember her," volunteers Seth. "She was cute. She single?"

Levi acts as if he's turned to stone. Thank God for Rusty, who comes charging back, still breathless with excitement over Charlie's win.

"DAD," she shouts. "THEY WANT A PICTURE WITH YOU."

"You don't need to scream," I tell her, but she's already grabbed my hand and is dragging me toward the podium.

"I got him!" she shouts, depositing me next to Charlie

"Thank you," says the photographer. "Very helpful."

She's middle-aged, a streak of gray in her pulled-back brown hair, and amused at Rusty's antics in a no-nonsense sort of way. I should probably know her name, but I can't think of it. My mom probably knows. Seth probably knows. They're both good at stuff like that.

"All right, smile and hold up the duck, please," she says,

lifting the camera to her face again. "Turn? Chin up. Duck lower. Get closer."

I've never liked having my picture taken — it makes me feel like an ant under a magnifying glass, in danger of getting burned — but I smile and turn my face and hold my arm around Charlie's waist anyway as she holds up her winning duck.

That part, at least, is pretty nice.

After the first set, Rusty gets in the picture. Charlie lets her hold the duck. Rusty's inability to stand still makes this set take twice as long, but finally, the photographer lowers her camera.

"All right," she says. "If you don't mind, can I also get a few for the engagement announcement?"

"There's an engagement announcement?" Charlie asks, her back muscles tightening under my arm.

"Of course," the photographer says. "You're engaged, aren't you?"

"Did you send that in?" Charlie asks me.

"Seriously?" I ask, and Charlie laughs.

"It was probably my mom," she says. "Knowing her, it'll be on the front page tomorrow."

"All right put down the duck and get closer," the photographer says. "This is gonna be a tighter shot so it's not too obvious that you're both wearing the same clothes in the regatta picture and the engagement picture."

We both press in. My right side is against her left, and even though there are thirty things going on at once — the photographer instructing us, my brothers in the crowd talking amongst themselves, Charlie's arm around my back, Rusty tossing the winning duck up and down in the air — it still sends a sizzle through me, an instant hit of longing, of nerves, of the wish that none of these other things were happening right now.

The shutter clicks a few times, and then she frowns. Rusty drops the duck and it bounces between the photographer and us. Just as I'm about to ask her to stop, Eli materializes to one side.

"Rusty," he says. "Want to pet a goat?"

"A goat?!" she yells, excitedly, the duck already half-forgotten. Eli takes her hand, flashes me a thumbs-up, and heads off. I take a deep breath.

"You two switch," the photographer orders, looking down at the camera, then frowning up at the sky. "I want to get the ring in the shot."

There's more direction, and Charlie and I probably look like robots trying to act like they're filled with human emotion, because having your picture taken is hard and having your picture taken while you're trying to look blissfully in love with your best friend who's pretending to be your fiancée is harder.

Finally, we're face to face, arms around each other, her left hand perched just-so on my shoulder as I gaze down at her and she gazes up at me. We're so close that her irises don't look hazel anymore, but like a kaleidoscope of green and brown and gold around her pupil, and I feel a little like I'm falling in.

The shutter clicks.

"Smile," the photographer says.

We smile.

"Not like that," she says.

I smile… less? Charlie's trying her best not to laugh, her eyes dancing beneath black lashes, her freckles twitching with the effort of holding it back.

"Closer," the photographer orders.

We pull closer, the heat of the warm day combining with our body heat, my fingers on her back aimlessly playing with the bow I tied earlier today.

"Don't undo my dress," Charlie murmurs to me. "Inappropriate, Daniel."

Her eyes are still laughing.

Her bra and panties match, I think, then banish that thought as thoroughly as I can.

"The bow's decorative," I point out.

"Doesn't mean you should undo it," she says.

I tug on it the tiniest bit and think about everything and anything besides undressing Charlie.

"Dammit," she hisses, and pokes me in the ribs.

"Please don't move," the photographer says, clicking away.

I tug again, just hard enough that Charlie can feel me doing it.

"Yeah, Charlie, don't move," I tease, keeping my voice low so the photographer can't hear me.

"If it comes out and she has to re-pose us, it'll be your fault," she says.

"Accidents happen," I say, and give another tiny tug. Charlie's freckles collide as she tries not to laugh, and the photographer lowers her camera, flipping through her photos.

"All right, these'll do, almost done," she says then lifts it back to her face. "Just a few of you kissing and we're good."

There's a sudden shift in everything: the air, the light, the timbre of the background noise, the way Charlie's standing.

The camera clicks. There are fifty sets of eyes on me, on *us*.

Suddenly I have no idea how to kiss.

I lower my face toward hers anyway. Charlie's on her tiptoes, eyes wide and slightly alarmed, and the last thing I think is *we should have practiced this*.

Then our noses collide.

"Ow," Charlie whispers, and I tilt my head to one side and now our mouths are half-together, hers partially in my beard, mine a little on her cheek. I move again but so does she and now we've got the opposite problem and somehow her mouth is slightly open, my lip against her teeth, the photographer clicking away.

"All right," she says. "Tilt the other way?"

We do. Our noses mash. We recover a little, manage to get our mouths together, but then the photographer is telling Charlie to close her eyes and telling me to lean in and the shutter is just clicking away.

I open my hand against her back. I force myself to ignore everything except Charlie.

Suddenly, there it is: the spark, the fire, the reason I've been thinking about this since we kissed in the driveway on Wednesday. Charlie relaxes too, moves closer, her mouth suddenly soft and warm and—

"Okay, that'll do," the photographer says, and we both pull away. "I think I got something useable."

Useable. Great. High praise for my modeling abilities.

"Thanks," Charlie says. I take her hand in mine again. "When's it running?"

The photographer slips her camera into its bag and slings it around herself carefully.

"The regatta's running tomorrow," she says. "The announcement, probably Monday, unless they decide to do a story."

"A story?" Charlie echoes, and the photographer just nods.

"That's up to the section editor, though," she says, and checks her watch. "Congrats on the win and the engagement!"

Then she's gone, before we can ask any more questions like *what kind of story* or *why is this a story at all?*

"Okay," Charlie says, mostly to me, after she's gone. "Sure. A story."

"There's no way they're going to do a story," I tell her, trying to sound reassuring. "A story about what?"

"Are there any abandoned buildings we could burn down?" she asks.

I raise one eyebrow at her and wait.

"So the paper runs that and not a fluff piece about us," Charlie explains.

I still don't say anything.

"I did specify abandoned," she says, a little defensively.

"True," I drawl.

"Sometimes you need to be creative," she says, sighs, and leans her head against my shoulder again. "Should we go find Rusty?"

"Probably," I say, but I don't move.

This is all turning out to be infinitely more complicated than I thought it would be — I thought Charlie would wear a ring to a hearing, and now here we are, kissing awkwardly for photographers and hoping that the newspaper doesn't run a story about us.

But I don't hate it. I don't like lying to people and I don't like the spotlight, but moments like this — Charlie's hand in mine, her head against my shoulder, the two of us sharing a secret — make it almost fun.

We should probably practice kissing, though, I think. My heartbeat picks up for a split second.

"All right, what do we think Eli did with my kid?" I ask.

"Probably juggling knives," Charlie says, and I sigh, scanning the crowd. Caleb, Levi, and Seth are still standing where I left them.

Caleb and Levi are talking about something, but Seth is just watching Charlie and me, looking contemplative.

I don't like it.

"All right let's go rescue him," I say, and we walk off to find Rusty.

CHAPTER ELEVEN

CHARLIE

Silas leans forward, the neck of his beer bottle dangling in his fingers.

"Look, she's not really going around telling people this, but her asshole boyfriend also dumped her the same day she got laid off," he says.

I gasp dramatically. It's probably a bit much, but it's the first Loveless Sunday Dinner after we announced our engagement, and I'm one-point-five beers in on an empty stomach.

"*After* she got laid off at the paper?" I ask, also leaning forward conspiratorially. "He knew she'd gotten laid off and then he dumped her too?"

Silas just nods.

"That seems unkind," says Levi, frowning.

"Well, he's a scummy asshole who wasn't fit to be cleaning gum from the bottom of her shoes, let alone dating her, so I wasn't terribly surprised," Silas says, swigging some more beer.

Then he looks at me.

"Don't tell her I said that," he says. "June already thinks

I'm a Neanderthal, so I'm trying to be reasonable about this when I'm within earshot of her."

"Sounds like he sucked," I say, sympathetically.

"He did suck," Silas agrees. "She thinks I'm just being an overprotective big brother, but that dude *sucked*. He was some trust fund asshole, so even though he supposedly had a job with his dad's company, it sure seemed like he mostly played golf and went on stupid weekend trips with his buddies."

"Fuck trust fund kids," I say, and hold out my own beer bottle.

"Fuck Brett in particular," says Silas, and we clink bottles.

Levi doesn't clink. He's just watching us thoughtfully, not saying much of anything. We're sitting in three deck chairs in one corner of Clara Loveless's back porch, slightly away from the general hubbub.

There's plenty of hubbub. Rusty and two of her friends are tearing around the back yard. Eli's in the kitchen, making something that smells amazing, and Seth is in there assisting. Last time I checked, Clara and Violet, Eli's girlfriend, were having some sort of in-depth discussion in the living room, and a few minutes ago Caleb came out the back door, frowned, and went back inside.

I haven't seen Daniel in like fifteen minutes. He's probably hiding somewhere.

"Luckily, I think she's more bummed about the job than the guy," Silas admits. "Like maybe, deep down, she knew all along how much he sucked, and now that it's confirmed that he sucked pretty bad, she's at peace with the end of their relationship?"

I just nod. I've never really had a bad breakup. Honestly, I've never dated anyone I really *liked* that much. I just tend to get bored after six months or so, then break things off amicably.

Levi clears his throat lightly, like he's about to say something, but instead the back door opens, and Clara walks over to the three of us.

"Try these," she says, and holds out a plate with three cookies on it.

"Thank you!" we chorus, instantly reaching for them.

When Clara Loveless offers you a baked good, you accept. It's a smallish shortbread cookie, crumbly and buttery when I bite into it.

Crumbly, buttery, and tasting a little like... pine trees?

"Ah, you made them," Levi says, nodding.

"I had to freeze the needles for a while because I got swamped with work," Clara says. "I think with fresh they might be a bit brighter."

Levi takes another bite. Silas is already brushing crumbs from his hands, having wolfed it down.

"That was excellent, ma'am," Silas says, and Clara smiles, looking amused.

"Thank you," she says.

I nod enthusiastically.

"Kind of strange, but good strange," I say.

"Yes, I think they're a bit piney," she says. "But I found this recipe for shortbread cookies made with evergreen needles, and Levi offered to collect some for me, so..." she shrugs.

"Delicious," says Silas, who thinks that everything is delicious, and Clara laughs.

"Thank you," she says. "I'll put some aside for you to take home."

As she leaves, I lean in toward Levi and point after his mom.

"Hot tip," I whisper. "That's when you call someone ma'am. Your friend's mom, not your friend's little sister."

Levi just sighs.

"Don't worry, I've gotten quite the earful on correct forms of address since yesterday," he says, taking another sip of his beer. "I think I've settled on never using one again. From now on everyone will just be *hey, you*."

"That's probably for the…"

The back door is open again, and I suddenly realize that Eli is standing in it, staring at me and pointing.

"…best," I trail off, frowning at Eli.

He points more emphatically. I point at myself, eyebrows raised, and he nods. Then he crooks his finger.

"I'll be right back?" I tell Silas and Levi, and head into the house, leaving my half-finished beer on a side table.

"My mom found her wedding dress and wanted to know if you were interested," Eli says as I walk up.

No, because there's never going to be a wedding, I think.

"What's it look like?" I ask, wondering how to be diplomatic about this.

Eli shrugs.

"Like a white dress," he says. "Come look at it, it's up in my old room."

He points at the stairs. I ascend. He follows me.

I wonder, briefly, why I need to look at this dress *right now*, why Eli is the messenger about it, and why this all seems so hush-hush, but I don't wonder that hard.

He follows me up two flights of stairs, to the attic room where he was living before he moved in with Violet last year. As soon as we're outside I hear Daniel's voice.

"—did you need me to come all the way up here to ask me *that*—Charlie?"

I step into the room. There's no wedding dress. There's one Daniel.

I've been tricked.

The door shuts definitively behind me, and Eli stands in front of it, arms crossed, looking for all the world like a bouncer.

"This is an intervention," he says.

"For *what*?" I ask.

"For kissing," Seth says, taking his place next to Eli, mimicking his stance. "Y'all are terrible kissers."

Several thoughts all trip through my brain at once. Heat flushes my face. I take a step back.

"Neither of us is kissing you, Seth," Daniel says, also crossing his arms over his chest.

"Don't speak for the lady," Seth says, suddenly grinning.

Next to me, I can feel Daniel's whole body go rigid.

"The lady's not kissing you either," I say before Daniel can say anything.

"No one is here to kiss Seth," Eli says, shooting him a look. "We're here to help you kiss each other, because I've seen puppets kiss more convincingly than you two."

A quick flutter of anxiety moves through my chest, waving through me like wind through a wheat field.

"What puppets have *you* been watching?" I ask, after a second.

"You can find some real weird stuff on the internet," Daniel offers.

"Spoken like an expert," says Eli.

"He's not the one who brought up puppet porn," I say. "Apparently, you've been watching—"

"Everyone quit talking about your perversions and focus," Seth says, raising his voice. "No one is kissing anyone, except that you—" he points at Daniel, "are kissing her—" he points at me, "because you need people to think you're actually engaged."

The flutters are only getting faster, stronger, a gale force wind through the wheat fields because I really do want to kiss Daniel and I really don't want to do it in front of his brothers, presumably while they shout helpful make out tips at us.

"They're Eli's perversions," I say. "I've never even seen—"

"No one is leaving this room until you stop talking about puppets fucking and start kissing," Eli says, firmly planted in front of the door.

Daniel just sighs.

"Is this because of yesterday?" he asks.

Despite being trapped in an attic and being told to kiss me or else, he's somehow the calmest person here right now because of course he is. Daniel's almost always the calmest person around.

"Yes," Seth says.

"Obviously," Eli confirms at the same time.

"I'd be the world's shittiest brother if I saw that travesty and didn't do something about it," Seth goes on. "You," he nods at Daniel, "have somehow gotten yourself into a ridiculous situation where you need to convincingly make out with her," he nods at me, "to keep custody of Rusty, and you," he nods at me again, "have inexplicably agreed to this farce. I agreed to do your taxes, by the way."

"Thanks," I say.

"And by God, Daniel, I'm not letting Rusty move to Colorado with the progeny of a demon and a swamp beast, so you better shut up and kiss Charlie."

"No one kisses normally in front of cameras," Daniel says. "Look, we kiss just fine. Yesterday there was a photographer saying something, practically everyone we knew was there—"

"Is it just me, Seth, or do those sound like reasons to

practice?" Eli says, turning to his brother. "Call me crazy, but maybe they should get *better* at kissing in public instead of just hoping it never happens again."

"I do believe you're correct, Eli," Seth says. The two of them are talking like they're in an infomercial, and it might be the most irritating thing I've ever heard. "And since they're not leaving this room until you and I are satisfied, they may as well get—"

"Fine," Daniel finally says, then unfurls his arms and looks over at me. "Sorry," he says, his voice softer, gentler.

"They do kind of have a point," I say, even as my insides twist. "Yesterday wasn't great."

Finally, Daniel half-smiles, and he smiles at me, not his dumbass brothers, runs one hand through his hair in his nervous-and-trying-not-to-show-it gesture.

"It was pretty bad," he admits.

"You jammed your nose into my eye," I say, laughing.

"You bit my chin," he teases.

"You—"

Eli clears his throat obnoxiously.

"Come on," Seth says, spinning a finger in the air in the universal *can we get a move on* gesture.

I take a deep breath, turn to Daniel, quiet the flutters, and look up into his sky-blue eyes for a split second.

Then we kiss.

It's slow, gentle, tentative. It's polite. I can feel his brothers' eyes on me as I kiss him back, mouth closed, one hand on the back of his neck. I can't forget where I am, and I can't lose myself in it like I want to. I can't pretend for just a few minutes that he's not my best friend, that this isn't all for show.

It still thrills me. I can still feel the kiss as a shiver down my back that goes all the way to the soles of my feet.

I rock back slightly. Our lips separate but Daniel's hand

cups my back, draws me in again, and then his hand is on my face, thumb on my cheekbone and we're kissing again. Harder. There's still no tongue and I'm still acutely aware that we're being watched, but now it's fervent, needy, barely constrained.

After a long moment, feet shuffle. Someone clears his throat. One more beat and we both pull back, still standing in each other's arms. I glance over at Eli and Seth though Daniel doesn't, his eyes still on me.

Eli and Seth look at each other, both suddenly uncomfortable.

"Um," says Seth.

"Probably tilt more," Eli says.

"Yeah, needs a little more head tilt," Seth says. "Just, you know…"

He tilts his head slightly to demonstrate.

"Thank you," Daniel says sarcastically.

"Anything else?" Eli asks Seth.

"I think the tilt is all," Seth says. "Is Caleb still down there with the sauce? Did you need to—"

"Yeah, I should make sure nothing's exploding in the kitchen," Eli says. "Dinner's in ten, guys."

They open the door. Eli steps through. Seth flashes us a thumbs up, and then follows.

I'm still in Daniel's arms.

"I am *never* letting you talk me into anything again," I hear Eli mutter as they descend the stairs.

"I didn't think it would…." Seth protests, but then they're gone and I don't hear the rest.

I pull back. Suddenly, I'm blushing, a full-body blush that I can feel rising from my chest and blossoming. My knees are probably blushing.

I step back and Daniel's hands fall away from me, his eyes still on my face. I'm lost for words. I'm a little lost for everything, so I swallow, and I rub my palms along my jeans just to ground myself, and then I smile because that seems like the right thing to do with my face right now.

"Dinner's in ten," I say, jerking a thumb at the open attic door. "We should probably go round up Rusty and help set the table."

Daniel doesn't move, so I turn and walk to the door but before I get two steps he catches me by the wrist and stops me.

"Wait," he says. I turn.

My eyes lock with his, and suddenly I'm stuck under the intensity of his blue gaze. I can feel my heart squeeze in the space between my heartbeats, and before I know it, I'm back in his arms, our bodies pressed together, and he kisses me again.

CHAPTER TWELVE

DANIEL

I 've been waiting years for this kiss. Six, I think, though as Charlie presses her lips against mine, as she goes on her tiptoes, as her hand settles against my hip and I pull her against me, fingers on her back, her mouth opening under mine — as all that happens, math's not my strong suit.

I don't have a strong suit. Not right now. Right now, I'm weakness itself, giving into impulses and fantasies and a wanting so deep I could swim in it.

She moves closer, presses against me. My hand finds its way into her hair and tangles there as our heads tilt the other way and my tongue meets hers, and she grips the back of my neck even tighter, drawing me down, and somehow two of my fingers find their way onto her skin against her back, under her shirt.

I am unmoored, swept away. I'm caught in a riptide as I push her backward one step, then two, guided by the vague notion that somewhere in this room there's furniture and I want her on it and then Charlie's pulling at me, the tide herself.

There's a table. It shudders as I push her against or she pulls me against her, against the table, impossible to know which, and she tilts backward as I lean over her, my whole hand against her bare skin now, her fingers tugging at my shirt like she's looking for a way in.

Then, suddenly, her hands are on my chest and she's not kissing me anymore. Charlie shoves me away and I let her, standing up straight and taking a step backward, her hazel eyes wide.

Too late, I realize there were footsteps.

"Eli told me to come—"

The door swings open, and Levi's bearded head pokes through.

"Get... you... for dinner," he says slowly.

I say nothing. I couldn't think of a word if my life depended on it right now. All I can do is watch the expressions moving over Levi's face, like clouds across a clear sky, from surprise to confusion to reluctant understanding.

"Dinner," he says again, unnecessarily, and then he's gone. Footsteps thunk down the attic stairs and I shove one hand through my hair as I feel like a pool float, slowly deflating.

Except my dick. That particular part of me is so hard it feels like it might shatter.

Charlie and I turn our heads, look at each other again. She's wide-eyed, nervous, her lips slightly parted and her hands perched next to her on the table, fingertips tented, like birds ready to take off at the slightest provocation.

"Fuck dinner," I say.

It works. It gets a smile from Charlie, her hands flattening against the table, the uncertainty washing out of her face.

"We should go down," she says. "Unless you want your

family members tromping up here one by one and asking increasingly nosy questions about what we're doing."

"The door locks," I offer, my voice low, even though I know she's right.

"How long do you think that would work for?" she says, head tilted to one side.

"Maybe today's the day they start respecting boundaries," I say as she hops off the table.

"I wouldn't put money on that," she says.

The neck of her shirt has gone lopsided, and I tug it back into place over her bra strap, my fingers brushing her neck. Her bra's black. I wonder if her panties match today, which doesn't help my erection.

"Me either," I admit.

She reaches up and moves a strand of hair off my forehead, her fingertips barely brushing my face.

I catch her hand again as she lowers it, pull her fingers back, plant my lips in the very center of her palm like a promise.

"Daniel," she whispers, that single word filled with uncertainty, with a thousand possibilities both good and bad.

"Right here," I say, my voice low, quiet, rough.

"That was weird," she says, nearly whispering. "Are we good?"

"DAAAAAAAAAAD!" Rusty shouts, and I close my eyes for a moment. I love my daughter more than life itself, but sometimes I really wish she would chill.

"I said *go see where they are*, not *scream at him*," my mother's voice says.

"Coming!" I shout unromantically toward the door. Charlie clears her throat.

"Not like *weird* weird," she says, her words rushed. "But,

I mean, that was definitely not what we talked about and it was kind of sudden—"

"I've wanted to do that since I kissed you on the truck at the bonfire," I say. "When we were drunk, and you spilled your beer on me."

Charlie blinks, surprised.

"I thought you forgot that."

"I tried."

"DAD, you're not coming!" Rusty shouts, and suddenly Charlie laughs.

"If you find out tomorrow that you've got a second child, I *will* kill you," she promises.

I let her hand go, open the door, let my fingertips drift to her lower back, guiding her even though she knows the way.

"Don't worry," I say. "This one was *very* effective birth control."

· · · · · ★ ★ ★ · · · · ·

DINNER IS SOMEWHERE between awkward and pandemonium. Levi won't look at me directly, but Seth doesn't seem to want to look anywhere else. Eli's just smirking, and every few minutes his girlfriend Violet shoots him a *stop it* look. Or maybe a *be nice to your brother* look.

Or maybe it's a *please take the trash out when you get home* look. I don't know girlfriend looks. I can't interpret them.

Caleb's the only of my brothers managing to act normal, a fact which makes him my current favorite. I know that either Seth or Levi told him about the whole fake engagement situation, but he is somehow managing to pass the mango-cashew slaw and curried veggie skewers like a normal human being.

"I thought it was a ski resort," my mom is saying.

"I thought you said it was an outlet mall," Eli says, frowning.

Levi clears his throat, pulling a chunk of pineapple off a skewer with his fork. He's barely said a word all night, so everyone stops and looks at him.

"We think he might be exploring the possibility of mining," he says solemnly.

"*Mining?*" says my mom, incredulous.

"He can't do that on National Forest land," Charlie pipes up. "It's protected."

Eli snorts.

"Walter Eighton doesn't understand the meaning of the word *no*," he says. "If someone tries to tell him he can't do something, he'll just throw a fit until he gets his way."

I'm listening, but barely, because Charlie's right here, next to me, and I'm trying not to watch her hands as she drinks her beer and slices into her carrots and swirls a bite in tamarind chutney and then lifts it to her mouth, closing her lips around it.

"He's reported us to the alcoholic beverage control board what, five times?" Seth says. "Six?"

She bumps me slightly, her elbow against my side as I reach for my water.

"Daniel," Seth says, and my head snaps up.

He looks entertained, and I quickly run back the last thirty seconds in my head.

"Six," I confirm. "He keeps telling them that we're distilling onsite, but our license is only for brewing."

"Are you?" asks Silas.

"No," Seth and I chorus together.

"You should give it a shot," my mom says. "You know, your great granddad Lowell made the best whiskey in three states."

"*Mom.*"

135

"I mean you should do it legally, Daniel," she teases.

"Great-Granddad Lowell also had quite the mugshot collection," I point out.

"Yeah, looks like he knew how to have fun," Seth says. He shoots me another look. I don't know what this particular look means, so I ignore it.

"Lowell bought the ring, right?" Charlie suddenly asks. She's holding her hand flat in front of her, watching it sparkle.

"He did," my mom confirms. "Three days on horseback to Richmond—"

"Last time I heard this story he also had the fastest car in the county," Caleb suddenly says. "What happened?"

"It was briefly in the Sherriff's possession," my mom says lightly. "What makes you think Walter Eighton wants to mine on National Forest land?"

There's a brief pause as we all switch mental gears from my bootlegging ancestors to the topic at hand. Levi's the first to get there, sharing a quick glance with Caleb.

"Do you know what a thumper truck is?" he asks the table.

"Is it a truck that thumps?" Silas guesses, gesturing with his fork.

"It is," Levi confirms. "It uses seismic activity to identify possible sites for natural gas drilling, and for the past few months, we've had backcountry hikers and campers reporting possible minor earthquakes around Laney Caverns, but they weren't being picked up by any seismic equipment anywhere."

Levi cuts a mushroom cap in half and carefully places it in his mouth, despite the fact that everyone is paying attention to him.

"But then you also found a thumper truck?" Seth asks, always the least patient brother.

"Tracks," says Caleb. "Large, deep, fresh tracks on a fire road that's supposed to be off-limits to public vehicles, in the vicinity of where the seismic activity was reported."

"That's not proof," Seth points out.

"It's not," Levi agrees. "But it's sure worthy of some suspicion, and Walter Fucking Eighton—"

"*Levi*," I say as Rusty suddenly perks up.

I look over at her. She's grinning from ear to ear.

"You're not supposed to say *fucking*," she says, delightedly.

"Excuse me?" I say sharply, and the grin drops off her face.

"Uncle Levi said it first," she says.

"It wasn't okay for him to say it and it's not okay for you to say it," I tell her, shooting a glare at my oldest brother. He at least has the grace to look ashamed.

"Sorry, Rusty," Levi says. "That was rude of me."

Rusty sighs, dramatically rests her chin on her hand, and stabs at a piece of eggplant. She's not that much taller than the tabletop, so the effect is more funny than anything else.

"Please don't use language like that," I tell her.

She sighs again, and I silently pray that we're not about to get into our *but why can't I say those words, they're just words* conversation. Frankly, I agree with her, but I also can't have another meeting with a teacher about her teaching her classmates the word *asshole*. Or *clusterfuck*. Or *shitshow*.

"Okay," she finally says. "Sorry, Dad."

"Thank you," I say.

"Walter Eighton," Caleb says, reminding us where we all were.

"Right," Levi says. "He's been petitioning for mineral rights in Cumberland National Forest, and the first step in the convoluted process of getting them is to show that there's actually something there to mine…"

I stop listening to them discuss the finer points of land use legislation and federal protection levels, because right now, I couldn't care less.

Instead I feel like a travel commercial I saw once: rocky cliffs overlooking a deep blue ocean, a color so rich it seems unreal. There was a man standing on top of the cliffs, and I'm sure the announcer was saying something like *come on this great vacation and conquer your fears, after this you'll be the billionaire CEO of your own company* but all I remember is the guy suddenly leaping off the cliff, flailing on the way down, landing with a huge splash.

I feel like I just leaped off the cliff. I feel like I've stood there for years, looking out at the ocean, not even knowing there was a cliff. I'm pretty sure I'm flailing now. I think there might be rocks at the bottom. I have no idea what's in store.

Casually, I lean back in my chair, take a sip of water, wipe my hands on my napkin. Then I put one hand on Charlie's leg. My heart kicks and next to me, she takes a deep breath, her shoulders moving.

Then her hand settles on mine.

* * * * * ★ ★ ★ * * * *

I DON'T GET her alone again that night. When there are nine people in a house, four of whom are the world's most interfering brothers and one of whom is your own seven-year-old daughter, secret alone time is hard to come by.

I do the dishes with a blissfully ignorant Silas while Violet and Charlie plan a day of cake tasting. Seth keeps wandering in and out of the kitchen, shooting me more and more significant looks each time until he's practically a caricature of himself, and I do my best to ignore him.

Silas ends up telling me about his sister, June, who just moved back to town. Because I'm a good brother, I just nod along, mention that we were in the same high school class, and don't bring up how Levi called her *ma'am* yesterday.

Call it pre-payment for Levi not telling anyone what he saw before dinner.

After that, Rusty wants to play Chutes and Ladders, so we do. I try to let her beat me, but the game is pure luck, so I win by accident but she's a good sport about it. Then she ropes Charlie and Violet into playing, then Caleb, then Candyland comes out, and before I know it, she's playing a version of that with Caleb and Eli that seems to involve bribery and negotiation.

I think she wins both games. I'd be tempted to say that they let her win, except I'm not sure Eli's ever *let* anyone win anything in his life.

We have dessert: blackberry cobbler that Levi made from the bramble near his cabin. Silas leaves. Levi and Seth both go home. Rusty tries to negotiate her way out of bedtime, and I let her get away with ten more minutes, but then it's lights out.

We don't even get through a full chapter of *Apprenticed to Dragons* before she's nodding off, heavy eyelids fluttering on her pillow. I leave her room and close her door, then stand on the second-floor hallway of my mom's house and have my first alone time of the day.

Rusty's room is right across the hall from mine, and as I stand there, mind jumbled, trying to make sense of every-thing, I'm looking into my own bedroom. I'm trying to clear my head, trying to get just a few seconds of clarity on today before I go back downstairs, but I find myself mostly wondering why there's a single pink shoe on my desk, when the last time I read the book on my nightstand was, why I've still got a picture that Rusty drew four years ago taped to my mirror when she's got much more recent artwork I could be admiring while I got ready.

The bed is made. The small desk is neat, laptop plugged in, charging. All the drawers shut on my dresser, the closet door is closed, dirty clothes only in the hamper and nowhere else. If I bent down, I'd see all my shoes under the bed in a neat-enough row, a single novel on my bedside table, a few necessities atop the dresser.

I wasn't neat until I had a kid, but after Rusty slammed into my life like a category five hurricane, I had to control every single thing that I could, because my day-to-day was filled with things completely beyond it.

One day, I was kissing Charlie on top of a pickup truck by a bonfire. We'd been best friends since we were eleven, and suddenly — finally — our relationship took a turn to something else, something I'd thought about for ages but had shoved down, deep inside myself.

She spilled a beer on me. We laughed. We went home separately but the promise was there, hanging unspoken in the air like a harvest moon.

The next day, Child Protective Services knocked on my door and told me that a woman named Crystal Partlow was claiming I was the father of her nine-month-old daughter. I denied the claim for about five seconds, until they showed me a picture of a baby named Rustilina, and instantly, I knew.

I got a DNA test anyway, but I knew. I'd slept with Crystal a handful of times about a year and a half before, during a rough, directionless period in my life when I drank too much, did some things I shouldn't have, and made plenty of questionable decisions. She was one of them.

CPS was there because Rusty had been removed from

her mother's home and placed into foster care due to neglect. If I was competent and willing, they'd consider placing her with me, her father, instead.

I was willing. I got competent. After a series of talks, my mom offered her help, so I moved back home. We set up a nursery. I read every parenting book I could find in the Burnley County Library, and one week after I found out that Rusty existed, I met her for the first time, in a supervised visit in the basement of an office building.

It was only love at first sight for one of us.

Rusty sat near the door the whole time, sobbing. She refused the bottle I offered. She would barely interact with me.

Same thing next day, but then the third day, she only cried for a few minutes. The day after that she smiled at me.

A week later, I took her home, and now she's been with me for six years.

I didn't forget about the kiss. I couldn't. I wished I could, but the memory would pop up no matter what: while I was bent over, helping Rusty toddle around the house, when she woke up crying for her mom in the middle of the night and I did my best to soothe her, when I tried to convince her that broccoli was delicious by playing the airplane game.

Charlie stuck around. Our relationship waxed and waned in intensity, but she was always there: dropping by with dinner, inviting the two of us hiking with her, teaching Rusty cool animal facts like *sharks have infinity teeth*. In no time at all, Charlie was the fun aunt, we had a new relationship, and the past was past.

I couldn't forget the kiss, but I could bury it. I could tell myself that it was in everyone's best interest that I never think about it again and I could hide it, shove it down into a hole, only revisit the memory when I couldn't help myself.

But buried things have a way of resurfacing, of exploding forth, of demanding to be reckoned with.

I hit the lights in the hallway, smile to myself, and head downstairs to do some reckoning.

CHAPTER THIRTEEN

CHARLIE

"It's not weird to taste wedding cakes before you've got a date and a venue locked down?" I ask Violet.

We're sitting on the couch, looking at her iPad. She's got about thirteen tabs open of different bakeries in the region, and for the past few minutes, we've been working up an itinerary that lets Daniel, Rusty, and me visit each of them in the most efficient manner possible this Saturday.

Violet's getting really into the efficiency part of it. There's a map open in a tab, and she keeps switching the order of the bakeries to see if she can figure out a way for us to drive one less mile.

"It's weird, but not that weird," she says, swapping the order of Francesca's Cakes with Betty Bakes, then frowning because the total driving distance is now half a mile *more*. "If anyone gets nosy about it, say you're still deciding between a couple of venues, but you expect to have the date and place locked down very soon."

"Right," I say, even though all this wedding talk may as well be Greek to me.

Thank God for Violet, who spent years working at a wedding venue and can supply me with all the wedding-related phrases I'll need for the next few months.

"Make sure you give them a fake phone number," Eli advises from the far end of the couch, where he's sitting next to Violet, playing something on his phone. "And a fake email address. Otherwise you'll be getting ten emails a day about cake."

"Doesn't sound so bad," I say.

"You'll just be constantly hungry for cake," Violet points out. "And it'll be even worse, because it's not like you're ever actually going to get to eat any of these cakes, so you'll just be torturing yourself with delicious, delicious sugar porn and no chance of satisfaction."

Eli raises one eyebrow and looks over at her.

"Is there something I don't know?" he teases. "Everything all right over there?"

"I'm talking about dessert," she says.

"I know."

"The pastry kind," she teases.

"You sure?"

"There are other people in the room," Caleb calls. He's lying on the other sofa, reading a paperback by holding it up over his face.

"She brought up sugar porn, not me," Eli says, leaning back again. "Why is today the day for weird porn conversations?"

That gets a look from both Violet and Caleb, who lowers his book just to stare at his older brother.

"Should I leave?" he asks.

"No, you're gonna help me find the shortest route to all these bakeries," Violet says.

"Is it gonna be dick-shaped? We talking algorithm porn here?"

"Well, that depends on what you come up with, doesn't it?" she says. "You can ignore Eli, I don't know what he's talking about."

She grins at Eli, and he narrows his eyes at her teasingly.

"The porn is a long story," I say, glancing at the staircase. Daniel left a while ago to put Rusty to bed, and I'm not antsy to see him again, but... okay, I'm a little antsy.

Not because I don't like hanging out with his family. They're great. I just want to see him again, want him to be here, because I feel like a lot of things got weird today.

"That's unusual for porn," says Eli. "Usually there's not much story at all."

There's a sound on the stairs, and then Daniel appears, tripping lightly downwards. My heart thuds faster and I sit up straighter.

"Are we talking about Eli's thing for puppet porn again?" he asks, walking to the couch where Caleb is sprawled and making a *move over* motion with one hand.

Caleb makes a *what the hell, I'm comfortable* gesture at him, but Daniel just rolls his eyes, and Caleb sighs, sitting up.

"Puppet porn," says Violet, resting her hands on top of her head and raising an eyebrow at Eli. "Do go on."

"Or don't," offers Caleb, tucking his feet under himself to sit cross-legged. "You could always not."

"I don't think puppets even have genitals," Eli points out.

"Well, not all puppets," I say.

"I'm *positive* that puppets with genitals exist," Violet says. "It's a big world, there's someone into everything."

"And Eli's into puppet porn," Daniel says, grinning.

He glances at me. I can't help but smile.

"Eli's an innocent man whose sole mistake in this life

was having brothers who latch onto the wrong part of everything he says," Eli sighs.

"*Sole* mistake?" says Violet.

"One? Seriously?" says Caleb. They're both grinning.

"Could you guys please finish your itinerary so we can all go home?" Eli says, ignoring the two of them.

"Fine, but not because you asked," Violet says, swiping at the iPad again.

"Of course not," Eli says, smirking.

"Daniel, come over here," Violet orders.

He gets up. Caleb sprawls again. Violet scoots down, squishing Eli, until there's room for four people on this couch, and Daniel settles in, smashed against me.

We share a look. A smile. He puts his arm around me like it's the most natural thing in the world, and strangely, it is.

It still gets a knowing eyebrow raise from Eli, though, so I focus on the iPad and ignore it.

"All right," she says, pulling up a document. It's a rough itinerary. I didn't even see her make it. "Your first cake appointment is at eleven a.m. At Susie Q's Cakes in Grotonsville, and your last appointment is at five p.m. at the Frosted Fig in Dry Run."

"Are there any in-between?" Daniel asks, leaning into me.

His beard catches slightly in my hair, which is medium-large right now, and I pull the strand back, tuck it behind my ear.

"There are five in-between," Violet says, and switches to the map on the iPad. "Caleb's figuring out which order they should be in, so you have the least amount of driving to do."

"Circle," Caleb calls.

"They're not *in* a circle," Violet says.

"Make the route as circular as you can," he says, back to reading his book. "There it is. The algorithm magic."

Violet sighs.

"What are we keeping you around for, then?" she teases.

"My charm and good looks," Caleb answers, going back to his book.

I lean into the crook of Daniel's shoulder, trying to look like I'm not sort of smelling him while definitely smelling him. The scent of the brewery has pretty much soaked into his skin, the smell of earthy-sweet roasted grain, plus there's a note of something else, something rich but faint.

Beard oil? I think. *Does he use beard oil?*

"Okay, I'll draw a circle and put together an itinerary for you guys," Violet is saying. She flips the cover of the iPad closed and tosses it onto the coffee table, then leans back. Eli puts his arm around her as she yawns.

"I should get home," I tell Daniel. "I've got work in the morning."

I don't need to tell Daniel that I've got work in the morning. I've got work every weekday morning. That's what work *is*, but I need something to say.

He looks over at me, his arm still around my shoulders, his face quiet and thoughtful and smiling all at once, and I'm pretty sure that right now he can read my mind:

I just need to be alone with you.

"I'll walk you out," he says, and we rise.

· · · · ★ ★ ★ · · · ·

LEAVING the Loveless house always takes twenty minutes, no matter what. I could be taking someone to the emergency room and somehow, I'd be waylaid anyway.

I bid farewell to Violet and Eli. I say goodbye to Caleb,

147

then to Clara, then, somehow, to Eli again. Daniel needs to go get shoes so Clara strikes up a conversation, and when Daniel comes back we're so embroiled in a discussion of whether there should be a stoplight at the intersection of Lawton Drive and Sheers Road that he has to wait another five minutes to walk me out.

Violet and Eli have already managed to leave without discussing a stoplight. Someday I'd like to learn their ways.

Finally, we go. He opens the door for me, his hand on my lower back as we leave, head down the porch stairs, the porch light fading behind us. Daniel glances back, takes my hand.

Then he gives me the wickedest grin I've ever seen and pulls me behind the cab of Caleb's truck, pushing me against the cool glass and metal, his lips on mine again before I can think.

It's fierce, ferocious, hungry. He's got a hand in my hair again, my head back against the truck window and my own fingers somehow find his belt loops, tug his hips toward mine.

We kiss so hard that teeth scrape my lip. I open my mouth under his and deepen the kiss. My hands find their way to skin, his muscles shifting underneath. He's got a hand on my face, cupping my chin, like he's making sure I can't escape.

When it ends, we're both breathing like we ran a mile. He leans his hand next to my head, on the glass of the truck window, and I put my hand on his forearm.

"They think we're engaged," I say, still trying to catch my breath. "We don't have to hide."

Daniel just chuckles.

"You really want to do that where my mother can see us?" he teases, still breathless. "Maybe we can go back in there, see if Caleb will give us some pointers."

He moves his hand to my face, traces the bottom of my lower lip in the dark with his thumb.

"We're going to need a flow chart," I murmur.

"Of who thinks what?" Daniel asks, and I just nod.

He puts his forehead against mine.

"And what do you think?"

"I think you should kiss me again," I say, and he does.

It's slower, more deliberate, just as deep. We explore each other, fingers and hands and tongues, and I'm surprised at how familiar it all seems, like I'm finally visiting a place I've only seen in photographs.

It's new, but it's not strange.

Suddenly, the porch light goes off, and we both turn around. I peek through the windows of the truck, but nothing seems to be happening.

"Did we just get busted?" I whisper.

"You know, we *are* adults," Daniel says, his lips so close to my ear that his voice buzzes.

"I think making out behind your brother's truck in your mom's driveway negates any possible adulthood we may have reached," I say, and Daniel laughs.

"They probably don't realize we're still out here," he murmurs. "Eventually I'm going to have to knock to get back in because I don't have my keys."

"You can't climb back in that window?" I ask.

"The last time I did that I was about a foot shorter and fifty pounds lighter," he says. "Besides, I think we cut that tree branch down. Not that I'd trust it anymore."

"So you're stuck out here until you work up the nerve to go back in," I tease.

"Yeah, it's terrible," he says.

We kiss again. We kiss some more. We make out like teenagers who've just discovered tongue kissing. It's dark now, the moon thin tonight, foliage waving overhead. His hands wander under my shirt and I wonder for several desperate moments whether we could just hop into the back of this truck and not get caught.

I don't suggest it. I have at least that much dignity; not to mention the thought of getting caught bare-assed by Clarabelle Loveless is enough to keep my pants on.

"Okay," I finally say, one hand on his chest.

"That's all?" he says, the smile in his eyes evident even in starlight. "*Okay?*"

"What, it's not good enough for you?" I tease.

"I was hoping that breaking my own rules after six years would at least get a *great*," he says.

Right. There were six years between the first kiss and tonight.

Six years of friendship, of constant texting, of watching Rusty get bigger and learn to speak and ride a bike and read books, six years of Daniel surprising me with Chinese takeout and brownies when I'd had a bad day, six years of coming over after Rusty's bedtime and pouring him whiskey and commiserating while he talked about Crystal.

Six years of forgetting our kiss and in its place, building something else entirely.

"We should talk," I say, and Daniel nods.

"Tomorrow," he says. "It's Monday."

"Ballet?"

"Can I come over?" he asks.

My breath catches in my throat, a rush suddenly swirling through me.

"To talk?"

We just look at each other for a long moment. Every Monday at five-thirty, Rusty has ballet lessons downtown, three blocks from my apartment, so Daniel has an hour to kill. Sometimes he comes over and we hang out. Sometimes we meet for coffee, or for beer, or just to walk around Sprucevale and talk about nothing.

If he comes over tomorrow, we're not going to be talking, and we both know it.

"Come on," he says. "This time I'll actually walk you to your car."

CHAPTER FOURTEEN

CHARLIE

"Rusty's welcome, of course," my mom says. "Just like any other dinner. I'll make macaroni and cheese along with the roast."

"I think she likes roast," I say. "She's not that picky."

"Then I'll make macaroni and cheese because I want to eat it," my mom says, laughing. "You know, I always did think that mac and cheese was underrated as..."

It's 5:05 on Monday and I'm not listening to my mom. Right now she could say *aliens just landed in our back yard, could you go see if they prefer red or white wine?* and I'd agree because one hundred thousand percent of my attention is focused on my five-forty-five-ish rendezvous with Daniel, a rendezvous for which I'm already running five minutes behind schedule.

I even wrote the schedule down, because I feel like a bucket full of ants and I can't focus for shit. I swear I had to measure a plank five consecutive times today because I couldn't remember how long it was for more than three seconds.

Daniel's coming over. Daniel's coming over. Daniel's coming over.

Alone.

The schedule is on a post-it that's currently scrunched in the pocket of my coveralls as I power walk to my car, in the parking lot out back. It reads:

5 p.m. in car

5:15 arrive at apartment

5:20 shower FAST

5:30 dry hair

5:40 BRUSH TEETH, get dressed

At 5:06, I actually get into my car, my mom still on the phone.

"I wanted to ask you something else," she goes on. "Since Daniel gave you that gorgeous ring, we wanted to get him something as well, but we don't know what. Sort of a 'welcome to the family gift,' even though he's sort of already family, but I guess it's official now? He doesn't really seem like the jewelry type, so unless he secretly wears a lot of ankle bracelets that's probably out…"

"Yeah, he's not really into jewelry," I agree, glancing at my speedometer, going precisely 5 mph over the limit, because that's probably fast enough not to get pulled over. I mean, don't cops have something better to do than pull me over for technically going over the speed limit?

"Do you have any other ideas?" my mom is saying. "Your father suggested a nice paperweight for his office, but I don't know, a *paperweight*, and then he said a tie, but does Daniel ever wear ties?"

What do I do when he shows up? Should the lights be low? Should I offer him a drink? How do you seduce someone?

What if he decides he just wants to talk after all?

We texted some this morning, but they were totally normal texts: hey, how's your day, come to dinner at my parents' house on Wednesday, Rusty says she likes the mermaid book better than the wilderness survival book.

There's a part of me that's afraid Daniel's going to back out. That, after having a chance to think about it, he'll realize that this friendship is too much to risk, and he'll want to go back.

There's a part of me that's afraid he'd be right. There's a part of me — a small, quiet part, but a part nonetheless — telling me that this friendship is the best thing that's ever happened to me, and if I lose it, my life will have a hole that'll take me years to fix.

I'm not listening to that voice. I don't like that it has some good points.

"Charlotte? A tie?"

"A tie," I repeat, coming to a stop sign and trying to sound like I've been paying attention. "I think he really only wears those to court."

"Oh," my mom says, sounding disappointed. "What about—"

My phone beeps. It's stuck in its holder on my dashboard, and Daniel's name flashes on the screen.

Please don't let him be early.

Please don't let him be canceling. And please don't let him want to talk about us right now, while I'm driving home too fast and wildly horny.

Oh, God, I just realized I'm horny while I'm on the phone with my mom, which has to be pretty weird. In my defense, I was thinking about other stuff, not listening to her.

"Mom, can I call you back tomorrow?" I say, shoving all those thoughts aside.

"All right," she says. "You'll remember, right?"

My phone beeps again, and my heartbeat speeds up.

"Yep!" I say, finger hovering over the button. "Love you!"

"Love you," she says, and I switch lines.

"Hey," I say.

"Hey, Charlie," says Daniel.

Instantly, I know he's not coming over. I don't know how I know, I just know that he doesn't sound like he's coming over.

"What's up?" I ask, hands gripping the steering wheel too hard.

"Rusty's got a fever and a pretty nasty stomach bug," he says. "I had to pick her up early from school. No ballet tonight."

I bite my lips together to fight the wave of disappointment that's washing over me. I want to say *get your mom to take care of her and come over anyway*, but I don't. I know when I'm being selfish.

"Poor kid," I say instead. "Tell her I hope she gets better fast."

"Hi Charlie," I hear Rusty's small voice say. "Tell Charlie hi."

"Rusty wants to say hi," Daniel says.

There's some rustling on the other end. I take a deep breath, letting disappointment filter through me, willing myself to let it go because this isn't the end of the world.

It's not like he'll never come over. He just won't come over tonight.

Shit happens.

Goddammit, though.

"I'll be okay by Saturday and we can still go eat cake," Rusty says in my ear, with a level of absolute certainty achievable only by children.

"If you're not, we'll reschedule, sweetie," I hear Daniel say, his voice distant.

"I'll be better," she says, matter-of-factly. "Bye, Charlie!"

Even through my considerable disappointment, I can't

help but smile. I guess she just wanted to make extra sure that I wouldn't cancel cake tasting.

"Bye, Rusty," I say, even as there's more rustling on the other end.

"I'm back," Daniel says, then pauses, briefly.

"Sorry about tonight," he goes on. "I'll see you another time."

Even though it's totally G-rated, it sends a tingle down my spine. Never in my life has the phrase *I'll see you* held such promise.

"Oh?" is all I manage to say.

"Of course," he says, and I can hear the smile, the rasp in his voice. "I'll let you know when the munchkin is better and we'll make plans."

"I'm not a munchkin," I hear Rusty's small, quiet voice say.

"Sorry, kiddo," he says, and she sighs very dramatically. I laugh despite my disappointment because I just imagine it: Rusty pale, pink-cheeked, probably under a blanket and hugging Astrid, her stuffed wombat, still protesting being called a munchkin. I swear, nothing gets past that kid.

"And Charlie, I'd *much* rather be taking her to ballet right now than being on puke watch," he says, and his voice is quieter, hushed, low. "Promise."

"Aren't most things better than puke watch?" I tease, keeping my voice low so Rusty can't hear.

"Sure, but there's better and there's *better*," he says. "And I owe you the latter."

I bite my lip in the car. I'm pretty sure my whole torso, from bellybutton to scalp, is currently pink. Daniel hasn't said a single thing even remotely inappropriate for a seven-year-old, yet I'm absolutely certain he's talking dirty to me.

Oh my *God*.

"Go take care of Rusty," I say. "And call me."

"I will," he says, and when we hang up I'm still blushing, still smiling, and still horny, though I feel much less weird about it this time.

I sit in my driver's seat for a moment. I pull the utterly useless post-it from my pocket, give it a quick glance just in case I also wrote down anything important on it, and toss it into the passenger seat.

Then I go upstairs to my apartment, get out of vibrator, and put it to good use. *Again.*

CHAPTER FIFTEEN

DANIEL

Rusty falls asleep at six-thirty that night after I manage to get half a cup of chicken broth into her. It's literally the earliest I've ever seen her fall asleep, but the poor kid is really down for the count. She's got a fever of 102. She's thrown up twice since I got her home. If she's not on the mend tomorrow, we're going to the doctor.

My mom gets home after Rusty's already asleep, but she comes in the door with her arms full of shopping bags: chicken soup, crackers, soda, and the biggest piece of ginger root I've seen in my entire life.

"Feed a fever, starve a cold," she says knowingly as she puts the bags on the table.

"That doesn't sound very scientific," I tease her, grabbing a bag and putting cans of chicken soup away in the pantry. My mom laughs.

"Double-blind studies have got nothing on folk remedies," she says. "I've told you the story about my father, right? When he was seven, he got—"

"Mumps, measles, and scarlet fever all at once, and the doctors told his mother he was going to die, but she gave him willow bark and chicken soup and he made it through?"

"I guess I have," she says.

"Thanks for the remedies," I say.

· · · ★ ★ ★ ★ ★ · · · ·

RUSTY'S FEELING BETTER the next morning. Not all the way, but her fever drops to 100. She only pukes once, and then I take the day off work and we spend it snuggling on the couch, watching animated Disney movies: 101 Dalmatians, The Jungle Book, Robin Hood, Mulan. She's never had much use for princesses who don't save themselves. I respect that.

I make her chicken soup with crackers and keep her water cup filled. My mom is in and out, packing to leave tomorrow for her conference. She's leading a panel on the various ways to measure gravitational forces of neutron stars, or something. I'm pretty sure I have that wrong.

And I spend the day texting Charlie: updates on Rusty, updates on the plot of whatever movie we're watching at the moment. At one point, she confesses that she had a crush on the animated Robin Hood, even though he's a fox. I remind her of that fact. She just says *yeah, he is*, and I laugh.

I'm disappointed about yesterday. She was all I thought about, all day long, at least until I got the call from Rusty's school nurse.

The kiss in the attic. The make out session in the driveway, pushed up against Caleb's truck, like we were teenagers.

Hell, I *feel* like a teenager right now, like I'm the first person to ever discover kissing.

I text Charlie again: *I think Rusty's on the mend.*

That night, I start to feel nauseous.

. . . . ★ ★ ★ ★ ★ . . .

THE FIRST THING I do Wednesday morning is vomit. It's 4 a.m. when I wake up, because Levi's there to pick my mom up and take her to the airport in Roanoke. I barely make it to the bathroom, and then I kneel on the tile floor in my pajamas, lean against the bathtub, and catch my breath.

Fuck.

Suitcases go down the hallway. Low voices. I stand, splash my face off, brush my teeth quickly even though that makes me nauseous, then head downstairs to grab a glass of water.

"Oh, no," my mom says when she sees me. Levi nods once but takes a step back.

I grab water. Levi takes my mom's suitcases and puts them in his truck. I try a couple of sips, and they seem to stay down. Jesus, it's cold in here.

"Don't hug me," my mom says. "Feel better. Get lots of rest, there's plenty of chicken soup in the pantry and don't forget to stay hydrated. Call Charlie or your brothers if you need anything, and you should really give the ginger a try, it always helps me…"

I nod along. Mom reaches out and squeezes my arm once, then feels my forehead and nods.

"Go," I tell her. "Before I get you sick too."

She blows me a kiss, and then she's out. I get back in bed.

. . . . ★ ★ ★ ★ ★ . . .

RUSTY, of course, is fine. Somehow, I get myself out of bed, take her temperature, pour her some cereal. I'm deeply grateful that she's old enough to get ready for school on her own with little more than supervision, and I watch from the front window as she gets on the school bus.

Then I text Seth that I'm not coming in today and get straight back into bed.

· · · ★ ★ ★ ★ · · ·

THERE'S someone outside the front door.

No. Some*thing*. The house is dead quiet around me, the windows dimmed, like there's a storm outside. Everything is exactly where I left it yesterday except, for some reason, the old couches are back in the living room, two ugly plaid monstrosities that don't even match each other, let alone anything else in the room.

And the shoes. My father's shoes are by the door, and something is outside, and it should be daylight right now but it's not.

I have to push a couch against the door. The thing outside moves, rustles, and suddenly I know it's some kind of enormous bird, feathers and talons and a beak so I bend down in front of one of the ugly couches and start pushing, fear spiking through my heart because I'm the last one here and I don't know what happened but I *cannot let this thing into the house*.

I get the couch in front of the door and now it's beating against the wood, scraping, clawing. I'm soaked through with sweat, ready to push the second couch, trying to see this thing through the tiny window on the front door.

Then it calls to me, and its voice is human.

"Daniel," it says. "Daniel?"

And the door opens like the couch isn't even there.

"Daniel!"

161

I wake up thrashing, shoving blankets away from my face, half sit up on one elbow.

"Jesus, dude," says Seth's voice. He's standing in my bedroom doorway, one hand still on the knob, and I flop back down onto my bed.

It's cold. Wet. I touch my chest and my shirt is soaked. My whole body tingles. Moving feels like a Herculean effort.

"Hey," I croak out as he crosses the room. "What's... is it Wednesday?"

"Wednesday morning," he confirms. "About ninety minutes ago, you texted me 'I'm dying' and then didn't answer my calls or texts, so I came over."

I make myself sit up in my bed. My stomach doesn't like it, but I take a deep breath and maintain control. I grab my phone from my nightstand and look at it.

After *I'm dying*, there's a text to Seth that I apparently fell asleep before I could send: *I got whatever Rusty had, I'm staying home today.*

I show Seth. He nods.

"That would have helped," he says, then sighs, pushing one hand through his hair, exactly the way Eli does. I swear, sometimes I think they're twins.

"Sorry," I say.

"Come on," he says. "You need to go shower while I at least change your sheets. You think you can keep anything down?"

I shake my head.

"I'll bring you some ginger ale," he says, and points at my bedroom door. "Go."

· · · · · ★ ★ ★ ★ · · · ·

THE SHOWER IS TERRIBLE. Standing takes too much effort, so halfway through it I sit down in the bathtub for a few minutes and just let the water run over me. It feels like needles against my skin, but it also feels sort of good, so I deal with it.

Afterwards, I put on a fresh t-shirt and pajama pants. Seth has re-made my bed, and I think I hear the washing machine going downstairs. On my nightstand is my phone charger, which I normally keep on my desk.

Seth is an okay nurse. Who knew?

"Figured you'd need it if you wanted to watch movies in bed," he says, poking his head back through the door. "That shit'll drain your battery with the quickness."

"Thanks," I say.

"You look terrible," he says, sympathetically, from the doorway. "Get some rest."

I just nod and crawl back into bed.

CHAPTER SIXTEEN

CHARLIE

Me: He's definitely alive, right?
Seth: Yep. False alarm.
Seth: Looks like shit, but he's alive and I do believe he'll stay that way.

I thank Seth, then toss my phone onto my workstation and take a deep breath.

For the record, I wasn't *actually* worried, like *worried* worried. But he did text Seth that he was dying, and when he didn't answer Seth's texts or calls, Seth called me to see if I knew what was up.

And, obviously, you read stories about people who are perfectly fine one day, then somehow ingest the wrong amoeba and next thing you know, they're dead.

But this isn't that, this is a stomach bug that he got from his kid, so I shake my head, put my goggles back on, and get back to the band saw.

· · · · · ★ ★ ★ ★ · · · ·

THAT AFTERNOON, Seth picks Rusty up from school, and when I get out of work I swing by his place and grab her since Seth has a *prior commitment*. I don't ask what — or who — his prior commitment is, because chances are, I'll hear about it sooner or later.

Rusty and I have Charlie's Special Pasta — spaghetti with jarred black olives and broccoli — for dinner, and then we head to my workshop, in a garage I'm renting from one of my mom's church friends.

Right now, I'm refinishing a two-hundred-year-old table for the Monteverte Historical Society, because they're reopening Monteverte House as a historical attraction next year. They found this table in one of the junky antique stores that line the rural roads out here, and in the 70s, someone glued comic book pages all over the top.

Getting them off has been a several-step nightmare, but it's nearly done.

Someday, I'd love to work for myself. I'd love to own all my own stuff, work on my own schedule, be my own boss. For now, it's just a side gig, though.

I set Rusty up with her homework at a table in the corner and start sanding the comic book pages off the two-hundred-year-old table. Even though she's well away from the particulates, I make her wear a mask anyway.

I'm finally making some progress on the stuff when she calls my name.

"Charlie!"

"Yeah?"

"Is this a cat?" she calls.

I perch my goggles on my head and walk over to where she's standing on her tiptoes, looking at a bunch of small carved animals I've haphazardly arranged on a shelf.

"It's a bear," I say, trying not to laugh. "See, it's got a super stubby tail."

"It looks like it could be a cat with no tail," she says.

She puts it back in its place and picks up another one, frowning at it for a moment.

"What's this?" she asks.

Very diplomatic of her.

"That's a raccoon," I say. "See, it's got the stripes on its tail?"

"Raccoons have masks."

"It's hard to carve a mask, though," I point out.

"You carved stripes."

What are you, kid, an art critic?

"That was easier," I say.

She puts it back with that exaggerated caution kids have when they're being extra-careful. I'm relieved that I tossed the voodoo doll I carved of her mom, not that she'd be able to tell what it was.

Whatever I may think of Crystal — namely, that she's half demon and half swampthing — I've never said anything negative about her in front of Rusty, and I've never heard Daniel say anything bad, either. Despite her many, many, *many* faults, the woman is still Rusty's mom, and the kid loves her to death.

There's going to come a day when she doesn't. Rusty's a sharp, perceptive kid. Sooner or later she's going to see Crystal's bullshit for what it is, and just like everything else, the damage control is going to fall to Daniel.

"This is an elephant," she says confidently, pulling another one down.

Inwardly, I sigh.

"Anteater," I confess.

"Why'd you make an anteater instead of an elephant?" she asks. "Elephants are cooler."

"But anteaters eat ants," I point out. "Giant anteaters can eat thirty thousand ants in one day."

I don't remember where I learned that. I can only hope it's right, or Rusty's going to correct me next time I see her.

"Gross," she says. "Can I make one?"

I open my mouth to say *no*, but then I close it without making a sound, because I was around her age when my Granddad first taught me woodworking. Somewhere, I've still got the snake I made under his supervision, even though he's been gone for years now.

It's a quiet, artistic task. Rusty's smart for her age and good with her hands. I'll keep a close eye on her.

"As long as you promise to be very, very careful," I say, and her eyes light up as she nods.

I find her a small block of pine — it's soft — and a penknife, then show her how to start. I suggest that for her first carving she try something simple, like an egg, but she informs me that she'll be carving a wombat.

I drag her table over next to me, both of us wearing masks again, and I swear I look over at what she's doing every thirty seconds. Every few minutes I put down the sander, go over, and give her a few pointers, stress safety again and again.

When it's time to wrap things up, she hasn't made a wombat, but she's made progress toward one, and she positively beaming with pride.

"Nicely done," I say, examining it. "You sure this is your first carving?"

"Can I keep the knife and finish it at home?" she asks.

"No," I say, a little too suddenly and too harshly.

I clear my throat.

"You can't have the knife, but you can finish it next time you visit, all right?"

"Please?"

"Sorry, kiddo," I say. "You ready to head back home? I think your dad misses you."

She walks back to the shelf of wooden animals and places the not-quite-wombat among them, and once it's back, I turn and start putting the belt sander away.

"He tried to pour orange juice in my cereal this morning," she says, matter-of-factly.

"Your dad's not feeling very good today," I tell her over my shoulder.

"Yeah," she says. "I know."

I manage not to laugh. Rusty hates it when we laugh at her being serious.

I close up the shop, load her into my car, drive to Daniel's house, knock on the door.

It opens three inches, then stops short when it hits the end of the chain.

"Hey, guys," half of Daniel's face says.

He doesn't look good: pale, a circle under the eye I can see, his hair slightly greasy and sweaty-looking, beard a little scruffy. I immediately have the urge to put him back in bed and put a cool cloth on his forehead.

Rusty shoves at the door, but it doesn't budge.

"Daaaaaaaaaad," she says, leaning against it with two hands.

"Just a sec, Rusty," he says, then looks at me. "You can't come in."

I stand on tiptoes, trying to see past him.

"What happened?" I ask, alarmed.

I'm imagining a bodily-fluid nightmare. It's gross.

"Nothing happened," he says quickly. "I just don't want you to get sick."

"I promise not to lick your doorknobs," I say. "Now can I please come in?"

"Nope."

"I'll help put this one to bed."

"Uh-huh."

168

"Daniel."

"I'm not letting you get Ebola, and that's final," he says, a slight smile around the single eye I can see.

So at least he feels well enough to smile.

"You don't have Ebola," I say. "If you had Ebola, you'd already be—"

I stop myself before I say *bleeding from the eyeballs and probably dead.*

"—sicker," I finish, glancing down at Rusty.

Rusty just glares up at her dad and lets out a long, annoyed sigh.

"Charlie's gotta get off the porch before I let you in," he says to her.

"Seriously?" I ask.

"Seriously."

"I can't even come inside and make you Gatorade or something?"

"Away, Charlie."

"You let Seth in."

"Seth has a key," he says. "Seth let himself in. Besides, if you miss the cake tasting Saturday…"

He trails off, one eyebrow arched, and even though he looks pretty rough at the moment, my stomach flutters.

Rusty shoves at the door again, this time leaning against it with one shoulder.

"Fine," I tell Daniel. "I'll call you tomorrow."

"Thanks," he says. "I'd give you a kiss, but…"

"You really don't need to," I laugh, and then I ruffle Rusty's hair. "Later, kiddo."

"Bye, Charlie! DAD NOW CAN I COME IN?"

I descend the porch steps as I hear the front door opening and Rusty's little voice saying *finally.* Glancing over my shoulder, I see Daniel for a split second: white undershirt, gray sweatpants, bare feet.

Before he shuts the door, he looks up and sees me, standing twenty feet away, and waves.

Then he blows me a kiss. Laughing, I catch it, and he closes the door.

· · * * ★ ★ ★ ★ * · · ·

THURSDAY:

"You're not even contagious anymore."

"Says you, a noted infectious disease expert."

"Come on. I'll bring you chicken soup."

"Charlie, there's so much chicken soup in the pantry here that I'd outlast the zombie apocalypse."

I sigh.

"You don't even need someone to hang out with Rusty?"

"Levi's taking her to her piano lesson."

"Does that have anything to do with the fact that June's been at the Mountain Grind a lot lately?"

The Mountain Grind is two doors down from the Sprucevale School of Music.

Daniel snorts. I'm pretty sure he's feeling better, but he swears that if I show up at his house, he won't let me in.

"I'm not going to ask him that," Daniel says. "Are you going to ask him that?"

I just laugh, because I think asking Levi that would result in a stone-faced denial that he'd ever met anyone with the name *June*.

"I'm not," I say.

· · * * ★ ★ ★ ★ * · · ·

FRIDAY:

"You're serious."

170

"I'll see you tomorrow morning."

"You could see me tonight," I point out.

It's been five days since I saw him. Peeking through the door Wednesday doesn't count. That's five days of thinking nonstop about being pushed against a truck on Sunday night. Five days with the promise of *more* dangling over my head.

It's five days of working on an antique table and carving staircase parts for some yacht and wondering what to wear Saturday.

It's five days of quietly wondering if this is the universe giving me the signal that going *there* with Daniel is a bad idea. It doesn't feel like a bad idea. It feels like a great idea. But deep down, there's a part of me that's afraid of change, afraid of taking the risk.

There's that part of me that's afraid that if I leap, I'll be left with nothing.

On the other end of the phone, Daniel pauses. I know he went back to work today, so he's at least that much better.

"Charlie, if I get you sick before tomorrow I will lose my goddamn mind," he says, keeping his voice low. He's in his office and I'm on my lunch break.

I swallow my piece of sandwich.

"You're just that excited to taste cake with me?" I tease, even as my pulse picks up.

He just laughs.

"Sure," he says. "I'm really excited to taste *cake*."

Just then, one of my coworkers who also happens to be in the break room glances over.

I jump out of my chair so fast I nearly knock it over and walk out of the break room, into the empty back hallway, face flushing pink.

"You still there?" Daniel asks.

"Still here," I say. "And you still haven't given me a good reason I can't come over tonight."

"I threw up seven times in two days and sweated through all my bedsheets twice," he says. "How's that for a good reason?"

I sigh.

"And if there's four *more* days when I can't see you, I'm going to start flipping tables over from frustration," he goes on.

I lean my head back against the wall, close my eyes.

"Don't do that, someone worked hard on those."

"I'm pretty sure my desk is from Ikea."

"Then someone Swedish worked hard on that."

"I'll see you tomorrow morning," he says. His voice is low, quiet, shiver-inducing. "And I won't flip any tables."

"All right," I finally acquiesce, because despite being the most even-keeled Loveless brother, he can be stubborn as a goddamn pig-headed bull sometimes. "Tomorrow."

"Ten?"

"Ten," I confirm, we say goodbye, and we hang up.

I shove my phone into my pocket. I kick the cement floor once and make a face at it, because it's there. I pack up the remnants of my lunch, put it back in the fridge, and go back to work.

That night, it's me and my vibrator. Again.

CHAPTER SEVENTEEN

DANIEL

"What kind of cake are you going to taste first?" Rusty says, taking the stairs to Charlie's apartment two at a time. "I want to taste red velvet first, and then chocolate, and then strawberry and then vanilla but then chocolate again because that's always the best. Sometimes weddings have carrot cake, but I don't like those weddings…"

I'm barely listening as my daughter goes on about cake. She's been pumped for this day all week, and now that we're here, picking up Charlie before heading out for a day of sugar consumption, she can barely hold still.

I feel pretty much the same way, only it's not cake-related. I haven't seen Charlie in almost a week, and I'm not counting the day that I was feverish and talked to her for a minute through a door.

"…but the best cake is birthday cake. I like when it's got the colors in it…"

I knock on Charlie's door, feeling like a car with the clutch down and the engine revving. Vroom. Vroom.

The door opens and there she is, all freckles, curls, and

hazel eyes, looking a little bit haphazard like she always does, like somehow despite confirming what time I'd pick her up seventeen times, she wasn't expecting us.

"Hey, come in," she says.

She's wearing a purple bathrobe, the waist cinched shut but she's got one hand over her chest anyway, like she's just making sure it doesn't fly open.

"Charlie you're not even dressed!" Rusty exclaims, waving both arms over her head. "We have to eat cake in *forty minutes*."

As she says this, she checks the bright green watch that her uncle Seth gave her last year, like she's a CEO late for an important meeting or something.

"Well, the first bakery is twenty-five minutes away, so we've got time," Charlie says as a ball of pure energy — that is, Rusty — sweeps into her living room.

"Are you wearing that?" I ask, my voice low enough that Rusty, already flipping through a carpentry book on Charlie's coffee table, doesn't hear me.

Charlie's hand holds her robe closed a little tighter.

"Give me five minutes, I still gotta get dressed," she says. "Sorry, I was a little late getting out of bed and then I hadn't washed the coffee maker last night so I had to do that and make coffee before I could function, and—"

I lean in and kiss her. It's nothing but a quick greeting of a kiss, a hello-how-are-you kiss, but I've been waiting a week for it and I swear I can feel it ripple through my whole body.

I want more. I want so much more, but Rusty's not even ten feet away, so I give Charlie one polite kiss and back up.

"Be right back," Charlie says, and disappears into her bedroom.

This time I hear the door click shut, thank God, so I sit on her couch and Rusty clambers up next to me, flipping through the pages of *Premodern Jointing: An Enthusiast's Guide*. Apparently, she doesn't find anything that interests her, because ten seconds later she hops off the couch and grabs another book.

A few minutes later, Charlie comes out of her bedroom.

She's wearing another dress. This one's a deep purple with bright flowers, sleeveless, the waist tight and the hips loose, the skirt ending at her knees.

"Ooooooh, pretty dress," says Rusty as she looks up. "How come you wear dresses all of a sudden?"

Charlie just shrugs, grabbing her purse.

"I just felt like it," she says, darting a quick glance at me.

"They look nice on you," I offer.

There's that word *nice* again. *Nice*. The least good, technically-complimentary thing I could possibly say right now, but what the hell am I supposed to say in front of my daughter? *Ravishing? Fuckable?*

"Thanks," she says simply. "Elizabeth evaluated my closet and found it lacking, so we went shopping. Shall we?"

Rusty doesn't even say *yes*, she just leaps to her feet and makes a beeline for the door. Seconds later I can hear her clomping down the wooden steps like she's an elephant.

"You need to wait," I call out, following her.

The clomping stops. Charlie and I leave. Rusty's halfway down the stairs, looking impatient, and Charlie turns to lock her door behind her.

The dress doesn't have a back. At least, it doesn't have half a back, just two purple straps criss-crossing over Charlie's shoulder blades, attaching to the fabric halfway down her spine.

Instantly, I wonder if she's wearing a bra. I can't help it. That's not what I want to be wondering right now, with my kid stomping impatiently ten feet away, but I am.

Charlie turns back to me, stops short.

"What?" she says, alarmed. "Is this dress okay?"

"It's fine," I manage to say. "It's nice. Great. Ladies first."

I gesture toward the steps, and Charlie descends them.

Nice? Come on.

. . . ★ ★ ★ ★ ★ ★ . . .

THE MOMENT we walk into Susie Q's Cakes, Rusty gasps like she's just been crowned Miss America, only more dramatic because she's way more interested in cake than in beauty pageants.

Then she stops short, standing in the middle of the entryway, and stares around in childish, slack-jawed wonder.

"Move it, kiddo," I tell her. "You're in the walkway."

Rusty wanders in, still agog, and Charlie and I follow, her hand in mine. There's cake everywhere: inside the massive glass-fronted bakery case, a cupcake display behind the counter. There are cakes under glass domes on the counter itself, not to mention a few beautifully decorated five-tier cakes in the front window.

I don't think those are real.

Rusty's eyes are the size of saucers, and she stands in the middle of the store, hands clasped together, looking for all the world like a sweet, charming second grader.

Which she is, but she's also a lot of other things.

"So, cake," Charlie says.

"Cake," I agree, sneaking another glance at her.

I can't stop staring, because I never see her this way. Charlie's always in regular clothes, jeans and t-shirts, sometimes coveralls, occasionally shorts. I can't remember the last time I saw her bare shoulder, the notch of her collar-bones, the sharp curve of shoulder blades.

I feel like I'm watching a striptease made just for me.

It's not the dress, which is perfectly modest. It's the way her body moves under it that has me transfixed. It's the suggestion that she might not be wearing a bra. It's how I see a flash of thigh when she sits down and the material shifts.

"I've never exactly been wedding cake tasting before," Charlie says, still looking around. "Do we just start pointing at things, or—"

"You must be Charlotte and Daniel!" a voice says, followed quickly by an apron-wearing woman who bustles out from the back. "Welcome to Susie Q's Cakes! I heard all about you from Violet, she's just so excited that the two of you are finally making it official. Here, go on, sit down."

Suzie ushers us to the café portion of the bakery, where a table is already set up with three place settings, complete with delicate teacups on saucers, plates with flowers, and forks with curlicues. Rusty plops right down, but Charlie eyes the whole setup a little warily.

"And *you* must be Rusty," Susie said. "I've heard all about *you*. This will be your first cake tasting, then?"

She's still addressing Rusty. It's quickly becoming clear who the star of the show is going to be today, and it's not either of the people getting fake-married.

"Yes," Rusty confirms, as seriously as she possibly can.

"Excellent," Susie says. "I'll be right out with your samples and tea."

"There's tea?" Charlie murmurs as Susie walks back into the kitchen, the ruffles on her apron fluttering.

"Is this Violet's doing?" I ask, keeping my voice low.

Rusty leans over the table, examining the delicate teacup and saucer, then finally picking it up.

"There's a flower on the bottom," she tells us.

I settle back in my chair, even though it's wildly uncomfortable, and stretch one arm over to Charlie, my hand on the back of her neck. She's tense, so I rub the knots lightly, my fingers edging under the crossed straps on her back.

I don't think a single dirty thought. It would be inappropriate.

Okay, maybe one.

Possibly two. But they're quick.

"I thought we'd be eating cake bites out of tiny paper cups while standing at a counter," she says, crossing one leg over the other. There's a flash of thigh. I keep rubbing her neck, and she leans into my hand, ever so slightly, and brush away a third dirty thought.

"Not dining off of fine china?" I ask. "Just hold your pinky out when you drink the tea, that way it's proper."

"Says you, noted etiquette expert," she teases.

Rusty's already pretending to drink tea, the cup held carefully in her fingers, both pinkies out.

"Like that," I say, nodding at Rusty. "See, she knows how to do it."

"Don't worry, I can teach you," she assures Charlie.

"Thanks," Charlie says.

Just then, Susie bustles back out, a tray held in front of her.

"Here we are!" she says and puts it down on the table in front of us.

It's filled with small squares of cake and one ornate, flowery, delicate teapot.

"Ooh," says Rusty, leaning over, her mouth forming an O, and Susie laughs.

"First things first," she says, and picks up the tea pot. "Our own special cake tasting blend, black tea with a hint of bergamot and ginger. Helps cleanse the palate."

Susie pours us each tea. Charlie is sitting ramrod straight in her chair. I wonder if I should have dressed more nicely than shorts and a t-shirt, but it's eighty-five degrees outside.

"And now, of course, the cake," she says, beaming. "We've got five different flavors for you to taste today, and of course, we can combine any of them however you like. First is one of our most popular, the bridal white."

The cake is in small, bite-sized pieces about an inch square, each with a frosting swirl on top. I spear it with the fork and pop it into my mouth, careful to avoid getting frosting in my beard.

It's good. It tastes like cake.

Across the small table from me, Rusty nods very seriously.

"What do you think?" Susie asks her.

Rusty thinks for a moment.

"The almond is coming through very strongly," she says carefully. "It's overpowering the other flavors."

Charlie raises her eyebrows, and for a moment, Susie is struck speechless. I force down a laugh.

Rusty *has* been hanging out with my brother Eli a lot. I didn't realize that he was training her palate or that Rusty could tell when a cake had too much almond extract in it.

But I'm one hundred percent sure I know where she got those phrases from.

"Well, I'll make sure to add a little less almond in the next batch," Susie says, her face somewhere between amused and taken aback. "What did you two think?"

"I liked it," says Charlie.

She keeps giving us single bites of cake. They follow more or less the same order as a beer or wine tasting, from the least to most powerful flavors: white, rose, lemondrop, spice cake, and finally, chocolate.

"Your ring is absolutely beautiful, by the way," Susie says when Charlie has a mouthful of lemondrop cake. "I so rarely see colored gemstones on engagement rings."

Charlie looks down like she's only just realized it's there, then swallows cake.

"It's a family heirloom," she says.

Susie just sighs.

"I love jewelry with a history," she says. "So romantic. How did you propose?"

That last question is to me, a forkful of cake halfway to my mouth.

Shit. We never came up with that part of the backstory. It never even occurred to me.

I glance over at Charlie. She's laughing at me, eyes sparkling.

"I think you should tell the story," she says, delicately putting one hand on my knee. "It was so unique and romantic, and I never suspected in a million years."

Her touch sets off a wave of warmth, impossible to ignore even as I'm trying to frantically think of a romantic-yet-unique way that I could have proposed to Charlie.

I put my hand on top of hers, bring it to the table, and hold it. She watches me, eyes still laughing.

"Well, if there's one thing to know about Charlotte, it's that she's absolutely crazy for ceramic figurines of angels," I start.

Her eyebrows dip ever so slightly.

"Her apartment is lousy with them," I go on. "It's her biggest hobby. She's always on eBay, looking for more, and I knew that there was this particular figurine, only produced for a few years in Belarus, that she was absolutely mad about."

Charlie is now half-skeptical, half trying not to laugh.

"Go on," she says, squeezing my hand in hers. "This is my favorite part, about the ceramic angel from Belarus."

"Well, I managed to find one and outbid her for it," I say. "And it's got its arms sort of outstretched, so one day while Charlotte was at work, I broke into her apartment, set the angel on the kitchen table, and left a note that said *come into the bedroom.*"

"I especially loved how that wasn't creepy at all," Charlie murmurs.

"And of course, I was in there, hiding with the ring, waiting on one knee," I say. "And she said yes!"

"Of course I did, pumpkin," she says, smiling a little bit too wide. "You'll always be my sweet banana muffin."

I have to bite the inside of my lips to keep from laughing. I take a deep breath, staring into Charlie's hazel eyes, and try to ignore the fact that we're both moments from losing it.

"You'll always be my gooey honey bun," I tell her.

Charlie's eyes start watering. She takes a deep, controlled breath.

"My darling pookie bear," she says, somehow keeping a straight face.

"My favorite cuddle gremlin," I say back.

I'm squeezing her hand way too tight, because I'm half a second from completely losing my composure, but Susie rescues me.

"That's just the sweetest thing," she says. "Is the wedding going to be angel-themed?"

"Absolutely," says Charlie, looking up at her, dead serious. "Angels everywhere. Nothing but angels."

· · · · ★ ★ ★ ★ · · · ·

WE BID SUSIE FAREWELL, promise to be in touch about cake, and then none of us says a word until we're back in the car, doors shut.

The second we look at each other, we both burst out laughing. I laugh so hard I snort. There are tears running down Charlie's face, and she shoves them away with the back of her hand.

"What?" says Rusty frantically, from the back seat. "What's funny?"

"Nothing, sweetheart," I manage to gasp out.

"Why are you laughing?" she demands.

I can see her serious little face in the rearview mirror, and it only cracks me up harder.

"Stop laughing," Charlie gasps. "Oh, my God, Daniel."

"Charlie told a funny joke," I manage to gasp out.

"What was the joke?"

"That she likes ceramic angels," I say. It's the best I can do.

"Cuddle gremlin," Charlie mutters from the passenger seat.

We both crack up again.

"Why is that funny?" Rusty demands. "Charlie doesn't like angels."

I close my eyes and take a deep breath, because if I look at Charlie right now, I'm going to lose my shit again and make Rusty even madder.

"That's the joke," I explain. "She doesn't really like angels, but we said she does."

"That's just a lie," Rusty points out.

"You're right, sweetheart," I say. Charlie clears her throat.

"Sorry, Rusty," Charlie says. "It's not really that funny."

I open my eyes again, Charlie's staring straight ahead, like she's trying not to laugh.

In the back seat, Rusty sighs dramatically, still frowning. I put the car into drive.

"Where's the algorithm taking us next, pookie bear?" I ask Charlie.

She snorts and unfolds the itinerary.

CHAPTER EIGHTEEN

CHARLIE

Thank God, the next stop doesn't have delicate, flowered teacups and saucers set up at their tasting table, just three plates with forks. Everything about this already makes me feel like a bull in a china shop: the beautifully, carefully crafted cakes; the signs on the wall with sweet sayings like *Live, Laugh, Love*; the other patrons who are inevitably women and inevitably have their hair and nails done and keep saying things like *lemon chiffon Victoria sponge*.

I'm not particularly delicate. I'm not great at being careful, unless it's around power tools. I've never in my life had a manicure that lasted longer than three hours without chipping, not that I've painted my nails in at least five years.

Also, I'm wearing a dress, so I'm constantly afraid of accidentally flashing people, and Daniel won't quit staring at my back and then saying that he's not. I'm starting to think I've got a KICK ME sign back there.

But despite all my discomforts with traditional markers of femininity, this is the best day I've had in weeks. Cake is delicious. Rusty's being her usual precocious, hilarious self.

And I think I might jump out of my own skin if Daniel touches me one more time. I don't know how I'm supposed to wait until *Monday afternoon* when Rusty has her ballet lesson for him to come over. That's over forty-eight hours away.

Maybe one of his brothers will take Rusty for a while tomorrow. I love the kid, but I'm trying to jump her dad's bones over here and she's not helping.

"All right," says the woman at The Cake Walk as she brings out a platter of cake pieces. "Here's our sampling of wedding cake options. All the way on the left is our basic white cake, which we've spruced up with a little bit of coconut to make it extra moist, and then there's our raspberry chiffon, a really moist cake that we usually serve with a simple buttercream, and third is the angel's food cake, which is dense but moist and really holds up well as the bottom tier of a cake."

I shoot Daniel an alarmed glance.

How many times is she going to say the word 'moist'?

"Next is our bakery specialty, the pistachio mint cake, which is probably our moistest and most popular..."

Oh, God.

She says the word *moist* at least five more times. She describes the red velvet cake as *moist* twice in the same sentence. I can no longer concentrate on cake. I can only wait for her to say the word *moist* again.

Midway through, she gasps. The three of us freeze, me with a bite of cake halfway to my mouth.

"That's a *beautiful* ring," she says. "Is that a ruby?"

I lower my fork.

"It's a garnet," I explain. "Family heirloom."

Daniel briefly tells the story, and the woman is now sitting with her chin on one hand, leaning over the table.

"That's so romantic," she sighs. "How did you propose? I'm sure it was amazing."

Daniel and I look at each other.

Is everyone going to ask us that? I wonder.

Before I can say anything, Daniel alights one hand on my shoulder, his rough hand on my bare skin. I take a deep breath and ignore the sizzle it sends along every nerve in my body.

"Charlotte loves to tell the story, so I'll let her do it," he says. There's a gleam in his eye that I don't like. "And don't forget the part with the skywriting, sweetheart."

I reach up and put my hand over his and smile at him sweetly, because I know I probably deserve this.

"How could I forget?" I ask.

· · · · ★ ★ ★ ★ · · · ·

THERE MUST BE some wedding cake marketing seminar where they teach people how to make small talk during cake tastings, because the same thing happens at every single bakery. It's bizarre. It's also kind of hilarious.

First, there's some variation on, "What a beautiful ring!"

Then, the big one: "How did he propose?"

If we were smart, we'd have come up with a story ahead of time. We didn't.

First was the ceramic angels. I have no clue where he got that idea from.

Next, at the Cake Walk, he threw it to me and I told the nice lady all about how Daniel took me for a picnic on a lake, and when we went out on a rowboat, a skywriter wrote MARRY ME CHRALOTTE overhead, and I said yes despite the misspelling.

"I know how to spell your name," he says as we walk

out, his hand steadily on my lower back, and I. Am, Losing. My. Mind.

"Of course *you* do," I say. "The skywriter made the typo."

"That was also a lie," Rusty points out as she climbs into her booster seat. "You're lying to people."

"Think of it as telling stories," Daniel says, and Rusty considers this all the way to the next bakery.

· · · ★ ★ ★ ★ ★ · · · ·

AT FRANCESCA'S CAKES, Daniel puts a hand on my knee and tells the lovely older woman who admired my ring that I really, really love sloths, so he took me to the zoo, then disappeared and came back wearing a giant sloth costume and proposed.

At the Magnolia Bakery, we're standing at a counter, and he slides his arm around my waist while I detail the elaborate treasure hunt that he sent me on, which ultimately culminated in finding him on one knee in his back yard.

None of us is very hungry for lunch, but we get sandwiches and find a park by a river. Daniel teaches Rusty to skip stones, or at least, he tries. I just watch them, shoes off, toes in the grass, and try not to notice that Daniel's extra-hot right now.

At Sugar Momma, Daniel tells the woman that he organized a flash mob for his proposal, but then joke's on him because he has to explain what a flash mob is. The whole time he's got one hand on my back, one thumb stroking the triangle of bare skin right below my shoulder blades.

At Cherry on Top, I tell them that we're both total adrenaline junkies, and he proposed while bungee jumping off a bridge in West Virginia. When I'm done with the story, including a description of how romantic the bouncing was, I lean over and give him a quick kiss, right on the lips.

It's a mistake. I want more. I want to climb onto his lap and wrap my legs around him, but we're in a bakery with plenty of onlookers and a seven-year-old, so I quietly pull away and pretend I'm not clenching my toes.

By the time we get to the Frosted Fig, our last cake stop, we're all tired. If there's such a thing as too much cake, we're approaching it. Even Rusty's enthusiasm is waning slightly, though she's still through the door before either of us.

At the Frosted Fig, there's a counter with stools. We sit. We each take bits of cake from the same tray, and when the inevitable question comes, Daniel quietly laces our fingers together.

"We took a hike to her favorite waterfall," he says. "When we got there, I asked her to marry me. Then we went skinny dipping."

I take a bite of cake, waiting for the punchline, but Daniel's just watching me as I chew and swallow red velvet.

"That's so sweet," the woman says. "I always like hearing about the simple proposals. They're the most heartfelt."

I nod, Daniel's hand still in mine. He's still looking at me, his face oddly serious, thoughtful.

"Yeah," I say, quietly. "It was really nice."

· · · · ★ ★ ★ ★ · · · ·

DINNER IS the rest of the sandwiches we got for lunch, eaten on the back porch of Daniel's mom's house as the sun sets. It's early May so it stays light pretty late, and long after we're done eating, we sit there, carefully reviewing the day's cakes.

Well, Rusty is doing most of the reviewing. As much as I like cake, they all kind of blended together after a while.

"I liked Sugar Momma," Rusty is saying. I wonder, briefly, if she has any idea what that means, but I don't think so. "Their chocolate was good. And they had the best chocolate frosting, too. There should be more chocolate wedding cake."

"Well, people always want it to be white," I say, lazily, my feet up on the low glass table, my shoes off, a slight breeze pushing against my hair.

"Why?" Rusty asks.

"White's the wedding color," I explain. "Wedding dresses are white, the cakes are usually white. Lots of wedding stuff is white."

Even as I'm saying it, I'm perfectly aware that this explanation isn't going to cut it with Rusty.

"But *why* is white the wedding color?" she asks. "How come everyone wears a white dress?"

I open my mouth, then close it, suddenly aware that I don't want to be the one who explains the concept of virginity to Rusty, nor do I want to explain the fact that almost everyone wears white, and yet, almost no one is actually a virgin when they get married.

So instead, I look over at Daniel.

"It's tradition," he says smoothly. "Like eating ham on Easter."

"But *why* is it tradition?"

"Why don't you research it?" he suggests. "I bet there's an interesting answer to that question."

Rusty just looks thoughtful.

The subject changes. Daniel reaches over, takes my

hand in his like he's been doing it for years and it almost feels like he has.

Finally, he glances at the time, then looks up at Rusty.

"All right, kiddo," he says. "It's shower time."

Rusty makes a face.

"You need me to come start it for you?" he asks, not moving.

"Dad. No," she says, as though he's asked if she'd like to lick a beehive. "I can do it."

"All right," he says, a little wary. "I'll be up in fifteen minutes to check your progress."

"Don't come in the bathroom without knocking," she orders, standing from her chair.

"Do I ever?"

"Just don't, okay?"

Daniel holds up one hand.

"I won't," he promises, and Rusty heads back into the house.

"When did she become a teenager?" I ask, and Daniel just sighs.

"She gets mad when I insist on double-checking her shower progress," he says. "But if I don't, she'll just stand under the hot water until the well runs dry, pretending to be a mermaid werewolf or whatever it is this week."

"You mean a were-maid?"

"That just sounds like she'll clean the house during a full moon."

"I'd take it," I say, and Daniel laughs. He pulls out his phone, sets the timer for ten minutes, and tosses it onto the table in front of us.

"You told her fifteen," I point out as he stands, our hands still linked.

"She needs a five-minute warning," he says, and pulls

me up, catching me by the waist. "I'll go knock on the door."

The sun went down half an hour ago and it's nearly dark, but not quite, the forest and the house all draped in the indigo of nearly-night. My arms are around Daniel, our bodies pressed together. His fingers find my chin, the rough pads skipping along my jawline.

"I shouldn't kiss you," he murmurs.

The words tug at me like a string, a jolt I feel in my chest.

"Why?" I whisper.

If he's about to tell me we should just be friends, I might punch him.

"Because in ten minutes I have to go hassle Rusty for taking too long in the shower," he says. "I'm going to have to stop kissing you and go be a responsible father, and I've been a responsible father all goddamn day."

"Language," I tease. His thumb finds my cheekbone, and I can't help but lean into his hand, his touch electric.

"Exactly," he goes on, his voice low, deep, quiet. "When I first saw you this morning, I should have said that you look goddamn amazing, but Rusty was there so I said *nice* instead of *fucking incredible.*"

His thumb finds my lower lip, traces it, and my eyes stutter closed.

"Now we've got nine minutes," I whisper.

He kisses me. It's gentle, slow, full of barely held restraint, like a horse straining at a harness.

We press our lips together, stop. Separate, millimeters between us. Kiss again, lips at a new angle by a few degrees, then stop. Separate, stop, each new kiss an adventure, an exploration. I want to map his mouth, chart his lips, discover him inch by inch and I'm starting here, now, with this single chaste kiss.

The kiss is glacial, an aeon, because Daniel's timer is ticking and soon we have to end this and it's better to not get too far. It's better to not get too breathless, better to not push my hands under his shirt, better to not straddle him in this chair.

So we're patient. The minutes tick down. I spent years waiting for this, not knowing that I was waiting; I can last a few more minutes.

Finally, the timer goes off. Daniel's hand knots in his hair, his forehead held against mine. We're both breathing hard and trying not to. I relax my hand when I realize I've got his shirt tight in my fist.

"I gotta go wrangle the merwolf," he murmurs. "Charlie, you're staying, aren't you?"

"Here?"

"Until she's asleep," Daniel says. His alarm is still going off, quiet beeping on the table below us.

"She can't put herself to bed?"

"I don't even fully trust her to rinse shampoo out of her hair," he says. "Just say you'll stay."

"Of course," I tell him, and he gives me one last, light kiss, then releases me. He grabs his phone off the table, shuts off the alarm, and vanishes back into the house.

I take a deep, deep breath of the twilight air. It even feels purple in my lungs, and I rub my hands together, calluses skipping along each other, trying to quell the rising wave in my body, the feeling that I'm buzzing like a high-tension powerline.

I grab the plates we used for our sandwiches, the glasses we drank lemonade from. I take them inside, decide not to bother with the dishwasher, and wash them by hand. I can hear Daniel and Rusty upstairs, the old wooden floor creaking above my head, occasional snippets of conversation — *pajamas, did you get your molars, I need the tortoise pillow.*

I can't hold still. When Daniel's voice leaks down to me it's low, steady, calm, just like always. I bite my lip and remind myself to breathe.

I find myself putting away clean dishes. I wipe down every surface: the counters, the table, the sideboard, even though they're already pretty clean. I find myself on the back porch with a broom in my hand, sweeping at the light dusting of bright green pollen that's collected in the corners, because I feel like a shark: if I stop moving I might die.

The porch is practically sparkling when I hear the scrape of the screen door opening.

"What the hell are you doing?" asks Daniel's slow, deep voice.

I turn, the broom still in one hand.

"There was pollen?" I say.

"Yeah, it's outdoors," he says, and then he's crossing the porch to me, taking the broom from my hand, tossing it down with a clatter. "Who are you, Cinderella?"

He grabs me by the waist, sliding his hands up my ribcage, and already I'm hanging onto his shoulders, the thick muscles there moving and flexing under my hands.

"You just think that because I'm so meek and tidy," I say, and he laughs.

"My two favorite things about you," he teases, his nose brushing mine, his fingers finding the bare skin on my back. "You never speak your mind and you're never a mess."

I kiss him, and this time it's like floodgates open. He leans into me, pushes me against the porch railing, the wood solid against my back. I wrap an arm around his shoulders and an arm around his waist and already the kiss is deeper, hungrier, my tongue against his.

Daniel sinks a hand into my hair, tilts his head, presses himself against me. I realize with a warm jolt that he's already hard, his length pressing against my hips, and the knowledge is a shockwave. I pull him even closer, hook two fingers through a belt loop and tug.

He crashes against me, a low sound coming from somewhere deep in his chest. He skims one hand along my thigh, grabs my skirt in his hand, hikes it until his fingers can steal underneath it and I sigh.

I reach a thumb underneath his shirt, right above the waist of his pants, brushing the fuzz there and the kiss slows, suddenly less furious as Daniel's hand moves to my inner thigh and I shift my stance, hoisting one leg, a noise escaping my throat.

"What was that?" he teases, his lips still brushing mine. Now my hand is fully under his shirt, and I can feel the vibration of his voice there.

"Shut up," I whisper, taking another kiss.

His thumb brushes the edge of my panties, and I bite his lip, but he doesn't go further. I've got one foot propped against the porch railing, my knee against his hip, balancing on one leg. Daniel presses into me again, harder, his thumb still teasing at me, his length like iron.

Then he pauses. His thumb sneaks under the elastic of my panties, the pad rough against the soft skin of my hip.

"This was a bad idea," he says.

I go rigid instantly, his thumb still stroking my hip underneath my underwear.

"What?"

"I thought this would work better," he says, and lets me go.

For a second, I'm completely dumbfounded, and then Daniel catches my hand, backs up, pulls me along.

"Daniel, what the *fuck* are you—"

He backs up against the wicker couch, sits, pulls me so I'm straddling him, my skirt covering his lap.

"You're an asshole," I laugh, his hands already up my skirt.

He grabs my hips and pulls me down, against him, and I have to bite my lip so I don't make a noise.

"Why, you don't think this is better?" he says.

I kiss him again. I can't stop. I roll my hips against his erection, separated by what feels like a hundred layers of fabric, the friction delicious. He pushes back, sits upright, anchors me tightly to him. For one wild second I think *we could just do it right here*. I'm wearing a skirt. There's no one around, the farmhouse surrounded by forest.

Except Rusty's upstairs, asleep, and sometimes kids wake up.

Daniel breaks the kiss. He leans back, heavy-lidded eyes looking up at me, one hand on my ribcage as his thumb traces along the bottom of curve of one breast. I'm breathing hard, and with every swell of my chest his hand moves more until he's cupping me with one hand, a slow smile spreading across his face.

"You *are* wearing a bra," he murmurs, mostly to himself.

"Of course I'm wearing a bra," I say, my own hands on his chest.

"I couldn't tell," he said. "It drove me crazy all day long."

"You think I'd go cake tasting with no bra on?" I tease, bending down. He palms my breast harder, grins, shrugs.

"I entertained the thought," he says. "And I kind of enjoyed imagining that your nipples were just one layer of fabric away."

"Sorry to burst your bubble," I murmur, teasing.

His other hand is on my thigh. It slides up and I lean my forehead against his, my hips rolling automatically, my own body out of my control.

He skims a thumb along my panties, right over my clit, my swollen lips, nothing but a single layer of thin cotton separating us, and I gasp. There's a hitch in Daniel's breathing, and then he does it again, this touch slower, more deliberate.

"That much, Charlie?" he murmurs. I'm pretty sure my panties are soaked straight through, and all I can do is nod and then he's kissing me again, pulling me in, his thumb tripping over my clit, moving to one side, swiping under the fabric and suddenly there's nothing at all between us.

I grab his hair. I make a noise into his mouth, a single note of a moan, and he answers me with another low rumble. I'm a ticking time bomb. I'm a powder keg. Primed, ready, dangerous, about to alter myself and everything around me when I explode.

This is the cliff's edge: this touch, this moment, this heady rush of skin to skin.

"Daniel," I finally whisper. "We can't undo this."

His hand stops moving.

"Do you want to?" he asks.

I'm still over him, the porch light off, everything draped in the blue-black of night. It feels like we're wearing a cloak, like we're alone in this world of our making.

"No," I say. "But I just—"

I take a deep breath. I have no idea how to say what I'm about to say. I just know I need to say it.

"—this will change things," I say in a rush.

"I know," he says, his voice low, soft, steady.

"Before, the one time we kissed, I could forget that," I say, the words still spilling out of me. "But this is more—"

"I didn't forget it," he says.

"I didn't *forget* it forget it," I say. "I moved on. Life moved and I pretended it didn't happen and after a while everything was fine, it was better than fine, but I can't forget again."

"I don't want to forget anything," he says. "I've got no intention of forgetting this, or of undoing it, or of letting this slip through my fingers again."

"You had a good excuse," I say, mostly teasing.

"I want to change us," he murmurs. "I know there's no taking it back and I want this anyway, Charlie."

We kiss again. I think I'm trembling, a seismic shift somewhere deep inside my core.

"I want this too," I whisper, and I kiss him, a kiss that turns into a full-body plea, Daniel's hands on me. He moves me to one side, tangled in my legs, until I'm on my back on the wicker couch and he's on top of me, skirt hiked around my hips as I tug it down on one side because despite everything I know that Rusty's in the house, and I know she *cannot* learn about the birds and the bees from witnessing us.

Finally, Daniel rises, holding himself up against the arm rest, his powerful arm stretched over my head.

"Come on," he says, and stands up, holds out one hand.

I take it, rise, my skirt falling back to my knees.

"Where are we going?" I ask, still breathless.

"My bedroom," he says, hand on my back, pushing me toward the house.

I stop, stiffen, look at him.

"The door locks," he says, opening the sliding screen door.

"She won't hear us?"

"Not if you're quiet," he says, one eyebrow raised.

Now we're in the kitchen, and he kisses me, up against the counter.

"Is that legal?" I ask, but Daniel just laughs, pushes a hand up my skirt.

"It's safer than the kitchen, that's for sure," he says. "If we fuck in my bedroom she at least has to knock. And don't you *dare* say 'language' right now, Charlie. We're clearly having a very adult moment."

I laugh as I kiss him, even as he snaps the elastic of my panties against my hip and makes me gasp.

"I would never," I protest between kisses.

"You would and you have," he teases, and now both hands are under my skirt, the hem going higher and higher. I've got one hand under his shirt again and I slide it down until I find the hard ridge of his cock, and I squeeze.

Daniel groans, both hands closing around the flesh of my upper thighs, pushing me so hard against the counter that I'm sure it'll leave a bruise. Not that I care.

"I wouldn't when you've got both your hands up my skirt in your mom's kitchen," I manage to say against his ragged breathing.

He just presses against me harder, leaning me back over the counter until my head hits the cabinets and he presses his lips to my neck, his beard tickling me. Another noise escapes me, and I clench my teeth together, trying to control myself.

Be quiet be quiet be quiet.

Then he pulls back, lets my skirt fall. He gives me one more firm kiss and pulls me away from the counter, spins me, smacks my ass.

"Go," he orders.

We're up in the stairs in ten seconds. In fifteen he's closing his bedroom door quietly, clicking the lock into place, twisting it once.

"See?" he murmurs. "Locked, and I'm pretty sure she hasn't even opened the lock-picking kit I got her last Christmas."

He's to me in three strides and he hasn't even kissed me

when I'm taking his shirt off, desperate to feel his skin on mine.

"Tell me that was a joke," I ask between kisses, my mouth still pressed against his, and I can feel his smile.

"Fuck yes, it was a joke," he growls, his hands roaming my back, pulling me closer. His skin is warm against mine, intoxicating, and already I'm pulling at the button on his pants, trying to get them off without looking down.

I yank it. The button finally pops off and I get the zipper down and Daniel groans quietly as his boxer-clad cock springs into my hand, long and thick. His head drops to my shoulder as I stroke him once, twice, hard, root to tip. He's big, but I've seen him in gym shorts before so it's not a surprise.

I stroke him again and he inhales sharply, kisses me on the neck, puts his lips to my ear.

"Charlie," he whispers, his fingertips climbing the column of my spine. "How the fuck do you get this dress off?"

I let him go, lift it over my head.

"Oh," he says, as I reach behind myself, unhook the strapless bra, let it fall to my feet.

For a long moment, he just looks at me. He looks at me like he's taking notes, like he's memorizing. His gaze feels like a caress, like a kiss, like some sort of worship and at the same time I take him in: the wide shoulders, the thick arms, the muscled chest, the dusting of light brown hair that thickens at his bellybutton, leads below the band of his boxers, his pants splayed open around his cock.

Then he reaches forward, the backs of his hands against my breasts, pinches my nipples between two fingers, flicks them with his thumbs.

"Oh *fuck*," I say, my own hands reflexively going to his wrists as he captures my mouth with his. He pushes me backward and then his bed is there, behind me, and then I'm on my back, Daniel on top of me, my blood rushing through my veins with the pounding, unceasing rhythm *yes please, yes please, yes please.*

I grab his pants and shove. Somehow, they come off and he's kneeling between my legs, boxer-clad, one ankle in his hand, resting on his shoulder, the other roaming up my thigh. This time he doesn't hesitate, but slides his fingers under the thin fabric instantly, his eyes on my face.

I'm soaking wet. I know it. I know my panties are soaked through and I know that Daniel's fingers are already slick as he runs a thumb over my lips.

I gasp when he finds my clit, reflexively grab the bedsheets and Daniel leans in, my ankle still on his shoulder as he massages it again, the thick pad of his thumb sliding over the sensitive nub with a jolt. His eyes don't leave my face as he does it again and again, pushing my leg to one side, leaning down, planting himself on one elbow.

Now he's rubbing me with his soaked fingers, panties shoved to one side. He lowers his head, takes one nipple between his teeth and I grab his hair in one fist, fighting the urge to shout as he moves faster and faster, one of my legs flung over his back.

Suddenly, he stops. He sits up, grabs my panties, yanks them off and I kick, sending them flying into some corner and then we're both kneeling on his bed, torso to torso, my hand wrapped around his cock.

Not good enough. I reach into his boxers, grab him bare, bring his head down to mine for a deep, hard kiss as I pump him slowly, listen to the noise he makes.

It's beautiful, a low growl, a note I've never heard before. I want to hear it a thousand times, want to feel the vibration of it echo through my own mouth that many times again. His hand is tight on my hip, on my lower back, his fingers leaving divots.

I let him go. The boxers come back and we move until I find myself against the brass bars of his headboard, cool stripes running the length of my back. Daniel's on his knees and he lifts me, mouth on mine, my legs splayed, until I'm sitting on him.

I'm stroking his cock again. He's pinching a nipple with one hand and holding onto the bars with the other, pressing me back, pressing me against them. He's brutal and soft all at once, gentle, teasing, rough.

He reaches between my legs again, and this time he finds my clit instantly and I sigh, my head back against the bars, my hips bucking against his hand as he kisses me, drags his lips against my jaw.

"You like that," he says into my ear. It's not a question. I nod anyway.

He pauses, strokes my entrance.

"You're so wet," he whispers, his voice wondrous.

Daniel slides his fingers into me smoothly, slowly, and I grab the top bar of his bedframe, somewhere over my head. I make a noise, eyes half open, and Daniel kisses me.

His cock is in my hand, hard and thick, a drop of precum running down the tip as I stroke it. It's taking all my self-control not to guide it to my entrance, not to lift myself up and lower myself onto him even as his hand moves inside me, stroking my front wall, thumb still massaging my clit.

Then he pulls away from the kiss for a moment, pauses. There's a flash of foil, a flutter, and then his mouth is on mine again as we're rolling a condom over him, his hand over mine. He groans softly into my mouth and I let the sound wash over me, through me, his fingers still spiking pleasure through my nerves with every stroke.

He pulls them out, grabs my hip, pushes me harder against the bars and I hang onto his shoulders, lift my hips. I kiss him again, nearly out of my mind with need as the tip of his cock finds my clit, parts my lips.

"Charlie," he whispers. "No takebacks?"

I can't help but smile.

"No takebacks," I whisper, and he eases into me.

My body feels like someone flips a circuit breaker, all the lights suddenly ablaze.

"Oh *fuck*," I whisper, one hand in his hair, clutching his face close to mine.

He stops.

"You okay?"

"I'm fine," I whisper, and he moves again, sinking into me, pulling back, pushing me against the bars, going deep and hard and slow and leaving me breathless. "Oh fuck, Daniel, I'm fine, I'm fine."

He grabs me, pulls me down, kisses me hard.

"Fine?" he asks mid-kiss, his voice a growl.

"It's good," I manage to get out, my voice barely working as he hilts himself again, so deep it makes my toes curl.

"It is," he says, and then we stop talking. We move together like two parts of the same machine, like we were designed with each other in mind. It's better than *fine*, better than *good*, better than *great*.

I can't keep my mouth off his. I can't stop whispering his name, usually with some version of *oh fuck* thrown in there. I keep telling him not to stop, chanting it over and over even though I know he won't.

He's whispering my name back, his face buried in my neck, his lips on mine as we hold onto each other, entangled, still trying to get more and more and more. The wave inside me crests, higher and higher, the feeling that I'm floating, flying.

I grab the top rail on his headboard, the cool metal anchoring me to reality as he hits that spot over and over again, my whole body attuned to his like a radio antenna.

"Daniel," I whimper. "Fuck, Daniel—"

He claps his hand over my mouth just in time, because a second later I explode, a chain reaction that rattles through my body, all the way to my fingers and toes, a cataclysm from somewhere deep within. I clench my teeth against the noise, but it escapes me anyway, bubbling up unbidden.

"Holy shit, Charlie," Daniel gasps, his hand still over my mouth, as he thrusts so hard I see stars. "Holy fucking shit—"

I grab his shoulder, tighten my legs around him, draw him in as if to say *come inside me please god come inside me* but he's already there, holding me so tight I can barely breathe, rocking like the aftershock of an earthquake, every muscle in his body tense and rigid.

It's beautiful. It's mesmerizing. I want to make him come a thousand times. I want to feel every single one just like this, the two of us together, so close that I can feel every single jolt as it travels through his body.

He finishes but he doesn't stop. He kisses my neck, bites my earlobe, takes his hand off my mouth, replaces it with his own. I can't stop touching him. I can't stop needing him, wanting his body to still be on mine, craving this closeness, this oneness.

He bites my lower lip. He pinches a nipple, rolls it between his fingers, my body jolting at the sensation and I laugh, softly.

"You're addictive," he murmurs, then pinches it again and I gasp lightly. "See?"

"Is that bad?" I whisper.

He slides his hand down my torso, and I realize I'm damp with sweat and so is he as he pulls out of me carefully.

"Fuck no," he says, and before I know it his thumb is on my clit, rubbing me slowly, firmly.

I lean my head back against the brass bars. My breathing gets shallow, my legs still splayed around his waist, my hand still on the top bar.

It doesn't take long. Neither of us says a word as he watches me as I come apart for the second time in three minutes, exploding again, this time with my own fist jammed against my mouth. I'm gasping when I finish, eyes closed, one hand in Daniel's hair because I can't stop touching him.

He kisses my neck. I'm still breathing hard, fingers and toes clenched, and as he kisses me again, I unfurl, breathe deep, his hands on my legs, waist, his arms around me, his mouth on mine.

We untangle, kiss again, untangle some more. Finally, we're sitting up in his bed, backs against the brass bars of the headboard, his arm around me and his other hand in mine, my head against his shoulder.

"Are we different now?" I murmur.

I feel him press his lips against my hair, keep them there for a long moment.

"Not in the ways that matter," he finally says.

CHAPTER NINETEEN

DANIEL

"So it doesn't matter that now I've seen you naked?" Charlie says, keeping her voice low, turning her head toward me, teasing.

"You didn't just see me naked," I say, still talking half into her hair. "You've *experienced* me naked."

"The Naked Daniel Experience sounds like a band," she says. "They'd play psychedelic rock and they wouldn't be very good."

"Unlike the actual experience," I say, and she laughs, tilts her head back over my shoulder so she's facing me.

"Right," she says, and her eyes search my face.

And then, simply: "That was good."

Good isn't a big word or a fancy word, but right now, Charlie's eyes looking into mine in the dark afterglow, it feels like it encompasses the universe. I know exactly what she means, and I know what she's trying to say, and yes, yes, *yes* to all of it.

"It was really good," I agree.

Charlie curls into me even more, her face against my

shoulder, her hair tickling my neck. She rubs back and forth once, twice, adjusts, rubs her face on me again.

"What are you *doing?*" I finally ask, and she stops.

Then she looks at me.

"My forehead itched," she says.

She's trying not to laugh.

"You've got hands," I point out, also trying not to laugh.

"They're far away."

"They're literally attached to you."

Now she's laughing, biting her lips, still trying to quell it.

"I didn't think you'd notice."

"You thought I wouldn't notice you rubbing on me like a cat?"

"Sometimes you don't notice things," she laughs.

"Is this how it's gonna be now?" I tease. "We have sex and suddenly you get super weird?"

"You think that's super weird?" Charlie says. "I'll show you super weird."

"You don't have — are you biting me?"

She's got her teeth on my shoulder, not hard enough to hurt.

"Grrr?"

"Oh, my God," I mutter, laughing. "I've unleashed a psychopath with the power of my dick."

That gets a snort-laugh out of her, her shoulder shaking under my arm.

"Sorry," she finally murmurs, and kisses the spot she just bit, still laughing.

"If I go get rid of this condom can you be normal for three minutes?" I tease.

"One way to find out."

I kiss the top of her head again and then pull myself

away from her and throw on pajama pants.

· · * * ★ **★** ★ * * · ·

"*SHIT.*"

I come awake all at once, already up on one elbow, always primed for middle-of-the-night problems.

"What?"

"I fell asleep," Charlie says, pushing herself to sitting, facing away from me on the edge of the bed. She's naked, her wild hair a halo around her head, both hands already in it. "Fuck. Shit."

I roll over enough to see my alarm clock glowing green on my bedside table: 5:45 a.m.

"I gotta go," Charlie's already saying, whispering at me in the quarter-light of early morning. "Shit, I didn't mean to fall asleep, I just meant to stay a little while…"

She bends down, comes up with her bra, wraps it around herself. Somehow, she does the clasps behind her own back, without looking. I'm impressed.

I toss off the sheets, get up myself, get dressed as Charlie tosses the purple dress back over her head.

"Where's my underwear?" she whispers.

"Floor?"

I pull on boxers, pants.

"I can't find it."

"It didn't disappear into a wormhole."

I open a drawer, grab the first t-shirt inside.

"Fuck it, I'll grab it later," she hisses. "I gotta go."

I pull the shirt on, my body still half a step ahead of my brain.

"You good?" she whispers, hand on my doorknob.

"No," I say. She frowns at me, but I cross the room, bend down, kiss her. We're both still foggy with sleep, both rushed, slightly rattled but we kiss slowly, deeply, softly.

"We still haven't talked," she murmurs when it ends.

"We talked for like two hours last night," I point out.

"I mean about us," she says. "Not about how big a rubber duck would need to be before it doesn't float anymore."

"I still think any size would float."

"But you couldn't make it out of rubber, at some point it would collapse in on itself, and — no. We're not having this conversation again," she says.

I lean forward and steal another kiss. She's soft and warm in the morning, yielding. I never knew that before. I like it.

"All right, get outta here," I whisper. "Before Rusty wakes up."

Charlie opens the door silently, peeks out into the hallway. All clear. We both tread downstairs lightly, she grabs her phone and purse from where she left them last night, and we step onto the front porch, the cool morning air raising goosebumps on my arms.

Then we both stop short at the same time.

"*Fuck*," hisses Charlie, right as the same realization hits me.

I gave her a ride here yesterday. Her car's still at her apartment.

"Crap," she says.

"It's okay," I say, pushing a hand through my hair, trying to think. Rusty's still asleep upstairs, so we've got time, but probably not all that much. "I'll just..."

I glance back at the house, and for precisely one second I consider just giving Charlie a ride home right now, before Rusty wakes up. Chances are, she'll never know she was home alone.

But then I imagine what would happen if she woke up and I wasn't there, and I wipe that possibility from my mind.

"Look, we're engaged, remember?" I say. "We'll just wait for her to wake up and then we'll take you home."

She's already shaking her head.

"Rusty thinks it's fake," she says.

"We're going to tell her, aren't we?"

"Not like this," Charlie says, urgently. "She can't just wake up with me here wearing the same outfit as yesterday with no underwear on—"

"You didn't find it?"

"It's there somewhere, I was in a hurry, but Daniel, we can't just spring this on her."

"She doesn't have to know about the underwear."

Charlie just gives me a look.

"Sorry," I say.

"We need to at least plan how to tell Rusty," she says. "We can't just be like, hey, Charlie's banging your dad now, by the way has anyone told you what sex is yet? Well, they did it while you were asleep."

"I don't think I'd go about it that way, but I see your point," I say.

"I'm calling Elizabeth," she says, already scrolling through her phone. "She's a teacher, she's probably awake right now. And if she's not she has to forgive me."

Charlie holds her phone to her ear and waits. And waits.

"I got her voicemail," she says, and dials again.

Same result. Charlie makes a face, goes to dial her phone again, but I shake my head.

"Levi's awake," I say, pulling mine out.

Charlie looks doubtful for a moment, but then she nods.

He answers on the second ring. I keep it short and simply ask him if he can swing by the house and give Charlie a ride home.

"A ride home from Mom's house?" he asks, his gruff voice full of unasked questions.

"Right," I say.

There's a moment of quiet, and I can practically hear him stroking his beard.

"Be there in twenty," he says, and hangs up.

"Twenty minutes," I tell Charlie, and she exhales. "You want coffee?"

CHAPTER TWENTY

CHARLIE

W hen Levi pulls up in the driveway, Daniel and I are sitting outside on the porch steps, coffee in hand, talking about nothing, watching the sunlight slowly soak through the forest that surrounds the house.

I'm on my feet before Levi's truck comes to a stop. Daniel takes my coffee mug. Levi's truck stops. He gets out.

Daniel leans down and kisses me. I put one hand on his shoulder without thinking, a brief, chaste kiss, and then it's over.

"Ballet Monday?" he says.

"Sounds good," I say, and I walk toward Levi's truck, manage to climb into the passenger side without flashing him.

"Thanks for the ride," I say as soon as we're both inside, seatbelts buckled. "I know it's early, I just totally forgot that I didn't have my car here, and we didn't want to wake Rusty up, you know?"

Levi puts the truck into gear, and I swear there's a quick, sneaky smile hiding under his beard.

"Naturally," he says. "I imagine she'd have a lot of questions."

I steal a quick glance over at Daniel's oldest brother. Just because he tends to be the quietest, the last one to typically get involved in family arguments, and the least likely to interfere, doesn't mean he's the least nosy.

There's a part of me convinced that Levi somehow knows everyone's secrets, all the time, he just doesn't say anything.

"Are you trying to tell me you've got questions?" I say, leaning back in the seat, my arm resting on the window ledge.

He's giving me a ride home at sunrise. I probably owe him some answers. I think I can handle that. This isn't really a secret, right? We're supposed to be engaged, after all, though I think Levi is one of the ones who knows it's a ruse.

Shit, I'm gonna need a flow chart to keep track of who knows what.

"I'm probably the only person right now who hasn't got any questions at all," he says, downshifting to go around a sharp turn. "Unlike Rusty, I know what it means when a woman is still at a man's house at six o'clock in the morning."

"Right," I say. "So... how are the trees?"

The answer to that question is surprisingly complex and interesting. Most of the trees are well. Some of the trees are in trouble. He's trying to convince the Forest Service to do slightly more prescribed burns this year than normal, to clear out the brush, and just as I ask how many acres they usually burn, my phone rings. It's my sister.

"Sorry, one sec," I tell Levi. "Hey, Betsy."

"What happened?" she asks.

"I'm fine, it's nothing," I tell her.

"You called me at five-fifty in the morning," she says. "That's not a nothing time, Chuck."

"Is that Elizabeth?" Levi asks.

"Is that Daniel?" Elizabeth asks.

I nod at Levi.

"It's Levi," I tell Elizabeth.

The line goes dead silent for at least five full seconds.

"It's *Levi*?" she asks.

I've never heard my sister sound more astonished. I just start laughing.

"Surprise!" I say.

"*What?*" she hisses into the phone. Another silence.

Then: "Charlotte Alexandra, are you fucking with me?"

"Of course not," I say. "It's Levi. It's six in the morning and I am currently with one Levi Loveless. Hand to God, Betsy."

Levi glances over at me, one eyebrow raised, an entertained half-smile on his face.

"Tell her I say hi," he says.

"Levi says hi," I tell Elizabeth.

"You're definitely fucking with me," she says.

"Elizabeth, she's fucking with you," Levi says, raising his voice slightly. "I am merely your sister's conveyance. Our relationship is platonic."

"He's giving me a ride home from Daniel's," I say, still laughing. "That's why I called you, but your phone went to voicemail."

Next to me, Levi is just shaking his head.

"I see," Elizabeth says. "Just so I've got everything straight, you were at *Daniel's* at five-forty-five this morning?"

"Technically, it's his mom's—"

"*Charles.*"

"Yes."

"I see. You want to get breakfast in an hour? Mountain Grind?"

"Sure," I say. After a few more exchanges, we hang up, and I look over at Levi.

"Sorry for involving you in that," I say. "Sometimes I can't help but mess with her, she can be such a know-it-all."

There's that slight smile again as the truck comes to a stop and Levi looks left, then right.

"Oh, I understand completely," he says. "You know my family. Some of them rather well."

I blush, laugh, and change the subject.

· · · · ★ ★ ★ ★ · · · ·

WHEN WE GET to my house, Levi insists on walking me to my door. I accept, because I've learned it's pointless to argue with a Loveless man on matters of chivalry.

I make some more coffee, shower as fast as I can, put on new clothes, and head back out to the Mountain Grind. It's only about six blocks away, so I walk, but I'm somehow still ten minutes late.

Elizabeth's sitting by the window, messing with her phone, two cups of coffee in front of her, a plastic number eleven in a stand. She doesn't say anything as I sit, just pushes one of the cups forward.

"Thanks," I say, and start on my third cup of coffee for the morning.

"I got impatient and ordered already," she says. "I hope you wanted a breakfast burrito."

"That sounds magnificent."

She takes a long sip of her own coffee, and I take the moment to marvel at my older sister. It's seven in the morning, and she's wearing mascara and a necklace along with her jeans and shirt.

How does anyone accessorize this early? I just feel lucky that my shoes match.

"You boned him, right?" she asks. "Please don't tell me you were up all night just talking or something."

"What's wrong with that?" I ask, ignoring the first part of the question for now, just to fuck with her a little more.

"You've wanted his dick for like ten—"

An older woman I don't recognize turns and looks at Elizabeth, and she looks away, toward the window, clears her throat.

"—like ten years," she finishes, her voice considerably lower.

"It hasn't been that long," I protest.

"Charlie," she says, leaning in. "Did. You. Bang. Daniel—"

"Yes," I hiss, also leaning in.

"Atta girl," she says, and holds out one fist. I bump it with mine. "That was the first time, right?"

I just sip my coffee and lean my chin on one hand.

"I bought you breakfast," she says, narrowing her eyes. "Come on."

"Yes, first time," I say. "We went cake tasting yesterday and he picked me up and I forgot I didn't have my car there…"

I sketch the vague details: no car, sleeping Rusty, Levi to the rescue. She won't stop grinning like the cat that ate the canary, so by the end of my story, we're both giggling.

"I hope he finds your underwear," she says. "At least they don't have a dog, that could be a disaster."

I take a moment to imagine a golden retriever, running through Clara's back yard, my panties held aloft in its jaw.

"I probably should have found them, but I was kinda panicking," I admit. "They're there somewhere, right? Oh, God, tell me Rusty won't find them."

"Daniel is very responsible," Elizabeth assures me. "He's probably found them already. He does his own laundry, right? Tell me his mom doesn't still do it."

I just shake my head as the waitress comes over and delivers us food: an egg sandwich for Elizabeth, a breakfast burrito for me.

"He's twenty-nine," I say.

"That doesn't guarantee shit," she says, mouth full. "There are some man-children out there, Charlie. Years ago, before Jeff and I got married, I dated a guy whose mom packed him lunch every day at thirty-one. He had to go by her house on the way to work. How that was easier than just making his own lunch I'll never know, but I broke up with him when he told me that."

I dump hot sauce on the burrito and take a big bite, suddenly starving after not eating much but cake in the last twenty-four hours.

After a moment, she nods at my burrito.

"It about that size?" she asks, pure mischief in her eyes.

"What?" I ask, my mouth full.

"His dick," she says, like it's perfectly normal thing to ask.

I nearly spit my burrito out.

"You teach children with that mouth?" I hiss once I swallow.

"No, I swap it out for an appropriate one, like Mr. Potato Head," she says calmly. "This is my getting-breakfast-with-my-sister-after-she-finally-fucked-a-guy mouth. Also, last time you had a boyfriend, you were way more forthcoming."

"That was like two years ago, and also, you got me drunk," I say. "Besides, you *know* Daniel, I can't just tell you about his dick."

216

"I'm just wondering if it runs in the family," she says calmly.

I've got my mouth open for another burrito bite, and I freeze that way.

"See? I can fuck with you, too," she says, and takes a bite of her sandwich, then takes her sweet time chewing it. I narrow my eyes, waiting. She's the same age as Levi, but there's definitely no way, right?

I'd *know*, right?

"I went for drinks with some of the other teachers a few months ago," she finally explains. "Did I ever tell you about Jennifer? Super sweet girl, new to town, teaches first grade?"

Things click into place.

"Seth?" I ask, and Elizabeth nods.

"Really nice, total oversharer," she says. "*Very* enthusiastic about her fling with Daniel's little brother. Great dick, apparently."

I make a face at my burrito, because I like Seth a lot but really don't want to know about his dick. I'm aware that it's well-traveled, and frankly, that's more than enough information.

"I thought he swore off girls in town," I say.

For the record, I didn't really think that Elizabeth had first-hand knowledge of a Loveless dick, but she did still scare the hell out of me.

"Yeah, but Jennifer's really cute," she says, licking egg off a finger. "And apparently a little bit of a freak. Besides, did anyone believe that?"

She waggles her eyebrows, and I snort.

"She didn't get his name tattooed anywhere, did she?" I ask, and Elizabeth laughs.

"No, she seemed pretty clear that they weren't a thing," she says. "At least he's getting better at choosing, right?"

"Right," I agree.

"You have to tell me *something* about last night," she says. "I got you that burrito. And coffee."

"I thought that was from the kindness of your heart," I tease, taking another bite.

"You've got me confused with some other sister," Elizabeth says, her mouth full. "That's a bribery burrito."

"I had a nice time," I say, deliberately baiting her.

"A *very* nice time?" she asks, grinning, both eyebrows raised.

"A very nice time twice," I admit, heat rushing to my face.

"Hell yes," Elizabeth says. "I knew Daniel was a gentleman."

CHAPTER TWENTY-ONE

DANIEL

"Dance your butt off," I tell Rusty, leaning down to kiss the top of her head.

She giggles.

"Then what will I sit on?" she says. "Dad, I need my butt."

"Then don't dance it all the way off," I tease. "See you in an hour, kiddo."

Before I've finished my sentence, she's scampering through the door and into her dance studio, where she lines up with six other little girls, all wearing black leotards, pink tights, and high buns.

I'm very, very proud of my bun abilities. I've impressed many a dance mom by putting Rusty's hair up in less time than it takes to say *pirouette*. I've even been hit on as a direct result of being able to twist a seven-year-old's hair into that shape.

Not today, though. Today I nod at the dance moms and then I'm out the door of the studio in record time, walking toward Charlie's apartment as fast as I can possibly go.

I want to be the only thing on her mind. I've been

sending her innocent-but-teasing texts all day, imagining her pushing up her goggles, reaching for her phone, blushing when she reads it. I've spent the day wondering what she's wearing underneath her coveralls, or if when it's hot like this, she wears anything at all.

The thought of Charlie wearing nothing beneath her coveralls was a particularly disastrous one. I spent about ten minutes in cold storage after that, pretending that I was looking for a box of fresh Centennial hops that I know for a fact I never ordered.

I come to a red light on William Street. There are no cars coming, so I jaywalk. I've got my hands jammed in my pockets and I'm resolutely trying to remember the dance moves I'm supposed to help Rusty practice — plie, arabesque, sauté, which I could have sworn was a cooking term — but it's not helping because now I'm just imagining a naked Charlie doing all those things, and it's having the opposite of the intended effect.

I give up and just walk faster. I reach her building. I cut around back to where her staircase is. I take the steps two at a time, and at the top, in front of her door, I pause.

I take a deep breath. I brush my hair out of my eyes. I wonder, briefly, if I should have brought a breath mint, and then before I can even knock the door opens and she's standing there.

Wearing nothing but a thin, brightly patterned robe, the neck open almost to her bellybutton, her damp curls in a high, messy bun.

"Oh good, it's you," she says lightly, her eyes laughing. "I dunno what I'd say if you were my landlord."

The edges of the robe are barely covering the swell of her small breasts, her nipples tenting up the fabric, and I'm having a hard time thinking right now.

I step inside. I shut the door behind myself and lock it.

"I like your robe," I say, finally looking her in the eyes.

I put one finger at the hollow of her throat, step closer to her as Charlie tilts her head up.

"Thanks," she says, her voice breathy. "I just got out of the shower."

I slide my finger down her chest, between her breasts, to her sternum, and Charlie exhales hard, puts her hands on my waist.

"And I didn't get a shower text?" I ask, teasing. "No *Hey, Daniel, I'm slippery and wet right now?*"

"While you were with Rusty, not to mention the dance moms?" she says.

I move the edge of the robe over one nipple, then the other, and Charlie's eyes flicker closed. They're pink and pebbled, hard nubs tilted slightly upward. I flick my thumbs across both of them at the same time, sliding my fingers around her ribs.

"I can be discreet," I say, letting my thumbs circle her nipples.

"I wouldn't want to damage your standing in the dance mom community," she murmurs, her breath hitching in her throat. "Mmmm."

I'm so fucking hard right now. My jeans feel like a cage, my cock throbbing, pulsing, straining against the fabric because this is nearly all I've been thinking about for forty-eight hours.

"I'll worry about my standing in the community," I tell her. "You just worry about texting me shower updates."

I lean down and kiss her, thumbs still on her nipples. She grabs my hips, her hands already under my shirt, pulling me in toward her. It's a deep, hard kiss, and she moans softly into my mouth, grabs the waistband of my jeans, pulls me in, fingers an inch from my dick.

"Hey, Daniel," she says, her voice low, her lips brushing mine as she speaks. "I'm slippery and wet right now."

Fucking hell.

I untie the robe, shove it aside, capture her mouth with mine again as I slide my hand between her legs.

She's not lying. She's soaking wet, the tops of her thighs sticky, her lips swollen. The moment I touch her clit she makes a noise in her throat and bites my lip, her hand convulsively closing on the flesh of my side. If she didn't have short fingernails, she'd leave marks.

"Jesus, Charlie," I whisper, already sliding my fingers into her, like she's drawing me in. There's another little noise, one arm around my shoulders, her other hand suddenly squeezing my cock through my pants.

We're not going to make it to her bedroom.

I push her backward, five steps, and she lands on her couch. I stand over her, fingers still in her, kiss her deeply, my thumb now on her clit. She tries to move but I grab one thigh, hold her in place.

Then I break the kiss. I plant my lips on her neck, her collarbone. I bite one nipple. I get on my knees between her legs, her breathing ragged, my mouth on her inner thigh, fingers still in her tight, slick channel, and I pull her down until she's right in front of me.

I'm breathless, dizzy with desire, her scent filling my nostrils and driving me wild. I flick my tongue across her clit and her whole body jerks, her thighs clenching, so I do it again, then again.

Charlie grabs my hair in her fist and makes the best sound I've ever heard — a breathy sigh, a strangled moan, a wordless plea to lick her until she comes so hard her eyes roll back in her head.

I flatten my tongue, lick her again, harder, her hips move, and she tightens around my fingers so I do it again and again. I'm careful. Deliberate. I stroke her with my fingers in the same rhythm as I lick her, and I can feel her muscles flutter, tremble.

"Holy fuck, Daniel," she whispers, her voice hushed, faraway. "God that feels good."

I push her thighs further apart, bury my face in her even harder. Charlie overwhelms my senses, her hips rolling against me like she can't control herself, her juices on my fingers, my palm, sweet in my mouth.

I don't say anything. I lick her harder, faster. She flexes her toes against the floor, arches her back. I add a third finger and she squeezes me, trembling, gasping for air.

I never want to stop. I'm so hard I think my dick might simply turn to stone and fall off, and yet, I don't want to stop. I want to stay here forever, Charlie grinding against me, buried in her while she gets closer and closer to her climax, whispering my name while she does.

I move, lick, coax, stroke. Charlie whimpers *oh fucking please*, every muscle in her body tense, ready, and I don't stop. I want her to come undone. I need her like this, here, now.

"You're gonna make me come," she whispers, her chest heaving like she's running a marathon. "Oh fuck, Daniel—"

I lick her harder, faster. I watch her throw her head back, a dent in her couch cushions, and just as she tenses, back arched, I put my lips around her clit and suck gently, fingers curling in her tight, slippery channel.

Charlie *shouts*, coming. Her pussy clenches so hard around my fingers that I can't move for long moments, the bones of my knuckles grinding together as her hips lift off the couch, her feet flexed against the floor. She moans, no words, just one long animal sound.

I still don't stop, pressure light but steady on her clit,

face buried in her. I let her come in wave after wave. She rocks, shudders, gasps for air, and I feel every single tremor until finally, her waters are calm again.

The moment I pull my fingers out of her she leans forward, her mouth on mine, her tongue probing deep. I still taste like her, but she obviously doesn't care so I kiss her deeply, rise to my feet.

Charlie just about tears my shirt off. Seconds later she's got my pants undone, cock out, and she's stroking it hard and fast and I have to steady myself against the back of her couch.

She tears my pants off. I collapse onto the couch, finally naked, pull her on top of me so she's straddling my thighs, hand still stroking my cock as she's on her knees, kissing me furiously, her hips rolling against me.

Both my hands are clutching her ass, round and firm, springy with muscle, and I pull her in until my cock is crushed between our bodies, her tits in my face.

I suck one nipple into my mouth, roll my tongue around it. Charlie moans, her hand tighter, and I suck on the other one until her breathing goes ragged again, then I find her mouth and we kiss hungrily, desperately.

"Condom," I murmur, and she bites my lip softly. I can tell she's laughing as her hand leaves my cock for a moment and then she's got the foil packet in her teeth, ripping it open.

"Was that in your robe pocket?" I ask, pushing her back slightly.

She shrugs out of the robe in one fluid motion and it flutters to the floor.

"Of course," she says, rolling the condom on. "I knew why you were coming, and I didn't want to waste time."

She kisses me deep, strokes me again.

"I'm a practical woman, Daniel," she says, teasing. "Why do you think I was wearing just a robe?"

I pull her in again, lift her, my hands digging into her hips. She's warm and ready, hands on my shoulders, curls half-falling out of her bun, and she reaches down and finds my cock and steadies it at her entrance.

This time she doesn't say anything, just takes me in a single stroke. Her hands clench my shoulders hard enough to leave bruises as she envelopes me with a moan, her eyes going half-mast.

Fuck, it's good. It's better than good. She's warm and tight, her muscles squeezing me as I push myself deeper, her hips moving as I bottom out, shifting inside her.

"God, I like this," I whisper, her hips in my hands. We move together, her hips rolling against me, sliding me in and out, her inner architecture stroking me.

Charlie just nods. She's got her forehead against mine, eyes closed, hands on my shoulders, the curls slipping from her bun, wild around our heads.

She moves faster. She grinds her hips against me while I'm buried deep inside her, rises onto her knees, plunges back down with an exhale that's half-sigh, half-moan.

"That good?" she whispers, breathless. She does it again, pulling me all the way out and then sinking me deep into her slowly, deliberately. My fingers dig deeper into her hips with every stroke.

"Fuck yes," I gasp. "Jesus, Charlie, this is perfect."

She moves faster, harder. She grinds against me with every stroke, her eyelids fluttering as she moans and I move inside her, watching her face. We do it again and again until with every single thrust I'm hitting *that* spot inside her, the one that makes a breathy little *oh* come out of her mouth.

Finally, I let go of her hips, slide my hands up to her

nipples again. We're moving faster now, in a furious, desperate rhythm, and when I pinch both her nipples at once, Charlie lifts her head, leans it back, moans explosively.

"Lean back," I tell her.

She looks at me, wild and breathless.

"I want to watch your tits bounce while you ride my cock," I say, and Charlie gives me a slow, saucy smile.

"I didn't know you'd talk this dirty," she says, anchoring one hand and then the other on my thigh, arching backward.

I pull her back down my cock, and I can feel the jolt inside her body as I do, and she makes that *oh* noise again but it's deeper, guttural.

"I didn't know you'd fuck like this," I say, and I'm trying to tease her but the words come out, ragged, breathless as our bodies come together again and I'm buried in her and she's moaning, clenching, and I can barely take it.

Charlie doesn't talk any more. She rides me faster, harder, her small breasts bouncing with every stroke, her glorious body on full display. I've got a perfect view of my cock disappearing into her over and over again, our bodies meeting roughly, savagely.

I find her clit again with my thumb, circle it slowly, in time with her movement and I'm rewarded by a long, low moan, her walls clamping tighter around me. I clench my teeth and gasp, self-control hanging by a thread.

"Daniel, I'm gonna come again," she says, her voice a whisper, a moan. "Make me— oh *fuck*—"

I pull her down hard, slam myself into her as hard as I can. I see stars. The air feels like thorns against my skin.

"—oh fuck oh please Jesus Daniel—"

I do it again and again. I think the ceiling is cracking.

"—so fucking good Charlie—"

"—oh God oh God please, please, *please*—"

Charlie comes like an earthquake, shaking and trembling and rattling, her head thrown back and her fingers digging into my legs. My vision goes white as she clenches around me but doesn't stop riding, my thumb still on her clit, taking me in long, hard strokes.

I'm two seconds behind her. I'm a fucking feral animal, grabbing at her, hauling her in with all my might, coming and coming and burying myself in her and wanting to never surface.

I come so hard I forget where I am. I come so hard I forget *who* I am and only come to with my face in her neck, my arms around her. We're both panting for breath, both sweaty, hard to tell where I end and she begins.

I lift my face and kiss her. She's trembling. She pulls back, laughing softly, shakes her arms out, wraps them around me again. After another minute we manage to unwind from each other and Charlie collapses to the couch, limbs akimbo, a droplet of sweat slowly making its way down the hollow between her breasts.

I reach out and trace it with my thumb.

"Next time I'll turn the AC up," she says, flinging one leg over mine.

"I think I busted a nut," I say. "Now I feel like I truly understand that saying."

"*That's* your pillow talk?" she teases, grinning. "We have the best sex of your life and afterward you want to talk about busting nuts?"

I slump further down on the couch, stroking her thigh. It feels like it's a million degrees in here all of a sudden, and I'm pretty sure I'm also very sweaty.

I also think I might just melt into this couch out of sheer satisfaction, even though I know I've got about five minutes before I need to leave so I can be at Rusty's ballet

227

class at a respectable time.

"Presumptuous," I say.

"Is it?" she muses.

"I didn't say it was wrong," I admit. "Just presumptuous."

Charlie laughs, puts her arm through mine, leans against my shoulder.

"This is good," she says. "Whatever it is."

"I think we're dating," I say. "Is this dating?"

"Well, usually there are more dates," Charlie says.

I look down at her, a smile tugging at her lips.

"This wasn't a date?"

"This was more of a... sex appointment?" she says, thoughtfully.

"I'm not seeing the difference."

"If it were a date, you'd have had to find a sitter, and we'd have spent a frustrated hour in a restaurant or something first," she says.

"So we're not dating, we're sex appointing," I say.

"While pretending that we're engaged," Charlie points out.

I glance down. The ring's there, on her finger, glimmering away. I think she's gotten used to it, because she isn't constantly messing with it any more like she used to.

"Well, that was an incredible sex appointment," I say, and kiss the top of her head. Charlie snorts.

"Do you have any openings on your calendar later this week?" she asks. The twist of her mouth says she's making fun of me, not that I care.

"Well, Rusty's got a piano lesson Thursday at five-fifteen," I say. "Though that's only forty-five minutes long."

"We can make it work," Charlie says instantly.

"And she's with her mom this weekend," I say. "Friday night until Sunday night, if you're available."

"I could make some time for you," she teases.

I glance at the clock again. Now I've got two minutes before I need to be gone.

"C'mere," I say, leaning down. I run my hand up the inside of her thigh, her skin soft and warm beneath my fingers. She tilts her head up and my lips find hers, her body splayed on the couch, naked and glorious.

It takes all my self-control to pull away from her, Charlie's hand still on my face.

"Thanks for lying to a judge," she murmurs. "It turned out pretty well."

I kiss her again, quickly, then stand before I can be tempted further.

"You're welcome," I say, then sigh. I'm already running a minute late.

I *hate* running late.

"Be right back," I say, and head for her bathroom.

"Daniel!" she calls.

"Yeah?"

"Make sure you wash your face so you don't smell like vagina in front of the dance moms," Charlie says. "Don't go giving them ideas."

I laugh, hand on the doorknob.

"I would never," I say.

CHAPTER TWENTY-TWO

DANIEL

Tuesday night, Charlie comes over for dinner, and afterward I clean up while she and Rusty play Go Fish with the deep-sea deck. When I'm done, I lean against the doorway into the living room and just watch them for a while: Rusty constantly trying to get one over on Charlie, Charlie having none of it.

They finish that game. Rusty wins. They play another one, I tell Rusty it's bedtime, and she negotiates for one more game before she has to go to sleep.

I swear, she's gonna work for the UN when she grows up.

Finally, she comes down in her pajamas — narwhals leaping through rainbows, a gift from Violet — to say goodnight.

"You brushed your teeth?" I ask, and she nods. "Washed your face?"

She nods again.

"Tell Charlie goodnight, then," I say, standing.

"I want Charlie to read to me," she says.

I raise both my eyebrows and look over at Charlie.

Rusty's never requested a bedtime book from anyone but me, but Charlie looks at me and shrugs.

"You have to ask Charlie," I say.

"Charlie, will you read to me?"

"Sure," she says. "You'll have to fill in the backstory, though."

"That's okay," Rusty says, bouncing on her toes. "Good night, Dad."

"Good night, sweetheart," I say, giving her a quick kiss before she's gone like a flash, Charlie alighting the stairs behind her.

"Okay," I hear Rusty say, slightly breathless. "So Sophia is a princess but she thinks that being a princess is stupid, her parents just want her to marry a prince so instead she goes and finds a dragon and asks if she can work for her..."

And then they're gone. I sit back on the couch, suddenly unsure what to do for the next fifteen minutes.

· · · ✦ ★ ★ ★ ✦ · · ·

THURSDAY WE HAVE another sex appointment. This one's even shorter than the last, and we don't even make it to the couch. Charlie answers the door in a towel, somehow wearing even *less* than the last time I came over, and within minutes we're kneeling on the floor and I've bent her over the couch while I fuck her hard and fast and deep and she begs me to do it harder, faster, shouting into the couch cushions when she comes.

I can't get enough of her. I feel like an addict, unable to think about anything but my next fix. Even as I'm going soft inside her, my cock slipping out, I kiss the back of her neck, her shoulder, one hand cupping her breast. I pinch a nipple and she makes a soft noise, her back arching, the perfect globes of her ass against my hips.

I love how responsive she is, how she tells me what she wants, how her body moves under mine, and even though I should be going already I slide my hand between her legs again, her clit between my fingers. I stroke her until she comes again, moaning, bucking backward into me and then when she finishes, I kiss her hard and deep.

"You're gonna spoil me," she says, her voice dreamy.

"I'm okay with it," I tell her.

· · · · ★ ★ ★ ★ · · · ·

FRIDAY MORNING, Crystal calls. I'm already at work, and I seriously consider not picking it up. I'm going to see her in a few hours when she picks Rusty up for the weekend, I can talk to her then.

But one of us has to be the reasonable, level-headed adult, so I answer.

"Listen, Daniel," she says. "Can you do me a favor and bring Rusty over at three?"

"No," I say, managing to keep my voice reasonable.

"Bruce has dinner with the board tonight, and I need to have Rusty over here on the early side so I can get her cleaned up and dressed and everything," she says with the air of someone explaining some very basic to someone very stupid. "So I really need you to just bring her to—"

"For starters, she's got school," I say, already on my feet, pacing back and forth. "And for—"

"It's May," Crystal says.

"School goes through mid-June," I remind Crystal. I'm honestly not sure she knows when Rusty has school.

"Then they're not doing anything," she says, like it's obvious. "Everyone just screws around for the last month anyway."

I take a deep breath, step out of my office and into the

main brewery. We just started our Mountain Hollow Brown yesterday, so it smells like fresh, strange bread right now, and I breathe that scent deep.

"I'm not pulling her out of school early, and I'm not bringing her to your house," I say, struggling to maintain calm.

Crystal snorts derisively.

"It's just second grade," she says. "It's not important."

"How would you know?" I ask, patience fraying quickly.

"Because it's *second grade*."

"When was the last time you helped her with her homework?" I ask. "How the hell would you know anything about whether second grade is important?"

"I mean, *maybe* high school is important," she says. "Jesus, Daniel, can you do me a favor *once*?"

I don't believe in violence, but if Crystal were here, I might strangle her right now.

"No," I say curtly. "Pick her up at six at my house. See you in a few hours."

She says something else, but I hang up. If I talk to her anymore I might say something I regret, and I wouldn't be surprised if she were secretly recording our phone calls.

I'm not pulling Rusty out of school — which she *loves* — for Crystal's bullshit. I have no idea what Crystal says about me when Rusty's with her, but her whole life, I've been careful not to say anything bad about Crystal, because no matter what, Crystal's her mom and Rusty loves her to death.

I worry that someday she won't. Rusty's a perceptive, precocious kid, and I worry that it'll be sooner and not later that she starts asking questions about why she only sees Mom once a month, or why I don't have any baby pictures of her. Sometimes I lie awake at night, practicing my answers to those questions. I never get them right.

I stuff my phone in my pocket, and head out back of the brewery. It's a little outside town, on a rural road, so it's surrounded in the front by farmland and the back by forest.

For a moment I just stand in the gravel parking lot, fuming at Crystal.

Then I throw rocks at the trees until I feel better.

* * * * * ★ ★ ★ * * * *

CRYSTAL FINALLY SHOWS up at 6:30, half an hour after we agreed. When she knocks on my door, looking impatient, I don't ask why the hell she's late if she was in such a damn hurry to begin with.

Rusty practically bounces into her mom's arms. She pats Crystal's belly and whispers hello to her little sister while Crystal gives me a triumphant look that I can't interpret.

I try to tell Crystal everything that Rusty's been doing lately: that she wears long-sleeved pajamas because she kicks all her blankets off; that she doesn't like to sleep without Astrid, her stuffed wombat; that we're reading *Apprenticed to Dragons* and she's been helping me cook and can tell different pine trees apart thanks to her uncle Levi and sometimes pretends to be Jump Girl and leaps off the back of the couch, onto the cushions she's piled up.

"Great!" is all Crystal says. "Rusty, want to go to the waterpark this weekend?"

"YEAH!" shrieks Rusty, jumping up and down. I'm pretty sure that Crystal didn't listen to a word I said.

I get the booster seat out of my car and put it into Crystal's, since she doesn't have one of her own and I definitely don't trust her to install it. While I do that, I can

234

hear her telling Rusty about all the fun they're going to have this weekend, all the presents that Rusty has at her house, how they've got a gallon of ice cream in the freezer.

When it's time for them to leave, my mom and I give Rusty hugs and kisses, promise to call, and then we stand in the driveway and watch Crystal drive away. Rusty waves all the way down the driveway, until she's out of sight. My mom puts her arm around me and hugs me to her side.

On one hand, I hate watching Rusty drive away. I'll miss her every minute she's gone. The house will feel weird and empty without her.

On the other hand, it's really nice to get a break once in a while. Particularly this weekend.

"Daniel, I have a confession to make," my mom says, still side-hugging me, both of us still facing the driveway where Crystal's car disappeared.

"Is it that you hate Crystal and wish I'd impregnated someone better?" I ask.

"Yes," she says.

I just put my arm around her and pat her shoulder. She says more or less the same thing to me every time Crystal takes Rusty for a visitation weekend, and I can't say I disagree.

We stand there for a bit, just my mom and me, still facing the driveway.

"And you're staying at Charlie's this weekend?" she asks.

"Right," I say, suddenly standing up straighter. It doesn't matter that I'm a grown man with a child. Admitting — however tacitly — to my mom that I have sex is... weird.

"Tell her I said hello," she says, disengaging with a final back pat. "And don't come back without calling first."

"Sure," I say, turning and following her toward the house so I can get my stuff and leave.

Then I stop in the driveway, my mom still making her way to the house.

"Wait," I call. "Why?"

CHAPTER TWENTY-THREE

CHARLIE

Daniel: Heading over now.
Me: Everything good?
Daniel: Don't make me talk about Crystal.
Daniel: Can we just talk about what you're wearing?
Me: What makes you think I'm wearing anything?

I watch my phone screen, waiting for a response. I see him typing, then nothing. Typing, then nothing.

I start laughing to myself. I'm lounging on my couch, half-assedly watching TV but actually thinking about tonight. My room is lit by battery-powered tea light candles that I impulse-bought off the internet last week, because real candles make me nervous that I'll forget to put them out and burn my apartment down.

Daniel: I'll be there in ten.
Me: Door's unlocked, just come inside.
Daniel: My pleasure.
Me: That's the idea.

Daniel: Don't distract me, I'm driving eighty miles an hour.

Me: I'm not sorry.

He doesn't respond, which is good, because that means he's busy driving.

I get off my couch, get undressed, and hop onto my bed.

· · ★ ★ ★ ★ ★ ★ · · ·

I COME TWICE BEFORE EITHER of us says a word. Daniel comes in, locks the door behind himself, finds me on my bed, and not ten minutes later I'm on my hands and knees and he's buried balls-deep, hitting the exact right spot over and over and over again until I fall apart. Twice.

Once we're finished, we collapse onto my bed, both facedown, on top of my sheets and duvet. Idly, I wonder whether I should have taken the duvet off, since it's a pain in the ass to wash and it's too hot to use it anyway.

"Hi," Daniel finally says, turning his head toward me, his face smashed into a pillow. "How was your day?"

I can't help but laugh at the polite, mindless small talk in light of what we were doing two minutes ago.

"It was fine," I say. "Sanded some stuff. Sawed some stuff. You?"

"As good as any day where Crystal's concerned," he says. "She wanted me to pull Rusty out of school so I could bring her to the new house because her husband is having some shindig or something."

I just snort. I don't think there's been a single visitation where Crystal hasn't tried to get Daniel to do something extra for her. He used to say yes more often, until he realized that if he gave her an inch, she'd take two miles.

"You didn't, did you?" I ask, even though I'm pretty sure I know the answer.

"Of course not," he scoffs. "There's probably an ancient secret society devoted to hunting down and killing her kind, I'm not going to help her."

"When's the hearing?"

"Two and a half weeks," he says, and buries his face in the pillow, stretching. The muscles down the back of his entire body bunch and knot so I give him a good, long ogle.

"I should write it down," I muse, not moving a single muscle.

Daniel just gives me a look.

"Give me your phone," he says.

"Why?" I say, still not moving.

"Because you're making me crazy right now," he says, hoisting himself onto his elbows and reaching over me for my bedside table. "Thirty-six, huh?"

I finally turn my head as he grabs my phone and spy the thirty-six pack of condoms I bought earlier this week.

"Well, now there's thirty-three," I say.

"That's ambitious," he says, grinning as he types the code into my phone's lock screen and opens it.

For the record, I also know that his phone password is 0305, Rusty's birthday. My phone's locked so that if I lose it, whoever finds it won't have access to all my bank accounts, not so I can hide something from Daniel.

"We don't have to use all of them this weekend," I tease. "They're good for seven years or something."

"They're not gonna last *that* long," he says, typing away.

"They'd better not," I say, and he gives me a sideways glance, already grinning devilishly, still typing.

After a minute, he closes my phone and tosses it in front of me.

"There," he says. "The hearing is in your calendar, and

I set up both alert and email reminders for a week before, a day before, an hour before, and thirty minutes before."

"Overkill," I mutter.

"Is it?"

"I remember important stuff," I protest, but not that hard. Daniel's not really *wrong* to set up a thousand reminders for the hearing date, even though I'm sure he'll also be calling and texting. I'm almost definitely going to remember something this important, but getting the reminders can't hurt, and I feel better knowing that they're there.

"Well, now you'll definitely remember," he says, his hand sliding down my back. "You hungry?"

"I could eat," I admit.

· · · · · ★ ★ ★ ★ · · · ·

WE ORDER a ridiculous amount of Chinese food and, in a fit of indulgence, have it delivered even though I'm categorically opposed to having food delivered, because I hate paying someone to do something that's so easy to do myself.

"Are you putting on pants?" Daniel asks as I find an old pair of pajama shorts and tug them on.

"The delivery guy is coming," I say, rummaging through a laundry pile that I'm 90% sure is clean.

It's a small pile. A discreet pile, sort of hidden next to my dresser. I forgot to fold it before Daniel came over.

"You've got a robe," he says, still lounging on my bed, fully naked, though at least he got the condom off.

"I answer the door in my robe when you're visiting," I tease. "If you really think that's the way to greet the delivery guy—"

"New plan," he says. "Do you have a snowsuit?"

I throw a pillow at him, but he swats it away. I pull on the tank top, still laughing.

"I can see your nipples," he says, stuffing the pillow under his head. "Come on, Charlie, a parka at least."

"Don't you dare go caveman on me," I tell him, rummaging through the almost-certainly-clean pile again.

"I just don't want you to be embarrassed," he claims. "It's got nothing to do with the fact that the thought of another man thinking dirty thoughts about you makes me wildly jealous."

I find two socks and stuff them into my tank top's shelf bra, right over my nipples.

"How's that?" I ask, putting my hands on my hips and sticking my chest out. "Good? Any nip showing?"

Daniel laughs, sitting up in my bed. He moves like a tiger, big and thick and muscled, with the grace of a powerful animal.

He reaches out and squeezes both my sock-boobs.

"I'd still hit it," he says solemnly, then grabs me by my waist and pulls me between his legs. "How long did they say delivery would take?"

· · * * ★ ★ ★ * * · ·

IN THE END, I do put a sweatshirt on over the tank top, because Daniel is right that I don't really want the delivery guy getting the full highlights. We eat lo mein and kung pao chicken on my couch, right out of the containers, and watch half of *Pirates of the Caribbean* because it's on TV.

It's lovely. It's peaceful. It's the exact same thing we've done a hundred times before when Crystal has Rusty for the weekend, only this time my nipples are fully visible through my shirt, Daniel's wearing nothing but boxers, and

I'm snuggled against him with his arm around me as Johnny Depp prances and swashbuckles.

Daniel was right. Nothing that matters has changed between us, and it's the biggest, most overwhelming relief.

We only make it halfway through the movie before I snuggle Daniel a little too hard, and before I know it, I'm gripping his hard cock through his boxers and he's got my tank top pushed up over my tits and one hand up my shorts. I don't even get the tank top off before we're having slow, lazy sex on the couch, the movie still playing in the background.

· · ⋆ ⋆ ★ ★ ★ ⋆ ⋆ · · ·

IN THE MORNING, I wake up to Daniel getting back into bed. Everything is slow, hazy, so for a few minutes I just watch him, lying there naked with the sheet barely draped over his lower half, one arm behind his head, as he reads my battered, worn copy of *The Complete Sherlock Holmes*.

It's a good view, and I just watch it for a long time, letting myself wake up. Every so often he takes his hand from behind his head, flips a page, and settles back in.

Finally, I take a deep breath, exhale, and roll onto my stomach.

"He dies at the end," I say. "Moriarty pushes him over a cliff. I think."

Daniel puts the open book down on his chest, both hands under his head.

"Bummer," he says. "Though I think they brought him back. He was hanging on by his fingertips, or something."

"Sounds like a close call," I muse. "I guess I never read them in order. I thought the author killed him off so no one else could write Sherlock Holmes stories."

Daniel closes the book, tosses it onto my floor, and rolls toward me, his arm snaking over my lower back.

My body responds instantly, even though I'm half-awake at best. I push myself up on my elbows, back arched, and look at Daniel through my eyelashes.

Or, at least, I try. I probably look like a crazed muppet right now.

"Tell me more about Sherlock Holmes," I purr, my voice still thick with sleep.

As come-ons go, it's pretty bad, but it's the best I can think of at the moment and besides, I'm certain it's going to work.

Daniel grins. His hand slides beneath the sheet that's covering me and palms one ass cheek, his fingers sliding into the crevice between my legs.

"Well, there's my favorite Holmes story," he says, his voice lowering. "*The Mystery of the Soaking Wet Pussy.*"

He pushes his fingers inside me and I gasp, arch, bite my lower lip as my fingers clutch my pillow. Daniel moves closer, his stiffening cock brushing my hip, as he lowers his lips to my shoulder.

"How the fuck are you already this wet?" he murmurs, his lips against my skin. "You just woke up."

"I was watching you read," I admit.

"Is that all it takes?" he asks, his weight shifting on top of me, his mouth on the back of my neck. He's got his other hand in my hair, pushing my head forward, my shoulders still raised, my back still arched.

"I was thinking," I say slowly, my brain still fuzzy.

Daniel's fingers move deeper, pushing into my channel. My hips buck upward, already asking for more.

"About?" he prompts, my breathing faster, ragged.

God, what a beautiful way to wake up.

"Whether it would be rude to interrupt your reading by

hopping on your dick," I gasp out. "Or if I should ask first."

Daniel moves a knee between my thighs, pushing my legs wide, and before I can even grunt, he adds a third finger. I put my face against the pillow and moan as he strokes me from the inside, then gasp when he finally puts his thumb on my clit.

"For the record," he says, kneeling upright, his other hand moving down my spine, squeezing one ass cheek. "I will *never* consider it rude to hop on my dick."

He pauses. I look up at the sound of a condom wrapper, watch over my shoulder as he rolls it on one-handed, his hips driving forward as he strokes himself.

Then he pulls his fingers out and plunges his cock into me in one fluid motion and I groan into the pillow, clenching it in my fists as I push back against him, taking him as deep as I can.

It's relaxed, unhurried. Daniel and I settle into a slow rhythm and I swear I float, just savoring the delicious feeling of his cock filling me, taking me again and again, each thrust sparking a chain reaction that sizzles along my nerves. When I finally come it's not a thunderclap but a slow-building rainstorm that leaves me gasping and wrung out by the end.

When we finish, Daniel collapses onto the bed again, still breathing hard, and looks over at me.

"We could just stay in your bed all weekend," he says.

"Isn't that the plan?" I ask. "Who knows when we'll get the chance again."

"Very true," he muses, then closes his eyes. "If something explodes at the brewery and I get called in, I will be *pissed.*"

"Nothing bad will happen," I tell him, finally sitting up, facing the headboard, grinning at him. "Just sex until we can't possibly bang anymore, and then maybe Chinese food or something."

He leans in, his smile devilish, and kisses me.

"Agreed," he says.

· · · ★ ★ ★ ★ ★ · · ·

We do, in fact, get out of bed. I suck him off in the shower, water running down his body in rivulets, caressing his beautiful, sculpted muscles, until he comes growling *oh that's so fucking good Charlie*. Then he bends me over my kitchen table and eats me out while the coffee's brewing.

There's sex on the floor. There's more sex on the couch, in my armchair, and we try it against a wall but that becomes floor sex, too. Between rounds we have breakfast and read books and turn on the TV to see if it's worthwhile and play stupid games on our phones, but mostly we talk.

We talk about absolutely nothing. He tells me the long, dramatic story of two brewery employees who were dating, then broke up, then she fucked his cousin, then they dated again, *then* he found out about the cousin and hung some ill-advised signs up around the brewery, took them down when they got back together, but by then Daniel and Seth had found a sign so they fired him.

"And it wasn't Seth?" I tease.

"Seth has more sense than that," Daniel says. We're lying on my floor, my head on his arm. "Besides, she's the one who fucked the cousin, not him."

"Right," I say, laughing. "Though, really, who else is there to fuck in Sprucevale? Everyone's someone's cousin, you're bound to get into trouble sooner or later."

In return, I go over all the reasons that Elizabeth claims her new house is haunted, even though it was built in the

1970s and the original owners are still alive, they just moved to Florida.

"I keep telling her that I can probably fix most of the creaks," I say. "And, I mean, the doors coming open at night is just a mounting problem, but I think she kind of enjoys living somewhere allegedly haunted. Gives their life some spice."

"I'd make a dirty comment about *mounting problem*, but I can't follow it up right now," Daniel says, and I laugh.

Around three that afternoon, he finds my vibrator in the drawer of my bedside table. By three-thirty I've come so much that I'm begging him to stop using the toy and just fuck me, and he obliges by sitting me on his cock and letting me ride him as fast or slow as I want.

I come again. I have no idea how, except it might have something to do with him sucking my nipples and telling me he loves watching me while I fuck him.

For someone who usually reprimands me for saying *damn*, Daniel is dirty as hell.

We both collapse sideways onto the bed, the sheets all kicked off and in a heap on the floor. My vibrator is still going, buzzing incessantly a few feet away from me, and by a heroic effort I reach over and turn it off.

"I should have bought Gatorade or something," Daniel muses. "I didn't realize I was coming here for an endurance athletic event."

I take a deep breath, eyes closed, and ask something that's been on my mind the last few hours.

"Is it too much?" I ask.

"Well, there are limits to what the human body can endure," Daniel teases, then rolls toward me, eyes open. "But I think you're a ways away from literally breaking my—"

He pauses as he looks at my face, then reaches out, puts one hand on my cheek.

"No," he says.

"We're not moving too fast, are we?" I ask. "We only got fake-engaged, like, two and a half weeks ago."

It doesn't feel too fast. It feels just right, us being together like this, but I've seen a calendar. I can count weeks. I know it was fast.

"When did we meet?" he asks. "Sixth grade?"

"I think so," I say. "Was that the year we had math together with Mrs. Thompson?"

"Was she the one who wore the battery-powered light-up sweater at Christmas?" he asks, and I laugh.

"No, that was *Miss* Petchul and she taught English," I say. "Mrs. Thompson always wore about fifty pounds of costume jewelry. Including a tiara that one time."

"I'd forgotten the tiara," he admits.

"Anyway, you sat behind me and copied all my answers, only half of them were wrong, and when you got busted she gave us both detention because she thought we were in cahoots," I say. "It was sixth grade. I got in *so* much trouble."

"Eighteen years ago, then," he says. "We've known each other for eighteen years and been best friends for most of that time."

I see his point.

"By most reasonable standards that's glacially slow," he points out. "It's not like we barely know each other."

"Especially now."

"We've done plenty of talking," he rumbles, his fingers working their way into my hair. "I think we've earned one weekend-long sex fest."

CHAPTER TWENTY-FOUR

DANIEL

"And then I went down the big waterslide," Rusty says, so excited she's breathless. "Fifty-five miles an hour!"

I lean my arms against the railing on the landing outside Charlie's door, looking down at the cars in the bridal shop's parking lot, phone pressed to my ear. It's Saturday night. And yes, I'm clothed.

"That's pretty fast," I say, keeping my voice as light as I can. "Did they clock you?"

"No but that's what the sign says," Rusty goes on. "The Tropical Tornado waterslide make you go up to *fifty-five* miles per hour, and you have to cross your arms and legs and close your eyes but it still—" she breaks off for a moment, giggling, "—it still gave me a wedgie at the bottom."

I swallow hard, opening and closing one fist. I don't love the idea of my small, fragile seven-year-old hurtling down a water slide, but I also know I'm being a little over-protective. She's tall enough, the waterpark is lousy with lifeguards, and hardly anyone ever dies at amusement parks.

Though staph infections and mysterious rashes are another matter altogether.

"What next?" I ask.

"Bruce and I went on one of the tube rides," she says. "Mom couldn't go because she's having a baby, so it was just us. Bruce is nice."

I want to tell her *he is not fucking nice, he's trying to take you away from me*, but I don't. She's seven. It's not her problem, it's mine, and I'm damned if I'm going to let her worry about anything bigger than homework.

"Bruce sounds cool," I say, hating every word of it. "What else did you guys do?"

"We went to Friendly's and I got a burger and then I got an ice cream sundae with a banana in it," she says. "I couldn't finish it, so Bruce and Mom helped."

"Sounds like you had a great day," I tell her. "Are you having fun with your mom? And Bruce?"

"Yes," she says, and then stops abruptly.

I stand up straight, because even though the phone is silent, I can almost *hear* her using her index finger to softly poke her cheek, the thing she does when she's thinking.

"What's up, kiddo?" I ask, stomach in knots.

"Are you coming to Colorado with us?" she asks suddenly, and the simple question stabs me straight through the gut.

I'm going to murder Crystal. I am. I take a deep breath, frantically trying to think of what I should tell Rusty right now that won't make her freak out completely. Apparently, I'm the only parent who gives a shit how she feels.

"We haven't decided yet whether you're going to move to Colorado," I say simply. "You might be staying here with me, or you might be in Colorado sometimes and here sometimes."

There's another long pause.

"Oh," she says. "Okay."

"Your mom and I are still figuring some things out, okay?" I say. "There are a lot of big changes happening right now. You've got a new stepdad, you're going to have a little sister."

Charlie and I are together for real.

I don't say that out loud. One change at a time.

"I don't want a pony if I have to go to a new school," she says. "Dad, I don't even like horses that much. They smell weird."

I'm going to kill Crystal, but I smile despite myself at Rusty.

"No one will make you take a pony you don't want," I tell her.

I spend the next few minutes talking to Rusty, trying to convince her as soothingly as possible that everything will be okay. I wish I didn't have to. I wish Crystal would interact with me like a grownup instead of a petulant teenager, because I would fucking *love* to have a co-parent who was willing to work with me as a team instead of trying to win Rusty's heart via waterpark.

When it's time for her to get off, I ask her if I can talk to her mom for a minute.

"Mom!" she screams, not taking the phone away from her mouth, and I wince.

"What?" I hear in the background.

"Dad wants to talk to you!"

"Tell him I'm busy."

"You're just watching TV."

"I can't talk to him right now, Rusty, okay?"

There's some rustling, then Rusty's back on the line.

"She can't talk to you right now," she says.

"Thanks for trying," I tell her. "All right, kiddo. See you tomorrow. Love you."

"Love you, Dad!" she says, and the line goes dead.

I stand there, on the landing outside Charlie's apartment, for a long, long time, taking deep breaths and resisting the urge to throw my phone off her balcony and watch it smash on the pavement below.

I fantasize about ways to get Crystal out of my life for good that don't go quite as far as murder. I imagine the judge handing down a new custody agreement: I get all physical and legal custody forever and ever and Crystal relinquishes her parental rights, then moves to Siberia and I never have to see her again.

It's not what I really want. What I really want is for Crystal to love Rusty back, for her to want to be a good parent and treat Rusty like her own child, not a fun prop one weekend a month at most. Rusty deserves to have two parents, but God knows I can't make Crystal do anything she doesn't want to.

There's a creak behind me, and I turn. Charlie comes out onto the landing, her eyebrows furrowed in concern, and leans on the railing next to me.

"What's wrong?" she asks.

"Crystal," I say, finally putting my phone back in my pocket. "Apparently she told Rusty that they're all going to move to Colorado."

Charlie sucks in a quick breath, her eyes going wide.

"That motherfucking hose beast," she whispers. "Do you want me to help you hide the body?"

I half-crack a smile.

"She took her to the waterpark and bought her ice cream," I say. "Charlie, I fucking *hate* her. I can't believe I ever stuck my dick in that."

She snorts.

"No one was all that smart at twenty-two," she says. "You just got hit with particularly dire consequences."

"Rusty's not really *dire*," I say.

"Crystal is," Charlie says.

I tell her about the rest of the conversation: the water-park, the fifty-five-mile-per-hour slide, though that part doesn't really seem to concern her, the ice cream, the fact that Crystal refused to talk to me.

When I finish, I hesitate for a second.

"I haven't even told Rusty about us," I say.

"Have you tried, 'Hey, sweetheart, Charlie and I are fake engaged but banging for real'?" she asks.

I laugh, still looking out at the parking lot below her apartment.

"Hey, honey, Charlie and I aren't actually engaged but I'm absolutely tapping that ass," I say, and Charlie snort-laughs.

"We're hitting it super hard every time you go to ballet class," Charlie adds.

"I might explain it to my second grader in slightly more PG terms," I say, then lean over and kiss the top of Charlie's head. "Like with the word *girlfriend* or something."

"Sounds reasonable," Charlie says, tilting her head up for a kiss on the lips.

· · · ★ ★ ★ ★ ★ · · ·

OUR SEX fest weekend mellows a bit on Sunday, when we only fuck twice before finally heading out, back to my mom's house for Sunday dinner. Crystal is bringing Rusty back at five — in theory — so we'll all be there when she arrives.

We don't even have sex the first time until *after* breakfast. I'd say that it's because I'm showing restraint, but the truth is that I'm sore in muscles I didn't even know I had.

The first is on the couch, one of Charlie's legs thrown over my shoulders, the other around my waist, taking me so deep it makes the hairs on the back of my neck stand up. I fuck her slowly, lazily, wanting to stretch this moment out as long as possible.

Then, right as we're leaving, she kisses me and suddenly I need her again, just one more time, so I toss her over my shoulder and carry her to the bedroom while she squeals.

I toss her on the bed, pull her shorts down, bend her over. Two seconds later I'm pressing her vibrator to her clit, five seconds later she's moaning my name, and ten seconds later I'm balls-deep in her tight channel, vibrator still pressed to her clit as she arches her back, shouts my name, gasps *make me come* with her head thrown back.

I do. Twice. Then I come hard, pressing myself inside her like I'm trying to meld our bodies together.

When we're finished, we're both gasping for air. We're both still wearing all our clothes, and before I pull out, I lean forward, plant a kiss on the back of her neck.

We're only ten minutes late to my mom's house.

· · * * ★ ★ ★ * * · ·

THERE'S NO RUSTY, so there's more drinking than usual. Seth and Caleb get into some red wine and hassle Levi about calling June *ma'am* at Riverfest. Levi has slightly more bourbon than usual and asks Eli when he's going to make an honest woman of Violet. Eli has some gin and tonics and asks Caleb if an algorithm can predict when your brother should stay out of your damn business.

Charlie and I more or less stay out of it, though of

course we get dragged into the fray a few times. There's no avoiding it.

We eat dinner and dessert. We clean up. Five o'clock comes and goes, then five-thirty. At six o'clock a silver BMW finally pulls into the bottom of my mom's driveway, then inches its way up to the house.

Every single time she comes back, I'm relieved, weirdly giddy to see Rusty again. She's my daughter and I love her, but I also *like* her. She's a pretty cool kid, no matter how much she drives me crazy.

As soon as the car stops, the back door opens and Rusty bursts out, hopping from her booster seat and onto the gravel. I note that apparently Crystal doesn't have the child locks activated on her car, but then Rusty's running toward me and I pick her up and whirl her around before giving her a giant hug.

"Hi, Dad," she says, leaning her head against my shoulder.

"Hi, kiddo," I say, kissing the top of her head.

She squirms. I put her down and she's up the porch stairs like a shot, and as she opens the door I can hear her shout, "Charlie! My mom gave me a piranha—"

I can only pray it's not a real live piranha as Crystal finally heaves herself out of the car and comes toward me, carrying Rusty's duffel bag. She hands it to me like I'm the bellboy.

"Fun weekend?" I ask, determined to be civil.

"We took her to a water park," she says, and starts to walk toward the house, sort of rolling her eyes. "At least she had fun, I'm too pregnant to do shit. I can't believe I have two more months of this. Jesus, I have to move to Denver in this state."

I hoist the bag over my shoulder and stop right below the porch steps, turning toward her.

"You told Rusty she was moving to Colorado?" I say, quietly.

Crystal doesn't stop, but she's slow as hell.

"Sure, why not?" she asks.

"Because that's a long way from decided."

She gives me one of her *you must be the dumbest person on earth* looks.

"She'll be there some of the time," Crystal scoffs. "The court's not going to revoke my visitation rights. Hell, I think I've got a pretty good chance of getting custody back."

My entire body flashes cold, then hot.

"Baby!" she calls, opening the door. "Mommy's gotta go, come say goodbye."

Whirlwind footsteps come clomping through the house, and I see Rusty's arms wrap around Crystal's legs.

"Careful there," Crystal says. "Okay. Mommy loves you."

"Bye," Rusty says, suddenly serious.

"Bye, honey," Crystal says, patting Rusty's head. Then Rusty detaches and Crystal smiles at her, distantly, walks back through the door, comes down the steps.

"Crystal, we need to talk about this," I say. "We can't each be telling her different things, she's seven years old and she doesn't understand—"

"It's fine, she's smart," Crystal says, walking past me. "I have to go."

I follow her.

"It's not fine just because she's smart," I say, my voice lowering to a growl. "She's sensitive. She notices more than you think, and I don't want her to feel like this is because of anything she—"

"Seriously, it's fine," Crystal says, opening her car door and dropping herself in.

I'm at the end of my fucking rope with this woman.

"Don't just drive away," I threaten, even though I know I've got nothing to back it up with.

Crystal closes the door. The car starts. I'm itching to wrench the door open, turn the thing off, get in her face until she listens to me, but I can only imagine how that would go over in court.

"I fucking hate you so much," I whisper under my breath.

The window slides down, noiselessly, and for one thrilling moment I think she heard me. Good. I've been nice to her for *years*.

"I know you're not really getting married," she says. "Nice try."

Then she stomps on the gas pedal and gravel goes flying as she backs up, nearly hits a tree, executes a sloppy three-point turn, and drives back down the driveway.

I'm left standing there like an asshole, stomach churning, fury burning right through me.

CHAPTER TWENTY-FIVE

CHARLIE

"Piranhas are like sharks," Rusty is telling me. "They have infinity teeth, but they have to replace them a quarter-mouth at a time, so it's like if—"

She opens her mouth and points at the lower right half of her jaw.

"—ahh eez eef were missing but then they came back *even sharper.*"

"What do they do while their teeth are missing?" I ask. "Do they get dentures?"

Rusty giggles, still waving her new stuffed piranha around the living room. I think Crystal must have injected sugar straight into her veins or something, because this kid is hyped up beyond hyped.

"They just use the other side," she says. "A school of piranhas can eat a whole person in *one minute.*"

"Well, I'd imagine that depends on the size of the school and the size of the person," Seth says from a couch. "It might take them two minutes if it's a big person and a small school. There's probably some sort of linear regression—"

"AHHHHH CHOMP!" Rusty shouts, ramming the fish's mouth into Seth's leg.

"Nooooooo my knee!" he yells, flailing both arms.

"OM NOM NOM MUNCH MUNCH—"

"—Not my leg, my beautiful leg—"

"—CRUNCH CRUNCH CHOMP—"

"That's my foot, I need that to walk!"

"GULP. Ahhhhhh."

Seth's now slumped over sideways on the couch, moaning softly but dramatically as Rusty grins and giggles, two feet away.

"Best not to question piranhas," I tell Seth, laughing on the other couch.

"I regret everything," he says.

"He's still hungry," Rusty announces, waving the fish again.

"Your uncle Seth has another leg," I point out, just as the front door opens again and Daniel comes inside.

He looks *pissed*, his mouth a straight line, his cheeks flushed the faintest pink, the line of his body rigid and controlled, like he wants to slam the door but closes it gently instead.

"Dad!" Rusty yelps, then skips over to him. "This is Sparkles, he just ate Uncle Seth's leg."

She throws both arms around Daniel, stuffed fish flopping in one hand, her face turned against his middle, and I can see his body relax as he hugs her back.

"That wasn't very nice of him," Daniel points out.

"I'll get better," Seth calls from the couch.

"Well, he's just a fish and he was hungry," Rusty says.

"I still think that Sparkles should apologize," Daniel says, and shoots me a quick, meaningful glance.

My stomach tightens right away, because that was a *something has gone awry* glance.

"Piranhas have very primitive brains," Rusty says, detaching from her dad. He ruffles her hair with one hand, not letting go just yet.

"My leg," Seth moans, and Rusty sighs. Then she pulls away from Daniel and sticks her head over the back of the couch, looking down at Seth.

"Sparkles says he's sorry," she informs him.

"Tell Sparkles thank you," Seth says graciously.

* * * * ★ ★ ★ * * * * *

RUSTY TELLS us about her weekend for an hour, then re-tells us about her weekend when Levi and Caleb replace Seth, and then even after I head into the kitchen for some water and find myself discussing undiscovered Amazonian tribes with Eli for thirty minutes, I can hear her telling everyone about her weekend yet again.

Like I said, I think she may have had some sugar.

Finally, it's her bedtime. Daniel herds her around to everyone, and when it's my turn she throws her arms around me dramatically and squeezes for a long time. Then, just as quickly, she's moved on to Eli.

"Can you stay after I get her to bed?" Daniel asks quietly.

I raise one eyebrow, but he smiles and shakes his head.

"Sadly, no," he says. "I gotta tell you something."

Then Rusty's scampering upstairs, he's hustling after her, and Eli and I go back to debating whether or not there are still undiscovered indigenous tribes anywhere on earth. It's unclear who's on which side here, but I can tell it's defi-nitely a debate.

Though, then again, it might just be because that's how Eli interacts with the world. He debates it.

Forty-five minutes later, Daniel finally reappears. By

now I'm sitting in the living room with just Clara, Caleb, and Seth, all of whom are discussing who's going to win the current season of *The Bachelor*.

I'm just listening, having never seen an episode, and Daniel nods toward the kitchen, then disappears. When I come in, he's pouring himself a glass of whiskey from the sideboard where his mom keeps it, then holds up the bottle.

"Want some?" he asks.

I eye his glass, which is at least three fingers full. Daniel's not usually much of a drinker, despite owning a brewery, so I wonder what the hell Crystal said to him out there.

"I gotta drive home, but thanks," I say, and he just nods and corks the bottle, then takes a good long sip.

"I hate her," he murmurs, almost inaudible, swirling the brown liquid in the glass. "Charlie, I try so fucking hard not to, but I do. I hate her."

"What happened?" I ask, and he takes another drink.

"She says she knows that we're faking it," he says.

· · · ✦ ✦ ★ ★ ★ ✦ ✦ · · ·

"I DON'T UNDERSTAND what she wants," Daniel says, his eyes closed, his head in my lap as we rock gently. It's thirty minutes later, his whiskey glass is drained, and we're sitting on the porch swing.

Or, rather, I'm sitting and he's lying across me, legs splayed off the side as we swing gently through the warm night air. The porch light is off to keep the bugs away, and the only light is from a sliver of moon and the stars above.

"I mean, why try to get custody when she never actually wants to see Rusty?" he asks, rhetorically, his eyes closed. "She's cancelled so many visits, Charlie."

"I know," I say, stroking his hair back from his forehead.

"I think Rusty knows," he says. "I try not to make a big deal out of it when Crystal cancels, but there's no way to not tell her. She gets so disappointed, and I feel so fucking awful."

My left hand is on his chest, and he finds it in one of his, closes his fingers around mine.

"I don't even want full custody," he says. "I'd love to split it fifty-fifty. I don't want to keep her from her mom, I just want Crystal to want to be her mom and I don't think she ever will."

"I know," I say softly.

It's not the first time this has happened. Once or twice a year for the past five or so years, Daniel's gotten tipsy after Rusty comes back from a visit and told me all this: how much he hates Crystal, how he wishes she were different, how he's afraid that he's screwed his kid up for life.

"I almost married her," he says. "You want to know the craziest fucking thing, Charlie?"

My heart trips in my chest, takes a moment, beats again. I thought I knew everything, but I didn't know that, though it makes sense. Sprucevale is small, Southern, conservative; if you knock a girl up, you best marry her.

"You did?" I ask.

"Yeah, and I wondered for years if I should have," he says. "I swear I heard it a thousand fucking times, *do the right thing.*"

It hits me like lightning turning sand to glass; he says it and I harden, brittle, afraid that if I breathe, I'll break.

For years? How many years?

"Maybe it would have been," he goes on, his eyes still closed. "Maybe if I'd done the right thing like everyone said I should, Rusty would have a dog and a picket fence and a little sister and we'd be doing whatever the fuck happy married couples are supposed to do. I don't know. Bowl on a league or some shit."

I swallow. I make myself breathe, brush his hair back again.

"I couldn't make myself go through with it," he says. "I looked at rings exactly once and I had to leave the store to puke on the sidewalk outside because I couldn't stomach the thought of marrying someone I didn't love."

I had no idea. We weren't as close for a little while after he found out about Rusty — he suddenly had a child, I was working two jobs and trying to get my shit together — but he's never told me this before.

I look down at the ring on my finger, the light inside it moving with the rocking of the porch swing. I know he doesn't like Crystal. I know he's never liked Crystal, but I know he loves Rusty and I know his guilt over her is deep and real.

"Do you even like bowling?" I ask. It's the first thing that pops into my head that I can say out loud.

"No," he says. "I mean, I don't hate it, either. I guess I'm neutral on bowling."

"And picket fences?"

"Maybe if I'd married her she'd love Rusty," he says. "Maybe if we'd gotten together, at least lived in the same house, she'd have spent time with her and gotten to know her better, been there when she started walking and talking and reading, sent her off to her first day of school, come to her ballet recitals..."

I lean my head back, silent, try to control my breathing as tears prick my eyes.

I hate Crystal. I *hate* her. Not just what she's done to Rusty but for what she's done to Daniel, for making him twist himself into knots over not marrying her years ago. For making him think that her behavior is his fault. For letting him think that if he'd done something differently, they'd all a perfect, happy family right now.

And I hate her for making me glad that they're not. I hate her for the small, savage pleasure of knowing that instead of two kids and a loving wife and a dog and a picket fence, Daniel's drunk and holding my hand right now.

I hate her for making me glad that his happy ending hasn't happened yet because it means I get him.

"I'm glad I didn't, though," he says, after a moment. "Even if it meant she'd have come to ballet recitals. Because I'd be *fucking miserable* and I wouldn't be here right now."

I tap my thumb on his chest as he opens his eyes, deep and blue as the night sky. He taps one finger on the stone in my ring, absentmindedly, watching my face. After a moment he sits up on the swing and puts his arm around me, tilts his head back and I lean against his shoulder.

"And I'm really glad I'm here right now," he says softly.

CHAPTER TWENTY-SIX

DANIEL

"I would never kill a civilian in cold blood," Silas is saying, beer in hand, legs stretched in front of him. "But if I did, they'd never even find the body. That's a promise. Never."

There's a slight pause around the table, as the other three of us sip our beers and contemplate this statement.

"But how do you *really* feel about Brett?" Eli drawls.

"He does sound dedicated," Levi offers.

"Maybe he should come back with a herd of goats," I say.

"I don't *actually* believe in dowries, you assholes," Silas says. "And besides, wouldn't the goats go to our father? I wouldn't get the goats."

"You'd inherit them one day," says Eli.

"Eventually, the goats would be yours," adds Levi.

We're all quiet again for a moment, sitting on the lawn outside the brewery in four wooden Adirondack chairs around a low table. It's a gorgeous night out: warm, slightly humid, the stars all out. It's nine-thirty on a Tuesday night, so the brewery is pretty quiet. Rusty's asleep and my mom is home, so I'm here with my brothers. And Silas, who's sort of a fourth-and-a-half brother.

"I could use a flock of goats," Levi says, his feet up on the low table, his beer balanced on his armrest, held lightly in one hand. "The Forest Service has been looking into using them on hillsides as an alternative to mowing some portions of the Parkway. It's apparently possible to rent hungry goats by the hour."

"Or you could marry Brett," Silas says. "He's available. I know this because he *played a boombox at my sister's window.*"

"I don't think I'd trust Brett to choose his goats wisely," Levi says.

"I don't think I'd trust Brett to choose anything wisely," Eli says.

"Except women, you mean," Silas prompts.

Levi's face goes carefully neutral, and he takes another sip of his beer.

"Right," Eli agrees.

"Where did he get a boombox?" I ask, and everyone goes quiet again for a moment.

"That's actually a good question," Silas says. "I haven't seen a boombox in years. God, that's even more suspicious."

"What was he playing?" Eli asks.

"Guess."

"*I'll Be Watching You,*" Levi says.

"No, but congrats on finding the one song that would have *actually* been creepier," Silas says. It's hard to tell in the low light, but I think Levi blushes slightly.

"*I Will Always Love You,*" I guess.

"Come on, y'all," Silas says. "Really?"

"*In Your Eyes,*" Eli says, like it's obvious. "You haven't seen *Say Anything?*"

Levi and I just shake our heads, and Silas starts laughing.

"Brett didn't come up with the boombox thing," he says. "It's from a movie."

"That explains a lot, actually," Levi mutters.

"And then when you got there, he tried to propose to *you*?" Eli says. "That's not how the movie goes."

"Something like that," Silas says. "The asshole got down on one knee in my parents' driveway and requested my permission to marry my sister. Meanwhile, now that I'm there, June's come down and is loudly and firmly rejecting his offer of marriage, so I just told him that if I saw him anywhere near her again he'd learn the meaning of the word *no* right quick, because apparently when she said it several dozen times he didn't believe her."

"Was the ring at least nice?" asks Eli.

"Hell if I know," Silas says, taking another drink. "It was big. Probably cost a lot of his daddy's money."

He clears his throat.

"Speaking of rings, how's your *engagement* with Charlie going?" Silas asks, raising one eyebrow at the word engagement.

"It's going well," I say, levelly, and narrow my eyes at Levi.

"How does that work?" Silas asks. "Are you two gonna stage a screaming match on Main Street in a few months so you can break up, or just tell people it wasn't working?"

I'm still glaring at Levi. My oldest brother is usually excellent at keeping secrets.

Usually.

"You told *Silas*?" I ask.

"Hey," Silas says.

Levi sighs.

"I couldn't keep your web of lies straight," he says.

"It's not a web," I tell him, even thought my stomach twists slightly. "There's the one lie, Levi. It's not hard."

He crosses one ankle over a knee, then sticks one thumb out like he's about to list something off.

"First, you've got your whole *we're completely platonic best friends* situation going on for several years now," Levi starts. "Which, frankly, I'd have been a fool to believe. Next," he says, sticking out a forefinger, "You've got your *we're engaged for custody reasons but not really* situation, which involves a fair amount of public canoodling—"

"Canoodling?" Eli and Silas say in unison.

Levi ignores them.

"—which you seem more than happy to do, and thirdly," he says, sticking out another finger, "there's the matter of where you were all last weekend while Rusty was with Crystal."

There's a brief silence.

"He was at Charlie's, right?" Silas quietly asks Levi.

"Right," Eli and Levi both confirm, and I shut my eyes briefly in consternation. I don't bother asking how they know, because Sprucevale is tiny and everyone is nosy.

Just last year, Eli thought it was a huge secret that he was spending most of his nights at Violet's house for a full month.

It wasn't. Not even close.

"We're supposedly *engaged*," I say. "If we were really engaged, isn't that where I'd—"

"Oh, for fuck's sake, none of us is stupid," Eli says. "Jesus, Daniel, we're all glad that you finally got with Charlie. It was about damn time."

"So you really *are* engaged," Silas asks.

"No," I say.

"You're sticking it to her, but you're not engaged," he says.

"Right," I say, for simplicity's sake.

"And most everyone thinks you're really engaged for real, though some people think that you're still just friends and faking the engagement, and some other people—" he spins his finger around in the air, indicating the four of us in the circle, "know the truth, which is that you're getting freaky on the regular but aren't actually going to get married."

"Right," I say again.

"I got bad news, brother," Silas says. "That is a one hundred percent, grade A, bonafide web of lies right there."

"You want to hear the rest?" I ask, draining my beer, in the mood to share my problems.

Eli and Levi both lean forward.

"Hell yeah," Silas says.

"Crystal knows it's fake," I say.

Silas lets out a whistle.

"I think Rusty must have told her," I say, leaning back in the chair, my head against cool wood, and close my eyes.

I've called Crystal a dozen times since she pulled out of my driveway on Sunday. I've left her at least four polite voicemails, requesting that we discuss this matter like adults.

It's gotten me nowhere. I don't know what she knows or what she thinks she knows. I don't know if she somehow pulled the semi-truth out of her ass and is bluffing with it.

"You told Rusty?" Silas asks.

"Rusty wouldn't tell," Levi says, frowning.

"Rusty's good at keeping secrets," Eli confirms.

"You bring her wedding cake almost every weekend and think I don't know about it," I tell Eli, my eyes still closed.

The circle goes silent.

"How?" Eli asks, sounding genuinely baffled. I open my eyes, raise my head, and look at him.

"Because she's *seven*," I tell him. "Seven-year-olds aren't very good at keeping secrets."

"Yet you told her that you and Charlie were faking," Eli says.

"What was my other option?" I ask. "Letting her think that Charlie was gonna be her stepmom? She'd have been over the moon, and then devastated a few months later when we told her it was off."

"True," Eli admits.

There's another quiet moment. For the record, I don't blame Rusty for spilling the beans. Like I said, she's seven.

"When you think about it, an engagement is quite an ephemeral concept," Levi says slowly. "What makes two people engaged? Someone asks, someone accepts, there's a ring. Or there's no ring. Or two people discuss the matter and mutually decide that they'll marry."

Eli looks over at me.

"He's got a point," he says. "There isn't even an exchange of goats."

"Truth be told, you and Charlie are just as engaged as anyone," Levi goes on. "You asked. She accepted. There's a ring."

"Technically, I asked if she'd fake it," I point out.

"There's no proof of that," Eli says. "Crystal can say whatever she wants, but unless she's got some sort of proof, it's nonsense."

"Well, apparently everyone in town knows it's not real," I say, pointedly, to Levi.

"One person," he says, huffily. "I told one person."

"I know how to keep my mouth shut," Silas says.

"She's going to look like a lunatic in court with Charlie standing right there," Levi says.

"Just canoodle in front of the judge," Eli says, and Levi sighs.

"The burden of proof is going to be on her in this case," Silas says. "You make a crazy accusation like that, you best back it up."

"Family court is nothing but crazy accusations," I say. "Half the time I'm pretty sure it comes down to what mood the judge is in that day. There's hardly ever proof of anything, and I can keep track of what happened when to my heart's delight, but all Crystal has to say is *that's not what happened* and then our lawyers are going at it for twenty minutes."

"Tell the court her belly's fake," Eli offers.

"That's extremely provable."

"They've got some really good fake pregnancy bellies these days," Eli says. "There's even one that's got machinery inside that fakes the baby's movement—"

"Why the *fuck* do you know this?" Silas interrupts.

"I couldn't sleep, so I was watching one of those true crime shows," Eli says. "There was an episode about a crazy woman who faked a pregnancy and then stole her best friend's baby. It was nuts."

"Shit," Silas says.

"I don't think I can convince the court of that," I say. "No. Wait. I'm *certain* I can't convince the court of that."

"Daniel," Levi says, sitting forward, his elbows on his knees, his fingers laced together. "You and Charlie had most of the folks you know completely convinced for several years that you were secret lovers when you, apparently, were not. Show up, be yourselves, and your engagement will be the single most credible thing to ever occur in that courtroom."

I thump my thumb on the wooden armrest of the chair I'm sitting in, thinking.

Crystal's usually full of shit, and I'm tempted to think that this is more of the same. I want to think that the judge will dismiss her accusation out of hand, due to lack of evidence and also the fact that she's a psychotic hosebeast.

But I don't know. I don't know if she's got evidence. I don't know what evidence she could possibly have — the texts we've sent each other? Recordings of private conversations between Charlie and me? Signed testimony from someone who knows the truth?

Meanwhile, all I've got is a girlfriend who's wearing a ring.

Girlfriend.

The thought is weird as fuck, but I like it.

"He's right," Silas says, standing. "I gotta piss. Anyone want another beer?"

CHAPTER TWENTY-SEVEN

DANIEL

Then, suddenly, weeks go by. Charlie and I fall into a rhythm: I go to her apartment Mondays and Thursdays. Sometimes she comes over for dinner. Sometimes one of my brothers or my mom babysits, and we go on a date.

And the weirdest part is that it isn't weird at all. It doesn't even feel different, it just feels... *more*. It feels like this is the way things always were, or at least this is the way things always should have been.

Best of all, we don't hear a single peep from Crystal.

· · * ★ ★ ★ ★ ★ * · ·

"That one's pretty intense, especially with a pack," Caleb is saying.

He and Charlie are on the floor of the living room, the coffee table pushed out of the way, maps spread across the floor.

"It is?" she asks, leaning in for a closer look.

"Yeah, that part up to the Twins is all crazy switchbacks

across a rock face," Caleb says. "Hold on, I've got the USGS topo here somewhere."

He turns to one of the filing crates he brought with him. They're both indexed and sorted by color, each folder clearly labeled.

Say what you want about the Loveless Boys — and plenty of people have — but we can keep our shit in order.

"Here," Caleb says, handing her a green folder.

They both bend over the folder. I'm on one of the couches, reading, half-listening to them plan our backpacking trip for later this summer. When they first started this, the plan was for three days and two nights, but Caleb keeps suggesting longer and longer treks into the wilderness, and Charlie keeps agreeing.

At this rate, I'm going to be gone for a week. When I get back, Rusty will be half-feral and my mom, who's agreed to look after her during the trip, will be completely out of bourbon.

"There," Caleb says, pointing at a spot on the map.

Charlie head moves slightly toward him. They're both sitting cross-legged, both wearing jeans and t-shirts with no shoes. They've even both got top knots, though Charlie's is all wild curls and Caleb's is wavy and messy.

"Does that really say two thousand feet elevation gain in a mile?" Charlie asks.

"Yeah," Caleb drawls. "Plus, when I did this hike two years ago with a buddy of mine there was nowhere flat enough to sleep for a good six miles, so by the time we found somewhere we could even lie down it was dark and we were hiking by flashlight. I don't really recommend it, even though the views are amazing."

"All right, we're not doing the Twins," Charlie says, pushing the map to one side and reaching for another one. "What else?"

Caleb sighs, takes the map, and puts it neatly back in the folder, and I smile to myself because I know exactly how he feels right now.

"If you don't mind starting the trip with a long day, we could head to the Crystal Grotto," he says, just as the front door opens and Eli steps through carrying two big canvas bags, one of which has a froth of greenery sticking out the top.

"Hiking?" he says, looking down at the people and maps spread across the floor.

"Caleb's taking us backpacking for secret reasons," Charlie says.

"The same secret reason I owe you meatballs?" Eli says, hoisting one of the bags over his shoulder. "Do I even owe you those, now that you're actually f—"

I clear my throat and glare at my older brother.

"— *dating?*" he asks, throwing me a look.

"A deal's a deal," Levi's voice says from beyond the still-open door.

"There's always negotiation," Eli says.

Boots cross the wooden front porch, and then the door pushes open further, revealing Levi, wearing work pants and a t-shirt, standing there with a bundle of long sticks over one shoulder, a cast-iron dutch oven hanging from his other hand.

"Just make the meatballs," Levi says.

"That's easy for you to say, you didn't get a task."

"Seems I've got the task of listening to you bellyache about—"

"Out!" my mom calls from the doorway to the kitchen. Five heads turn as she comes into the room. "Levi Beauford, you know better than to bring a mess of kindling into my house," she goes on. "Take it around the side."

"It's not kindling, it's a spit roast," he says.

"Around. The. Side," she repeats, then looks at Eli. "You too."

"It's groceries," he protests. "The ducks need to go in the fridge."

"Ducks?" I ask as Levi sighs and turns back through the door.

"Have feathers, go *quack*," Caleb supplies.

"Thank you," I deadpan, and Charlie snorts.

"Please tell me they're already butchered," Mom says.

"They're already butchered," Eli says dutifully.

"All right, you can stay, I guess," she says, and steps back out of the room.

"You're spit roasting ducks?" Charlie asks.

"Wait, that's today?" I add.

"You two have gotta pay attention," Eli drawls, a slow smile coming onto his face. "Yes, today is Rusty's *Little House on the Prairie* feast extravaganza. Levi's been crafting the roasting mechanism for days."

"Where *is* Rusty?" Caleb suddenly asks, stretching his legs in front of himself and leaning back on his hands.

We all look around. It's been quiet for at least half an hour.

Too quiet.

"I think she's in her room," I say, suddenly suspicious. "I'll go tell her you guys are here."

I heave myself off the couch and head for the stairs. I know she's probably just reading a book in her room, but one of the very first things I learned as a parent was that noise is suspicious, but quiet is *extremely* suspicious.

"Hey, munchkin," I call out. "Your uncles are he——"

I stop short when I reach the top step. There's something on the floor between Rusty's room and the bathroom, four or five drops of dark liquid.

It takes me a second to realize what it is, and then my stomach leaps into my throat.

"Rusty!" I shout. I reach her bedroom door in one step, slam it open. It's empty and in the second it takes me to scan the room, I also see her desk chair pushed back, a sharp stick on her desk next to a bright red smear, the drops of blood on the floor closer together here.

I'm at the bathroom door in another second. Locked.

"RUSTY!" I shout, rattling the knob, shoving at it. I slam my hand against the door, full-blown panic blossoming through my chest even as I tell myself that it's not that much blood, just a few drops, she's not in there bleeding to death.

Nothing happens. She doesn't unlock the door and it doesn't magically unlock itself. I try the knob again, as hard as I can, hoping that maybe the old mechanism will break and when it doesn't, I slam my shoulder into the door. It's old, solid wood, as old as the house and it shudders but doesn't break.

"Hit it again," Caleb's voice says behind me. Pain spikes through my shoulder as I do and the door shudders, gives slightly, and then when I slam it one more time with my shoulder the frame splinters and the door comes open and I half-fall into the bathroom.

"Rusty," I gasp.

She's there, sitting on the toilet with the lid down, legs dangling, a mass of toilet paper pressed between her hands, bloody strands of it littering the floor.

Not covered in blood, not lying broken on the floor. There are no head wounds or severed limbs, no sliced arteries.

"I'm sorry!" she says, looking at me wide-eyed, her face already tear-stained.

I'm already on my knees in front of her, her hands in

mine even as I'm still checking her over: head fine, body fine, legs fine, one hand hurt.

"It's okay," I say. "Shh, sweetheart, it's okay, what happened?"

She sniffles, another sob breaking through as she holds out her left hand.

"It slipped," she whispers as I peel back the wadded mass of toilet paper, the last few layers soaked through with blood, until I can see the wound.

She flinches as I unstick the paper, more blood welling up from a two-inch gash in her palm, right through the meat below her thumb.

"Ow," she whispers.

"I bet that hurt," I say, trying to commiserate while my heart is still beating wildly, every nerve in my body still rattling even as I hold her hand, trying to assess the wound.

"It was an accident," she says, her voice still small, hurt.

"I know, honey," I murmur.

Sniffle. More blood wells up as I try to examine her blood-stained hand as well as I can. I don't think it's deep enough to need stitches, but it's hard to tell. Every time I touch her hand, she jerks it away slightly, fresh tears rolling down her cheeks.

I'm rattled. My heart is still pounding. I'm still sweating, still half-imagining the worst things that could happen, even though they haven't, and I take a deep breath and try to concentrate.

"Here," says Charlie's voice, and I realize that she's kneeling next to me on the bathroom floor, a first aid kit open next to her. "Can I see?"

"I don't think she needs stitches, but I can't tell," I say as Rusty holds out her hand to Charlie. I rub my knuckles across my forehead, trying to tamp down the quake making its way through my core.

She's fine, I tell myself. *She's fine. It's a cut.*
What the hell happened?

"Okay, Rusty, I need you to hold your breath for a few seconds because this is gonna hurt," Charlie is saying. She's got a pad of gauze pressed to the wound, holding Rusty's small hand in both of hers, totally calm and patient and in control. "Ready?"

Rusty nods and sucks in a breath, eyes still wide.

"Here we go," Charlie says, and pulls the gauze off. Gently, she touches Rusty's palm, pulling the edges of the wound apart. Rusty's turning pink, her feet kicking against the toilet.

"All right," Charlie says, completely unfazed. "Good news, kiddo, I don't think you need stitches."

Rusty exhales in a rush, then sniffles.

"Okay," she says.

"We'll bandage you up and have you out of here in no time," Charlie says. "Can you be brave again for a little while?"

"I think so," Rusty says.

Charlie coaxes Rusty to the sink, has her hold her breath again while she rinses out the cut and I slump on the bathroom floor, back against the bathtub. Rusty whimpers and I close my own eyes for a moment, listen to Charlie soothe her slowly, calmly.

She's always been good at emergencies. It's the strangest thing, because in the rest of her life she can be scattered, a space cadet, but the moment something goes wrong she's completely on top of it. Once we saw a car accident while we were getting coffee during Rusty's ballet class, and I swear Charlie was the first person out there, calming down the drivers and ordering me to call 911 and telling the other onlookers to direct traffic, all before anyone else had managed to stand up.

When they're done at the sink Rusty comes over to me, sits in my lap while Charlie bandages her up: gauze, medical tape, a big bandage to hold everything in place. By the time they're finished Rusty's smiling again, even though she's got the hiccups from crying.

"Plus, you'll have a cool scar," Charlie is saying. "You can tell everyone that you got into a knife fight and won."

"Don't encourage her," I murmur.

"What's a knife fight?" Rusty asks.

"It's a fight with knives," I tell her, resting my chin on her head. "They're very bad."

"Oh," Rusty says. "It wasn't a fight, just an accident."

Charlie finishes wrapped the bandage, presses it against itself.

"What happened?" she asks Rusty.

Instantly, Rusty goes silent, her little body suddenly tense in my lap.

"I wanted to help Levi make roasting sticks," she says quietly. "And my knife slipped."

Her knife?

"What knife?" I ask, just as Charlie's head snaps up and she looks at Rusty.

"The knife I borrowed," Rusty whispers. Now she's squirming in my lap, arching her back, trying to get up.

"Borrowed from where?" I ask.

Charlie's eyes meet mine, wide and hazel, guilt written all over her face. I swallow hard, fighting the rising tide of anger, because I'm pretty sure I know exactly who gave my second grader a goddamn knife.

"Charlie's workshop," Rusty finally admits. Charlie's gone pale beneath her freckles and her gaze drops from mine.

I take a deep breath, jaw clenching, and wonder what the *fuck* Charlie was thinking.

"I said you *couldn't* take that knife," Charlie admonishes her, gently, glancing at me again. "Did you take it anyway?"

"I just borrowed it," Rusty says. "I was going to give it back. I'm sorry."

"I didn't want you to take it because I didn't want you to get hurt," Charlie says, her voice sharper now. "Rusty, if you take something without permission that's stealing."

Rusty's breathing picks up and moments later a sob breaks through. She rubs her eyes with the backs of her hands, flopping sideways against my chest like she's trying to burrow in.

"I'm sorry, Charlie," she says. "I didn't mean to."

Charlie opens her mouth, looks at me, and shuts it again. I hold Rusty, sniffling and sobbing, against my chest and shake my head at Charlie.

I've got questions for her, starting with *why the fuck did she have a knife in the first place* and ending with *how easy was it for her to take it?* But I don't ask them right now, not while Rusty's having a breakdown on the bathroom floor.

"Just go," I tell Charlie, my voice tight, clipped.

"I'll clean up," she says, touches Rusty's shoulder one more time, and then she's gone.

I close my eyes, hold my kid, let her cry, and wonder if any of the parenting books I own cover this situation.

CHAPTER TWENTY-EIGHT

CHARLIE

Turns out there's nothing to clean up, because Clara, Eli, Levi, and Caleb did it already: the floor is spotless, the desk is no longer blood-smeared, and Levi is holding a thumb-width stick with one end barely sharpened in one hand and my penknife in the other.

"This yours?" he asks, holding it out on his palm, blade closed.

It's the one I let her borrow when she wanted to carve a wombat, when I gave her a hunk of soft pine and taught her to be very careful, cutting away from her fingers. The stick looks like it's oak, much harder. No wonder it slipped and she cut herself.

I feel awful, like there's a hand around my windpipe. Rusty's in there, sobbing to Daniel, and it's my fault. What the hell was I thinking, letting her use a knife and not watching where it went?

"Thanks," I say, and put it into my pocket, where it weighs heavy as guilt.

"She okay?" Levi asks.

I swallow, my throat tight. I just want to find a corner

where I can hide and cry away my guilt, but instead I'm faced with Daniel's family after letting Rusty slice herself open.

"We should make sure we keep an eye on her hand, but she should be fine," I say, not meeting anyone's eye. "Keep it clean, see that it doesn't get infected, but it should heal okay."

"I think she might be more upset than really hurt," Clara adds, sympathetically. "If she's anything like her dad, she's mad that she's not invincible. Come on."

She heads back downstairs. Caleb puts a hand on my shoulder and rubs it sympathetically, and I nod in thanks.

"I'll be down in a sec," I tell them. "I'm just gonna... you know." *Cry, probably.*

They leave, footsteps fading down the stairs, the hubbub from the kitchen rising again as I turn toward Rusty's room, put my face in my hands, and take a deep, deep breath.

Holy fuck, I feel awful. Rusty's hurt and now Daniel's pissed at me, all because I wasn't paying attention, because I totally forgot that she had that knife and didn't think to double-check—

The floor creaks behind me, and I whirl. Eli's standing there, alone, arms folded over his chest.

"Is he being a dick about it?" he asks gently.

I bite my lips together and shake my head, afraid that if I try to say anything I'll start crying.

"You sure?" he asks. "Daniel can be a real unforgiving, uptight asshole sometimes."

"It's fine," I whisper.

Eli sighs, and then he's in front of me, wrapping his arms around my shoulders, pulling me in for a brotherly hug.

"It's not your fault," he says. "Trust me, I know how he can be."

"Thanks," I mutter into his shirt. Eli pats my back a few times, then releases me, one hand on my shoulder. He's only a year older than Daniel. The two of them have always been close, so by the transitive property, I know Eli pretty well, too.

"Besides, that kid's in for way worse than a few cuts and bruises," he says. "Daniel seems to have conveniently forgotten all the hell he used to raise. Were you around when he ran into a sharp tree branch and it almost went clean through his shoulder?"

"Oh, my God," I mutter. "Yeah."

"He never would tell us how that happened," Eli says, casually.

It happened when we were eleven and had discovered that if you spray hairspray into an open flame, you can make a mini flamethrower. We were chasing each other around the woods, like idiots, and Daniel turned around to unleash a gout of flame in my direction.

When he turned back around, still running full speed, there was a pointy tree branch exactly at shoulder level.

"No?" I say, just as casually, and Eli laughs.

Even as I was practically dragging a bleeding Daniel back to his house, he made me swear not to tell anyone what we'd been doing, terrified of how angry his parents would be. I've kept the secret for eighteen years and I don't plan on telling anyone now.

"Well, I tried," he says, then reaches out and ruffles my hair like I'm his kid sister. "Sorry he's a dick. See you in a few."

With that, Eli leaves Rusty's room, and I'm alone, the bathroom door across the hall still shut. Behind it I can hear Daniel and Rusty's voices, one high and one low.

I give myself another thirty seconds, and then I follow his family downstairs.

* * * * * ★ ★ ★ * * * *

"YOU GAVE HER A KNIFE?"

I take two seconds before I answer him, finish mincing the stalk of celery I'm working on.

"No, she took it," I say, sweeping the small chunks to one side of the cutting board. "She asked if she could take it home, I said no, and apparently she just took it anyway."

"She said you let her carve a wombat," he says, standing in the middle of the kitchen, arms folded over his chest. I brush celery bits from the knife onto the cutting board, not looking at him.

"She was looking at the little wooden animals in my shop and wanted to make one," I say.

"So you *did* give her a knife."

"I didn't *give her a knife*, I let her use one temporarily while being supervised," I snap. "I was five feet away the whole time."

"Charlie, she's seven," he says, pushing a hand through his hair, voice rising. "You can't just hand a seven-year-old—"

"Jesus, Daniel, I didn't just hand her a machete and tell her to bushwhack a path into town," I say. "I showed her how to use a pen knife and then I let her carve something while I kept an eye on her from a couple feet away."

"Apparently it wasn't a very close eye if she managed to take it!" he says.

"She stole it!" I hiss, trying to keep my voice down, because I don't want this argument getting more public than it already is.

"You left it where she could take it!" he says, hush-shouting. "First you gave a second grader a knife—"

"— I didn't *give her a knife*, for fuck's sake, I just told you—"

"And then you just let her take it because you probably forgot she even had it," he says. "I guess I should be glad she didn't burn it down. I don't know why I ever let her go into your workshop, the last time I was there you had a hacksaw just sitting out on a chair—"

I put the kitchen knife down. It clatters on the cutting board.

"She didn't slice herself open on my watch," I point out, gripping the edge of the counter with both hands, glaring at the cabinets in front of my face, trying to maintain control and not lash out at Daniel. "Yes, sure, I handed her a knife and she sat quietly for an hour and made some progress on a pretty okay looking wombat, because contrary to what you apparently think, I'm perfectly capable of monitoring a situation."

"Until she took it."

Finally, I turn around and glare at him.

"Well, look at who her father is," I say.

Daniel doesn't say anything, but his jaw flexes, his short beard shifting, and even though I know the silence means he's *really* pissed I keep going because goddammit, this is not my fault.

"She asked if she could have it, I said no, and then she took it anyway," I say. "Remind you of anyone?"

"The fuck is that supposed to mean?" he asks, his voice dangerously quiet.

"It means how many times did you get dragged down to the Sheriff's station for stealing lighters and malt liquor from the Gas 'N' Go?" I hiss. "The only reason you don't have a juvie record is that every deputy in the county knew who your daddy was—"

"The shit I did has *nothing* to do with this," he finally says, stepping closer.

I fold my arms, glaring upward.

"Only that the apple apparently doesn't fall far from the tree."

"How the fuck is this about me?" he shout-whispers. "You can't keep track of the knife because I swear to God you'd lose your head if it wasn't screwed on and somehow—"

The sliding glass door to the porch slides open, and Levi steps through, then stops. He nods once, a plate full of foil-wrapped potatoes in his hands, then proceeds across the kitchen to put it down on the counter in complete silence, Daniel and I still standing about two feet apart.

"Eli said to tell you five more minutes," he says, not making eye contact, then heads back out.

"Thanks," I say to his retreating form.

"She sliced herself open with it!" he says. "An inch lower and she'd have gotten herself across the wrist, for fuck's sake, and it wouldn't have mattered if she'd stolen it or not!"

The sliding glass door opens again, and now it's Seth, who looks from Daniel to me and back again, one eyebrow raised.

"Sorry to interrupt, but can I steal you for a minute?" he asks.

"Yeah," Daniel says, giving me a hard look. "It's fine, we're done here."

He shoots me a look, then stomps off to join his brother.

I wait until his back is turned, then flip him off with both hands.

CHAPTER TWENTY-NINE

CHARLIE

I stay for dinner. I don't even know why. If I were smart I'd invent some excuse about needing to water my cactus and just leave, but I don't really want Daniel's whole family to know we got into a fight, so I stay.

As if the ensuing weird awkwardness doesn't make it *crystal fucking clear* that we got into a fight. His brothers are all way, way nicer to me than usual. After dinner I'm clearing some glasses off the back porch, and Seth sticks his head out, then follows me and takes the stack of glasses from my hand.

"He'll calm down," he says. "You know how he is."

"*I'm* not going to calm down," I huff. "I'm never calming down."

Seth gives me his slightly off-kilter grin. When he was a kid he got hit in the face by a large stick — all three of his older brothers deny being the culprit, but everyone knows it was one of them — so there's a tiny scar on his upper left lip that's just enough to make his smile the smallest bit crooked.

It's very, very charming. Everything about Seth is very charming.

"See if you feel that way tomorrow," he says, then shifts his stance, looks at me, a stack of glasses in both hands. "He's just being overprotective," Seth goes on. "You know how people are, they get up to all sorts of shit, then they have a kid and realize that the kid might get up to the same shit they did."

"That doesn't make it my fault," I grumble.

"He's never been good at staying pissed," Seth says. "I predict he'll start seeing reason by about eleven tomorrow morning, so by the time Rusty has her *ballet lesson* he'll conveniently be full-on sorry."

"Goddammit," I mutter. Does everyone in this town know what Daniel does during Rusty's ballet lessons?

"Sorry," Seth says, laughing, and turns to take the glasses back into the house.

"You're not," I call after him.

He opens the back door and gives me that stupid charming grin again.

"Nope," he says and disappears.

· · * * * ★ ★ ★ * * * · ·

AT FIVE FORTY-FIVE the next day, there's a knock on my door, the way there's been a knock on my door every Monday for the past couple weeks.

Briefly, I consider not answering it, because I'm still slightly annoyed that Daniel apparently thinks I'm irresponsible and untrustworthy.

But then he knocks again so I shut the fridge and go answer it. Because of course, Seth was right, and I didn't stay full-on mad forever.

"Hey," Daniel says when I open the door.

The man really is irritatingly hot, even now, when I'm still slightly mad at him. I take a moment and give him a once over, because I think I deserve a little eye candy right now.

"We can't have make-up sex until we make up," I say, leaning against the doorjamb.

His eyes light up in a teasing smile.

"I thought the sex *was* the making up," he says.

"Well, that's why you were single until you made me pretend to marry you," I say, but I'm laughing.

"Damn, Char, right for the jugular," he says.

"Sorry."

"Cleo's has two-for-one happy hour beers," he says, nodding his head toward my staircase. "Want to get a drink?"

· · ★ ★ ★ ★ ★ · · ·

"THIS BETTER NOT BE THAT Loveless shit," I tease as Daniel puts a beer in front of me. "I get that for free."

"It's that horrible peach IPA from River Run you love," he says, sitting across from me. "The one that tastes like licking a jolly rancher's butthole."

"At least call it tossing a Jolly Rancher's salad," I say, taking a sip.

"It tastes like heading to Downtown Jolly Ranch on the brown line," he says, and I nearly spit my beer out.

"You made it grosser," I say. "How the fuck did you make that grosser?"

He just shrugs and takes a sip of his own beer, looking pleased with himself. There's a long moment of silence.

"I'm sorry for being a dick," he finally says. "But I do wish you'd keep dangerous stuff away from her a little better, at least until she has some impulse control."

I bite my lip as my annoyance flares, take a deep breath, and tell myself not to restart the argument.

Particularly because he's being totally reasonable, and I know it.

"I'm sorry for not keeping better tabs on her," I say. "But it's also not my fault she stole something."

"I know," Daniel says. "We talked about that last night after you left. Also, she's grounded for a week. Missing Jody Richter's birthday sleepover this weekend."

I gasp, involuntarily, and Daniel pauses, his beer halfway to his mouth.

"Is that the unicorn themed party?" I ask.

"Yup."

"She's been looking forward to that for weeks!"

"Then maybe she'll remember not to steal things," Daniel says, calmly.

And *now* I feel bad that Rusty doesn't get to go to this cool sleepover. Kids are a total mindfuck.

"I'm also sorry I brought up how you were a total shithead when you were a kid," I say, looking down into my beer.

"You're not wrong," he says, shrugging. "I was pissed when you said it, but…"

"You really were an asshole," I say, finishing his sentence for him.

"The first time that Pat Sherman took me down to the station and gave me hell for taking a Snickers and a forty it scared the shit out of me," Daniel admits. "But then he just let me go because he felt bad about Dad, and I realized that nothing was ever gonna happen."

"Monster," I say.

"It's the worst part of being a parent," he says, sighing. "Being afraid they're going to turn out exactly like you."

"Don't worry, she's already smarter than you were," I say, grinning, and Daniel laughs.

"God, I hope so," he says, then takes another sip of his beer, watching me over the glass. "Do I have anything else to apologize for?"

I take a long look at him, trying to corral my thoughts into some sort of order, because I still feel bad on some deep-down level, still feel like I'm lacking somehow, like I'm forever the girl who forgets lit candles, forever the girl who leaves saws sitting on chairs and would forget her own head if it wasn't attached.

I wish I wasn't that girl. I wish I wasn't irresponsible, impulsive, flighty. I wish I had a daily planner that predicted my life exactly and I wish I had to-do lists with every item neatly checked off, but instead sometimes I lose my keys and find them in the fridge.

But none of that's an apology. None of it's in the scope of this conversation, a whole list of *ways I want to be different but can't be*, so I take a long drink of beer and say something else.

"You keep getting beard hairs on my sink," I say.

Daniel just narrows his eyes at me.

"And you rearranged my spice drawer," I go on.

"I put them in order," he protests.

"They *were* in order," I say. "It took me ten minutes to find garlic powder the other day. I had a system, Daniel."

He makes a face that clearly indicates what he thought of my system, but then he catches himself.

"I'm sorry about the beard hairs," he says. "And I'm sorry for organizing your kitchen."

"You mean de-organizing."

He makes a perfectly neutral face.

"De-organizing," he says, and then looks down and quickly checks his phone.

"You just looked to see if we've got time," I say, and he looks up at me, half amused and half guilty.

"I have to go get Rusty in twenty minutes," he says. "I have perfectly legit reasons for knowing the time."

"Nah, you checked to see if we have time for make-up sex," I tease.

Daniel just raises one eyebrow, then takes the last sip of his beer, puts the glass down, leans in.

"Cleo's has a bathroom," he says, his deep blue eyes practically sparkling.

I lean in too.

"No," I say, fighting a smile.

"Come on."

"They will *never* let us come back here," I say, and he just shrugs.

I'm tempted. He's definitely kidding, but I also think that if I said yes, he'd take me up on it.

"I'd live," he teases. "Come on, there's a bible study group in the back. Let's scandalize them."

We don't. Instead, ten minutes later he leaves to go get Rusty, and I head back home.

CHAPTER THIRTY

DANIEL

I knock again, then wait.

And wait. I lean back against the railing of her balcony. Her porch light is on, even though it's still bright outside. She probably forgot to turn it off this morning.

I raise my fist and knock again, a third time, as loud as I can, just for the hell of it. There's nothing inside. No footsteps, no sounds of her frantically throwing books into piles, shouting *sorry I was in the shower, I'm coming*, just dead silence.

Something in my chest squeezes unpleasantly, and I've got the distinct feeling that I don't get to see Charlie today. I know where her spare key is, but before I go get it, I call her.

It rings three, four times.

Maybe she's in the shower and lost track of time.

Maybe she's running late, coming home from work, maybe she ran an errand and got stuck somewhere....

Maybe even though I thought we made up, she's still pissed, and this is how she's telling me, by just letting me knock and knock and not answering the door.

Not Charlie's style. At least, I don't think so, but we've never gotten into a fight like that before. Not as a couple.

"Hey, what's up?" she asks.

"I'm at your place," I say.

I don't say, *It's Thursday, I haven't seen you alone in nearly a week and I'm crawling up the goddamn walls.*

"My place?" Charlie echoes.

I'm still staring at her door, the bad feeling in my chest expanding.

"Rusty's got piano right now?" I say. "Like she does every Thursday?"

"Today's Wednesday," Charlie says.

There's a pause. I say nothing, because it's not Wednesday, it's Thursday.

"Shit," she says, and then voice gets distant, probably because she's checking her phone to see if I'm right. "I could have sworn…"

I quietly resign myself to jerking off in the shower tonight. Again.

"I'm sorry," she says. "Shit. Fuck. I'm at the workshop, I'm finishing that table I told you about that had all the superheroes glued on and I totally just…"

"It's okay," I tell her, even as the disappointment coalesces in my chest, forms a ball of something viscous and unpleasant.

"I really thought today was Wednesday," she says.

Of course she did. My irritation, my impatience both flare at Charlie. Of course she has no idea what day today is, because today's the day I was too busy at work to text her about tonight. Of course she forgets something if I'm not constantly reminding her about it.

That's not the worst part.

The worst part is the small, nagging voice in the back

of my head saying *she wasn't excited enough to remember? You didn't think about anything else all day.*

"I'm so sorry," she says again, and now she sounds awful and I feel bad. "We were super busy at work all day, and I just... I don't know, sometimes I get the day wrong. I'm sorry."

"It's fine," I say, and already I'm wishing I hadn't made Rusty cancel her sleepover this weekend. When I grounded her, I didn't give a single thought to how it would affect *my* plans.

Parenting blows sometimes.

"Tomorrow," she says. "Which is *Friday*. I'll take you out."

"Rusty doesn't—"

"You just chill, I'll take care of everything," she says.

I pause, still staring at her front door, hoping that her idea of *taking care of everything* isn't leaving Rusty home alone, watching cartoons.

Of course it's not. Charlie's not stupid, she's just a space cadet, and even though right now I'm annoyed and tired and holy hell am I *frustrated*, I know that.

"Tomorrow meaning Friday," I say, just to double-check.

"Right," she says. "Friday. The day after today, which is Thursday. I'll pick you up at... I dunno, six?"

"If you're not there I'm calling the cops," I tease, and Charlie snorts.

"Accidentally leaving you horny isn't a crime," she says, laughing.

"It should be."

"Thank God it's not," she says. "Can you imagine the fuckboys at the police station, mad about some girl they got coffee with?"

"All right, I see your point," I concede, finally heading down her back stairs. "Six."

"Six," she says.

· · * * * ★ ★ ★ * * · ·

A FEW HOURS LATER, Charlie texts me.

Charlie: Is Rusty in bed?
Me: Yeah, why?

I'm in the kitchen, spreading peanut butter onto sandwich bread, packing Rusty's lunch for tomorrow

I've just dolloped strawberry jam on when the next text comes through.

I drop the knife, because it's a picture.

Of Charlie. Nearly naked, wearing nothing but panties in her bathroom mirror, one hand in her hair and one on her phone. Her nipples are stiff pink peaks. She's smiling, laughing, and I can practically feel the curve of her waist in my hands, hear the sound she makes as I pull her in, squeezing, wrapping her legs around me.

I go from thinking I should put peanut butter on the grocery list to hard as fuck in less than a second. In my kitchen. With my daughter's *Critters of the Outback* lunchbox in front of me.

Charlie: I really am sorry about today.

I shoot a glance toward the living room, where my mom is reading her book, then quietly put my phone in my pocket and go upstairs, to my own bedroom. The second I lock the door I've already got my dick out, my hand wrapped around the base.

I snap a picture and send it to Charlie.

Me: I forgive you.
Charlie: Good ;)

I pull up her picture again, conjure up a scene from last week: us standing in her bathroom, right where the picture was taken, her braced against the counter. I watched her face in the mirror as she came so hard her eyes rolled, and that's what I'm thinking about ninety seconds later when I come without ever taking off my pants.

Then I clean up, start some laundry, and google *how to hide naked pictures on your phone*, because I don't want anyone finding this, but like hell am I deleting it.

· · ⋆ ★ ⋆ ★ ★ ⋆ ★ ⋆ · ·

"We're going *where*?" I ask, pulling my milkshake straw out of my mouth.

"The skinny-dipping hole," Charlie says, like I know what she's talking about.

It's Friday night. When I got home from work, my mom informed me that she was taking care of Rusty, and my job was to go make myself presentable because Charlie would be there at six.

Miraculously, she was on time. Well, five minutes late, but for Charlie, that counts.

"There's a skinny-dipping hole?" I ask.

"Yeah, it's down past where Washtub Road crosses Pony Creek, right before you get to the mountain," she says. "There's a dirt road right after that, and if it's rained recently there's a couple of streams you have to ford but it's a great spot. The field hockey team used to go there all the time."

She's saying all this like I know what she's talking about, and I don't. I absolutely don't, and I thought I knew every secret nook and holler in Sprucevale.

"Field hockey? You mean in high school?" I ask, still trying to catch up.

"Was I on another field hockey team?"

"Did you go skinny-dipping?"

"Of course, it's the skinny-dipping hole. That's what we did after we won games, we'd get Becca's older sister to buy us some box wine and we'd come down here," she says, like it's common knowledge.

It is not. If I'd known that the whole field hockey team was routinely getting naked and drunk together, I'd probably have masturbated to different fantasies in high school.

"You're telling me that *while we were in high school* a bunch of girls were getting drunk and naked together," I say, just to make sure I'm crystal clear on what I was missing.

"I only ever went with the field hockey team," she says. "But I thought everyone knew about it."

"Definitely not," I say, still staring at her. "Are you kidding? If I'd known that it would have changed everything about my entire high school experience. I'd have skipped school to live at the skinny-dipping hole if I'd known that a team of girls was getting naked together there on the regular."

"Honey didn't put out?" she laughs, naming my on-again-off-again-on-again high school girlfriend. We'd get together for a few weeks, break up over something stupid, she'd hang all over some guy to make me jealous, I'd steal her a rose from the grocery store, we'd get back together. Repeat ad nauseam.

"If you want to know about my sex life in high school, you can just ask," I tease.

"Oh, I know that she once asked Paula Peterson if you could get pregnant from swallowing semen," Charlie says. "I drew my own conclusions from that."

I grimace at the window as we go around a curve in the road, because even though this is all long-gone history, I don't love talking about other women with Charlie. Especially because we were already best friends at the time — half my breakups with Honey were over the fact that I refused to stop being friends with Charlie — even though Charlie was dating Steve Fisher, who was on the football team and drove a very large truck.

It just feels wrong, like I'm comparing her to them. There's no comparison. She's the sun and any other girl disappears in her daylight.

We cross a wooden bridge, and two hundred feet later, Charlie slows and turns onto a rough unpaved road that's clearly not been maintained since at least 1990. Branches scrape my window, and I slurp my milkshake again, ignoring the gnawing suspicion that we're not supposed to be here.

Sure enough, in another few hundred feet there's a NO TRESPASSING sign. I point to it with my straw as we bounce by.

"It's fine," Charlie says. "They don't care."

"They cared enough to put up a sign," I say.

"Yeah, but that's all," she says. "Trust me, it's fine. I've been here a million times."

I steal a sideways glance and wonder what sixteen-year-old Daniel would have done with this new information.

Finally, just as the sun is going down and everything is turning blue, she pulls into a clearing, the creek on one side. We're at the base of the mountains, right where the ground rises from the valley back into the heights, so it's a rocky creek, dotted with boulders, the water white upstream where it rushes over fallen trees and slabs of granite disgorged from further up.

It's beautiful. It's also illegal, a fact that I wouldn't have cared about ten years ago but that bothers me now. At least my mom's got Rusty if I spend the night in jail, right?

Charlie stops the car, kills the engine and lights, turns to me. Her eyes are dancing, dark in the twilight, and she leans toward me, one hand on my leg.

"Come on," she says. "Live a little. You deserve to get wild sometimes."

"I'm not wild enough for you?" I tease, sliding my hand over hers.

"You're not wild enough for *you*," she says, her eyes sparkling. "You need to get naked in the wilderness and say a whole bunch of curse words sometimes."

She kisses me, and the heat of it floods my body. I'm insatiable when it comes to her, all the more because all of our encounters are over too soon, hemmed in by the demands of having a seven-year-old and the reality of living with my mom.

I don't mention that around these parts, people don't call the police on trespassers, they come out carrying a shotgun. I don't mention that if we get caught, we could spend the night in jail, get ticketed, worse.

It's been a long, long time since I did something not perfectly above-board. Too long, and she's too tempting, wild, impulsive.

She breaks the kiss, winks at me, and then she's throwing open her car door and I'm doing the same a step behind her as she pulls off her shirt, her bra, tosses them onto a rock. She loses her shorts and panties, her body pale and breathtaking in the fading light as she looks over her shoulder at me, laughing.

"Come on," she calls. I'm still standing by the car,

watching her undress because I'd hate to miss a second of it. "The water's great!"

Then she puts one foot in and gasps, jerking it back out, and I laugh, tugging my shirt over my head.

"Great, huh?" I say, stepping out of my shoes, my pants.

"I think I forgot how cold it is," she says, carefully sliding her foot back in. "Holy shit, did I really do this all the time?"

I stand next to her, naked, pretending that I'm not half-erect from the simple act of watching her disrobe, and dip a toe in as well.

It's cold, but it could be colder.

"Don't tell me you're gonna wimp out," I say.

"I'm not wimping," she says, making a face as she puts her other foot in, now ankle-deep. "Just... letting myself adjust."

"You gotta do it all at once," I tell her. "It's the only way. We'll be here until Monday otherwise."

"*You* do it all at once and leave me be," she says.

I'm still on the bank, just watching her. After a moment she turns her head, looks up at me.

I can't help grinning.

"Daniel, *no*," she says, her eyes going wide. "Don't you dare."

"I thought you wanted to be wild," I say. "I thought we were ignoring trespassing signs and being impulsive like a couple of badasses."

She holds out one hand, pointer finger up, and takes a step backward, even though she's trying not to laugh.

"No," she says, like she can ward me off. "Daniel, don't, it's fucking freezing, my tits are going to fall off—"

I lunge, grab, lift and Charlie yelps. The water's cold

but I ignore just *how* cold as I wade in, the pebbles on the bottom smooth under my feet.

"No," she gasps, upside down over my shoulder. "Nooooooooooooooooo!"

"Quit kicking, do you want me to drop you?" I tease, wading deeper.

She kicks one final time, and I grab a handful of ass to steady her, and also because I can. Below my feet, the bottom drops, and suddenly I'm a foot and a half lower, the water up to my waist. We're ten feet from the shore, and over my shoulder, Charlie just sighs.

"Ready?" I ask. "One…"

"Goddammit," she sighs.

"Two…"

"Can you at least put me down slowly?"

"Three!" I say, and toss her in, yelping.

Half a second later she comes back up, water dripping from her hair.

"HOLY FUCKING SHIT THAT'S COLD," she gasps, and splashes me. "God*damnit*, Daniel."

"You're welcome," I tell her.

"I," she says, sending a wave of water my way, soaking me, "Did not," she does it again, "Say," *splash*, "Thank you!"

She goes to do it again but this time I catch her wrist before she can get me. We've both got water dripping from everywhere, breathing hard, laughing. The water's deep here, just above her nipples, which are rock-hard and bobbing right below the surface.

"You haven't even been in," she says, her eyes sparkling with mischief. "If you're gonna toss me in, you have to at least go under yourself."

"Says who?"

"What, it's not too cold to throw me in, but it's too cold

to go in yourself?" she teases. "Don't make me sling you over my shoulder and toss you in."

Charlie's strong, but I've got at least eight inches and sixty pounds on her.

"I would *love* to see that," I say, sincerely as I can.

"You're such a dick sometimes," she laughs.

Then she puts both hands on my chest and shoves. Even though the rocks underneath my feet are a little slippery, I don't budge.

"Seriously?" I deadpan. "Is this your plan?"

Charlie makes a face and shoves harder.

"You're kidding, right?"

"Shut up," she says, still shoving.

"I don't think it's working," I say, as she lifts one of my arms, putting her shoulder to my sternum and shoving again. "You know, maybe if you asked nicely—"

Suddenly my knee goes out and I fall backward, my body plunging into the deep water before I can even take a breath, the cold enveloping me instantly.

I come up a second later, gasping for air, shaking the water out of my eyes and hair, breathless.

"Cheater," I say, the cold shaking the air from my lungs. "Shit, that's really cold."

Charlie laughs triumphantly, coming into the deeper water, just her shoulders in the air, bobbing near me.

"Told you," she says, and kicks her legs up, floating, her body pale ripples under the clear water, knees and breasts surfacing and sinking, hair floating around her head like a dark halo.

I float, too. I forget about everything that's not this moment in time: a landowner with a shotgun, if Rusty's in bed yet, the hearing that's scheduled for next week, my hurt that Charlie thought yesterday was Wednesday.

"See?" she says, her voice dreamy now. "Not bad, right?"

"Did I say it would be bad?"

"You weren't thrilled when you saw the No Trespassing sign," she teases.

I push off, float, look up at the trees above us.

"Well, I've tried to reform from my younger days," I say dryly. "You just keep dragging me down. I was a law-abiding citizen until I fell for your charms."

"Daniel Loveless, you lied to a damn judge without a single bit of help from me," Charlie says lazily, arms spread out on top of the water. She kicks. Her nipples crest, sink.

"That was an act of desperation," I say.

"That was an act of dumbness."

"Either way, I like the consequences," I tell her.

She's quiet a moment, floating, thinking.

"Was it an accident?" she finally asks.

I'm still floating, looking up at the trees, and I find the bottom and stand and look at her.

"How?"

"Did you just say my name because we'd been texting? If you'd been texting someone else, would you have said her name?" Charlie asks.

She's half treading water, half balanced on the bottom, arms waving just below the surface, her deep, serious eyes locked onto mine.

I don't have an answer. I've honestly never thought about what would have happened if I'd said someone else's name. I don't know whose name I would have said, because it's not like there are other women I think about.

"I said your name because you were on my mind," I say slowly, truthfully. "You're on my mind a lot, Charlie. You always have been."

She looks away, ripples moving under the surface.

"Sorry," she says.

"Don't be," I say, moving toward her, slowly. "But I promise you're always the very first person I text with tattoos of beloved children's characters performing sex acts."

That gets a smile, a laugh.

"I'm flattered," she teases.

"Except the time someone had a tattoo of the Giving Tree mooning Calvin from Calvin and Hobbes," I say, thoughtfully. "That time I texted Levi. But he never texted back. Probably because he still has a damn flip phone. I don't even know if he can get pictures."

"Does he seriously?" Charlie breathes.

"Yes," I mutter. "He claims he doesn't want to be beholden to modern technology or the tyranny of the screen."

"Nerd," Charlie says under her breath. "I should get drinks with June, now that she's back in town. Maybe I should tell her that her brother's best friend has a thing for her."

"Don't do that to poor Levi," I say, still staring up at the stars beyond the tree cover.

"What, give him a head start?"

"He's gotta muddle through it himself," I say. "The man is stubborn as anything, and if he finds out you tried to make something easier for him, he'll never speak to her again out of sheer pigheadedness."

Charlie just sighs.

"You're all ridiculous," she says.

"Just the others," I tell her, and she laughs. "I'm the reasonable one."

She splashes, and then her toe pokes my ribcage.

"Hey," I say, grabbing her foot.

"Is that why you chastise anyone who says *damn*?" she

teases. "Is that why you gave Eli shit for looking at his phone at the dinner table last week?"

I straighten up, pull her toward me through the water.

"I'm not hearing anything unreasonable yet," I say.

"Is *reasonableness* the reason you practically tripped over your own feet making sure I wouldn't go backpacking with Caleb without you?" she teases, wringing water from her hair as I slide an arm around her waist, her flesh warm against mine in the cold water.

"I like camping," I say.

Besides, backpacking tents are tiny. It's not that I don't trust either Charlie or Caleb — I do, completely — but that doesn't mean I have to love the idea of them sleeping six inches from each other.

"Sure," she says, laughing. "For the record, I wasn't going to go without you."

She puts one hand below the water and flicks droplets up at me, her other arm around my neck, her nipples barely peeking above the surface, pink and pebbled and hard as rocks.

They're not the only thing.

"Hey," I say, making a face, and she does it again. "Quit it," I say.

"Make me," she says, and it's barely out of her mouth before I've grabbed her wrist, my fingers encircling her bones, her upturned face luminous and beautiful and still laughing.

"What now?" I ask, letting my voice go low. I draw her in, my erection bumping against her stomach, and she just barely raises one eyebrow.

"Well," she says, looking up at me through wet eyelashes, a devious look on her face. "I seem to be wet, naked, trapped, and at your mercy."

"So I should dry you off, put your clothes on, and let you go?" I tease, lowering my face.

"Shut up," she says, and I find her mouth with mine. Her skin is cold, but her lips are warm as she opens them beneath mine, deepening the kiss instantly.

I swear I can feel every day, every hour since the last time we were together like this in the ache that shoots through my body. Moments like this, the rest of my life falls away and there's nothing but her.

Charlie breaks the kiss. She's breathing hard, the flat of my hand against her lower back, her hips underwater and moving against my erection, throbbing despite the cold.

"You brought me here because you wanted to fuck outside," I murmur into her hair, and Charlie laughs into my neck, her arms around me.

"The possibility occurred to me," she says.

"Did it?" I tease, reaching one, thumbing one of her bright pink nipples. It's stiff as cardboard, and I pinch harder than usual, wait to hear her gasp. She does. "*Did* it occur to you that getting naked and wet and giving me your fuck-me face might—"

She grabs my cock, and my words cut off with a groan.

"It's been a week and I'm horny as fuck," she whispers, stroking me hard. "My vibrator's practically begging me for a break."

I kiss her again, push her backward, the water now around our thighs.

"You never send me those pictures," I say into her mouth, rolling her nipple between my fingers.

"I'm shy," she says.

"Too shy to tell me what you think about when you're wearing out the batteries in your vibrator?" I ask. "Make a wish, Charlie, maybe it'll come true."

Now she's got both her hands in my hair, the water to our ankles. Charlie slips and grabs onto my shoulder, glancing behind herself at the rocks along the bottom. I take her hand, still steady on my feet, guide her back to the big flat rocks along the bank, stop her when she reaches it, her back to me.

"Well, this afternoon I was thinking about the time you came over and we took one of my dining room table chairs into my bedroom, where I've got the full-length mirror," she says.

I pull her tight against me, bury my face in her neck. She gasps, but I've already got my hand between her legs where she's still warm, fingers sliding through slippery folds until I've found her clit.

"And you rode me while we both watched?" I say, my cock jumping against her back, a tremor moving through Charlie's body.

"I like seeing us together," she says, her cold hands sliding around my neck, her back arching. Fuck, I'd love to have a mirror right now, so I could see her body as she's like this, stretched out against me while I pleasure her, her ribcage rising and falling with quickened breath.

"I like watching your eyelids flutter and knowing it's because of me," I say, massaging her harder, her clit sliding between two slippery fingers, a noise escaping her throat. "I like finding everything that makes you gasp and moan and whisper my name that way you do."

I lower my head, kiss the back of her neck, and Charlie sucks in a breath. Found that one last week, and I take her hair in my other hand, tilt her head to one side, follow her neck with my lips to her collarbone, my hand still between her legs, working her slowly, steadily while she moans, sighs, standing on her toes to get us closer together.

I bring her close, to the brink, before stilling my fingers. She holds her breath and lets it out, shuddering, arching back against me like she's trying to coax two more strokes, but I don't let her finish because sometimes I like to tease her, sometimes I like to turn her breathless, wild, incoherent.

She makes me breathless and wild all the time. It's only fair.

Charlie turns, pulls my face down to her with her strong hands and I move my hands over her hips, grab her, bring her body against mine, still wet so we slide against each other.

"Tease," she says, and grabs my cock, biting my lower lip at the same time.

"You bring me out here to get naked and I'm the tease?" I ask. I push her backward, toward the rock, until the backs of her thighs hit it. She strokes me again, hard, her thumb sliding over the tip and I kiss her as a reflex even as heat slices through me, my hips driving toward her soft warmth.

Holy God, I want her. I push her back again until she's on the rock and I'm over her, still standing with my feet in the creek, holding myself up on one elbow. She's still stroking me and without knowing what I'm doing I'm rubbing her again, her clit under my thumb, two fingers sinking into her heat.

There's something around my hips: her legs. I crook my fingers inside her and her eyes go shut, her thighs tighten, the tip of my cock against the soft velvet skin of her inner thigh, still slippery with water.

"Daniel," she murmurs, her grip on me still tight. Her channel flutters around my fingers, squeezes, and I pull them away, surge forward to kiss her.

When we break the kiss I can barely breathe. I'm holding myself up, over her, one elbow on the rock and the other on her thigh, hitched around my hips.

"Condom?" I whisper, even as I irresistibly buck my hips forward, my cock seeking her heat like a magnet seeking north.

"In the car," she whispers back. Her freckles all stand out in the dark, constellations across her face, the negative of the sky above, her eyes bright and her lips plush and I want her, I want her, I want her like it's the only thing I've ever felt.

Charlie guides me to her, the tip of my cock suddenly at her entrance, and my eyes slide shut despite myself.

"Wait," I say, leaning my forehead against hers, even though there's nothing I want to do less.

"It's okay," she says, her lips on mine, the words muddled. "Just pull out."

"We should—"

"Please?" she asks, and that's all it takes.

I know better and I've been careful for years but all it takes is that one breathy, murmured *please* and I throw caution to the wind and sink into Charlie's tight heat with a single thrust.

I go deep, deep enough to hit the spot that makes her fingers dig into my back, makes her legs tighten around me as she groans, her eyes closed, her head turned to one side.

"Like this?" I whisper in her ear, bending over, pulling her legs tight around me to get deeper. "You want me bare, like this?"

"You feel so fucking good," she whispers, her eyes opening to half-mast.

The hairs on the back of my neck are standing and there are goosebumps down my spine with the sheer pleasure of Charlie, skin to skin like this, nothing between us. It's dangerous and perfect all at once, all-consuming, unstoppable.

I try to go slow, to savor this. I want to etch every detail in my memory: how beautiful she is right now, eyelids fluttering and hair half-wild, my name on her lips. I want to make this last, the pure bliss of being inside her with nothing between us, the knowledge that I might never get closer to heaven than right now.

But I can't, not now, not when we're fucking outside, not when she begged me to fuck her with no condom, not when she's dragging her nails down my back and whispering *harder please God Daniel, please*. Now I fuck her hard and deep and I growl *you like that don't you* into her ear and she just gasps *yes* and it makes me want her harder, deeper, faster.

She brings out some primal, base instinct in me. Charlie turns me into a feral animal with no control, no power to stop my impulses. Right now, I'm nothing but a working cock slamming into her over and over again, feeling her twitch and shudder, feeling her body as it collides with mine and she draws me in, always wanting more, taking anything I can give.

I love this about her. I love that it's always been the two of us, through everything, and now it's the two of us here as close as two people can get. I love that she's never backed down from me and I've never backed down from her.

I lean over her, elbow over her head, the thumb of my other hand on her clit because I can't last much longer and her channel contracts around me when I do. I have to take a deep breath, clench my teeth, keep control.

I *have* to keep control.

"Come," I tell her, my voice low, guttural, pure growl.

Her breath hitches and her eyes meet mine, unsteady, unfocused.

"Don't stop," she murmurs.

"I can't last much longer like this," I tell her, my voice

bottoming out. "And I can't come inside you, so if you want to come with my cock in you like I know you like to—"

Her fingers curl against my back and I clench both fists, forcing myself to hold back just a little longer. I rub her clit harder and hit the spot she likes with every stroke and she flutters, squeezes, her back arching.

"Oh fuck, Daniel," she whispers, and I put my forehead to hers, every muscle in my body taut. "Oh *fuck*, I'm gonna come, Daniel, don't stop—"

She comes. She comes so hard it nearly knocks the wind from my lungs and my vision edges black as I bury my face in her hair, her fingernails cutting ribbons down my back. There's one second where I'm afraid I've lost control, too, that this was too reckless and too stupid, that of course there was no way I could resist her like this.

I come half a second after I pull out, spilling myself all over her thigh and hip in spurt after spurt. I'm still coming as she sits up and kisses me and puts her hand over mine, stroking me until it's done and I'm gasping for breath, holding her close, kissing her, tangled.

"That was close," I say, still standing between her thighs, my feet still in the cold water. I'm getting my own semen on me, but it's not like I care.

"That was good," Charlie says.

"It was," I say, her face in my hands. I kiss her, and I don't think about the next thing I say in this moment, I just say it.

"I love you," I tell Charlie.

"I love you back," she says instantly, and I kiss her, and the water's cold on my feet and the night air is cool against my now-overheated skin and Charlie kisses me slowly and I feel like I'll never want anything else, ever again.

We break the kiss. She looks up at me, hazel eyes wide,

face pale and freckles dark in the moonlight, and her lips part like she's about to speak.

Whoop!

We both freeze, and it's been so long that it takes me a moment to realize what the sound is.

But then I see the blue lights blinking through the trees, and I remember.

CHAPTER THIRTY-ONE

CHARLIE

A blue light strobes through the trees across the creek, behind Daniel's head, and for a second I just freeze. I shut my eyes, then open them, thinking that maybe if I do nothing they'll just pass by or go away and I won't have fucked up royally yet again.

Instead, there's the slow crunching sound of tires on a crappy dirt road.

"Shit," I hiss, jumping off the rock, pushing Daniel backward. "Shit, shit, I'm sorry."

"At least it's not an old man with a shotgun," he says, but his voice is tight, clipped.

"They never actually shoot," I say, still pushing him backward, into the water. "They just shout some and then let you go."

He grimaces as he goes deeper, behind a stand of rocks, but he doesn't say anything.

"Sometimes they shoot," he says, watching the shore behind me as he goes still.

I turn my head. We're both waist-deep in the water now, the lights getting closer, my stomach in ten thousand knots. Daniel's tense, his jaw clenched, and I know exactly what's going through his mind.

He's wondering how an arrest would look at a custody hearing. He's wondering if skinny dipping with me would land him on the sex offender registry. He's wondering whether everyone in Sprucevale will know about this by tomorrow morning, whether *Crystal* will know about it, how she'll use it against him.

I hate her. I really do.

The crunching stops. I'm holding my breath, the lights still playing on the trees above us. There are a couple big rocks between us and the police cruiser, but I've got a pretty good suspicion that they've stopped behind my car and, at the very, very least, they're issuing me a ticket.

Please just give me a ticket, I think. *Just give me a really expensive, obnoxious ticket and then drive away, I can't let Daniel get caught trespassing naked—*

A car door opens. The lights are still going, the glow of the headlights reflected off the trees, making it harder to see here in the shadows. The door closes with the heavy *click* of a serious car, and I realize I've got my hands in prayer formation, the knuckles of my thumbs against my forehead.

"Just go," I'm whispering. "Just fucking leave."

A powerful flashlight beam plays across the creek, lighting up the rocks and fallen trees opposite of us.

Please. Leave.

"All right," a man's voice calls out. "I know someone's over there and by the looks of it you're not wearing a lick of clothing, so just come on out with your hands raised."

Daniel and I look at each other. My heart's hammering wildly, so loud I can hear it over the rush of the creek.

"If you're thinking that I'll just turn around and leave if you don't come out, you have got another think coming," he calls. "You're trespassing on private property, and if you make me put my waders on and come into that creek, I can assure you I'll be in a much less good mood than I am right now."

"Charlie," Daniel murmurs, and I shake my head.

"He's bluffing," I murmur back. "He'll just give my car a ticket, do some more shouting and then decide we've left—"

"Old Man Williams is talking about pressing charges, you know," the officer calls. "And right now, I'm inclined to talk him out of it, but make me look any harder and I might not be."

Oh *fuck*. Daniel exhales, his jaw clenched, but before he can step forward, I put a hand on his chest.

"Stay there," I murmur, and before he can do or say anything, I cross my arms over my boobs and step out from behind the rock.

Instantly, there's a bright light in my eyes and I can't see a goddamn thing.

"Just one of you?" the voice says. He sounds *very* skeptical.

"Just me," I say, still squinting. I want to shade my eyes, but I don't want to move my hands.

"Is that so?" he asks. Footsteps come closer, then stop.

"Yes, it's so," I say, annoyed despite myself at the light. "I just… I was really hot today, so I wanted to take a quick swim. Alone. By myself. Officer."

I tack that last bit onto the end in the hope that it sounds respectful enough to work.

"There seem to be two pairs of pants on this here rock," he points out.

I say nothing. He sighs.

"Miss, if you can't tell me the truth, I'm still going to have to—"

There's a splash off to my left, and Daniel steps from behind the rock. We're still both waist-deep in the water, so when the light hits him, he shields his face instinctively.

"Daniel," the officer says, and now that the light's not on me, I squint through the dark, trying to see him. I can make out that he's stout, middle-aged, but that's all.

Daniel clears his throat.

"Hello, Officer Sherman," he says.

"I thought you'd cleaned up your act, son," Officer Sherman says. "I haven't seen you in years."

Daniel doesn't say anything.

"It's my fault," I say, still hugging my boobs. "This was my idea, I talked him into coming here."

"And you're the fiancée, correct?" he says. "Congratulations, by the way."

"Thank you," Daniel says.

"Right," I say. "Charlotte McManus."

Finally, he turns his flashlight off, though the police cruiser's headlights are still on, bright in the dark night.

"McManus," he says, both hands now on his hips, his feet shoulder width apart, still in a fighting stance. "Do you know an Elizabeth McManus?"

"She's my sister," I say.

"She's coordinated with the department for career day at the middle school the last few years," he says. "Very nice woman. Responsible. Responds promptly to all my emails."

"Yeah, she's good at that," I say, still cold and hugging my boobs, wondering how long we're going to have to talk about how great my sister is.

"All right, you two," he finally says. "Since there seems to be no actual harm here, I'm going to turn my car around and wait for you to appear at the mouth of this road. If you're not there in five minutes, then we proceed according to the letter of the law. Otherwise, I came down here and couldn't find a damn thing. Got it?"

"Yes, sir," Daniel responds promptly, and I echo him.

Officer Sherman nods briskly, then turns. He starts to walk away, stops, looks back at us.

"Thomas was a good man and a good officer," he says, suddenly. "I don't believe I ever gave you my condolences after he passed."

Daniel's stone-still, momentarily struck dumb. Then he swallows, his hands rubbing each other mindlessly.

"Thank you," he calls, and Officer Sherman walks off. He gets back in his car, slams around a three-point turn in the small clearing, and then bumps back up the road, leaving us in the moonlight.

We waste no time getting dressed, getting back into my car, and driving off.

CHAPTER THIRTY-TWO

DANIEL

"You gonna walk me to my door?" I ask as Charlie makes her way up the long driveway.

"Does that make me a gentleman?" she says, laughing.

"I hope not," I say, leaning one elbow on the windowsill of her car, the windows rolled down to the night air.

After the swimming hole, we went out and got a drink at Strangeways, one of a few bars in town, and then we talked until they kicked us out at midnight. I told her how much I always hated it with the cops in town called me *son*, especially after my dad died.

I don't bring up the close call with Officer Sherman. I don't bring up what an arrest or prosecution could have meant for me; I don't bring up that if I'd gotten really unlucky, I could have landed on the sex offender registry.

I know she didn't think any of that through before taking me there. She wanted to do it, and she did. There's a beauty in the simplicity of it, a beauty that I envy when I feel like every decision in my life is a complex flow chart.

She parks, we get out and walk to my house, bumping into each other's sides as we walk, glancing up at the stars.

In front of the door she turns, and we kiss, ignoring the bugs buzzing around the porch light over our heads.

"You want to come inside?" I ask, my hand on her back, even though my mom is home and nothing can happen.

"Isn't that supposed to be my line?" she teases, eyes sparking.

There's a slight rush of blood downward at the mere words, and I ignore it, looking away.

"I'm kidding," she says, one hand on my chest.

"I know," I say, leaning my head down, my forehead against hers. "That was reckless of us."

We were half a second from having to find an open pharmacy that carried the morning after pill, I think. We're in the rural Virginia boondocks. I have no idea how far we'd have to drive. Hours, maybe.

"It was good, though," she says softly, and I bite my lips together, so I don't agree with her aloud.

"We should be more careful," I say, pushing my fingers through her wild curls, some of them still slightly damp. "Of all people, I should know better."

Charlie sighs, takes my hand in hers, kisses the back.

"I'm sorry," she says. "I'll be more responsible."

It's not really what I want. I want her wild, impulsive; I want her skinny dipping and fucking me bare on the rocks, and I want to come inside her and hold her close and never let go.

But I don't want another kid, at least, not yet, and I know full well that Charlie's not on birth control. She'd never remember to take it every day.

"I love you," I tell her.

"I love you too," she whispers, and we kiss, and then I go inside and Charlie drives away and I wish, for at least the thousandth time, that instead she were staying with me, that I could fall asleep next to her, wake up next to her, that when Rusty jumped on my bed in excitement for breakfast cereal and cartoons, that Charlie could be there, too.

I fall asleep wishing for her, wondering how soon is too soon.

· · · ★ ★ ★ ★ ★ · · ·

"IT NEEDS BLUEBERRIES FOR EYES," Rusty says critically, standing on a step stool by the stove. "And a nose. And you weren't supposed to give it a tail."

"I'll cut the tail off," I tell her, carefully plonking two blueberries onto her pancake, approximately where a wombat's eyes should be.

Suddenly Rusty hesitates, then looks up at me.

"It's okay, Dad," she says. "I'll eat it anyway. It's fine."

I flip the pancake over on the griddle, the bottom perfectly golden brown. I'm no Eli, but I'm pretty good at blueberry pancakes these days, even if my art direction could probably use some help.

"How was your date with Charlie?" she asks, still watching the pancake, suddenly sounding seventeen and not seven. She's been doing that sometimes lately. I'm not sure how I feel about it.

Well, sweetheart, we barebacked on some rocks because I thought with my dick instead of my brain and then we nearly got arrested, and I had a great time anyway, I think.

I do not say that out loud.

"It went well," I tell her. "She says hi. How was your game night with Grandma?"

"I won," Rusty says, matter-of-factly. "I don't think Grandma's very good at games."

My phone buzzes on the counter, and I glance at it as I

flip the wombat off the griddle and onto a waiting plate, then hand it to Rusty.

"It's Uncle Seth," she says, leaning over to look at it.

"Yo," I answer.

"We have a code fucking red goddamn disaster," he says, more than a note of panic in his voice. "Someone didn't put the release valve on the wort tank that's brewing the double and it exploded last night, and now there's fucking sticky half-beer everywhere—"

"It *exploded*?" I ask, frozen in place, a wombat pancake in one hand.

"Yes!" he says, sounding exasperated.

"They're not supposed to explode—"

"No shit."

Rusty walks over, takes her plate from me, and starts eating quietly at the table. She can definitely tell something's wrong.

"It's a whole batch, Daniel, we already had the orders in for the kegs and now we're gonna have to delay those, not to mention that every goddamn thing in this place is sticky right now plus the floor is still covered in beer," he says.

Fuck. *Fuck.* The double IPA is one of our biggest sellers and missing a batch of it hurts.

Not to mention that I have no idea what else went wrong when it exploded. Was it infected with bad yeast? Is everything in the brewery infected? Is it all just waiting to explode because someone didn't sanitize the equipment properly?

Fuck.

"I'll be down," I tell him, and hang up before he can start ranting in my ear again, because when Seth gets worked up, he can *really* get worked up.

"What happened?" Rusty asks, still chewing, and I sigh.

We were going to go to the park, take a short hike, maybe follow it up with a swim. Definitely ice cream downtown, just the two of us, since lately I've felt like I haven't spent enough one-on-one time with my kid.

"There's a problem at the brewery, I've gotta go in," I say. "Do you mind eating the rest of that in the car?"

CHAPTER THIRTY-THREE

CHARLIE

"I need a huge favor," he says. It sounds like he's in the car, on speakerphone, his voice slightly distant.

"Bigger than faking an engagement?" I ask, instinctually glancing down at my finger, even though the ring's not there right now. It's in the NO BUTTS ABOUT IT mug on my dresser, because I'm afraid that if I sleep in it, I'll break it.

"Well, smaller than that," he says. "Are you busy today? Can you take Rusty? Something exploded at the brewery and I've got to go make sure we can still sell beer to people next month."

I'm still leaning against my kitchen counter, drinking my second cup of coffee, but the word *exploded* sure wakes me up.

"What exploded?" I ask, alarmed.

"Beer," he says. "I don't know what happened yet, Seth called in high dudgeon and said that there was something wrong with the release valve, but I'm worried that it's infected…"

He goes on about the problem, clearly stressed. I'd been

planning on using today to finish up the antique table so it's ready to go back to the mansion next week, then maybe hit up a few junk shops along the rural roads and see if they had anything worth fixing up and selling.

Sounds like my plans have changed. I'll have to finish the table tomorrow, hopefully.

"Yeah, no problem," I say. "Want me to come pick her up?"

"Meet me at the brewery," he says.

· · * * ★ ★ ★ * * · ·

IT's obvious that something's wrong the second I open the side door, since there's a big SORRY, CLOSED TODAY sign across the front: it smells like beer.

I mean, it always smells like beer — it's a brewery — but this is a warm, wet, punch-you-in-the-face beer smell. I think I can taste it in my mouth.

Also, the floor is sticky. There are still a few puddles here and there, and as I look for Daniel, there are several people diligently mopping.

The beer smell doesn't fade like smells usually do. When I find Daniel a few minutes later, it's as beer-y as ever, and he's standing in front of one of the giant metal tanks, surrounded by puddles, talking to one of his workers and gesturing madly.

"Hold on," he tells the guy when I come up, walks up to me.

"Thanks," he says, tugging one hand through his hair. It's obvious that he's been doing that nonstop today, because it's completely insane, sticking up in every direction like it's trying to escape his head.

"The tank in the corner exploded," he says, jerking his thumb over his shoulder. "I still don't know whether something got into the beer and made it produce way too much carbon dioxide, or whether someone fucked up the gas release valve, or whether the tank lid itself is just defective, and Seth is pissed as *hell* about the whole thing—"

"Don't worry about it," I say, reaching up and combing my fingers through his hair, trying to get it to lay flat. I'm medium successful. "Stay as long as you need, I've got Rusty. If you're here late, I'll put her to bed."

Daniel shakes his head, his hand in his hair again, messing it right back up.

"I'll come back and do bedtime," he says.

"I don't mind," I say, trying to keep it light. "I'm pretty sure I can get it right."

His face is tight, his eyes serious. Someone behind him shouts his name, and he holds up one finger, the gesture quick, jerky, stressed.

Of course he's stressed. His brewery just exploded. Rusty's final custody hearing is Tuesday, and his sea-hag of a babymomma claims she's got something on us.

And then there's last night, when I didn't think a single thing through, I just *did*, and it could have fucked us both over. What if he'd pulled out half a second later? What if it hadn't been Officer Sherman? What if the landowner had come down there with a shotgun?

Actually, I think Daniel would have preferred the shotgun over getting arrested, at least with the hearing on Tuesday.

Suffice it to say, I feel guilty about the whole thing, and will never be more than an arm's length from a condom again.

Also, I won't trespass.

Finally, Daniel nods, a smile twitching at his lips.

"Right, of course you can," he says. "Just don't forget Astrid."

"I would never."

"Rusty's in my office," he says, then digs in his pocket, comes out with his keys. "Just take my car, it's already got the booster seat."

We swap keys. I head to his office and grab Rusty, who hops off the chair, shoves her coloring books into her rainbow backpack, and practically bounces out the door.

"Can we go to the waterpark?" she asks as we wind between massive tanks, something bubbling in all of them.

"I don't think so," I say.

"Can we go to the beach?"

The beach is four hours away.

"Probably not," I tell her.

She huffs. We turn a corner, and there's Daniel again.

"Can we go to the sliding rocks?" Rusty asks me. "*Please?*"

"No," Daniel says, frowning.

"I asked Charlie," Rusty points out.

"He's the authority here," I say. "Sorry, kiddo."

She sighs dramatically and rolls her eyes. Daniel and I exchange a look.

"I never get to do anything," she mutters, kicking at the ground.

"Well, have a fun day with Charlie," Daniel says, leaning down and kissing the top of her head despite the sulking. "If I'm not back, she's gonna put you to bed, okay?"

"Fine," she mutters, still not looking up.

"C'mon," I say. "We'll find something fun to do. Bye," I say to Daniel, lean in for a quick kiss.

It's a second longer than quick. It's perfectly chaste and appropriate, but we linger. When we pull back, I look down.

Rusty's making a half-grumpy, half-grossed-out face at me, and it takes everything I've got not to laugh.

"Bye," he echoes as Rusty precedes me to the parking lot.

· · · · · ★ ★ ★ · · · · ·

"COME *ON*," she says from the backseat, where her small, still-slightly-grumpy face is in the rear-view mirror. "The sliding rocks are no big deal. Everyone goes there. Valerie goes there all the time and she can't even do a cartwheel."

I reach below the driver's seat of Daniel's car and slide it about a foot forward, then flip the lever on the steering wheel and adjust that, too.

"Your dad said no," I say, even though I secretly agree with her.

The sliding rocks are exactly that: a bunch of big, flat-tish rocks in one of the mountain creeks that form a natural slide. As long as you wear sturdy shorts over your bathing suit, it's pretty harmless, and it's *really* fun.

"Dad thinks I'm a baby," she huffs. "He won't even let me cut my own sandwiches. With a *butter knife*."

"Want to go to the park?" I ask.

"I guess," she mutters.

"How about the one in Flintburg that's shaped like a castle?" I offer, even though that one's an hour away.

Rusty just sighs.

"The one near my house is fine," she says. "Even babies go to the sliding rocks. I know *first graders* who go."

"Nope," I say.

"We don't have to tell my dad," she says, leaning forward. "Charlie, I *promise* not to tell him if we go to the sliding rocks. He'll never ever know. Cross my heart and hope to die. Uncle Eli brings me wedding cake from his job all the time and my dad has *never* found out."

I glance in the rear-view mirror at her small, earnest face.

Daniel knows about the wedding cake. He's known for ages. I don't have the heart to tell Rusty.

"I never told about the rides at the state fair," she cajoles.

"Rusty, knock it off," I say, sighing.

I'm bummed, because I'd also like to go to the sliding rocks instead of the park. It's hot out. They're fun. The park is kind of lame, and besides, Rusty won't get hurt.

She's silent for about five minutes, just looking out the window, thinking to herself.

Then, at last, she speaks up again.

"Are you and my dad sleeping together?"

To my credit, I don't react. I don't jerk the wheel to one side, I don't shout *what?* I don't even suck in a breath, despite being unprepared for that question.

Instead I pause. I remain steady. I look in the rear-view mirror at her incredibly serious face, and I decide that Rusty is a young woman deserving of respect and straight answers.

"Yes," I say.

"Huh," she says thoughtfully, then looks out the window again.

I wait.

"What's the point?" she finally says.

"Of sleeping together?" I ask, still maintaining perfect calmness.

"Yeah," she says. "Sleeping is *boring*. Why don't you go out or something?"

Right then, I make a choice.

I choose not to explain euphemisms. I decide not to tell

her that *sleeping together* actually means *having sex*, because I don't think she knows what that is yet, and I'm unprepared to tell her right here, right now, on this car ride.

"Adults are weird, I guess," is all the explanation I give.

"When you sleep together are you naked?" she asks, making a face. "Valerie says adults sleep together naked."

I look at the double yellow line on the road in front of me and consider my options for a long moment. Then I take a deep breath and look into the rear-view mirror again.

"If I take you to the sliding rocks, do you *promise* not to tell your dad?"

· · * * ★ ★ ★ * * · ·

IT WORKS.

Rusty doesn't ask another question about sex for the entire car ride, even though we have to go to my apartment for my bathing suit and then her house for *her* bathing suit, and the whole thing takes forever.

The rocks are a half-mile hike into the woods, and I think Rusty skips the whole way there, practically floating on a cloud that she finally gets to go. She jumps. She leaps. She uses her towel to pretend that she's a woodland-themed superhero named *The Fearsome Fawn*.

There are a few other people there when we show up, and I recognize most of them, but not too much. I'm pretty sure that none of them know Daniel well enough to rat me out, so we're good.

We spread out our towels on the rocks. We jump into the pool at the bottom to get wet, Rusty shrieking with the cold, and I don't think about Daniel throwing me into the creek last night even once.

In fact, I don't think about a single thing that happened

last night at all. Not about watching him float, naked, in nothing but moonlight. Not about him tossing me over his shoulder and throwing me in.

And I most certainly don't think about fucking outside on the rocks, the air cool and his body pure fire.

Once she's in, I show her the best way to the top of the rock slide, because it can be tricky if you don't know how to go.

"All right," I tell her, sitting at the top, watching another kid slip and slide down the rocks, shrieking with delight as he tumbles into the pool at the bottom, "Do you want to go first or do you want me to go?"

She bites her lip, nervous, kicking her water-shoe-clad feet on the rocks.

"You go," she says.

I clamber over her to the trough where the water escapes the top pool and put my butt in.

"See you at the bottom!" I say, pushing off.

Holy *shit* is it fun. It's over in five seconds and then I'm splashing into the pool at the bottom, breathless with the thrill, water up my nose. I surface and wave at Rusty, who waves back, then gets into position.

For a second, my heart squeezes. Just because everyone in Sprucevale takes their kids here doesn't mean it's *safe*. Sliding down a bunch of rocks into a creek isn't necessarily *safe*, and for a minute I wonder if taking her here on an impulse was dumb as fuck, and then she pushes off.

And screams with delight the whole way down.

I catch her when she splashes down at the bottom, laughing like a maniac.

"Again!" she shrieks, slithers out of my arms, and is already clambering up the rocks.

She must go down the slide twenty, maybe twenty-five times. The second she hits the water at the bottom she's already racing back to the top, impatient when she gets stuck behind someone slower on the climb, tapping her foot dramatically if someone else is on the slide when she gets to the top.

I go down plenty more times, but I can't keep up with her. I swear Rusty's rocket-powered or something, and after a while, I head to the towel we spread out in the sun and sit down.

Sitting feels great. I lean back on my hands, let the sun warm me up, bright behind my eyelids, and try to wash everything else but this blissful, perfect moment away.

The table will get finished in time. The brewery lost some beer, but they'll be fine. Crystal will never get custody.

I'm going to be more responsible, quit being impulsive, start remembering shit like I'm supposed to. For once, I'll get Elizabeth a birthday present next month instead of just texting her at 9 p.m. like I usually do.

A scream jerks me out of my sun-drenched reverie, and before I even know what I'm doing I'm already on my feet, every nerve in my body alive and tense, heart hammering.

It's Rusty, and she's wailing, the sound agonizing and pain-filled and it strikes terror deeper into me than I knew terror could go and oh *fuck* where is she, is she drowning is she stuck did she hit her head and get a concussion—

I spot her. On the rocks, halfway down, and half a second later I'm scrambling up to her, more terrified than I've ever been in my life, more terrified than the time Daniel impaled himself on a branch and even more terrified than the night I woke up to the garage on fire.

"Rusty!" I shout, even as my foot slips and my knee slams into a rock, slides along a sharp edge, but I get up and keep moving toward her.

She's sitting, legs akimbo, one half in the rushing water,

her face bright red and her mouth open, her cheeks already soaked as she screams and sobs and then screams again.

Her left arm is out, held stiffly away from her body, and it's *wrong*. I don't even know how it's wrong — not bent backwards, not snapped in half — but there's something wrong about it and it's swelling up like a pufferfish.

"What happened?" I ask, uselessly, when I reach her.

She just sobs and holds out her arm, still swelling.

Strangely, I'm relieved. Even as I scoop her up in my arms, crying, even as I make my way carefully down the rocks and people gather around us and someone hands me our towels and my bag, I'm relieved that she's not bleeding to death, that she didn't hit her head, that it's just an arm.

I've never hiked faster than I hike back to Daniel's car, half-running even with a sobbing seven-year-old over one shoulder, breathlessly telling her that she'll be okay. I get her into her booster seat, I wrap her arm in a towel, I kiss her and tell her we're going to the hospital and it'll be over soon, and then I drive like hell to Sprucevale General.

It's not until she's in a room, a nurse and a doctor hovering over her, looking so small in that hospital bed, that I realize my hands are shaking.

CHAPTER THIRTY-FOUR

DANIEL

I feel like someone's driven a stake through my gut as I powerwalk through the emergency room at Sprucevale General, heart pounding, hands clammy. I feel like someone's reached down my throat and is trying to pull my heart up through my mouth, and I swallow again and again like it'll keep all my organs in place.

"Sign says this way to 132," Seth calls, and I follow him.

Charlie's voice was shaking on the phone, even though I hung up on her after a dozen words — *hey it's me, Rusty's okay but she broke her arm, we're at the emergency room* — and bolted out of the brewery, Seth practically chasing me down.

He took the keys out of my hand and drove here. He navigated the stupid parking lot, talked to the front desk, charmed the nurses, and got her room number all while I stood by, unable to think anything but *it must hurt so much, I hope she's okay, I'm glad Charlie's with her*, and now he's pushing me down the hall to the right room, and I shove back the curtain and there they are.

"Hi, Dad," Rusty says softly when I come in. "Hi, Uncle Seth."

She looks so small in her hospital bed that it knocks the air from my lungs. I swear she outgrows all her clothes every six months and I'm so used to looking at her and thinking that she's so big now, so tall, so grownup, that seeing her like this spears me with pity.

"Hi, sweetheart," I say, coming over, sitting next to her hospital bed, right on the edge of the chair. "How are you feeling?"

"It hurts," she says, her voice small, her eyes big. "It hurts less, though."

Her forearm is propped up, wrapped in bandages, looking too big for the rest of her.

"They gave her ibuprofen," Charlie says, sitting opposite me, on the other side of the hospital bed. "The ER doctor already looked at it and thinks it's a spiral fracture, so they probably won't have to do anything but put a cast on, but we're waiting for X-rays."

I just nod. I feel like a can of soda that's just been shaken, fizzing and ready to blow.

"It's pretty boring," Rusty says, sighing.

"What happened?" I finally ask. "Did you fall?"

Last year a nine-year-old at the playground told Rusty that he didn't think she could jump off a swing high enough to land on the grass, a good seven feet away.

The phrase *you can't* is like catnip to my daughter. There's no better way to make her do something. She sprained her ankle and had to wear a brace for a week.

She made it all the way to the grass, though.

"Um," she says, and suddenly she won't meet my eyes. "Yeah. I fell."

"I took her to the sliding rocks," Charlie says.

She's leaning forward, her elbows on her knees, and she

looks me dead in the eye as she says it, her face tense, drawn, her curls half-wet and half-ragged. Suddenly, I realize she's also got a hospital gown on, the gap turned to the front.

"I thought I said she couldn't go," I say, and I sound shockingly reasonable, even to myself.

Charlie swallows, takes a deep breath, puts both hands on her head like she's trying to tame her hair.

"You did," she says. "And I took her anyway. I'm sorry."

Rusty's just watching me, her eyes red-rimmed, her face splotchy, her hair sproinging everywhere. For just a second, I wonder if anyone's ever thought that Charlie was her real mom.

I just nod. I shove my hand through my hair again, crack my knuckles, try to bite back the sudden fury riding through me, borne of panic and then relief.

"Sweetheart, can you talk to your uncle Seth for a little while?" I ask, reaching out and stroking Rusty's hair. "I need to talk to Charlie for a minute."

"It was my idea," Rusty says urgently.

"I know, honey," I say, leaning forward, kissing her hair.

"We'll be right back," Charlie says, and when she stands, she also drops a kiss on Rusty's head, like it's normal, natural, like she's done it a thousand times.

I walk out of Rusty's room, past a nursing station, down a hallway. I'm pretty sure that Charlie's behind me but I don't even turn and check. I don't know where I'm going, I just know I don't want to be around other people right now.

Finally, I turn a corner and there's an alcove, windows, a couple of chairs, and no one else, and I stop.

"I'm sorry," Charlie says before I can even turn around.

She's about to cry, her jaw clenched, her eyes bright with tears.

"I didn't think she'd get hurt," Charlie says. "I went to the rocks all the time as a kid and nothing ever happened, and I know you said she couldn't—"

"What the fuck?" I interrupt.

She goes quiet.

"Seriously. What the *fuck* were you thinking?" I ask, taking a step closer to her. I'm on the edge right now and I want to shout at her, yell, scream.

She closes her eyes, shakes her head.

"I'm sorry," she whispers again.

"You didn't give it half a second of thought, did you?" I ask, my voice still low, dangerous. "You didn't *for one fucking second* stop and think, maybe there's a reason Daniel doesn't want Rusty doing this yet?"

"I thought you were overreacting," she says, jaw clenching again.

"I didn't want her going because when he was her age, Caleb got his arm stuck on the way down and broke it," I say. "I was ten and I *still* remember the way he screamed, Charlie."

"I never broke my arm," she points out. "You never broke your arm. Hundreds of people have gone to the sliding rocks and haven't broken—"

"I still said she couldn't go," I say.

"You won't let her climb trees," Charlie says. "Last year, when I took her to fair, you didn't want her going on the carousel—"

"Do you know how fucking dangerous those things are?"

"It's a carousel, Daniel! It goes half a mile her hour, and if it breaks loose or something *you just get off it*," she says. "You can't wrap her in cotton. She's gonna go out into the world, and she's gonna get hurt sometimes, and you can't always be there to protect her."

"Not now," I say. "She's seven, Charlie. Seven. She's only just figured out that the tooth fairy isn't real and you're handing her knives and letting her jump off of rocks—"

"She loved it," Charlie says, her arms crossed over her chest, like she's protecting herself. I see a flash of something bright beneath the hospital gown she's wearing and realize she's still got her swimsuit on, a bikini top over shorts.

"I don't care," I tell her.

"She also loved the Scrambler, last year, at the fair," she says. "And the Ferris Wheel. And that ride where you get in the car and it goes around in a circle really fast, whatever the fuck it's called."

I take a deep breath, trying to corral my frustration, my anger. I put a fist on my forehead, turn, walk a few steps away, turn back. I don't know how to make her agree with me, how to make her understand that she can't just do whatever the fuck she wants, when she wants to do it.

"I have to tell Crystal," I say, simply.

The look on Charlie's face tells me she hadn't considered that, either.

"I have to tell her mom, and this is sure as *shit* going to come up in court on Tuesday," I go on, and as I say it the enormity of the thing hits me. "I'm going to be the dad that got his kid's arm broken because I let her do something dangerous. I'm already the dad who got her hand sliced open, and you can be sure as *shit* that both those things are going to be cited as reasons that she should be heading to Colorado next month."

Charlie swallows, looks away. A single tear slides down her cheek, but it only makes me angrier that she pulls this shit, then cries about it.

"We could have gotten arrested last night," I say,

coming closer, dropping my voice. "Did you know that public nudity is a sexual offense in Virginia, Charlie? What do you think my chances of keeping Rusty would be if I were on a registry?"

"I didn't think about that," she whispers.

No shit.

"You're going to make me lose her," I say.

Charlie looks at me like I've slapped her. She goes white, then pink. She rubs her swollen eyes with the heels of her hands, then takes a deep breath.

"No, I won't," she says.

Then she turns. She leaves, practically fleeing down the hallway, and I watch her until she's gone around the bend.

I'm still furious at her: for going behind my back with my own daughter, for getting Rusty hurt, for never thinking a goddamn thing through even once in her life, for never knowing what day it is.

And I'm terrified.

I'm terrified that I'm right, that falling for Charlie came with the price of losing Rusty.

CHAPTER THIRTY-FIVE

CHARLIE

I'm a fucking mess. People on the elevator stare at me — sobbing, snotting, wearing a hospital gown over a bikini top and shorts — and subtly move away.

I don't care. Daniel's right. He's fucking right about everything, about the sliding rocks and the carousel and the skinny dipping. He's right that I'm a walking disaster, that I'm a human wrecking ball.

And he's right that if he loses Rusty it'll be my fault. The knife? That was me. The broken arm? Me. Almost getting arrested?

Me, me, me.

There's a loose end in Daniel's life and her name is Charlotte McManus.

When I get to where I parked a few hours ago, Daniel's car is sitting there, and for a second I'm confused and then I remember we switched cars because of Rusty's booster seat, and fuck everything.

Fuck booster seats. Fuck cars. Fuck rocks in mountain creeks and fuck arms for breaking and most of all, fuck Daniel for being right about me.

For a hot second, I consider just taking his car and letting him figure it out when they release Rusty in a few hours. Fuck, that's probably what he thinks I'm going to do, because I'm sure *Daniel* has remembered that I had his car and his keys and *Daniel* probably keeps a spare set on himself at all times, just in case.

I'm sure *Daniel* has a backup plan for getting home because he expects me to forget that Rusty still needs a booster seat, and he thinks I'm so brainless and selfish that I'll just take his car.

He's so close to right, but I don't. I crouch down next to the car and put his keys on top of the back passenger-side tire, the heat radiating off the black rubber.

Then I text Seth, because I know he's still upstairs, and I cannot handle texting Daniel right now. I turn my phone off before he can text me back.

Then I turn and walk home, still wearing a swimsuit and a hospital gown. If they want it back, a nurse can chase me down.

* * * * * ★ ★ ★ * * * * *

SUNDAY MORNING, there's a knock on my door. I'm still in bed, spread-eagled and face down on a pillow, staring at a pile of stuff on my bedside table because I don't want to get up.

I fucked up. I've gotten Rusty hurt twice now because I'm an irresponsible dumbass who can't even keep track of the days of the week. It's a miracle that I haven't burned the whole town of Sprucevale down yet.

And what do irresponsible dumbasses do? They stay in bed all day.

Whoever it is knocks again. It's not Daniel, because that's not how he knocks — his is always a firm *knock knock*, and this is a more impatient, slightly softer *knockknockknock-knockknock.*

The third time I hear it, I realize it's my sister's knock, and even if I don't answer it right now there'll be no escaping her, so I may as well get out of bed and see what she wants.

"Hi!" she says brightly when I open the door. "I was just popping by to see if you wanted some reusable grocery bags, since someone left literally three hundred of them in the school's donation box — are you okay?"

"I'm fine," I say, leaning against the door frame.

"Uh huh," she says, sounding completely unconvinced. "You're wearing a swimsuit?"

I didn't manage to get undressed last night, just sort of... laid on my bed and woke up later.

"It's a new thing I'm trying," I say.

"Are you also trying getting sunburned on only one side of your face?" she asks.

I put my hands to my cheeks. Sure thing, the left side of my face is hotter than the right side. It's probably courtesy of my two mile walk home yesterday.

"Goddammit," I mutter.

"You fall asleep in the sun?" she asks, eyes narrowing suspiciously.

"...yes," I lie.

"Where?"

"Outside."

"Can I come in?" she asks, tilting her head to one side.

I don't want her to come in. I want her to give me the stupid bags and then leave and I want to crawl back into my bed in my swimsuit and feel bad for the rest of time.

Instead, Elizabeth pushes the door open.

"Let me rephrase that," she says. "I'm coming in."

SHE SITS me down at the kitchen table and makes me coffee. She finds a comfy t-shirt in a pile — probably the clean pile but I'm not 100% sure — and puts it on me. She raids my fridge and makes us breakfast, and she doesn't even comment on how much of the stuff in my fridge is past its expiration date.

"I fucked it up," I say, shoving away a half-eaten plate of eggs and toast, my other hand locked around a mug of half-drunk coffee. "God, I fucked it up so bad."

I take a deep breath and push the heels of my hands against my eyes again, like I can stave off tears, but all I can think about is how easy it would have been *not* to fuck it up and how I didn't do that.

Across the table, Elizabeth sets her coffee mug down with a light *clonk*.

"You're supposed to say *no, you didn't, Charlie,*" I tell her. "Maybe also *he won't be mad forever, he'll forgive you, love will conquer all*, shit like that."

"How bad was the break?" she asks instead.

"Not what I asked for."

"Sorry," she says.

"It was just a hairline fracture," I say, still rubbing my eyes. "She put her hand out and it got sort of stuck between two rocks for a second and jerked the wrong way."

Elizabeth sucks in a breath, and I think about Rusty's scream, the way it felt like an icicle to my heart.

"That's how I sprained my ankle," she says, matter-of-factly.

"It got stuck?"

"At the sliding rocks," she says. "I was kinda sliding off-track, so I kicked a rock, only my foot got stuck and got yanked the wrong way. Mom just about had a heart attack, made the doctors do about fifty x-rays because she was convinced it was broken, but it wasn't."

"You called Mom?" I ask, feeling like I'm one step behind.

"I was five," Elizabeth says. "She's the one who took us. You don't remember that?"

Slowly, I shake my head.

"I guess you were only two," she muses. "You gave me your stuffed bunny Arthur, so he could make me feel better, but I was really grumpy and told you that bunnies were stupid and ate their own poop and we got in a big fight about it."

"That doesn't sound like us," I say sarcastically, and Elizabeth laughs.

"Come on," she says, standing up and taking my half-eaten plate. "Finish that and go put some real clothes on. Also sunscreen."

"Why?" I ask, taking a gulp of coffee.

"Because we're gonna go do some fun shit, dumbass," she says. "Come on."

"Bossy," I mutter under my breath as I put the empty coffee mug into the sink and she turns on the water.

"Call me whatever you want, just go change out of the swimsuit you've apparently been wearing for twenty-four hours," she says.

I do it.

Big sisters, man.

· · · ★ ★ ★ ★ · · ·

"How is this not stupid?" I ask, staring at the enormous tire, perched at the top of a grassy hill.

Elizabeth rolls her eyes.

"Just get in, loser," she laughs.

"How did you even find out about this?"

"Jeff's students," she says, a trifle evasively. "Come on, it's fun."

"How do you know?"

Elizabeth shrugs, grinning, and I narrow my eyes. Her husband Jeff is also a teacher who teaches English at Sprucevale High.

"Which students?" I demand. "The college-prep class or the remedial class?"

"Does it matter?"

"Yes," I say, looking at the old tractor tire that Elizabeth's standing on its side, its diameter about six inches less than my height.

"Listen, Chuck," she says, sighing. "The remedial English kids *do* know how to have fun."

I cannot believe my sister, *a teacher*, is saying this to me.

"You're the worst role model," I tell her.

"Oh, the college prep kids will be having a much better time four years from now," she says. "But they're not the ones rolling down a hill in a tractor tire."

"But you think I should."

"I think you should take your mind off the fact that your boyfriend is being kind of an uptight dick right now," she says.

My stomach squeezes. I press my lips together, look away, and the voice in my head says *he's not being a dick, he's being right because you can never be what he needs.*

"Chuck," Elizabeth says. "Shit, Chuck, I'm sorry. C'mere."

She ducks through the middle of the giant tire, and it falls away from me and hits the ground with a *whump*.

"We can't even be friends now," I say as she steps out of the tires and wraps her arms around me, my voice going sky-high at the end. "How the fuck are we supposed to even be friends after I know what he looks like naked?"

She holds me, rocks back and forth.

"I'm sorry," she murmurs, one hand stroking my hair.

"It was so dumb," I say. "This whole thing was so dumb. I mean, who even lies in court anyway? *Dumb*. And it was dumb to say I'd go along with it and then it was dumb to actually fall for him, because, you know, if it was for real, we'd have done this ages ago—"

I break off, sucking in air.

"Not necessarily," Elizabeth says. "You needed a kick."

"He still wishes he'd married Crystal," I say suddenly, the words spilling out of me before I even know what they're going to be, like someone's got a string and tugged at it. "He got drunk and told me that one night, that he thinks he should have married her so they can have a dog and a fence."

I gasp for air again, because I'm trying to keep control of myself, keep from sobbing again next to this giant truck tire that my sister wants me to get inside of.

"He said that?" she asks, sounding genuinely baffled. "About Crystal?"

I just nod. I breathe deep again, trying to maintain control.

"Daniel Loveless said that he wishes he were married to his trash-ass babymomma?" Elizabeth says. "He said *those* words? To you?"

I look at my sister in some alarm.

"Don't use your murder voice," I say.

"I'll use my murder voice if I'm going to kill someone," she says. "Come on. Sit down."

She tugs me onto the grass, and I more or less crumple, lean back against the hot rubber of this massive tire. It smells like asphalt and dirt and grass out here, and Elizabeth gets on the ground next to me, one arm around my shoulder.

"He didn't say *that*," I admit. "He just sort of said it, what's the thing where someone doesn't say what they mean but you're supposed to understand it anyway?"

"Subtext?"

"Yeah, he said it in subtext," I say. "Like, he thinks that if he'd married her when he knocked her up everything would be great and perfect and she'd love Rusty and they'd, like, have family movie night and shit, and she'd be in the PTA and bake cookies and knit sweaters and they'd go to Disney World on vacation and everything."

Elizabeth's quiet for a moment, her arm around me, her fingers gently springing through my hair.

"He thinks his dick is *that* powerful?" she asks, and I snort. I snort so hard that snot comes out of my nose, and I wipe it on the grass, and it's gross.

"Don't all men?" I say, my voice shaky.

"True," she says. "Did his dick teach *you* to knit?"

I just shake my head.

"Has it spurted out a dog and a fence yet?"

"You're disgusting."

"I'm not the one wiping my snot on the grass," she says, gently.

"I can't join the PTA and organize bake sales," I sigh, resting my head against her shoulder. "I can't even remember what day it is half the time, Betsy. I got Rusty's arm broken and she took a knife from me—"

"Not your fault," she interjects.

"—and I nearly got Daniel landed on the sex offender registry—"

"Also probably not true."

"And... he's right," I say. "I'm gonna get Rusty taken away from him."

347

She pulls me in, kisses the top of my head gently.

"I can't even be mad," I say.

We're quiet for a long time. The birds chirp. A few stray clouds pass over the sun. The wind waves through the grass.

"Are you still gonna go to the custody hearing?" she finally asks.

"Why, so he can tell everyone how I got Rusty's arm broken in person?" I say. "So that when Crystal gets custody the judge can point to me and tell Daniel how it's my fault specifically that his daughter's gone? Oh God."

I burrow into her. Elizabeth wraps both her arms around me, and I sob.

CHAPTER THIRTY-SIX

DANIEL

"Dad!" Rusty calls.

I take a deep breath, my hand still on her door-knob, then open it again.

"Yes?"

"I need a glass of water."

"There's a glass on your nightstand," I point out.

In the dark I can just barely make out her small form in the bed, Astrid the wombat snuggled up on one side, her bright green cast on top of the covers.

"That one's old."

"Is this what you're using your coupon on?" I ask.

It's an idea I got from one of the ballet moms, actually. Rusty likes to fight bedtime by asking for a million things after lights out, so I gave her a coupon that she's allowed to use once, and that's it. One post-bedtime request, and then she has to go to sleep.

Of course, now I'm wondering whether having a broken arm merits a second coupon, the guilt twisting deep in my chest, intertwined with anger at Charlie, because I specifically said *no sliding rocks* and she still threw caution to the wind and now Rusty's paying—

"Yes," she says. "Can I get it myself?"

I step into her room and take the glass.

"Not a chance, kiddo," I say, because I know what she's really after — most of her uncles are still downstairs after Sunday Dinner, and she thinks they're having fun without her. "I'll be right back."

Rusty sighs dramatically as I leave, but she doesn't put up too much of a fight. I head to the kitchen and get her a new glass.

As I walk back through the living room, I realize everyone's quiet and looking at me.

"What?" I ask.

Levi, Eli, Seth, and my mom all raise their eyebrows and shake their heads in the exact same way. They're clearly up to something.

"Sure," I say, and head back upstairs to give Rusty her fresh water.

She does her best to put off going to sleep: she needs to say goodnight to Grandma again. She wants socks. Her pants are itchy. She needs a different stuffed animal, she has to tell Seth something *really important*, she left the milk out.

I shut it all down, kiss her one more time, and close the door on her protests.

Usually, I don't. Usually I have a little more patience with her, but not tonight. Not after yesterday, when Charlie got her arm broken after the knife thing and after nearly getting us arrested.

Not after I made Charlie cry and run away from me like that. Not after watching her leave felt like someone sucking all the air out of the room.

Ten minutes later Seth left the room and came back with my keys. Charlie texted *him*. She wouldn't even text me to give me my keys back, and I have no idea how she got home. I've been telling myself I don't care.

When I get back to the living room, they're all still sitting there, and I stop dead in my tracks.

"*What?*" I ask again, more sharply than I meant to, but they're all watching me like I'm the latest addition to the freak show, and I'm over it.

My brothers exchange glances, and finally Seth shrugs. I shove one hand through my hair, patience hanging by a string, cross my arms in front of my chest.

"You," he says, walking up to me and putting one hand on my shoulder, "are coming with us."

"Coming where?" I ask.

"My place," Levi says.

"Did you not just see me put my daughter to bed?" I ask, jerking a thumb over my shoulder. "Whatever the hell you want, just do it—"

"I've got Rusty," my mom says. "You go on with your brothers."

"I have work to do," I say.

I have no desire whatsoever to go to Levi's cabin in the woods and do whatever the fuck they think I'm going to do. I want to go back upstairs, to my own room, and I want to sulk and be angry at Charlie and worry about Tuesday's hearing and wallow in my guilt about Rusty.

"No, you don't," Seth says.

"Who asked you?"

"We can lift you," Eli chimes in. "There's three of us and one of you."

I grind my teeth together, annoyance and irritation and anger at everyone in my life gnawing at me from the inside.

"I don't want to go to Levi's house," I say, as patient and slowly as I can. "Right now, I just want to be alone—"

"Fascinating," interrupts Seth.

I consider punching him. Not that hard, just hard enough to make him fuck off.

"Unfortunately, you're terrible at knowing what's good for you so we're taking charge now," he continues. "And you'll be coming with us."

I look from one face to another, all wearing the same expression: total sincerity.

Shit. They mean it. They're actually prepared to lift me up and take me out of here if I don't come of my own free will. For a second I think about just punching *one* of them — a gentle punch, they can take it — and then running upstairs and locking my door before the others catch me, but I only give that tactic about a thirty percent chance of succeeding.

"Fine," I mutter, and head for the door.

· · · ★ ★ ★ ★ ★ · · ·

I STARE at the brown liquid in the tumbler in front of me as Levi re-corks the bottle and puts it back on the shelf.

"How long have you been barrel-aging your own whiskey?" I ask, sniffing it. "*Where* have you been barrel-aging your whiskey?"

It smells *good*. Almost good enough to make me forget that I'm mad with them for dragging me to Levi's mountain man shack.

Okay, it's not a shack. It's actually a pretty nice house, and he did build it himself. But I'm still pissed, and I've sure never seen barrels of whiskey anywhere.

"Approximately five years," he says. "And I've been aging it in a suitable place."

I give him a look for being obtuse, but I take a sip anyway.

It's *good*. It's a little weird — it's smokier than a bour-

bon, a little sweet, and has a distinct note of wet rock —
but it's also delicious.

I take another sip. We're all gathered around his fireplace, on two couches facing each other, a coffee table in
front of us, a bear skin rug in front of the fireplace, which
doesn't currently contain a fire because it's almost summer.

Yes, Levi the vegetarian has a bear skin rug. He didn't
shoot the bear himself. It's a long story. Its name is
Jebediah.

"Okay," I say, leaning back onto my couch, Eli next to
me. "Let me guess, I'm here because you think I'm wrong
for being pissed at Charlie and you're going to tell me to
get over it and forgive her, because you all like her and
think she's fun and don't want her to stop coming around."

I take another sip. The weird/good balance is starting
to tip in favor of good.

Also, I didn't drive myself here.

"Not even close," Eli says, propping his feet on the
coffee table, which is a long, glossy slice of …tree, I guess.
"You've been a total dick to everyone for the past twenty-
four hours and mom needs a break from your shit."

"I'm being a dick because——"

"Stop it, we know why you're being a dick," Seth says,
his posture matching Eli's. I put my feet on the table too,
just for the hell of it. "We don't care, we just need you out
of the house before Mom kicks you out and locks the door
behind you."

"Be mad at Charlie all you want," Levi says, swirling his
own whiskey. "Just stop stomping around and snapping at
people about using coasters."

"I specifically said *don't go to the sliding rocks*," I say,
ignoring the fact that we're not talking about Charlie.
"Seth, you were there. Did I not say that?"

"You did," he says. "Heard it my own self."

"And she took her!" I say.

"Indeed," agrees Seth.

"And now her arm is broken, and it wouldn't be if Charlie hadn't just decided to do whatever the fuck she wanted to do—"

"She could have broken it anyway," Levi points out. "There's about a million ways to break an arm."

"Caleb broke mine when I wouldn't give him back his Lego Darth Vader," Seth volunteers.

"You deserved that," I say. "And it was an accident. He tackled you at the top of the stairs because he was seven and didn't understand consequences very well."

"Whereas Charlie snapped Rusty's arm herself, on purpose," Eli says sarcastically.

"That's not what I'm saying," I snap, and take another long sip.

The bourbon also has a slight aftertaste of… sage?

"You're saying," Levi says, crossing one ankle over the opposite knee, "That if only everyone listened to you and did exactly as you directed at all times, life would be a Norman Rockwell painting because you'd be in total control of everything."

"I'm obviously not saying that," I go on. "But she's reckless, she's impulsive, she's a scatterbrained mess who nearly got us arrested Friday night—"

"Hold on."

"What?"

"Yeah, we need that story," Seth finishes, leaning forward. "Daniel, did you have… fun?"

I just give him a long, withering look. Or, I try. Seth doesn't wither. He just waits, glass between his hands, leaning forward.

"The question is," Levi says. "Would Daniel know he were having fun if he had it?"

"Oh, for sure," Eli says, grinning. "Daniel was real fun once. How do you think he got Rusty?"

"Do you still have your badass snake tattoo?" Seth asks.

"I've still got a tattoo of the constellation *Serpens*, yes," I say, draining my whiskey glass.

"You mean the one you got because, and I quote, 'snakes are badass'?" Seth says.

We all have constellation tattoos. We got them together, on Caleb's eighteenth birthday, all five of us. I've got *serpens*, the snake, Levi's got *corvus*, the crow, Eli's got the dragon and the north star, Seth's got Scorpio, and Caleb's got the sextant, because he's always been a nerd.

"At least I didn't get my ex-girlfriend's zodiac sign," I counter.

Seth's face goes flat. Everyone goes quiet.

I regret saying it *instantly*, even though it's been at least five years.

Then he drains his whiskey glass.

"She wasn't my ex at the time," he says, his face lightening. "Besides, scorpions are also badass. Tell us the story of how you had fun already."

I tell them, mostly because I feel bad for bringing up Seth's ex, Delilah: the milkshakes, the trespassing, the skinny dipping, Officer Sherman.

I leave out the part about barebacking and barely getting away with it, because there's such a thing as oversharing.

When I finish, Levi and Eli are smirking, and Seth is full-on grinning like it's Christmas morning.

"You," he says. "Naked. Outside. *On someone else's property.* My God, Daniel, that's about two steps away from some real law-breaking, like changing lanes without signaling or jaywalking."

"You're such a dick," I say, but he's already getting up

and grabbing the weird whiskey off the shelf, pouring it into my glass.

"I'd like to submit a thought for consideration," Levi says, settling back into his couch like it's a throne.

"Submit away," says Eli.

"I think this is why you like Charlie," he says.

"Because she gets me in trouble and got Rusty hurt?"

"Daniel, we went over this," says Eli. "Rusty could've fallen off the swings and broken her arm."

"The swings have a rubber mat underneath them," I say.

"You can be a dick all you want, but I *know* you understand the point I'm making," he says.

"You like Charlie because she's exciting," Levi continues, acting like Eli and I aren't bickering. "She's fun. She's unpredictable. She takes you on nude excursions."

"That's one way of putting it," Seth mutters into his glass.

"For all you act like you want safety and stability and a home life that looks like a Coca-Cola ad from the fifties, you've never liked someone half as much as Charlie and you never will," he says.

I swallow hard and stare down, right into Jebediah's glass eyes, his furry face forever frozen in a snarl. Levi's right and I hate him for it, but that's not the worst part. It's not the real problem.

"She's bad for Rusty," I finally say, my voice quiet. "It doesn't matter how I feel about it, she's not — we can't have a future if she's not good for Rusty."

There's a brief moment of stunned silence, and I look up into three faces, all leaning forward and looking at me like I have two heads.

"Are you fucking kidding me?" Seth asks.

"That," Eli says, pointing at Seth.

"Charlie's awesome with Rusty," Seth continues. "So she fucked up. All parents fuck up."

"I got a black eye once because I was riding on Dad's shoulders and he walked me into a door frame," Eli says.

"Mom forgot me at the grocery store when I was six," Levi says.

"When Dad was teaching me to ride a bike, he steered me straight into a tree by accident," Seth offers. "And didn't Mom give you a huge gash on your arm once when you were hiding in a pile of leaves to surprise her and she raked you?"

"Oh, I remember that," Levi says. "We all had to go to the hospital so you could get a tetanus shot."

"They weren't having a custody battle," I point out. "Mom and Dad didn't have some other parent just waiting for them to fuck up so they could use it against them in court."

They fall quiet.

"I can't fuck up," I say. "I'm already the wrong parent, I already put her in public school and don't live in a gated community and won't give her a pony and don't have a spouse—"

"You've got Charlie," Eli says.

"Not a spouse, Eli," I say.

"She's been more of a presence in Rusty's life than her own mother," he says softly. "You think that other shit matters to Rusty?"

"It matters to a judge," I say. "This school they want to send her to has a ninety-nine-point-nine college acceptance rate, last year they sent *seven* kids to Harvard and ten to Yale—"

"And Rusty was nearly a year old and barely able to sit

up by herself, let *alone* crawl when you got her," Eli says, his voice rising. "That's in the file too. You know what else is in the file? That Swamp Thing has seen her about six times in the past year."

"Don't call her—"

"Rusty's not here so I'll call her garbage mother what I want, thanks."

Somehow, my whiskey's gone again. I stand up, then wobble, drunker than I was expecting.

"It's on the table," Levi says.

I pour more. I drink more. I sit back down on the couch, with my brothers, and lean my head back against the cool leather and close my eyes.

And I see Rusty, so small in her hospital bed, big eyes glassy from crying, still in her swimsuit, her wrapped arm propped up while she waited to get a cast put on. All I can hear is her soft voice saying *hi, Dad.*

Charlie on her other side, holding her other hand tight, looking ragged and terrified herself. Charlie who must have carried Rusty back through the woods, who must have been the one to get her into her booster seat, soothe her, get her to the hospital.

It suddenly occurs to me that when I got there, Rusty wasn't crying, even though she was still in pain. She wasn't scared even though she was in the emergency room, she wasn't freaked out.

Even though her arm was broken, Rusty was fine, and it's because Charlie was there. Because she loves Charlie and trusts Charlie and even if Charlie does dumb shit sometimes, she's never once failed Rusty in the ways that matter.

"Are you asleep?" Levi asks.

"No," I say.

"Are you considering our sage advice?" he asks.

I say nothing.

"That means yes," says Seth.

"It's good advice," says Eli.

I just sigh, then lift my head and take another long sip of whiskey.

CHAPTER THIRTY-SEVEN

CHARLIE

I'm in the cereal aisle again, trying to decide which anthropomorphized cartoon animal has the sort of sugar that I want right now.

Which cereal will quell the hollow, gnawing feeling in my chest?

Will Froot Loops make me feel better about tanking the most significant relationship of my life with one bad decision?

Will Cookie Crisp let me go back in time and take Rusty to the playground instead?

Perhaps Tony the Tiger, who seems very charismatic, can give Daniel the *give her one more chance* talk.

It's six in the morning. I didn't sleep for shit last night, even though I was up late with Elizabeth, drinking Slurpees in the 7-11 parking lot because we're classy like that. She still thinks I should go to the hearing. I disagree, and since it's my life, I get to decide.

Fuck it. I want Lucky Charms, because those marsh-mallows are delicious. My arms are already full, because yet again I underestimated the amount of stuff I'd be buying this morning, so I put my phone on the shelf by the Cheerios, grab the Lucky Charms, shove the box under one arm, and promptly knock several boxes of Grape-Nuts and Raisin Bran off the shelf with the huge bags of tortilla chips I'm holding in my other hand.

"Dammit," I whisper under my breath.

I put everything on the floor. I pick up the cereal, put it back. I put the Lucky Charms back, remember why I'm there, grab it again, shove it under my arm, pick up the tortilla chips and the salsa and the queso dip and then finally maneuver myself to the checkout, where I take a plastic bag because *obviously* I forgot the reusable ones.

Then I put my pity food into my car and drive off.

· · · · ★ ★ ★ ★ · · · ·

IT'S close to noon when I realize I left my phone in front of the Cheerios. I'm at work, shaping a dovetail joint on a side table, when I suddenly have a vision of it, sitting there in front of the yellow box where I put it down for *just* a second.

I don't know why I didn't put it in my pocket. I just didn't.

I borrow the phone in the office and call the grocery store. While I'm on hold I sit back in the uncomfortable upholstered chair from 1970, a spring sticking straight into my butt, and look at the knickknacks that Donna, who runs the office, keeps on her desk. One is a small ceramic dog peeing on a ceramic fire hydrant, and I wonder why on earth anyone would want such a thing.

"Hi. Miss?" the voice on the other end of the phone says. "No one's turned it in and there's no phone in the cereal aisle."

For a moment, I just look at the peeing dog.

"It's not there?" I echo. Somehow, that hadn't occurred to me — Sprucevale is a small, safe town, so I assumed I'd just waltz back to the store after work and grab my phone.

"Sorry," he says. "But I'll put a bulletin out for it if anyone's seen it."

I lean back in the uncomfortable chair and do my goddamn best not to cry, because of *course* I did something dumb and lost my phone. I mean, I'm constantly misplacing it — I found it in my medicine cabinet a few weeks ago with no memory of putting it there — but this is the first time it's actually gone *missing* missing.

Shit. Now, on top of everything else, I probably need a new phone.

"Thanks," I say, give him the office number, and we hang up.

Then I go to the bathroom, and for the first time ever, I cry at work.

· · · · ★ ★ ★ ★ ★ · · · ·

I'M WATCHING stupid TV that night when Elizabeth knocks on my door. I've still got my coveralls on, and I'm probably coating my whole apartment in sawdust right now, but I just can't be bothered to care.

"What?" I shout.

The door opens, because it wasn't locked.

"You stopped answering your phone again," she says.

"It got stolen," I say, still slumped on the couch.

Elizabeth frowns in alarm and comes inside. She has dry cleaning in one hand, and it swishes inside, the light plastic rustling.

"What happened? Was it stolen at work? Did your car get broken into? Did you—"

"I left it in the cereal aisle for six hours and someone took it," I say.

I see her eyes flick to my coffee table, which has an empty cereal bowl, a giant bag of tortilla chips haphazardly opened, and the jar of queso dip on it.

"Oh," she says. "Well, I hope they find it. That sucks."

"I called. They didn't," I say.

"Did you go check yourself?"

"Yes," I say, feeling a little exasperated. "It wasn't where I put it, because either someone stole it or it fell through a very small wormhole that doesn't seem to have affected the rest of the fabric of our reality, just my phone."

She just sighs again, then comes over to me, the dry cleaning in the garment bag swishing, and drops a kiss on top of my head.

"I'm sorry," she says. "But I brought you a suit."

At last, I actually look at the garment bag. All day I've felt like I was watching the world through a haze, like something was separating me from everyone and everything. A fancy shower door or something.

"Thanks," I say automatically.

I pause for a moment, looking at the suit.

"...why?" I ask.

"For Daniel's hearing tomorrow," she says, as if we've discussed it, decided that I'm going, and I had any idea that she was letting me borrow a suit for the occasion.

Finally, I stand from the couch and turn off the trashy reality TV show I was watching, grab my empty cereal bowl, take it to the kitchen.

"I'm not going," I call, putting it in the sink and balancing it carefully on several other bowls. "I promise you that if I go, I'll make everything worse, because that's what I do, and Daniel has made it pretty clear that I should stop making everything worse for him—"

"Daniel said what he said standing the hallway of the emergency room," Elizabeth says. I turn back to my living room, and she's still standing there, freshly dry-cleaned suit hanging off of one finger. "No one is their best self in an emergency room. Except maybe the doctors and nurses, or at least I would hope——"

"I'm not gonna be the reason he loses his daughter," I say.

"Charlie."

"Elizabeth."

"You should go," she says. "If nothing else, prove that Daniel wasn't lying."

"He was," I point out, but she just waves one hand in the air.

"Only technically," she says.

"That's lying! Technically lying is still lying!"

Elizabeth turns, walks to the door to my room, and hangs the suit from the top of the door.

"You should go," she says, simply. "You said you would, and right now you need to be the bigger person and go to the hearing, even if Daniel never speaks to you again afterward."

I look at the suit, hanging on the door. Of course Elizabeth would both try to push me down a hill inside a tractor tire and be responsible enough to dry-clean her suit before lending it to me. Even though I know I'm lucky to have her, right now I'm annoyed at her for being so much better at life than I am.

"I'll think about it," I lie. I'm not going to think about it, because I'm not going.

I'm not going, and I'm never going to feel better, and I'm just going to wallow in my sadness and self-pity and eat Lucky Charms and queso until my butt literally fuses with my couch, and I'd like to see my stupid, responsible sister try to stop me.

"Thank you," she says.

Then she walks over and wraps me in a hug.

I'm surprised. It takes me a minute before I hug her back. Her hair smells like flowers, of course, and mine probably smells like sawdust, but she squeezes me a little tighter and then releases me.

"Call me when it's over, I want to hear how it goes," she says, giving my hair a light ruffle.

"I'm not going, and I don't have a phone," I remind her.

"Use Daniel's," she says, heading for my door. "Bye, Chuck. Good luck. Love you."

"Love you too," I call out, ignoring the part about using Daniel's phone, and then the door closes behind her.

I take the suit and put it in my closet, and then I go back to dumb television and queso dip.

I'm not going.

I'm never going to feel better.

I will become one with this couch, and that's what I deserve.

· · · · · ★ ★ ★ ★ · · · ·

THAT NIGHT, I sleep like the dead, and I wake up late because my alarm was on my phone. I shower as fast as I can. I eat cereal. I run out the door, hop into my car, start on my way to work.

I'm halfway there when a rabbit runs across the road, right in front of me, and I slam on the brakes. I lurch forward into my seatbelt, bracing my whole body for the sickening *thump* of flesh under my tires, but it doesn't come.

A second later, the bunny disappears into the grass on

the side of the road, safe and sound, probably with no idea that it nearly met a gruesome death just now.

I feel it like a fist right to the chest, like my ribcage is being squeezed, my organs shaken, and I start sobbing. Right there, still stopped in the middle of the road, I start crying hysterically about the bunny who didn't die and about the sister who's too nice to me and about Rusty who was so brave about getting her arm broken and mostly, I cry because I'm sorry and because I already miss my best friend.

I pull into someone's driveway so I'm not in the road anymore, and I stay there for at least ten minutes, crying. I wonder if Elizabeth is right and I wonder if she's always right, if maybe I should listen to my sister who can remember her reusable bags and who responds promptly to emails.

Finally, I reach for my phone, but it's not there. I cry a little more, but then I turn around and head back to Sprucevale, where I have to find a pay phone — a *pay phone* — before I can call my boss and tell him that I have horrible food poisoning and won't be coming to work today.

CHAPTER THIRTY-EIGHT

DANIEL

"She knows it's today, doesn't she?" Lucinda asks, glancing down the long hallway of the Burnley County courthouse.

"I reminded her," I say.

That's a slight understatement. Besides the reminders I put in her phone a few weeks ago, I called her yesterday after waking up on Levi's couch feeling less-than-stellar.

He was right. I'm never going to like anyone else half as much as I like her, fuckups and all.

Charlie didn't answer. She didn't answer two hours later, or around lunch, or any of the other three times that I called her and apologized and rambled into her voicemail, telling her that I was sorry, that I needed her, that I fucked up just as much as she did and we were both imperfect and that's what made us beautiful together.

She didn't pick up once. She hasn't called. She hasn't texted. Not even a smoke signal, and I'm starting to panic. I'm wondering how badly I fucked up on Saturday.

Lucinda checks her watch just as the doors to the courtroom open, and she looks at me.

"She knows where to go, doesn't she?" she asks.

I just nod. I told her in the voicemails.

We go in. We sit. We're five minutes early, and I pull out the same things as always: report cards and teacher statements, testimony from her ballet teacher and her piano teacher, the schedule of every visit over the past five years, and finally, her drawing.

Shit.

I packed all this last week. The drawing has Charlie in it, next to me, her hair a cacophony of squiggles. We're both smiling and standing next to a castle surrounded by palm trees.

Looking at it feels like a trap door just opened under my heart, and I nearly put it back, but I don't. I keep it out because if Charlie doesn't come, I'm prepared to lie my damn face off and say that she had a work emergency or her dog died or her grandma is sick or whatever bullshit used to work when I was a kid in school.

"Cute," Lucinda says. "No wombat?"

"Not in this one," I say. "She's still on that kick, though."

The door opens again. I turn towards it too fast, but it's not Charlie. It's Crystal, coming belly-first, her lawyer and husband behind her, and she doesn't so much as look in my direction as they sit, talking amongst themselves, her husband helping her into her chair like she's got two broken legs or something.

"Do you want to try texting her?" Lucinda murmurs.

I think she's getting antsy, and that knowledge makes the hairs on the back of my neck prickle, my palms start sweating because Lucinda is rarely *antsy*. She's cool and calm and collected and a legal badass, but she's not *antsy*.

"I'll try," I say, pull out my phone, text Charlie: *Where are you?*

I wait thirty seconds, a minute. There's no answer.

I want to throw up.

The bailiff — Pete Bresley, officially Sprucevale's biggest gossip — pulls the huge wooden doors closed, folds his hands in front of himself, stands by them.

"All rise," he intones, and we do. Lucinda throws me a look. The judge walks in from chambers, casts a glance around the assembled parties, sits. I'm sweating, anxious, and I feel like someone's put chains around my heart and thrown it into the ocean.

She didn't come. She ignored all my voicemails and texts and apologies and pleas and even if she doesn't want to forgive me, she couldn't get over it and come for Rusty's sake.

"Be seated," the judge calls. "I hereby call into session the matter of Thornhill vs. Love—"

The giant wooden door creaks open again, and everyone turns, but we can't see anything. It's open about three inches and there's nothing on the other side but the sunlight in the hallway.

I don't hope. I don't let myself. It's probably someone looking for another courtroom, someone who got lost on their way to a bail hearing or something.

"Bailiff," the judge calls, and Pete steps over, pushes the door open, and even though I'm not hoping, my heart is beating on my ribcage like it's trying to break down a door.

"Thanks Pete," says Charlie. "That thing's heavier than it looks, huh?"

She steps in. She's wearing a suit and her face is bright red. Her hair's wild. She's breathing like she's just run a marathon but trying to pretend she's breathing normally as she looks around, uncertain until her eyes land on me.

Relief douses me like a summer rainstorm, leaves me shivering. Pete points in my direction and Charlie walks over, careful in heels, drops neatly into the chair to my right.

Up close I can see tiny rivulets of sweat on her temples, and without being told I can see it: Charlie knowing she's late again, knuckles white on the steering wheel, Charlie taking off her shoes and running barefoot through the courthouse, ignoring the weird looks and mutters that followed her.

I love her for it. She'll probably never change, and she'll probably never be on time, but I love her for the flaws, the cracks, for the fuckups and mistakes.

She scoots her chair in, still trying to catch her breath, and glances over at me.

"Sorry I'm late," she whispers.

I reach over and take her hand. She's got the ring on, and I lace our fingers together, raise it to my hand, kiss it.

"You're fine," I whisper back.

·· * * ★ ★ ★ * * ··

IT FEELS ENDLESS. Crystal's lawyer talks about schools and gated communities and college acceptance rates and *opportunities unavailable to the child in her current situation.* He suggests that Charlie and I aren't actually a couple. He goes on and on about the fact that she's going to have a sibling, that a child *needs* her mother, that it's a shame to raise a child in any situation that isn't a picture-perfect nuclear family.

We hear about the knife, about the broken arm, and I look over at Charlie. She's staring dead ahead, glassy-eyed, jaw clenched.

I can't say anything, so I just squeeze her hand.

Then it's Lucinda's turn.

The report cards. The teacher statements. We hear about how Rusty is in second grade and reading at a seventh-grade level; how she's ahead of the rest of her class in math; how she has an interest in abyssal fish and *Little House on the Prairie* and brain teasers.

Lucinda reminds us it's a miracle, given how delayed Rusty's development was when I got custody. She details every single time in the past five years that Crystal has cancelled visitation. She points at Charlie and reminds the room that I'm in a long-term, stable relationship with a suitable woman.

Then there are the questions: about my intentions with Charlie and with schooling and with the brewery, to Crystal about the move to Colorado and the new baby. I tell him what I know, and what I don't know I make up and state confidently.

Finally, the judge stops asking questions. He looks down at his notes. He adjusts his glasses. He frowns. My heart is a kick drum in a punk band, thrashing away. It's a wave in a hurricane, pounding against the rocks and dissolving.

"Let's take a ten-minute recess," he says, stands, and leaves the room.

My fingertips go cold as I watch him go. I can feel the blood draining, coming back to my heart, my brain, my lungs, my body's stress reaction. There's a hand on my shoulder.

"It's a big decision," Lucinda reminds me calmly. "It doesn't mean you're losing her. It means he wants to get it right."

I nod. Charlie squeezes my hand so tight the band on her engagement ring cuts into the webbing between my fingers, her hand strong and firm in mine. I'm not normally a weak man, but I am right now.

If I go straight from here and get her from school, we could be across state lines by this afternoon, I think. *We'd use cash. Go to cheap motels, stay under the radar, and we'd live like that and I'd never have to be without her...*

"Tell me something," I say to Charlie, leaning my forehead on my fist, trying not to think.

"Tell you what?"

"Anything," I say. "Distract me."

"The sound llamas and alpacas make when they mate is called *orgling* and it sounds like a jalopy trying to turn the engine over," she says.

My eyes are still closed, and I take a deep breath.

"Orgling?" I say.

"Sounds exactly like you think it does, kind of a... *bludabludabludabluda*," she says, then clears her throat, lowers her voice. "I'm not doing a very good job. Turtles squeak when they fu— uh, mate, like this high-pitched *ennnhhhh*. Though in most of the videos I've seen they were actually doing it to shoes, which I guess look like female turtles."

"Were there feet in the shoes?" I ask.

Kidnap Rusty and get fake names, maybe Charlie will come...

"Some of them," she says. "Apparently Crocs *really* look like hot lady turtles, which is kind of ironic given the name."

"I knew there was a reason my mom hates them," I say, and Charlie smiles.

We keep talking about nothing, or rather, Charlie keeps talking: about the weird noises animals make when they mate, about how speed walking is an Olympic event, about how President Andrew Jackson was once gifted a 1,400 pound block of cheese and threw a party at the White House so people would come eat it.

Then the door at the back of the courtroom opens again. Charlie stops cold. Our palms are sweaty against each other's, but I couldn't care less.

"It's fine," she whispers. "It's fine."

Despite myself, I glance over at Crystal.

She looks bored. Court resumes. Formalities are said, and finally, Judge Hughes takes his glasses off and leans forward.

I swallow, waiting, Charlie's ring digging into me.

"After serious consideration, I've decided to amend the custody agreement between Mr. Loveless and Mrs. Thornhill," he states, and I hear Charlie gasp. She squeezes harder.

His words push the breath from my body, like I'm in a vise.

I lost. The last six years don't matter, because I lost my daughter to a woman I can't stand, to a woman who doesn't love her—

"In light of Mrs. Thornhill's new life circumstances, I'm awarding you partial custody," he goes on.

I might throw up. Charlie might break my hand. I think, desperately, of everything I might be about to miss: watching her run through the sprinkler and reading her bedtime stories and teaching her to make scrambled eggs, all the simple, day-to-day things that seems like nothing until they're gone.

Please, don't let them be gone.

"That custody will consist of four weeks per year at your new home in Colorado, to be divided as you see fit," he says.

I was so set for bad news that it takes me a moment.

The information reaches my brain like snow melting through cracks in the asphalt, and I don't understand it right away because I'm still thinking of singalongs in the car and games of Candyland.

"Mr. Loveless will retain custody for the other forty-eight weeks..." he goes on.

I finally get it.

She's staying with me, and she'll be gone once in a while, but day to day, morning and night, it'll still be me.

Just as I realize it, Charlie gasps. I look over, and she's crying, tears streaming down her face, and she grins at me, and the next thing I know our arms are around each other and her face is in my neck and she's sniffling and I'm burying my face in her hair.

A month is nothing. It's nothing. That's fall break, spring break, and two weeks over the summer. It's less than she theoretically has in visitation right now.

"I'm sorry," Charlie says into my neck, whisper-laughing as she sniffles. "I'm sorry. Shit."

I just laugh, my face still buried in her hair. For the first time in years and years, my own eyes are wet, and I blink against tears because Rusty is staying with me and I'm so happy and grateful that I don't know what to do.

There's more court. Lucinda handles it, I assume, because I sure don't. I don't hear anything that anyone else says, I just know that Rusty's staying with me and Charlie showed up and while life is never perfect, it feels damn close right now.

Court adjourns. We all stand, and after the judge leaves, I finally give Charlie a proper hug, holding her against me, her breathing ragged and deep to match mine. Crystal, her husband, and her lawyer leave, dry-eyed, looking annoyed.

Charlie pulls back, wiping her cheeks, her face bright red and her eyes highlighter pink.

"I think that went quite well," Lucinda says, snapping the latches on her briefcase shut, the hint of a smile on her face. "A month a year isn't too bad."

I just laugh.

"A month a year is fine," I say. "I never wanted her not

to get to see Rusty, I just... didn't want her to take her away."

Lucinda reaches out, takes my arm.

"I know, Daniel," she says. "Pleasure working with you. Call me next time she gets up to her tricks again."

She offers her hand. We shake. She leaves, and I pack up all my papers that are scattered over the table, shove them back into a folder, put them back into my bag. Pete Bresley watches the whole thing, and though part of me wonders whether he's taking notes so he can tell his mother Mavis the most accurate version of what happened, I don't care.

Let him tell everyone that Charlie sprinted in and that we held hands the whole time and that I cried tears of relief when I found out I got to keep Rusty. Fuck it, I don't care.

We walk out of the courtroom holding hands.

CHAPTER THIRTY-NINE

CHARLIE

I let Daniel lead me, since he knows where we're going and I don't. We head down the hall, around a corner, through a passageway and at the end, there's a staircase. This building was built at least a hundred years ago so the staircases are beautiful, made of stone and brick, wrought iron balustrades, big windows on every landing.

I wobble, wearing the only pair of heels I own. I'm out of practice, and that makes me slow, uncertain, and I'm hanging onto Daniel for dear life.

At the first landing, we stop. We're next to a window that looks out over a green field and the Burnley County detention center, and he turns, faces me.

"I'm sorry," I say instantly.

"Charlie, that's not—"

"I fucked up and I'm so, so sorry, and I wasn't even sure if you wanted me to still come today so if you didn't, I'm sorry for that, but I think it worked out ommph."

He covers my mouth with one hand, still slightly sweaty. I look up into the alpine lakes of his eyes, and they're smiling.

"You didn't get my voicemails?" he says.

I clear my throat, and he takes his hand off my mouth.

"No," I say, offering no further explanation.

"I left at least five," he says. "And I texted?"

"Uh, I guess they didn't come through," I say, and he raises one eyebrow.

"You didn't come because I apologized?" he says.

"For what?"

"For being an asshole to you," he says, like it's obvious. "For acting like you're the only person who's ever made a mistake with a child."

I swallow hard and look away, out the window, because I still don't feel like he was *wrong*. Everything he said was true. I fucked up. I keep fucking up.

"For forgetting that we're all human, and we all fuck up, but it's the wanting to be better that matters," he goes on.

"Is it?" I ask, still looking away.

He pulls me close, his fingers on my chin, makes me look at him.

"You're the sun and I'm the moon," he says slowly, carefully. "You shine and I reflect, and that's how we always were. Without you I'm a dark, cold, dusty rock hurtling through space."

"You're not dusty," I whisper, eyes already leaking.

"I love that you're the sun," he goes on. "I've been in love with you for years and I didn't know it because you were always there, always letting me bask in your light and your warmth even if sometimes I didn't deserve it."

"What?" I say, my voice barely above a whisper. "You always deserved it. You were always, I don't know, my anchor in a storm. My safe harbor. I always had you."

"You still have me."

"I don't ever want to not have you," I say, the words

spilling out of me. "But I'm gonna fuck more things up, Daniel."

Now he smiles, leans in, kisses me on the forehead. I'm still doing my best not to cry in the staircase of a courthouse, but it's a losing battle.

"You're gonna fuck things up and I'm gonna fuck things up and all I want is to be together when we do," he says. "We're people. We're human. We're imperfect, and giving in to love is the best we've got, so say you forgive me and let me fall with you."

I take a deep breath. I still feel awful, like my insides are circling a drain. I still feel guilty about Rusty, about all the damage I've done or almost did, about the things I know I'll fuck up in the future.

"Of course I do, Daniel," I say. "Yes. You knew I'd say yes."

"I hoped," he teases, resting his forehead against mine. "I thought I was done for when you didn't text me back or answer your phone. Not just because of the hearing. Because of me. I thought I was going to have to live out my life as a dried husk of a man, Charlie, if I couldn't have you back."

"Stop it," I whisper, eyes closed, smiling.

"Stop what?"

"You're not a husk," I say.

"Well, not now."

"Not ever."

"You promise?" he asks, his voice low, quiet. He slides one hand down my arm, intertwines our fingers.

"I promise," I say. "When we fuck up, we fuck up together."

He leans in and kisses me, his lips hot against mine. I'm three inches taller than usual and the angle is different, more direct, and I grab his tie and pull him in, his other hand going around my back, under the suit jacket. His fingers press into my spine, and I arch against him.

It's the heels. I swear. If I weren't wearing heels I'd never be wondering where the nearest janitor closet was and whether I could talk Daniel into pulling out again, after the first time was a close call.

We pull back. I flatten my hand against his chest, feel his heartbeat, his warmth.

"I love you," he says, quietly, seriously. He pushes a curl out of my face, and it sproings right back. "Even when I didn't know I loved you, I loved you."

"I love you back," I say.

"I have a proposition for you," he murmurs.

"I like it when you proposition me," I say.

"Come to dinner," he says. "And if traffic isn't too bad on the way back, maybe we'll get there in enough time for a quickie before my mom gets home."

I just laugh. I push my fingers into my eyes, wiping away the last tears, and I laugh.

"A quickie before your mom gets home," I say. "How'd we go from _you are the sun_ to that?"

"_Maybe_ a quickie," he corrects me, his smile lighting up his eyes. "Depending on traffic."

"How could I forget the most erotic part?"

"Beats me," he says, shrugging. "But we should hurry up if we want to make it."

He kisses me again: brief, thorough, hungry. He takes my hand and we descend the rest of the stairs.

"What happened to your phone?" he asks as we walk slowly through the courthouse, since I'm a little iffy in these heels.

"Why do you ask it like that?" I say, my voice totally neutral.

"Did you lose it?" he asks. "Or drop it in the toilet? Or did you saw it in half or something?"

I give him a quick sideways glance. He's laughing.

"It got stolen," I say.

"From where?" he asks.

"You're supposed to say *that's terrible, what a pain in the ass, I'm so sorry*," I correct him.

"Charlie, where'd your phone get stolen from?" he asks again.

There are times I wish he didn't know me so well.

"The cereal aisle at the grocery store because I left it on the shelf for six hours," I admit.

Daniel just starts laughing.

WE GET BACK to his house with twenty minutes to spare.

They're twenty minutes well-spent.

CHAPTER FORTY

CHARLIE

D aniel turns his Subaru onto a gravel road, though *road* is a generous term. It's more like two gravel ruts pointing into the forest and then disappearing behind trees.

"Now you're definitely not trying to find a McDonald's," I say.

He just grins, not taking his eyes off the road.

It's Friday, two and a half weeks after his court hearing, and this afternoon he told me to pack whatever I needed for a weekend away and be ready by six, because Eli and Violet volunteered to take Rusty all weekend.

I didn't need to be told twice, though I'd imagined more of a… location. You know, a nice little bed and breakfast, a hotel, even a motel.

Frankly, I don't care as long as it's got a bed and the sheets are clean.

You know what? I don't even need a bed. I'll take any flat surface where pine needles aren't jabbing me in the ass.

"You'll see," he says, carefully rounding a bend in the road, the car jostling.

"Glamping?" I guess, peering between the trees. Since

it's summer, the sun still isn't down, but the light is slowly fading. Regardless, I can't see anything besides brown trunks and the bright, nearly day-glo green of summertime Virginia woodland.

"What's glamping?" he asks.

"Glamor camping," I say.

"Okay," he says after a moment, clearly waiting for more explanation. Guess I was wrong about glamping.

"You're technically in a tent, I think, but it's a permanent tent, with a floor and a bed and stuff. And heating. And air conditioning?" I say, trying to remember the details of something I read once.

"So glamping is just a flimsy cabin with no windows," Daniel says. "Unless the tent has windows."

"Some probably do," I say as he goes around another bend in the road. "I don't know, I'm not a glamping expert. I think there's usually also kombucha. It's that kind of thing."

"I tried kombucha once," he says, reflectively. "Some lady kept calling the brewery and *insisting* that we should start making it to sell, but honestly, it just tasted like I ruined some perfectly good iced tea. Maybe I was doing it wrong."

"No, kombucha's kind of gross," I agree. "And it's got that big weird fungus — is *that* where we're going?"

Daniel doesn't answer, just grins as he pulls his car into a clearing next to a cabin and parks.

"Hopefully it's better than glamping," he says.

It's a log cabin perched above a creek in the middle of a small clearing. I hadn't realized we were going uphill, but clearly we were, because even the parking spot has an incredible view of the unspoiled valley below, the mountains beyond, blue and purple and green. I feel like I can see straight to West Virginia, or Tennessee, or Kentucky or whichever state I'm facing right now since the geography way down here gets a little confusing.

"How'd you find this place?" I ask as we get out of the car, still staring around.

"I know a guy who knows a guy who rents it out," Daniel says, pulling out his phone. "Okay, he says the key is under the ceramic frog with the bowtie…"

I peek through the window in the front door while he finds the key. There's a curtain in front of it, so it's hard to see, but I'm fairly sure there's a big stone fireplace, a high vaulted ceiling, and a light fixture that's not even made from deer antlers.

"Did you want to actually go inside, or just peek through the window all night?" Daniel teases from behind me, and I move. He unlocks the door, then pushes it open so I can go in first.

The opposite wall is nothing but windows, overlooking the creek below and then the mountain vista beyond, the sun just dipping below the horizon, painting the sky pink and orange and purple.

It's gorgeous, and I walk over to the wall, just looking out at the view.

"Holy shit," I breathe, and Daniel comes over. He drapes his arms over my shoulders and rests his chin on top of my head, his beard tickling my scalp through my hair.

"Jim Bob wasn't lying," he says.

"Someone named Jim Bob owns this place?" I ask. Based on my personal experiences, I'd expect a Jim Bob to be more of a trailer guy, but what do I know?"

"Jim Bob is very enterprising," Daniel says.

We stand there for a long moment, and I lean back into his solid form, reveling in the moment. Aside from the crickets and the grasshoppers and the birds, it's quiet. The view is beautiful. There's no piles of probably-clean-I'm-pretty-sure laundry, there's no seven-year-old in the next room. We've got all weekend, not thirty minutes.

I might be in heaven.

"I'm gonna go get our stuff," Daniel says, and drops a kiss on top of my head.

"You want help?" I ask.

"I got it," he says, and disappears outside.

I wander back into the cabin and look around. It's only got one bedroom, but the bedroom is glorious — a view, a sitting area, a jacuzzi bathtub in the bathroom, and a bed that I'm pretty sure is the next size up from a king bed. The rest of the cabin is open plan, the kitchen separated from the living area by nothing but the island in the center, rustic wooden stools gathered around it.

There's a stone fireplace. There's a light fixture — maybe it's a chandelier; what makes something a chandelier? — that's not made of antlers.

A minute later Daniel is back, a duffel bag over each shoulder and a giant cooler held in both hands, his biceps and shoulders bunched under his t-shirt.

I don't even offer to help again. I just watch as he walks to the kitchen island and sets the cooler on top of it, because I'm never going to get tired of watching him lift heavy things. He walks the duffel bags to the bedroom, comes back out.

"You want to check out the deck while I make mojitos?" he asks, opening the cooler and bringing out bottles.

I lean my elbows on the cool granite surface, narrowing my eyes at him.

"What?" he asks, a bottle of rum in one hand and a bag of limes in the other.

"You're acting suspiciously like a perfect boyfriend," I say. "What'd you do?"

"Are you saying I don't always act like a perfect boyfriend?" he says, grinning.

"I'm saying that last week you invited me over for a romantic dinner, only to call me fifteen minutes before I got there to ask if I'd pick up a pizza," I say.

He puts the limes on the table and grabs two glasses from the cupboard behind himself.

"Listen, I thought I could handle using the broiler," he says. "I was wrong. Besides, I ordered the pizza and everything, you just picked it up because it was on your way."

"Too many ideas above your station," I tease as he uncorks the rum with a small *pop*. "I'd say you should have gotten Eli to supervise you, but that would have been an even less sexy time than Papa John's."

"I'm sure Eli can be a very sensual man," he says.

Then he makes a face, and I burst out laughing.

"I'm sure Violet thinks so," I say.

"Well, she gets off on the arguing," Daniel says, pouring rum into a shaker. "I mean, she must, right?"

"She gets off on something," I say.

"Gross," Daniel mutters.

"You just called your own brother *sensual*," I point out, still laughing.

"Go look at the deck and stop ruining my cocktail concentration," he teases. "They'll get done faster without you harassing me."

"All right, *fine*," I say, step over, kiss him on the cheek, and go through the side door to a huge redwood deck on the side of the house.

It's also gorgeous. It's also got stunning views of the creek and the mountains and the sunset, nothing but trees and sky as far as I can see.

There's a hot tub, a simple round one with wooden sides,

set into one corner of the deck, four cushioned loungers on other side, all facing the sunset, and I lean my elbows on the railing, looking out, thinking about absolutely nothing.

After a few minutes, Daniel comes out, stands next to me, and hands me a mojito. We clink our glasses together.

"Here's to weekends in the middle of nowhere without Rusty," he says.

"Here's to swearing like a sailor for two days straight," I laugh.

"Goddamn right," Daniel agrees, and we both drink, leaning against the railing, watching the sunset.

"I brought Eli's meatballs," he says. "I think that's everything."

"They're good, but I'm not sure they're *everything*," I say.

"I mean I've fulfilled your requirements," he says, counting on his fingers. "You already got free beer, Seth agreed to do your taxes, we're going backpacking with Caleb next month, and Eli made you meatballs."

"You still haven't let me win at horseshoes," I point out.

"We haven't played horseshoes," he says. "Besides, I don't think I'm good enough at horseshoes to let you win. Everything I do in that game is completely accidental."

I sigh and lean my head against his shoulder.

"Same," I admit. "It's a stupid game."

I tap the engagement ring against my mojito glass idly, a habit I've developed over the past two months. I glance down as it catches the fading light of the sunset, flaring with internal fire.

Suddenly, I remember the last thing that was on my list of demands.

"We never had the world's most amicable breakup, either," Daniel says, putting his hand on my back, tucking his body against mine as we watch the sunset together.

"I can let that one slide," I say, looking down again. "Though I should probably give the ring back to your mom, and we can tell the gossips that, I don't know, we're still together but not getting married because we don't believe in putting labels on relationships or something."

I tap it against the glass again, leaning into Daniel, the fuzzy feeling of contentment floating through my body. He doesn't say anything for a long moment, his thumb just idly stroking my lower back.

"It was a joke," I say, turning my head toward him, though now I'm just talking to a pec because his chin is resting on top of my head. "I think labels are useful."

"What if we didn't?" he says suddenly.

"Use labels?"

"Give the ring back."

"I can't just keep it, your mom would kill me."

"Not if we were really engaged."

He pulls back, turns to face me, his hand still on my hip, and I stare up at him.

It's still him. Even if our relationship has been flipped upside down and then right side up in the past two months, it's still Daniel. He looks the same, he sounds the same. When we talk, he talks the same and he acts the same, and thank God for all of it because if we had lost anything we had, I'd have been heartbroken.

But we didn't. We added, multiplied, built on the bedrock foundation that we'd laid down over the years.

And I think he just asked me to marry him.

"Too soon?" he says, his eyes running over my face, taking in my surprised silence.

I look into his eyes like I'm diving into a perfect blue lagoon, and I realize I don't know how long I've been in love with him. I'm not even sure whether I count that time in weeks, months, or years.

"No," I say. "It's been eighteen years."

"Then will you marry me?"

He gets down on one knee. He literally does that as I'm standing there, still feeling one step behind, still trying to trace how we went from meatballs to proposal as he takes my hand, slides the ring off. I'm still holding a mojito as he turns the ring slowly in his fingers, and my heart feels like it's blooming.

"Charlie?" he asks, and I realize I haven't actually said anything yet.

"Yes!" I say. "Yes, Daniel, of course yes."

He slides the ring back on my finger, kisses my knuckles, stands. He takes my face in one hand and kisses me, and I wonder for half a second if a really-engaged kiss will be different from all the others, but it's not.

It's just as good.

"I love you," I murmur, our lips still touching.

"I love you back," he says.

It's a tender kiss, a slow kiss, lit by the last rays of the sunset, a kiss that's got all the time in the world.

Slowly, I step in. Slowly, my body presses against his, harder, tighter, his warmth bleeding into my skin through our clothes. The kisses quicken, deepen, grow more urgent because it doesn't matter how much time we have right now, it matters that most of our moments are stolen, brief, and that's made us ravenous for each other.

Daniel pulls back, his lips an inch from mine. I gaze up, the fingers of one hand already twined through his belt loop, pulling him toward me, the other wound around the back of his neck. He's got one palm flat against my back and he gazes down at me, an expression in his eyes I can't read.

Carefully, slowly, his thumb traces my bottom lip, a look of total concentration on his face. Then he follows his thumb with his lips, his tongue, taking my head in his hand and holding me to him, so tight I can barely move but I open my mouth under his anyway, aching for him.

Daniel moves me backward, step by step, until I walk into something. The side of the hot tub, and then he's grabbing me, hoisting me, pushing my legs wide and stepping in between them as I throw an arm around his neck, trying to keep my balance.

"I won't drop you," he teases, nuzzling his face along mine "Probably."

"Don't," I gasp. "My phone's in my pocket, and I can't go through two in one month."

Daniel just laughs and wraps one strong arm around my back, holding me in place while he pushes my legs wider with the other hand, his fingers digging into the soft flesh of my upper thigh, roaming beneath the hem of my shorts.

"I forgot to tell you the real reason I found this place," he says, his voice rough, deep. "And it hasn't got shit to go with the view."

"Don't tell me there's a secret sex dungeon," I say.

"Better," he says. "We're smack dab in the middle of a hundred acres of private property with no one else on it."

He kisses me hard, our tongues tangling. His fingers find the crease of my thigh, the leg of my panties, and they slide underneath.

"So you can indulge your exhibitionist tendencies all you want," he says. "You can spend the whole weekend naked outdoors, and I sure wouldn't mind."

"Is it as much fun if we can't get caught?" I tease.

His body is up against mine, his hard cock right against my heat, the friction of the denim between us almost unbearable.

"I guess we'll have to find out," he says, and in that

instant his thumb slides under my panties and finds my clit. I jolt. He catches me before I fall into the water, holds me tight against him. I cling to him, roll my hips, grind myself against him and listen to the soft groan that escapes him.

It lights me. I'm dry brush, the forest floor after a long drought, and he's a spark. In moments I'm aflame, ravaged, the heat racing through me like a wildfire.

I grab his wrist, pull his hand out of my shorts before he can stop me, push him back from the hot tub and hop down.

"No?" he says, a devilish smile on his face as he pushes forward again, pinning me against the side of the hot tub. "We're engaged and suddenly I can't get you off on the side of the hot tub, should I be worried?"

"Maybe," I tease, finding the thick ridge of his cock under the zipper of his jeans and sliding my palm along it. Daniel groans, louder this time, and I twist my other hand in his shirt, drawing him in. "Next thing you know I'm going to be all baking, sewing, and sex only on Saturday nights."

"It wouldn't work," he says. I slide my palm down again, hard, the friction sending sparks through my whole body. "I'd find some way to seduce you, even on a school night."

I pull him closer, kiss him, his hands sliding under my shirt.

"How?" I ask, biting his lower lip between my teeth.

He grinds his hips against me and a thrill rocks through my body. Before I know it, I'm pulling at the button on his jeans, getting it undone, fumbling for the zipper.

"Just like this seems to work," he says. "Kiss you. Tell you I love you."

He undoes the clasp on my bra and in one movement,

pulls both that and my shirt over my head so I'm suddenly topless in the evening air, my nipples puckering.

"Very romantic," I murmur.

"Tell you I want you to ride me like a wild mustang," he says. "And if that doesn't work, I'm out of ideas."

I pull the zipper down and his cock springs out, still half-constrained in boxers. I wrap my hand around it, stroke, feel the muscles in his whole body tense and relax.

I grab his shirt, pull it off, kiss him again with my hand stroking his cock and he moans into my mouth, primal and guttural. I pull his boxers down until we're skin-to-skin and he groans again, digs his fingers into my sides.

We kiss again and I *want* him, and I don't want to wait, I want to turn around and bend over this hot tub and let him bury himself in me until I'm seeing stars, until I'm shouting his name into the wilderness. I want to tell him to come inside me so that I don't have to sacrifice a second of *us*, even if it's risky, because I want him with a desire so deep I can't fathom it.

I don't. I kiss his neck, his shoulder. I drop to my knees and before his hands have even wound through my hair, I've got the head of his cock in my mouth, sucking, swirling my tongue around the thick ridge, swallowing his salty precum.

"Charlie," he whispers, and I take more of him, opening my mouth as wide as I can, stretching my tongue along the underside of his cock, one fist at the base.

He's huge, almost too big to manage, but then his fingers tighten in my hair and I push my lips down just another inch, eyes watering, and he whispers my name again.

I love this. I love the way he tastes, the way he says my name, the way he breathes when I've got his cock in my mouth. I love giving into him like this, getting on my knees, worshipping at his altar.

Daniel sighs, moans. He works his fingers into my hair, his entire body full of barely held restraint as I move faster, suck harder. He's leaking precum now, groaning every time I swallow, and I don't stop. I don't want to stop, because even though I want him, I want *this*, too.

But suddenly, he pulls my head back and I'm looking up at him, fist still wrapped around the base of his cock. Delicately, I open my mouth, lean forward, swirl my tongue around the head of his cock, wrap my lips around it as he groans, his eyes going to half-mast before he pulls my head back, grabs me by the arm, pulls me up.

"You're sure?" I murmur.

In response, he undoes my shorts, shoves a hand inside, swipes two fingertips along my slit and grins.

"I'm sure," he says, finding my clit again, circling it with slick fingers.

My shorts come off, his pants fall, and then I'm on one of the lounge chairs, sinking into the cushion as Daniel pushes me backward, mouth on mine until I'm at an angle against the back.

"I packed condoms," I say, breathless, before I can say something irresponsible like *fuck me bare and come inside me.* "They're in my duffel bag, in one of the outside—"

He holds up a foil packet, rips it open with his teeth.

"Pocket," he says, kissing me again. "I learned my lesson."

He rolls it onto his thick cock, his tongue in my mouth. I can hardly breathe for anticipation, for wanting, for *needing* him like this again like he's oxygen and I'm on Everest.

"I learned my lesson too," I say, grabbing his cock again, guiding him toward me. "Fucking outside is fun."

He finds my entrance, pauses, teases me. He nips at my lips with his teeth, kisses me hard and fast, slides the tip of his cock between my lips and I grab the top of the chair behind my head, roll my hips.

Daniel tweaks one nipple, rolling it between his thumb and finger, and I moan in helpless frustration.

"I love you like this, you know," he says, his voice velvet against my ear.

"Like what?" I whisper.

"When you want me," he says. "When you need me to fuck you so bad you can't stand it, but there's nothing you can do."

"Tease," I whisper.

"You know what else I love?" he asks.

He doesn't wait for an answer, just hilts himself in one stroke, and even though we've done it dozens of times I still feel a little like I'm being split in half, like he's knocked my soul free from my body. He collapses into me and I sink my fingers into the hard muscles of his back, curling one leg around him.

"I love it when I finally do," he whispers, his face in my neck, his beard ticklish and scratchy, sending quick shivers through my whole body.

I don't say anything. I can't. My mind is so blank it feels spiritual, ascendant. When we're together like this is when everything else suddenly goes quiet and there's nothing but Daniel and me, our bodies together, flesh become transcendent.

When we move, we move together, like different parts of the same machine. I've always found solace in physicality and in him I find deliverance, redemption, something more than pleasure.

It's pure, wild lust but it's lust for *him*, for his body and his mind, for the way he growls *love you* in my ear so low I almost can't hear, for the way he pulls me against him and kisses me like he'll never be able to get enough.

We crash together, meld, waves in a storm. He fucks me hard and fast and deep and he whispers my name as he holds himself over me, his other hand sinking into my thigh, pulling me, seeking more.

Suddenly he pulls out, kisses me, breaks it.

"Roll over," he gasps.

"Why?" I ask, already on my hands and knees, grabbing the back of the lounge chair.

He plants a hand over mine, runs a hand down my back. He sinks himself into me again, slow but hard and deep and I gasp, pushing back against him, taking him until my toes curl.

"Because I like it when you fuck me back and come hard," he says, holding me against him.

I can feel every inch, every millimeter, can feel myself pulsing and clenching while he fills me. It feels good. It feels right. It feels like home.

"Because I like the way you whisper my name and tell me to make you come as if I wasn't already going to," he says, his voice dipping as he starts moving.

My knuckles go white on the iron bar of the lounge chair.

"And because I don't want you to miss the view," he says, laughing.

He wraps an arm around me. He kisses my cheek and fucks me hard, one hand over mine and the other snaking down my body as we crash together, relentless.

It builds. He drives into me and I take him, push back, ask for more. Our words are guttural if they're words at all, just sounds, begging and pleading and praising. I'm laid bare, helpless, utterly vulnerable to my own want and

Daniel takes me, protects me, gives himself to me until I'm gasping his name because I've forgotten my own.

I beg him *don't stop please don't stop* and I beg him *make me come oh God make me come* and then there are fingers on my clit and sparkles in my vision and I come like an earthquake.

I shout his name. I rock back and forth, taking everything, a seismic shift in my body. I moan and I whisper and I think I howl and then his hands are on my shoulder, pulling me into him as the aftershocks rattle through me and he's whispering *I fucking love it when you come* into my ear and I respond with *come inside me please Daniel I want you to come inside me* and he does.

He kisses the back of my neck. He slides his fingers down my spine, slick with sweat, and finally he pulls out, both of us shuddering. I roll back over, onto the lounge chair, and he collapses onto me, his face on my belly, my fingers in his hair.

It's nearly night, the whole cabin and deck and valley and mountain range different shades of blue, stars popping out of the sky above.

Daniel pushes himself up, pulls me down, gives me a long kiss on the lips.

"You enjoy the view?" he asks, a smile on his lips, and I laugh.

"Of course," I say. "The view was great. Very satisfying."

He rolls over, his head against my chest. I put a hand on his shoulder, and he takes it in his.

"Plus, I don't have to see Officer Sherman now," he teases. "That man really knows how to kill a mood."

I just sigh dramatically.

"Hell, we don't have to put on clothes all weekend if we

don't want to," Daniel goes on. "I don't even know why I brought them."

"Because it's better than putting sunscreen on your dick," I say, and Daniel laughs.

"I've never had cause to sunscreen my dick before," he muses. "It's never even occurred to me."

"You're welcome," I tell him. "And don't act like you didn't enjoy everything that happened *before* Officer Sherman showed up, either."

"Of course I enjoyed it," he says. "I went to great lengths to make a version of it happen again, didn't I?"

I laugh, fingers winding through his hair, my other hand in his. The ring sparkles, even in the night, and I think: *we're engaged.*

"I have a question," I say, my voice slow, lazy.

"Shoot."

"Did you mean to propose?" I ask, still stroking his hair.

He twists, looks up at me.

"Of course I meant to," he says, his eyes the color of the night sky, filled with stars.

I swirl his hair around one finger, the night breeze soft against my bare skin.

"That doesn't mean I was planning on it, though," he admits, and I laugh.

"You really booked this super-romantic cabin just so we could fuck outside," I say as he sits up, offers me a hand, pulls me upright.

"I thought you'd like it," he says, that rakish smile on his face.

"I did."

He puts one hand on my face. I'm still flushed with heat and his fingers are cool, dry, slightly rough against my skin.

"The plan was to wait a couple months at least," he says, thumb on my cheekbone. "The plan was to give you a little time, maybe start looking at houses together, have a couple discussions about marriage, figure out all the logistics, *then* ask you to marry me."

"Nice plan," I say.

"It was really well thought-out," he says. "And then I ruined it by suddenly not wanting to wait."

He takes a deep breath, leans his forehead against mine, and I close my eyes.

"I'd have waited," I say.

"I know," he says. "I'm the one who couldn't."

We kiss gently, tenderly.

"I love you," he says. "And I have for a long time and I will for a longer time yet."

"I love you back," I say. "Long time, longer time."

He kisses me again, and then we get up. We eat spaghetti and meatballs and we soak in the hot tub and we sleep in the same bed, Daniel's arm thrown across my back.

When we wake up, we wake to the sun streaming through the bedroom window. We snuggle for a long time, saying nothing, just Daniel and me together, alone, the two of us.

And it's perfect.

EPILOGUE

DANIEL

ONE MONTH LATER

"Do you think he'll like it?" Rusty asks from the back seat. "At first I had unicorn stickers on it but I'm not sure Uncle Seth likes unicorns, so I put the shark stickers on it instead."

I glance in the rearview mirror. She's holding up a novelty cowboy hat, the words HAPPY BIRTHDAY emblazoned in gold on the front.

"I think he'll definitely like it," my mom says, reaching over and touching the hat. "Look at all those different sharks."

"I also had a princess hat," Rusty says, still contemplating.

"Seth's not much for princesses," my mom says, and in the passenger seat, I can see Charlie press her knuckles against her mouth and look out the window, probably before she says something inappropriate about my little brother.

"He'll like the cowboy hat much better," I say, loud enough that Rusty can hear me.

"More appropriate," Charlie mutters, casting me a quick, conspiratorial glance.

"Ridden everything in town," I agree *sotto voce.*

My mom gives me a *look* in the rear-view mirror, but I don't think Rusty heard us.

She's still chattering away as I pull into Eli's driveway and park behind Seth's mustang. Rusty's the first one out, impatiently rattling the door handle against the child lock until I let her out, then racing up the stairs to Eli's deck, already shouting for Seth. I watch her long enough to confirm that there are, indeed, responsible adults up there, and then I open the back and grab the cooler.

"Don't jostle it too much, please," my mom says. "It's loaded very particularly, you know."

"I would never intentionally harm a pie, mom," I say. "You know that."

I heave the cooler out of the back. Charlie comes around, gives me a quick once-over look, then grabs a few more things.

I flex a little harder and lift the cooler a little higher. She notices, but my mom's there so she pretends she doesn't and closes the lift gate after me.

"You can touch if you want," I tell her the moment my mom's out of earshot.

"The cooler?" she asks, blinking up at me in faux-innocence.

"C'mon, squeeze one," I say, lifting the cooler a smidge higher. "No one's looking."

"Daniel, get your pies upstairs," she says.

"I know you want to."

"If they get jostled, it's not gonna be on me."

"Just a quick squeeze, I already caught you looking," I say, grinning down at her.

Charlie sighs, glances over at the deck where Rusty is currently presenting Seth with a cowboy hat and Seth is acting very impressed.

"Fine," she says, and slides her hand around my bicep.

I flex.

Charlie laughs but she also blushes, her cheeks going faintly pink under the freckles, and I wink at her.

"Told you," I say.

"Ridiculous," she says, and then we head up the stairs just in time to see Seth ever so carefully perch the hat on his head.

"That's a real good look, pardner," Silas says. He's standing next to Seth. On Seth's other side, his younger sister June rolls her eyes and drinks her beer.

Seth touches the brim of the slightly-too-small hat and ducks his head.

"Thank you kindly," he says, his accent matching Seth's.

Rusty's grinning from ear to ear, and I duck inside to where my mom's instructing me to relinquish the pies in the kitchen.

"Thank you," she says, opening the cooler again. "Oh good, the new pie system worked. I was afraid the blueberry would get crushed on the bottom, but—" she holds up a pie, inspecting it, "—it's right as rain."

Outside, it already smells amazing. Eli and Violet have a very small but very adorable house on Deepwood Lake, and over the past year they've built a huge deck onto one side. It's making its debut today at Seth's birthday barbecue.

Because it's Eli, there's a whole cooking section on the deck. Two charcoal grills. A gas grill. Something that's got a window in the front of it and somewhat resembles a bank vault. A turkey deep fryer, though that at least appears to be off right now.

Charlie walks up to me, a beer in each hand. I pick one, we clink our bottles together, and drink, wandering back over to the knot of my brothers and their friends.

"The monster's name is Dave?" June's asking Rusty.

"It's short for David," Rusty explains.

June has to bite her lip to keep from laughing.

"He's only Dave to friends and family," Levi says. "With everyone else he prefers Mr. Monster."

I shoot Charlie a quick glance. Levi? Acting like a normal human in June's presence?

May wonders never cease.

"Lake monsters are very formal, it's true," Seth says.

"Do you call him Dave or David?" June asks, and Rusty sighs, like she's being very patient.

"I've never met him, I don't call him anything," she explains. "But his name is Deepwood Dave."

"What's he look like?" June asks. "Have you ever seen him? Does he surface often, and what does he do when he does? How does—"

"Let her answer," Silas says. "You're not at a press conference, you can ask one question at a time."

"Sorry," June says.

"Dave is blue and green and wavy for camouflage," she says. "I've never seen him, but I've heard a lot about him, and he breathes water so he doesn't need to surface very often. Plus, he's crepuscular so he usually sleeps during the day."

I stand a little taller at *crepuscular*, because that's my kid.

"He's what?" Silas says.

"It means that Dave is mostly active around twilight," Levi says. "Like deer."

"Ah," says Silas, nodding solemnly.

"I brought my viewing equipment," Rusty says, very seriously. "And I also brought my bathing suit, in case my dad decides I can go in the canoe?"

That last part's directed at me as she looks over, lemonade in one hand, eyes big and pleading.

"We'll see," I say, and as soon as she looks away, Charlie nudges me in my ribs. I don't love the idea of Rusty — small, delicate, fragile Rusty — going on the lake in a boat, but I also know I might be overprotective. Besides, she got her cast off last week and has been begging to go swimming.

"Is Dave a dangerous sort of monster?" June asks casually.

"Well, he's got big teeth but they're only for defense," Rusty explains.

June frowns.

"From what?"

"Other monsters," Rusty says, like it's obvious.

"How many monsters are in Deep—"

"Eli!" Levi calls suddenly, and everyone turns.

"What?" Eli calls back from where he and Violet are leaning against the railing, laughing with my mom about something.

"Is that your dog?" Levi asks, nodding at the driveway.

"We don't have a dog," Violet calls, coming toward us.

Everyone on the deck turns, and sure enough, there's a dog casually trotting up the driveway, between the cars.

"Does it belong to one of your neighbors?" Levi asks, brow furrowed.

"I don't think so," Eli says.

At the end of the driveway, the dog sits, looking up at us. It's black and white, medium-sized, slightly shaggy. It's got no tags, there are grass and sticks stuck in its fur, and as I take a step closer, I realize its paws are filthy.

"She's hungry," Levi says, and hands me his beer. Before I can react, he's already down the stairs, carefully approaching the dog, crouching with one hand held out.

The dog sniffs his hand carefully. Suspiciously. Levi doesn't move a muscle, letting it get all the information it wants while the rest of us watch from the deck.

"I hope it's not rabid," Violet mutters.

"If it was rabid, we'd know by now," Eli says.

Then the dog licks him, its fluffy tail thumping on the grass, and Levi scratches gently behind one ear. When that goes well, he scratches behind the other. In a few seconds he's got her head in both hands, scratching away, a look of total doggie bliss on her face.

"So basically, he's Snow White," June says, still standing on the porch. "Animals just seek him out to love him?"

"He's only Snow White if the dog does his dishes," Charlie says.

"That part always grossed me out," June admits, still watching Levi and the dog.

Now he's on his knees and the dog is going nuts, wagging her tail so excitedly that the back half of her body is moving from side to side.

"When the animals licked the plates and acted like they were clean?" I ask. "Yeah, that was gross."

"It just made me want my own forest pets, so they'd do my chores for me," Charlie admits.

"Yeah, same," Silas says. "Who cares how the dishes get clean?"

"You're gross," June says, still watching Levi. "Animal spit isn't clean."

"It's clean enough."

On the ground, Levi's still scratching the dog with one

hand, the other holding one of her front paws while he frowns. Then he puts it down, stands, gives her another vigorous scratch, and comes back up the stairs to the deck.

"Eli," he says. "Have you all got a first aid kit anywhere? She's got a deep laceration on one paw and I'm afraid it might get infected."

"Under the bathroom sink," Eli says.

Levi nods and goes inside. Down below, the dog stands, alert.

Then, tentatively, she comes up the stairs to the deck. She sits on the top stair, and we all look at her uncertainly until June sighs, puts her beer down, and walks over.

"Hey, girl," she says, kneeling a few feet away and holding out one hand, just like Levi did. "You were supposed to stay down there, you know."

The dog licks her hand, and I can pretty much see June melt.

"Fine," she says, offering ear scratches. "Fine, you can stay."

The door opens, and Levi comes back out, first aid kit in hand, then stops. He slides the door shut behind himself, surveying the scene in front of him.

"She missed you," June explains, now giving full two-handed dog scritches. "Do you need any help bandaging her up?"

· · * * ★ ★ ★ * * · ·

An arm slides around my waist, and without looking, I drape mine around Charlie's shoulder.

"She's wearing a life vest, there's an extra in the boat, she knows how to swim, *and* Caleb's with her," she says. "Rusty's fine."

I watch my daughter's small form grow smaller as Caleb rows them further out onto the lake. He sees me watching and waves. Rusty waves, too, then puts her binoculars back to her face, methodically surveying the surface of the water.

The sun has already sunk behind the trees, casting the lake in shadow. Dave is crepuscular, after all.

"Does she think Dave is real?" I ask Charlie.

"I'm not sure," Charlie says. "I think she wants Dave to be real, since it would be cool to see a lake monster."

"They took flashlights, right?" I ask.

"I think so," Charlie says. "Also, I'm pretty sure that Caleb could make a lantern out of an oar and a cellphone if he needed to."

"An oar and a cellphone?"

"Shh, don't question it," she says, leaning into me.

I kiss the top of her head. We're standing on the shore of the lake, below Eli and Violet's house, on a narrow strip of mud that's not really a boat launch, but that sometimes functions as such regardless.

"You know you're doing a good job, right?" she says.

"Because she knows the word *crepuscular*?"

"I'm serious," Charlie says, poking me in the side. "Rusty's a great kid. She's gonna kick a lot of ass."

"She already is," I say. "Specifically, mine. You sure you're ready for this?"

"Bring it on," she says. "I'm looking forward to officially being her stepmom."

"Me too," I say.

We still haven't really started wedding planning, but last weekend we went on a grand tour of open houses in the Sprucevale area. We discussed master bedrooms, bathtubs, whether we want an open-plan kitchen. We debated carpet versus hardwood flooring. We argued over whether garages are extra space for hobbies and projects (Charlie) or a place to put cars (me).

It's all going to be a lot: buying a house, moving in together, her suddenly becoming a parent to a seven-year-old instead of just a cool aunt.

But it's going to be good, because Charlie's going to be there.

"Should we go back up?" she asks, still leaning against me. "They're probably looking for us."

"Let them look," I say. "I like being alone with you."

Charlie tilts her face up, so I lean down and kiss her. We move so she's facing me, in my arms, and we kiss again, her arms around my neck, my hands on her back, and it's good.

It's better than good, these quiet moments where nothing matters but her and me. It's nearly perfect.

We separate. I kiss her forehead, and she leans into my chest, face toward the lake. I know that soon, Caleb and Rusty will row back, that they're going to light the candles on Seth's birthday cake, that all the people gathered up above will sing to him in the warm Virginia night.

But that's not now. Now is Charlie and me, standing here, getting our moments where we can steal them.

There will be more moments like this. There will be a house that's half hers and half mine, where I rearrange the spices and she finds her phone in the cabinet with the mugs sometimes. There will be Rusty, growing up and getting older and someday leaving us. There might be more kids, a dog, some cats, maybe an iguana.

But always, there will be this, the two of us together, souls intertwined. An entanglement so deep it could never be undone.

"I think they're heading back," I say. We still haven't moved. "Think she found Dave?"

"Probably not," says Charlie. "I think she'd be more excited."

She's right. They didn't. Caleb drags the boat onto the shore.

Rusty comes up to us, still embracing, and wraps her arms around our legs. I rub her back, lightly, and think: *family is something you make out of love.*

"I didn't find Dave this time," Rusty says, breaking the silence. "It's okay. Let's go get cake."

Just like that she's off, running back to the house. Charlie and I both laugh.

Then I take her hand, and we follow our daughter.

THE END

ABOUT ROXIE

Roxie is a romance author by day, and also a romance author by night. She lives in Los Angeles with one husband, two cats, far too many books, and a truly alarming pile of used notebooks that she refuses to throw away.

www.roxienoir.com
roxie@roxienoir.com

Made in the USA
Middletown, DE
20 May 2024

54621100R00252